WHEN WINGS FLUTTER

LIANE CARMEN

ISBN: (paperback) 978-0-9984247-6-7

ISBN: (hardcover) 978-0-9984247-9-8

ISBN: (ebook) 978-0-9984247-5-0

Cover design by 100 covers.

Author photo by Bill Ziady. (www.matchframeproductions.com)

For Jone Salter.
I hope when my time comes, you're waiting
with a golf cart to pick me up.

THE OTHER SIDE

*T*his wouldn't be her first lifetime. On this side, pain didn't exist, so the challenges of a human experience were necessary for her soul to grow and evolve. In the selection room, she'd reviewed snippets of the possibilities for her next life and found one especially intriguing. She'd never been a household name before.

She'd chosen the body she'd occupy, and her parents were getting prepared to welcome their new daughter. They'd name her Kate. After she was born, memories of this realm would fade. An amnesia of sorts. She wasn't meant to remember her past lives or the blissful existence she'd leave behind. Her focus had to be on the new lifetime in front of her.

She joined her soul circle as it convened. It resembled a company meeting on Earth that might occur in a conference room around a large, mahogany table. But here, there weren't walls to contain them. No polished wooden surface to gather around. Only a warm golden hue and an overwhelming sense of peace and love surrounded the orbs in varying shades of white light.

These circle members had appeared repeatedly in her prior

lives to assist with the lessons she needed to learn. They'd gathered again now to sort through possibilities for yet another lifetime together.

As their work began, there were no voices. No need for words. Messages and intentions traveled seamlessly without the need for the senses their human forms required.

Kate felt a familiar tug toward a soul she'd been with many times before.

I've seen what I want to achieve, she conveyed. *I'd be a celebrity of sorts. Can you imagine? Leaving a legacy, my small mark on history, would be quite an accomplishment.*

His bright white orb drifted toward her. *Well, that would make for an exciting life this time around.*

What about you? she asked.

He tried on his new appearance for her. He was handsome, but it was his eyes that drew Kate in. They were an intense green —impossible to forget.

Not bad, huh? he asked with a grin. *I've also chosen my purpose for this next life.* He relayed his plan to her, then gestured toward two other members of their circle. *I'm hoping they will use this lifetime to finally resolve their issues.*

The pair of souls assumed their new appearances as well—a young boy and a man with a tattoo inked on his arm. A set of initials and two words.

I could help you, too, Kate. His green eyes sparkled with a love many lives together had perfected. *If you marry me, I could lead you to that success you have your heart set on.*

Another orb, not quite as bright as the first, moved toward her to give her a message.

I'd like to play a part as well—maybe use this lifetime to make amends.

Kate understood why this soul needed another chance. Still, she had objectives to accomplish and choices from her own past to revisit. After considering his offer, she laid out her conditions, then shared a pivotal moment she'd viewed on a screen in the selection room. It would serve as his sign she was ready.

When you see the rainbow of colored lights, she told him, *you'll know the time is right.*

He promised to wait, and the signal she gave him would sit deep in his subconscious.

Still, Kate knew if she failed to reach her goals, the celebration she'd seen in the selection room would never come to fruition on Earth. The opportunity for him to see the rainbow of colored lights wouldn't exist.

Other souls were then slotted like puzzle pieces into a flow chart of sorts. Kate's master plan. When their paths crossed, there might be a sense of familiarity. An instant connection she couldn't explain. She'd have to trust in that gut feeling some might call intuition.

The existence Kate was about to take on wasn't meant to be easy because, really, what would that teach her? For her soul to evolve, she'd have to challenge herself. Learn lessons where she'd fallen short before. It was important she find a way to believe in herself, so this time she could depart fulfilled and without regret.

When that time came, Kate would have no further need for her physical body. She'd leave it behind and take the lessons she'd learned on a familiar and comforting journey. Her soul would get to go home again.

CHAPTER 1

NEW JERSEY, 1983

"Sorry, I'm late." Kate's gaze bounced around the kitchen, searching for an empty spot to lay down the tray she held. Her cousin's spread was scattered over every counter. "Geez, Melinda, you must have cooked all day."

Frowning, Kate used her forearm to shove aside an enormous bowl of guacamole on the kitchen table. She set her platter of cookies next to the homemade salsa. Not a perfect spot, but her cousin would relocate it anyway.

"You're fine." Melinda gestured at the woman pouring vodka into a plastic cup at the makeshift bar. "That's Dawn. Her parents live next door."

The twenty-something woman teetered across the kitchen on four-inch heels, the smell of Aqua Net wafting in Kate's direction as she came closer. She was pretty but done up to perfection in a way that made Kate wonder how long it had taken her to get ready.

"Hey," Dawn said, offering a half-hearted wave before taking a long swallow of her drink.

"This is my cousin, Katie." Melinda removed the cling wrap from Kate's platter. "She's an amazing baker."

She lifted a football-shaped cookie to her nose, inhaled, and then scrutinized its appearance. "It's so gorgeous I'm afraid to eat it." After taking a bite, she let out a satisfied moan. "I didn't think it could taste as good as it looks, but it's delicious."

"Really?" Kate had spent the morning painstakingly decorating them but hadn't tried one.

Melinda nodded, then took another bite. "Way too good for today's crowd."

Kate scowled. "Then why'd you make so much food? It's just a football game."

"Just a football game?" Dawn huffed and shot her an incredulous stare. "Uh, it's the *Super Bowl*. I love football. NFL and college. I mean, I went to Penn State, after all." Her tone was matter-of-fact, as if the mere mention of her alma mater explained her affinity for the sport.

Kate had no intention of admitting she'd graduated from the local college. They didn't even have a football team—at least she didn't think so. She wasn't into sports.

"Adam and his buddies think Super Bowl is a national holiday," Melinda said, her shoulder lifting.

"So do most people." Dawn's grin revealed a smudge of red lipstick on her front tooth. "For me, any time good-looking men gather, it's a reason to celebrate in my book."

Melinda glanced over at Kate and rolled her eyes. "Dawn only stopped by to check out Adam's friends."

"Not entirely true," she said. "I came because you *said* you were having a Super Bowl party. But then you decided not to watch—"

"I see my husband and his friends enough," Melinda said. "I

like to cook, and they like to watch the game. We're all happy doing our own thing."

"It's okay, I'm patient. I can wait till halftime to make my move." A slow smile lifted Dawn's lips. "I already know who I want." She lowered her chin and fixed her gaze on Kate. "I call dibs on Will Kennedy." Her stare went on longer than necessary, then she drained the rest of her drink.

When Dawn took her empty cup back to the vodka and cranberry for a refill, Kate caught Melinda's eye and bit back a smile. *Dibs?* she mouthed. *Is she serious?*

Melinda waved her hand dismissively in Dawn's direction. "Do *you* care if we watch the game?" She was clearly only asking Kate. "We can if you want."

Kate tossed a pretzel in her mouth, then reached into the refrigerator for a Coke. She popped the top of the can and brought it to her lips.

"I don't understand the first thing about football," she said. "I wouldn't even know when to cheer."

When the swinging door from the family room to the kitchen opened, Kate paused mid-sip. The man who filled the doorway had dark brown hair with messy curls that swept over his forehead and partially covered his eyes. Piercing green eyes now anchored on her.

Kate froze while his gaze swept over her. After she'd finished baking, Kate had puttered around her small apartment until she'd finally bothered to check the clock. As usual, she'd been running late.

She hadn't given her appearance much thought as she'd rushed out the door. Her long blond hair was in a ponytail. She wore no makeup. She'd paired a bulky GAP sweatshirt with her favorite jeans—the faded ones with the gaping hole at the knee. Now, as she locked eyes with the handsome stranger, Kate wanted to thump herself for her lack of effort.

The idea that someone interesting might be at the party hadn't even occurred to her. Disillusioned with dating, she'd all but stopped looking.

Six months earlier, she'd broken up with Mike. It wasn't anything he did necessarily. It was more what he *didn't* do—he didn't make her feel "it."

Kate had tried to give the relationship time to see if she ever got that warm tingly feeling, but she hadn't. Not once.

As Kate soaked in the man in the doorway, her stomach flip-flopped in a way it had never done for Mike. Or anyone else, for that matter. Now she knew. *This* was what she was supposed to feel.

They both stood silent for a moment, but when Kate's cheeks grew hot, she was sure their telltale red hue betrayed her interest. She forced herself to look away, but her pulse was racing.

Kate sipped her soda and attempted to act casual. "I guess I know who you're rooting for."

The man stood rigid, his shoulder still propping the door open as he stared at her. "What?"

She held a flattened palm against her chest. "Your Dolphins shirt."

His teal T-shirt, tucked neatly into a pair of perfectly faded Levi's, had short sleeves that met the swell of his biceps. Katie was staring again. This time it wasn't his eyes that had her mesmerized.

"Oh, right." Full lips lifted into a grin as the man let the door swing shut behind him. "I'm actually a huge Giants fan. I only wore this to bust on Adam's brother, Paul. He's a die-hard Washington fan." The man's deep green eyes twinkled mischievously. "It's no fun if we all root for the same team, right?"

"Is the shirt working?" An amused smile played on Kate's lips.

"So far. We're up 7-0, but it's only the end of the first quarter."

Just then, Dawn's heels clattered in their direction. She edged her way in front of Kate and cleared her throat as if to announce her arrival. "Hi again, Will. Did you say the Fins are up?"

Oh, crap. Dawn's Will. As in "I call dibs on Will Kennedy." So much for that idea.

He took a step backward. "Oh, hey …"

"*Dawn*," she said, sounding annoyed he hadn't remembered her name. With a fresh drink in her left hand, her right hand went to her hip, her pose now blocking Kate's view.

"Right. Yeah, they're up by a touchdown." Will stepped to the left and back into Kate's line of sight.

Dawn moved as well, not willing to let him go so easily. "So, the defense—"

"Will, this is my cousin, Katie Matthews," Melinda cut in as she stepped forward.

Most people called her Kate, but she'd always be Katie to her family and relatives. She nodded in acknowledgment.

The smile Will gave her made the corners of his eyes crinkle. "Nice to meet you, Katie." He held her gaze one beat, then two.

Then, Melinda spoke up. "Did Adam send you in for more beer?"

"You know your husband well," he said, and his attention shifted. "Chips too."

"I can get those for you." Dawn tripped as she raced toward the bag on the kitchen counter.

Kate took the momentary lapse of eye contact to study Will Kennedy. Maybe five-ten or so. He couldn't be that much older than her. She put him in his late twenties, and he wore stubble on his face that seemed like maybe he'd given himself permission to skip shaving for the weekend.

She felt Dawn's eyes bore into her, but Kate couldn't help herself. Her focus moved to Will's broad shoulders and then to the defined muscles in his arms. They left no doubt he played sports or worked out regularly. Those jeans hugged him in absolutely all the right places.

Kate's metabolism was kind to her, but she wasn't in the shape he was in. Not that he would have any idea what she looked like under her frumpy, oversized sweatshirt. Even on her best day, Kate couldn't compete with Dawn, who had her assets on full display.

Dawn returned with the party-sized bag of potato chips held possessively in her grasp, seemingly determined to play defense. She positioned herself by Kate's side as if to prevent her from making an unapproved move.

When Will reached for the beer Melinda handed him, Dawn seized the opportunity to hiss in Kate's ear. "Dibs, remember?"

Kate pursed her lips. She wasn't usually one to rock the boat, but she'd felt something when she met Will. Besides, she didn't even know this woman. Dawn couldn't expect to lay claim on Will without his consent. Didn't *he* get a say?

With the six-pack of beer in one hand, Will's gaze drifted toward Dawn. "I, uh, need the chips."

"Right." She hurried to the counter to retrieve a bowl, then poured a generous amount. Dawn glanced up seductively at Will through her long, dark lashes. "Here you go." She handed the bowl to him, and let her fingernails drift up along his forearm before he pulled away.

He glanced at the door that would take him and his provisions back to the football game but then strolled instead toward Kate. He tipped his head to the side as he stood there, one disobedient curl falling forward into his left eye. Kate worked to resist the urge to reach forward and brush it off his face. She could almost feel his soft hair entwined in her fingers. Imagined her hand drifting down to cradle the side of his face, her mouth moving slowly toward his.

Her face grew hot, her body tingling. Kate sternly reminded herself about social etiquette. Grabbing a stranger in her cousin's kitchen was not appropriate behavior. Not to mention, Dawn might tackle her and throw her down right there on Melinda's harvest gold linoleum.

If Will noticed Kate's longing, he didn't let on. Instead, he blew out a puff of air, but his wayward curl lifted only momentarily out of his eye. He set down the beer and chips on the kitchen table and ran a hand through his hair.

His endearing smile was back.

"That's better. You know, I could swear when I walked in, I heard you say you don't know the first thing about football."

Kate gave a slight shrug she hoped looked coy and not pathetic. "You heard right. My dad watches it, but I never really understood the game."

Dawn emitted a dramatic groan, but Will didn't flinch.

He rubbed his thumb against the stubble on his chin, his focus on Kate. "I'd love to be your teacher if you want to watch the game with me. I mean, you'd have to cheer for the Fins." He grinned. "And if Washington scores, we glare at Paul as a team."

The sound of cheering erupted in the living room.

"Uh, oh. Looks like we need to get in there." Will picked up the beer from the table, then lifted his shoulders. "So, are we a team?"

Kate's heart thumped wildly. Every part of her wanted to go with him—to watch the game or anywhere else he wanted to take her. She opened her mouth to respond, then closed it.

She spun around to find Dawn staring daggers at her, her lacquered lips pinched as if they'd just sucked a lemon dry. Kate didn't care. She was much more concerned about leaving Melinda high and dry. She hated girls who did that.

Her cousin noted her conflicted stare and moved to Kate's side.

"Don't forget these," Melinda said as she handed her the bowl of chips. "Have fun and report back at halftime."

Kate gave a grateful nod and avoided further eye contact with Dawn.

She turned and faced Will. "Okay, Professor Kennedy. I'm ready for class."

The corners of his mouth lifted into a satisfied smile. "So, you know my last name. Seems you've done a bit of homework before our class even starts."

Kate's cheeks burned, but as they walked toward the swinging door to the family room, Will rested his hand against the small of her back. Butterflies raced in her stomach.

She hoped she hadn't created problems for Melinda with Dawn, but resisting Will would have been impossible. Kate wanted to nestle herself into those strong arms of his and gaze into those beautiful green eyes. Maybe for the rest of her life.

* * *

At halftime, the group streamed into the kitchen. Kate cast a nervous gaze, but Dawn was nowhere in sight. Her shoulders lowered in relief, but as she reached for a plate, Melinda grabbed her arm.

"Well?"

"We're tied," Kate said. "Coach Shula is *not* happy."

Melinda huffed. "Not the *game*, silly." After a quick glance to see if anyone would notice, she pulled Kate into the laundry room and slammed the door.

Kate pouted as she stared at the empty plate in her hand. "So, I don't get to eat?"

"Not until you tell me what's going on out there."

Kate's nose wrinkled. "Was Dawn pissed?"

"Oh, she left after a few choice words, but too bad." Melinda rolled her eyes. "Dibs? C'mon. This isn't high school."

"I agree." Kate bit back a smile. "*Obviously*. I just didn't want her mad at you."

"I don't care. Honest. Dawn only noses around when Adam's friends are over, but it's not like Will was interested in her. How could he be? The only sparks flying in that kitchen were between the two of you."

Kate lowered her voice as if someone might hear. "I think he actually likes me."

Melinda's hands flew up in the air. "Well, duh. He couldn't take his eyes off you."

"I can't believe I came to your party looking like this." Kate glanced down at herself and sighed.

"Oh, please. You couldn't look bad if you tried." Melinda bobbed her head as she smiled. "Besides, it didn't appear Will had a problem with the way you looked."

"How do you even know him? I can't believe you've been hiding him from your favorite single cousin."

"You're my only single cousin," Melinda said as she opened the dryer.

Kate groaned in frustration. Her cousin couldn't just hide out in the laundry room for a covert gossip session. She always had to be doing something. Right now, Kate wanted her full attention. She had an urgent need to learn as much about Will Kennedy as possible.

Melinda reached for a laundry basket and then pulled out a towel. "I don't know why I never thought of him for you. Will was one of Adam's college roommates, but he's always been my favorite."

She held the towel in place with her chin while she folded it in thirds and then in half and then in half again. She placed it in the basket at her feet and reached for another.

Kate scowled at her cousin's complicated folding technique. In her apartment, she was lucky if she didn't just pull a towel out of the laundry basket of clean clothes when she needed it.

"Well, I certainly don't remember Will at your wedding. There's no *way* I wouldn't have noticed him." Kate moaned. "He must look incredible in a tux."

"Ah." Melinda nodded as she continued to fold. "You're right.

He wasn't there. He had a cousin getting married that same weekend in Connecticut." She tossed the folded towel in the basket and gave Kate her full attention. "So, how's it going out there?"

Kate released a contented sigh. "The guys tried to tease him for watching the game with a girl, but he told them they were just jealous. Can you believe that?"

"Actually, I can. Will's the kind of guy who's nice even when no one else is around." Melinda smirked. "So, is he teaching you about football?"

"He's trying. I'm nodding a lot, but mostly I'm trying to act cool, calm, and collected."

Her cousin snorted. "Which you're not."

"Not at all." Kate rolled her eyes. "Especially since we're sharing the armchair, and he's so close, I can barely breathe." She moaned and fell against the washer. "He smells like ... soap. But manly, incredibly sexy soap."

Melinda reached back into the dryer, then turned with a towel in her hand and cringed. "You're not *sniffing* him out there, are you?" She leaned closer to Kate, her eyes narrowed. "*Please* tell me you weren't sniffing him."

"No, of course not." Kate then slumped over and put her head in her hands. "I mean, not *really*. But it's not like I can help it." She offered a sheepish smile. "I mean, a girl's gotta breathe."

"Well, I'm glad you like him, and it's going well." Melinda shot Kate a pointed look. "See, you said Super Bowl was boring, and now look at you."

"I can't believe I almost wasn't going to come." Kate crossed her arms in front of her. "But now I know why I'm still single. Why it's never worked out with anyone else." She lifted and dropped her shoulders matter-of-factly. "Will's the one, Melinda. I just have to hope he feels the same way about me."

"Wow. So, maybe you'll have a date for Valentine's Day this year. One you actually like."

"Oh, it's more than that," Kate said with a determined nod.

"What do you mean?"

"I'm going to marry that man, Melinda. I just know it."

CHAPTER 2

TWO AND A HALF YEARS LATER

*K*ate sipped her mimosa and then closed her eyes as the makeup artist swept eye shadow across her lids. Her blond hair was already swept into an updo with delicate tendrils framing her face. Her veil was anchored in place, and the white tulle flowed down her back over the tube top dress she'd worn. When the time came, she'd slip easily out of it and into the stunning white dress waiting for her.

"What time are the girls coming?" Melinda asked.

"Will's sister, Lisa, should be here any minute with his parents," Kate glanced up at the clock on the wall. "Jane and Michelle should have been here ten minutes ago."

Jane had been Kate's best friend since she was a little girl, and she'd met Michelle at work. They'd become fast friends, and she'd been there for every phase of Kate's obsessive wedding planning. The two of them had dissected flower arrangements and DJs when they were supposed to be working.

"They should be all ready to go, except they're bringing their bridesmaid's dresses to change here." Kate waved a hand at her cousin but didn't turn her head so the makeup artist could continue working. "Come stand in front of me so I can see you."

Melinda twirled in front of her, and Kate let out a happy sigh. "You look beautiful. That dress was a perfect choice."

There was a knock on the bridal suite door, and then it opened slightly. Kate's mother peeked through the narrow crack. "Can we come in?"

"Of course," Kate called out.

After she greeted her aunt and uncle, Melinda crossed her hands over her chest. "To think this all started in my kitchen."

"It sure did," Kate said, trying to remain still.

Will had scoffed when she'd shared how Dawn had attempted to claim him that Super Bowl Sunday. 'I only had eyes for you, that day and every day since,' he'd told her.

She still couldn't believe Will would be hers forever. He'd chosen her to be his wife, and he was absolutely perfect.

Her mother interrupted her thoughts as she offered an approving nod. "You look beautiful, sweetie."

Kate's gaze drifted to her dad, standing in front of her in his tuxedo. She'd always been a daddy's girl, and he appeared as emotional as she did now that this day had arrived.

Her father's eyes were wet as he reached for her hand. "You sure do. I'm not sure I'm ready to give you away at the end of the aisle."

"But ..." Kate said, leaving her father to finish the thought.

"But Will's perfect for you," he added in an obligatory tone. The two of them had discussed this before. Her parents adored Will almost as much as she did. "But if it was anyone else—"

The door to the bridal suite flew open. Will's sister must have met up with Jane and Michelle in the hallway. They all came in laughing and toting their bridesmaid's dresses over their shoulders.

"I'll let you girls finish getting ready," Kate's father said as he placed a hand on her mother's shoulder. He winked at Kate. "I'll see you in the vestibule."

An hour and a half later, Kate appeared next to him in her dress, pink and white roses cascading from her hand in a perfect waterfall.

Her father stepped back so his eyes could take her in. "Oh, my."

"So many pictures," Kate said, shaking her head. "Get ready, because after the ceremony—"

"You look beautiful," her father cut in, his voice emotional. He leaned forward and placed a gentle kiss on her cheek. "I changed my mind, Katie. There's no way I can give you away. Even to Will."

"Oh, Daddy." Kate's voice wobbled. "You'll never *really* get rid of me."

The wedding coordinator tapped Kate on the shoulder. "Ready?"

"I love you," she whispered to her dad and then gave the nod.

The doors opened, and organ music began to fill the church. As Kate waited, swaying on her heels, nervous flutters filled her stomach.

The bridesmaids and groomsmen paired up and made their way down the aisle until she and her dad were the only ones left.

After a deep breath, Kate linked her arm into his and gazed up into his eyes. "Ready?"

Her father reached over and patted her hand. "I guess I'm as ready as I'm ever going to get."

The bridal march began to play, and with sunlight streaming through the stained-glass windows, Kate began to walk, her steps slow and measured as they'd practiced the night before. The spectators stood from the pews to watch, but Kate's gaze was anchored on the incredible man waiting for her. As she got closer, Will's eyes met hers with so much love Kate had to fight back the tears. How had she ever gotten so lucky?

Her father lifted her veil and kissed her cheek before stepping back. As Kate clasped hands with Will, the room faded away. With him, she felt complete, like two perfect puzzle pieces meant to be together.

Will leaned in close and whispered, "If this all gets to be too much later, you and I will escape and find someplace amazing to be alone. Start the honeymoon early." He caressed her with his eyes. "There's no way I'm wasting a minute of the way you look right now."

Kate's cheeks burned. That was Will. If he had something to say, he was going to say it, no matter where they were. Still, she was grateful there were no microphones yet, and the minister was far enough away not to hear. At least she hoped so.

Kate had no hesitation that Will was the right man for her. There was no one else she'd want to spend her life with. Nobody better for her to have a family and grow old alongside.

After opening remarks from the minister and several readings, the minister called upon them to share their personal vows.

Will squeezed Kate's hands, then released them to reach into his tuxedo jacket's inside pocket. He unfolded a sheet of paper and locked eyes with her.

"When we met a little over two years ago, I had no idea what I was getting myself into. In you, my sweet Katie girl, I found my best friend, my rock, the most genuine and caring person I have ever met. With every question I ever had, you were always the answer. The direction I wanted to go was whichever way you were going. You were the person I was meant to be with."

He shot a look at the groomsmen. "When you said I had to stand up here and make promises in front of all our friends, I have to admit, I was a little nervous about sharing my private thoughts. But here goes."

Was that a sparkle of mischief Kate saw in his eyes before they drifted down to his vows?

"I promise to accept that you enjoy long, hot showers." Will brought his gaze up to her, a playful gleam in his eye. "But with you around all the time, my need for cold showers will increase substantially, so that'll work out perfectly."

Kate rolled her eyes as laughter erupted from the pews. With a captive audience, could she have expected any less from him?

Will held up his hand. "Okay, okay. I just had to get it out of my system. I'm good from here on out."

Kate shot him a skeptical look.

He continued. "I promise to always give you my opinion, even though we both know it really doesn't matter."

Kate lifted a shoulder, then nodded at her bridesmaids. "Well, that's probably true."

Will licked his lips and then kept going, his gaze focused on the paper in his shaking hand. "I promise to be your test subject when you want to try out a new dessert. I promise to keep my cold toes to myself under the covers and to always tell you we have to be somewhere twenty minutes early." He glanced up. "You know, so we stand a chance of being on time."

Will stifled a smile. "I promise to always give you a bite of my food even when you *swear* you're not hungry." He leaned in close to her, his voice low. "I can't lie. That might be the hardest promise yet."

He held his vows out in front of him in one hand and reached for Kate's with the other. His expression turned serious, his eyes welling up as he held her gaze. "I promise you will always have a faithful husband, a man of values and integrity who will raise our family with the same standards. I promise to always encourage you to follow your dreams and help you achieve whatever it is you want most in life." He gave her hand a soft squeeze.

"Although today marks the official beginning of our life together, it can never be long enough. I promise to never take our time together for granted, to cherish every single day I have with you. For the rest of your life, I intend to take care of you, to show you just how much I love you. I am the luckiest man alive to have you as my wife."

As Will folded the paper and returned it to his jacket pocket, Kate felt tears threatening to fall.

She sniffled and shot him a hopeless look. "How am I supposed to get through mine now after that?"

Kate reached out for Will's hands. No need for paper. Her vows had been memorized. "From the moment I laid eyes on you that Super Bowl Sunday, I knew we were meant to be together. At the time, I worried maybe it was just wishful thinking. You taught me about football that day and asked if we were a team." She glanced in the direction of the groomsmen. "Never mind that our team was created for the sole purpose of rooting against Paul's team."

Paul scowled as there was a titter from the audience.

Kate's eyes were back on Will. "It didn't matter which team got the trophy. I was the clear winner that day because I found you. You've made me a football fan and a better person. I promise I'll *always* be on your team—to love and support you, no matter what. Your goals are my goals. Your wishes are my wishes." She gave a slight smile. "Even when it comes to the thermostat. I mean, as long as it doesn't get below seventy degrees in the house in the dead of winter. Let's not get crazy."

Sixty-eight, Will mouthed at her, his eyebrows lifting.

Kate ignored him and continued. "I promise to root for your Giants no matter how rough the season gets, and I accept you'll probably have your lucky sweatshirt until the end of time." She winced slightly. "I also know it's possible it might never get washed."

Will grinned, and his gaze bounced to his groomsmen, all nodding enthusiastically in their moment of male bonding. Kate had known they would love that part, and it provided a moment of levity before her vows turned serious.

"Will, I promise to be your best friend, through good times

and bad, laughter and tears. Love is a choice, and I choose you. I choose you today, and I will continue to choose you every day for the rest of my life. When the time comes that we're watching the world from our rocking chairs, my heart will feel the same as it does right now. We'll look back and know how blessed we were to have this life to spend together. I love you." Kate squeezed Will's hands, and her shoulders relaxed with relief that her vows were now behind her. She'd been terrified she'd freeze in the moment and forget what she'd written.

The minister nodded to acknowledge they were moving on. "I will also offer the traditional vows as you have both requested." With the book for the ceremony laid open in his hands, he turned to Will. "Will, do you take Kate to be your lawfully wedded wife? Do you promise to love and cherish her, in sickness and in health, for richer, for poorer, for better, for worse, and forsaking all others, keep yourself only unto her until death parts you?"

Will gave the minister an earnest nod. "Oh, I do."

Then he leaned in toward Kate, and his voice dropped to a whisper only she could hear. "Even death wouldn't stop me from loving you."

CHAPTER 3

TWO YEARS LATER

ate's fingers gripped the edge of the tub. Perched there, she squeezed her eyes shut and marveled how three minutes could feel like an eternity. Her right leg bounced against the white tile floor while she waited for the kitchen timer she'd set on the vanity. Still, she jumped when the bell jingled louder than she'd expected in the small bathroom.

Her stomach rolled. It wasn't proof, she convinced herself. Most likely just her nerves. But it also didn't mean she wasn't right.

Kate's heart raced as she stood to retrieve the long white stick. Other months she'd hoped, thought maybe, but she'd been wrong. Today, even before seeing the test results, Kate was confident. She just knew. The night it happened—several weeks ago—she'd had this feeling.

Kate squinted as she stared at the stick, but the tip had clearly turned blue. There was no misreading it.

She reached for the box and flipped it over to reread the

instructions. Doublechecking. Just to be sure. She'd done every-thing the way she was supposed to, but this new test seemed too easy. Kate bit her bottom lip as her eyes fixed on the beauti-ful blue color. A smile grew on her face until she was grinning.

She was pregnant.

There was an unexpected knock on the door. Kate flinched, a guilty heat on her cheeks.

"Hey, hon, you in there?" Will's voice was on the other side.

"Um, yeah. You're home early."

Grateful she'd closed the door before she started, Kate hurriedly shoved the test back into the box. Her gaze drifted across the countertop as she scooped up all traces of what she'd been up to. She threw the evidence back into the pharmacy bag and tossed it inside the cabinet under the sink.

She had a plan to tell Will he was going to be a father. If he saw something that gave it away, it would ruin her news. After a peek into the small trash can, Kate turned the doorknob and flung open the bathroom door.

"Hey." He drew her close and wrapped his arms around her.

Could Will feel her heart pounding? Kate tried to push down the feeling of guilt that she was keeping a secret from her husband. She would share the news soon enough.

"Everything okay?" she asked. "I thought you had practice."

Will pulled back to study her, a look of disbelief on his face. For a moment, she thought he suspected something. "Have you looked outside lately? It's storming like crazy."

The sky had been an angry gray when Kate dashed into the pharmacy on her way home. Since then, she'd been far too distracted with the pregnancy test to care about the weather.

She glanced casually out the bedroom window. "Oh, wow. It wasn't even raining when I got home."

He pushed her long hair back off her face and kissed her. "Yeah, well, I decided I wasn't quite in the mood to get hit by lightning today. I ended practice early and told the guys to work out in the weight room with Mac."

Will taught eleventh grade English and coached the football team. His students and players adored him.

Kate tilted her head as she looked up at him. "You feel okay? You never let Mac handle stuff on his own."

Will shrugged as he aimed a suggestive smile at her. "I missed you today, even more than usual. And besides, isn't that what an assistant coach is supposed to do? Assist the coach so he can go home and kiss on his wife?" Will leaned forward and brushed his lips against hers, gentle at first and then with more intensity as he pulled her body to his.

Kate closed her eyes and let out a soft moan. Even after two years of marriage, her husband's kisses still made her pleasantly woozy.

Will pulled back slightly, then nodded his chin toward the bed. A smile played at the corners of his mouth. "I mean, I am home early."

Kate gave him an eager nod, then let out a gasp when he scooped her up. Their baby was a tiny speck right now. Would he sense something was different about her?

Will rested his forearms on the bed, and as he held himself up over her, she got lost in his eyes. If they were the window to the soul, Kate was looking deep into Will's. What she saw was warm and comforting, the way sunshine feels on your face that first spring day after a long dreary winter. She couldn't wait to share their news with him. Will was going to be an incredible father.

The sky outside lit up and sent a flash of white light flooding into the bedroom. A moment later, a booming clap of thunder followed, so intense the windows rattled.

Will nuzzled into Kate's neck as he kissed her. "See. Out there." He shook his head at her, an exaggerated scowl on his face. "Very bad." He brought his lips to hers. "In here ... so very good."

He peeled off his shirt, and Kate's hands slid up and down his back and then toward his broad shoulders. Her fingers drifted into the soft curls at the nape of his neck. Very good indeed.

Afterward, Kate lay wrapped in Will's arms, her hands resting across his stomach. She giggled when it grumbled under her fingertips.

"Hungry? I didn't start anything for dinner when I got home. I was—" She lifted her gaze to him and raised her eyebrows. "Interrupted."

"Why, Mrs. Kennedy, are you complaining?" Will asked, feigning shock.

Kate shook her head and sat up, resting on her elbow. "Absolutely not. What I am doing is telling you I'll probably need to order a pizza."

"Fine with me. Order one with everything, and make sure Giuseppe's piles on extra mushrooms and onions." Will assumed a serious expression as he nodded enthusiastically. "Oh, anchovies too. Lots and lots of anchovies."

Kate playfully swatted him. He teased her all the time that her pizza preference was plain and unimaginative. "I'll get your usual on *half* of it."

Will yanked back the covers and slid out of bed. Kate rolled over and rested her chin in her palm as she watched him strut toward the bathroom. He spun around and flashed her a grin. "If you're done admiring the view, I think I'll take a shower."

With a laugh, Kate threw a pillow at him. It hit the bathroom door as it closed behind him.

"Don't take too long," she called out, hoping he wouldn't have a need to rummage through the cabinet.

Kate slipped back into her clothes, and when she made her way into the kitchen to place the pizza order, the fragrant smell of lilacs greeted her. Her favorite. Will regularly brought her flowers. Tonight, he didn't even know they were getting ready to celebrate.

With a glance at the phone number on the refrigerator magnet, she dialed the pizzeria. Kate stretched the phone cord to the kitchen table and inhaled deeply over the flowers until her call was answered. "Giuseppe's Pizza. Pickup or delivery?"

Kate was sitting at the kitchen table, strategizing her plan for telling Will about the baby, when he strode in freshly showered.

"The flowers smell great," she said. "They're beautiful."

"Beautiful flowers for my beautiful wife." Will leaned in over her and placed a kiss on her cheek.

Kate let out an appreciative sigh. The smell of his soap took her back to the day they'd met at Melinda's. It had left her intoxicated that day, and it still did.

She tilted her head back to look up at him. "Pizza should be ready in about fifteen minutes. Can you go pick it up?" She needed a bit of time to execute her plan.

"Sure. Want me to pick up a bottle of wine too?"

Kate narrowed her eyes and studied him. Was he baiting her? Had she not taken the test, she would have loved to share a bottle of wine. But knowing she was pregnant, the answer had to be no.

"Nah, I don't think so." Kate hoped declining wouldn't arouse his suspicion. She didn't usually turn down wine. "I told my boss I'd come in early to set up for a meeting, but there's some beer in the fridge if you want."

Will leaned down and gave her a quick kiss. "Okay, be right back." His eyebrows shot up as he grabbed his keys from the counter. "One pizza with absolutely everything coming up."

Kate rolled her eyes. "This is why I always offer to place the order. So, there aren't any surprises."

She waited for the click of the front door shutting behind him and then sprang into action. Although they hadn't been trying very long, she'd been prepared for this day.

When Will returned twenty minutes later, he brought with him the aroma of fresh pizza. He strolled into the kitchen, the box on his flattened palm.

"Are you ready for some delizioso—" He froze, his mouth open as his gaze fixed on the table.

"I have something to tell you," Kate said in a soft voice.

Resting on the back of Will's chair was the infant-sized Giants jersey she'd bought and stashed away for this moment. The over-sized foam finger that said #1 Dad was in his seat, and where his plate usually went was the sign she'd made. *Baby Kennedy, Coming Soon.*

Will slid the pizza box off his palm and onto the counter. He knelt down in front of Kate and searched her eyes for confirmation. "Really?"

Kate nodded, her lips turning up in a smile. "Really. I mean, it's still early, but—" She unwrapped the test she'd hidden in a napkin. "Blue means I'm pregnant."

"Well, that's definitely blue." Will lifted her from the chair and hugged her. "Oh, honey, I'm so happy. I can't believe I'm going to be a daddy. I want a boy. No, a girl. How about one of each? Or maybe two of each?"

Kate laughed at his excitement. "How about we do them one at a time, tiger?"

Will held her hands in his and kissed them. "You're going to be a wonderful mother. How far along ..."

"I can't be sure until I go to the doctor, but remember our anniversary weekend in Cape May?"

He whooped. "I knew it was good, but I didn't know it was *baby-making* good. How 'bout us?"

Kate nodded and laughed again. "How 'bout us, indeed."

"I can't believe we're going to have a family." Will held up the tiny jersey. "Us. Parents. This definitely deserves a slice of pizza with everything." He pulled the pizza box from the counter and flipped back the lid. "Okay, you deserve your favorite too, I suppose. One slice of naked pizza coming up for the mommy-to-be."

Still grinning, he slid a slice onto each of their plates.

"A whole football team. That's what we need," Will said, folding his slice of pizza to keep the contents from falling off. "My sweet Katie girl, do you have any idea how deliriously happy I am right now?"

"I do. Because I feel exactly the same way."

"A baby. We got it going on now, honey." Will took a large bite and smiled as he chewed. "I can't wait to be a dad. I'm going to do everything with our kid. I mean, even if we have a girl, she'll be into football, right? I mean, I got you into it, and she'll already have a jersey." He nodded to himself. "Yeah, she'll be a Giants fan."

Will's excitement over being a dad tugged at Kate's heart.

"You got me good," he said, shaking his head. "I don't know why actually. I mean, I *know* how babies are made." Will gave her a lopsided grin. "And we do *that* a lot. But we actually made us a baby, honey. You and me. How freaking amazing is that?"

He reached for a napkin and wiped the pizza grease from his lips, then picked up his glass. "A toast."

Kate lifted her glass and held it to his.

"To us," Will said, his eyes locked on hers. "To celebrate our love and this new life that's coming to change everything for us in the most spectacular of ways. You have made me the happiest man in the world. I love you, Katie girl."

She leaned forward and kissed him. "I love you too. Cheers." She tapped her glass against Will's and picked up her slice of pizza. She couldn't stop smiling even as she took a bite. Happiness had her heart dancing in her chest. She was going to be a mom.

They had no idea their celebration would only be practice for the next time she was pregnant. This baby would never make it into the world.

CHAPTER 4

A YEAR AND A HALF LATER

he pain woke her. Kate winced and then glanced at the glowing numbers on the alarm clock. Midnight. It had only been an hour since Kate maneuvered her oversized belly into a cradle of pillows so she was comfortable enough to sleep. In the darkness, she heard the soft sound of Will's snoring beside her.

Her pulse quickened, but she tried to convince herself it was nothing. This was probably Will's fault. He had insisted on tacos for dinner.

Kate settled back into her pillow and waited. One minute. Then two. When nothing happened, she took several of the deep, cleansing breaths she'd read about in her pregnancy book. She closed her eyes and tried to go back to sleep.

A couple of weeks earlier, she'd roused Will from a deep sleep. It had been a false alarm. Braxton Hicks contractions the nurse at the hospital called them before she'd sent them home. They'd both gone to work bleary-eyed the next morning.

After the miscarriage of their first baby, Kate was devastated. Will held her afterward, promising they'd try again. Deep down, she'd been petrified to consider it, but before she could even decide if she was ready, Kate was pregnant again.

She was grateful but finely tuned into anything that could be a problem. Headaches, the baby not moving, even indigestion— all met with dread that something was wrong. When she'd gotten past the four-month mark, the point where she'd lost the first baby, Kate tried to relax. Now she knew. Until she held this baby in her arms, she'd continue to worry something might happen again.

"Ow." Kate moaned as the pain briefly swept through her again.

The clock now said 12:15 a.m. The doctor had told her to time her contractions to see if they started coming at consistent intervals. Gritting her teeth, she glanced over at Will, blissfully sleeping through her discomfort. Dreaming peacefully with no idea her uterus seemed ready to painfully squeeze this baby out of her. Will had played his part in getting her pregnant. It wasn't fair he wouldn't have the opportunity to share in this as well.

Kate laid there in the darkness waiting. Sure enough, there were three more contractions by one o'clock. Before long, they started coming closer together, and each lasted longer. Now in pain, she'd forgotten what the doctor had said about when they should come in.

With a perfectly placed elbow, she nudged Will.

Her husband let out a sleepy, aggravated grunt. Then he rolled over to face the other direction, as if whatever was attempting to disturb his sound sleep would stop if he couldn't see it. No such luck.

Using two fingers, Kate poked his shoulder sharply. "Hey," she whispered into the darkness. When he still didn't respond, she spoke louder and instilled a bit more urgency. "It's showtime, and I'm not doing this alone, *Daddy.*"

Will whipped his body around, and his eyes blinked hard as he worked to keep them open. "I'm awake." He sat up and ran his hand over his face. "You're sure? This is really it this time?"

"Well, I've been timing the contractions and—ow." Kate's stomach tightened, and she tried to breathe rapidly through it until it was over. Finally, she took a deep, cleansing breath and nodded. "They're coming faster and lasting longer. About ten minutes apart now."

Will released a wide, audible yawn. "The nurse said to come in when they're five minutes apart and each one lasts about a minute." He laid back down and tucked his pillow under his head.

Kate frowned and poked him again. "Are you sure that was what she said?"

"Positive." Will turned slightly and opened one eye a crack so he could peek out at his wife.

"You know you're not going back to sleep, right?"

"Of *course* I'm not going back to sleep, my love." Will slid out of bed, came around to her side, and held out his hand. "The doctor said it would help to walk around."

Kate gripped his hand and groaned as she let him pull her up and out of bed. "What would help is to get this baby out of me."

"Soon, honey." Will winced. "You're squeezing my hand pretty tight there. Can you walk on your own?"

Kate let go and tried to stand up straight. "I can as long as the pain's not ripping through me. Ohhh, here comes another one." She lunged for Will's arm.

When the contraction was over, Will rubbed at the dents his wife's fingernails had left in his skin. "I'll call Dr. Lubetkin."

Kate followed him. "Hon, it's two in the morning." She leaned on the kitchen counter.

"I'm sure you're not the first expectant mother to get him out of bed." Will picked up the phone and began to dial.

While Kate did laps—through the kitchen, into the hallway,

through the family room, and back through the kitchen—she listened to his half of the conversation with Dr. Lubetkin.

"She's been up for a while," Will said into the phone. "Um, she just got me up. Let me ask her. Hon, how often are the contractions coming?"

Kate had reached the kitchen again, and she leaned on the table. "About every eight minutes, I think."

Will reported back to the doctor and then hung up. "We need to start timing them. I'll get my watch, but I was right. He said to wait until they're five minutes apart and they last about a minute. When they do that consistently for an hour, we need to head in."

Kate hung her head. That seemed like an eternity. Her eyes narrowed, a whine on her lips. "Is that when I get the drugs?"

Will laughed. "Yes, honey, we'll get you some nice drugs to make you comfy."

Kate let out a soft happy moan. "I have the best husband ever." Then she doubled over again.

* * *

"Okay, Kate, I need one more push."

Dr. Lubetkin let her know the finish line was in sight, but Kate was exhausted. She wasn't sure she had anything left. Not even one more push.

Will held her hand in his and squeezed it. "You got this."

Kate glanced at him, and then her head fell back against the bed. A trickle of sweat rolled down her face. "I don't think I do," she said, her voice sounding as weary as she felt. "I'm so tired, hon. I can't push anymore." She shook her head. "I just can't. You're going to have to figure out another way to get this baby out of me."

Will leaned over the bed, and his eyes met hers. In them, she saw the man she loved, believing in her with everything he had. At that moment, Will's face was all she saw, his love all she felt.

LIANE CARMEN

"You can do anything, Katie girl. You're absolutely amazing. One more push and we get to meet our baby. You can do this. I know you can."

Kate hesitated, then nodded slowly. Gripping his hand, she sat up and gave one last push accompanied by a husky groan. Will's wide grin accompanied the relief Kate finally felt.

She heard crying.

"It's a boy," Dr. Lubetkin announced as he held him up and handed him to the nurse.

Emotions flooded through Kate, her eyes wet. "Is he okay?" she asked, her nervous gaze volleying between the doctor and Will.

"He's absolutely perfect," Dr. Lubetkin said, smiling. "They're just cleaning him up for you."

Kate turned to Will. "Did you see him?" she asked, her sweaty brow wrinkled, her voice full of concern. "Is he really okay?" Her eyes pleaded with him for an answer.

Will swallowed hard and nodded. He used a finger to push Kate's hair, matted with sweat, off her face. "Our son is incredible, just like his mom." He kissed her lips and then glanced up as the nurse came toward them.

"Ready to meet him?"

When the baby was placed in her arms, a sob caught in Kate's throat as she gazed down. Everything she'd been through—the miscarriage and the fears she'd carried into this pregnancy. All forgotten. Her worries ebbed away as she held him and leaned over to kiss his soft forehead.

"Hi, Zachary," she said in a soft voice, trying out the name they'd chosen. She glanced up at Will and nodded. "He looks like a Zach."

"I can't wait to teach you how to play football, Zach." Will leaned in close and whispered, "You're going to be a Giants fan, little guy."

The baby let out a small, perfectly-timed whimper, and Kate struggled to stifle her laugh.

Will scowled, pretending to be offended. "Hey, now, buddy. Don't be like that right off the bat."

As Kate gazed down into Zach's sweet face, he let out a sleepy yawn. A small smile played on her lips. "Yeah, I get it. I'm tired too."

"I know, right?" Will stretched his arms into the air. "I'm absolutely exhausted."

Kate shot him a look, then ran the back of her index finger across Zach's cheek. "Your father thinks he's funny, but you know what? You couldn't have picked yourself a better daddy, and I get to be your mommy. How lucky am I?"

Will kissed the top of Kate's head, and together they gazed in awe at their newborn son. He was absolutely perfect. Kate's heart overflowed with an intensity she hadn't expected.

How was it possible to feel so much love for someone she'd just met?

CHAPTER 5

SEVEN YEARS LATER

*T*hrough the kitchen window, Kate heard Will's direction to Zach.

"C'mon, buddy, you got this. Go long."

She glanced out into the backyard. A football sailed through the air, and Zach ran barefoot in the summer grass toward it. When he turned, the ball thumped squarely into his small hands.

Will ran and scooped him up. "That was an amazing catch. You're getting to be quite the little receiver. Want to practice throwing now?"

"Hey, you guys," Kate called out. "You have about ten minutes, and then you need to come in and wash up for dinner."

"Okay, Mommy." Then Zach gestured in the air with his hand, directing Will to head toward the property line that separated their house from their neighbors.

Kate leaned on the windowsill and watched. Zach was only seven, but Will had ensured their son had a football in his hands before he could speak complete sentences.

"Dude!" Will yelled after he caught the ball, aimed directly at him. His gaze drifted up to Kate. "Did you see that, honey? This kid's got a quarterback's arm if I ever saw one."

"You'd better call the Giants. Let them know he's coming. Don't forget, ten minutes," Kate said before she returned to the stove.

A few minutes later, they bounded in the door. "I'm telling you, this boy's got it," Will said as he ruffled the messy curls on Zach's head.

"He certainly does." Kate gestured at the stool that stood near the kitchen sink. "But even famous quarterbacks have to wash their hands before dinner."

Will helped Zach and then washed his own hands. "Smells good, hon."

"Meatloaf, mashed potatoes, and corn on the cob."

When they sat down, Will portioned food onto each person's plate. "Did you get the corn from the farmer's market?"

When Kate nodded, he bit carefully into his as butter dripped from the cob onto his chin. "Freshly picked Jersey corn in the summer. Nothing better, Zach." He lifted his eyebrows as he caught Kate's eye. "Your mommy hooked us up."

Kate laughed and handed him a napkin.

"I like corn too, Daddy." Zach picked his up, letting it deliberately drip the same way down his chin before collapsing into a fit of buttery giggles.

Kate shook her head and dug into her plate before asking about Will's day. He taught summer school while Zach attended camp, but they were both home early.

"Great job on your dinner," Kate said as Zach made his way through his plate of food.

"Playing football's hard work. You gotta eat to get big and strong." Zach glanced at Will, who gave him an unmistakable wink.

The little boy smiled, gave a nod, and then turned to Kate. "Mommy, you know what I think we should do after dinner?"

Kate cast a suspicious glance in her husband's direction. "What's that?"

Zach threw both hands up in the air and grinned. "Dairy Queen!"

"Oh, I don't know about that, Zach," Kate said, trying to look serious. "Nobody here likes ice cream."

Zach's surprised gaze shot over to Will. "I do, and Daddy does. It was his idea. He *loves* ice cream."

Will groaned. "C'mon, buddy. You never rat out the other players on your team."

Kate laughed. "Like I wouldn't know there was a bit of a conspiracy here." She usually baked something for dessert but hadn't had time to make anything. "I could go for ice cream. But you have to finish your dinner." She pushed her own plate to the side. "So, how was camp today?"

As Zach launched into a long, overdrawn tale of dodge ball, her gaze drifted to Will, and she smiled. Kate's stomach and her heart were full.

* * *

When they backed away from Zach's bedroom door several hours later, Kate put her finger on her lips. "Shhh."

After the trip to Dairy Queen, a bath to wash off the sticky remnants of his chocolate-dipped cone, and two bedtime stories, he'd finally drifted off to sleep.

"Sit with me outside?" Will asked.

"I'll meet you down there."

Ten minutes later, Kate joined him on the patio. He held up a glass and patted the spot next to him on the swinging loveseat.

Kate reached for the wine and sank down, nestling in under his arm. She sipped from her glass and let out an appreciative sigh as Will's foot gently pushed off the concrete to rock them in a slow, soothing rhythm.

"I love summer," she said. "You two playing in the grass. Ice cream for dessert. Sitting outside like this after Zach goes to bed."

Will put his finger under her chin and tipped her face up toward him. He kissed her lips gently. "A perfect day. Did you see how good Zach's getting?" His face lit up, and Kate could tell he was bursting with pride. "He naturally picks up everything I tell him."

"Well, you *are* a football coach, hon."

"For *high schoolers*. Zach's *seven*. By the time he's in high school, I can't even imagine how good he'll be."

"Speaking of football, before you have to start practices in a few weeks, should we head to the shore this weekend? It's going to be ninety on Saturday."

Will shrugged casually and sipped his wine. "I wouldn't mind building another sandcastle with Zach."

Kate laughed. He'd said that casually as if the last one hadn't been worthy of a mention in *Architectural Digest*. He and Zach had spent all day making the massive structure with a moat around it, turrets, and a drawbridge. By late afternoon, other beachgoers had gathered around to watch them build it. Some even took pictures. When they were ready to leave, Will had simply high-fived Zach and walked away without looking back.

Kate had shaken her head in disbelief and asked, "Doesn't it bother you to spend all that time building it, only to leave and know it's going to get trampled on or washed away?"

Will had grinned at Zach. "Nah. We'll just build an even bigger, better one next time. Right, buddy?"

That was Will. He never felt the need to look back because he was sure something even better was ahead of him.

Kate sipped her wine as his hands caressed her shoulder, his fingers warm against her skin.

"I think I'm ready to go up," he said.

"You're tired?"

"Nope. Just ready to go up." Will lifted his eyebrows, and the smile on his face widened.

Now Kate knew what he meant. "Oh, you are, huh?" She tipped back her glass and finished her wine before setting it on the small table.

She cupped his face in her hands and kissed him. The wine and his hands tangled in her hair as he pressed her against him had Kate's entire body buzzing.

He pulled back and stood, leaning down to reach for her hand. "My sweet Katie girl, do you know how much I love you?"

She let herself be helped up from the loveseat. "I love you too, and…"

Will wrapped her up in his arms. "And what?"

Kate's eyes locked on his. "I can't imagine how our life could be any more perfect."

CHAPTER 6

THREE AND A HALF YEARS LATER

"*M*om, it's snowing!" Zach's excited voice called to her from the family room.

To her son's disappointment, it had been a mild winter so far. That morning as Kate drove him to school, the weatherman on the radio announced they'd finally get their first snowfall of the season. Zach was thrilled. Kate hoped it wouldn't start until Will was home from work.

Kate wiped her hands on a dish towel, then made her way to where Zach stood, his nose pressed against the sliding glass door. The tree branches and grass had turned white. It was beginning to stick.

Zach spun around with a satisfied smile. "We'll probably get a snow day tomorrow. Dad needs to blow up my new tube."

The snow tube had been a present under the tree a few weeks earlier, and he was dying to break it in. Kate sucked air in through her teeth and shook her head. "I hate to break it to you, but I doubt it. It's supposed to turn to rain overnight. Probably all be washed away by morning."

His face fell in disappointment. "No, way," Zach said, whining. "That's not fair at all."

Kate ruffled his hair. "Sorry, buddy, but I'm sure we'll have more before too long. If this keeps up, maybe we'll get enough that we can go out and play in it after Daddy comes home."

That would just add to the night she'd planned. Pot roast was in the oven, and she had Will's favorite cake glazed and ready for dessert.

Kate pursed her lips as she watched the snow falling. "Let me see if Daddy's left work yet."

Back in the kitchen, she lifted the phone and dialed the number at Will's school.

"Hey, Peg," Kate said when the secretary in the office answered. "Any idea if Will is still around?" The school day was over, but her husband tended to stay late to prepare for the next day.

"Well, I haven't seen him leave, Mrs. Kennedy, so hang on, and I'll transfer you to his classroom."

He answered on the second ring. "Will Kennedy."

That familiar rush went through Kate at the sound of his voice. "Hi, honey, it's me. It's starting to snow."

There was a pause, and Kate could picture Will turning to glance behind him out the window of his classroom. "Well, look at that. So, it is."

"Any chance you could leave now? It's supposed to get heavier, and I hate the idea of you driving home in it." She was being silly. It wasn't snowing that hard yet. Will was a safe driver, but Kate felt unsettled when it snowed unless he was home too. Then it felt cozy and safe.

"It doesn't look *too* bad out."

"Not yet, but I've already got a roast in the oven, and it'll be all dried up if you get stuck in traffic. You know people forget how to drive after the first snowflake hits the ground."

"Tell the truth," Will said, his tone serious. "You want a rematch on last year's snowball fight. I'll even give you Zach again, but you know you two can't take on the reigning champ." He let out an evil chuckle.

Kate laughed despite herself. "You got me. Actually, Zach's pretty excited it's snowing but not very happy the rain will probably wash it away. He was hoping for no school tomorrow." She stretched the phone cord to peek in on him. "So, there's probably only tonight to get out there and play in it. You wouldn't want to miss the first snow of the year with him, right? If there's not enough for snowballs, maybe he can at least use his new tube. He wants you to inflate it for him." She hated playing the Zach card, but she wanted Will home.

"Okay, you convinced me. I still have some work to do, but I can do it at home later after Zach goes to bed." Will lowered his voice. "No seducing me tonight, you hear me? I have papers to grade."

Kate rolled her eyes and laughed. "I promise."

"Okay, A's for everyone. That makes it easy, so don't you worry, we're back on for later."

"I wasn't that worried." Kate heard the sound of rustling papers.

"I'm packing up, and I'll get out of here now. Need me to stop on the way home and get anything?"

She glanced out the window. "Maybe hot chocolate? The kind Zach likes with the marshmallows." It would be a nice treat to warm up with when they came in.

"You got it. I'll see you soon. Love you."

"Drive carefully. I love you too."

Kate hung up the phone and glanced at the clock on the wall above the sink. The roast had already been in or over an hour, so the timing would be perfect. They might even have a chance to have a glass of wine before dinner.

"Hey, Zach," she called out. "Daddy's leaving now. If we get enough snow, he promised a snowball fight, or at least we can take your tube to the park." When the little boy turned, excitement in his eyes, Kate held up her hand. "But not until after dinner, okay?"

Zach's backpack lay in a heap by the front door where he'd dropped it when they got home. Kate carried it into the family room by one of its straps. "Do you have any homework?"

"I dunno. Maybe." Zach's eyes didn't stray from the television.

"Listen." Kate picked up the remote. "If you want to play later, you need to finish it. Get out your planner and see what you have. Just get it over with."

Zach groaned when the screen went black and then turned to her with his lips puckered into a pout. "But maybe it will keep snowing and not rain. Then I'll have tomorrow to do it."

Kate shook her head. "But you probably don't, so let's get going."

Zach trudged to the kitchen and plopped down in a chair. Elbow on the table, he placed his chin in his palm, a glum expression on his face. "Okay, let's have it."

"That's a lot of drama for about fifteen minutes of homework, you know." Kate pulled out his planner and tossed it on the table. "If you want, when you're finished, we can put on a movie until Daddy comes home."

Zach's eyes lit up. "*Air Bud?*" The movie about the golden retriever that played basketball had been a Christmas present. His new favorite.

Kate's shoulders drooped. "Again?" When he nodded enthusiastically, she sighed. "Okay. But let's get your homework done first."

"They should teach that dog to play football," Zach said matter-of-factly as he hunted in his backpack for a pencil.

Twenty minutes later, his homework was done, and they were snuggled side-by-side on the couch with a blanket tucked around them. Snow was still falling, and the smells of the roast cooking permeated the air. It was perfect. All they needed was Will.

Despite the fact she'd now seen the movie too many times to count, Kate found herself sucked in. Zach's hand rested on her arm, and every so often, he patted it and said, "Mom, watch."

"I am watching." Kate reassured him time and again as if she wasn't sitting right next to him doing just that.

"We should get a dog like him," Zach said when the movie ended. "Dad could coach him to play basketball *and* football."

"I bet he could," Kate said, and then she frowned. Where was Will? She'd expected him home well before the movie was over. "Hey, I need to get up and check on dinner." She handed Zach the remote, slipped out from under the blanket, and tucked it back around him.

The roast smelled delicious but would need to come out of the oven soon. A quick glance out the window at the driveway confirmed Will's side was covered with a layer of snow but still empty.

Kate pursed her lips. It was hard to believe Will would have stayed after he'd said he was leaving. That wasn't like him. If something had happened, he would have called back to let her know he'd be running late.

With a glance at the kitchen clock, Kate picked up the phone. She heard a dial tone. The phone was working, so it wasn't like he couldn't get through if he had tried to call. She wasn't optimistic anyone was still around, but she punched in the numbers for the school anyway. Kate sighed as it rang and rang.

She hung up, then dropped into a chair at the kitchen table so she could watch the driveway through the front window. Her heart raced as she forced herself to think through all the possible scenarios that might explain why Will wasn't home yet.

He only had a twenty-minute drive to the house. Even stop-

45

ping at the store, potentially packed with shoppers nervous about the snow, he should have been home—Kate calculated the time in her head. At the absolute latest, Will should have walked in well over an hour ago.

Maybe there was an accident, and he was stuck behind it. A road closure or something simple to explain why he couldn't pull over to call. He'd never let her worry like this if he could help it. Kate was the one who was generally late, not Will. Still, a twinge of uneasiness crept in. He'd said he was leaving over two hours ago.

In the distance, headlights lit up the street as they headed in her direction. Kate exhaled a sigh of relief and stood to greet her husband at the front door. He'd be getting an earful. As Kate peered out the window, waiting for him to pull in, the car drove past their house and turned right at the corner.

It wasn't him.

She sunk back down. With her elbows on the table, she held her head in her hands as her mind began to race.

She jumped when the timer went off for the roast. Her stomach was in knots as she got up and grabbed an oven mitt. Her dinner, which had smelled wonderful not so long ago, now held no appeal.

"Is Daddy home yet?" Zach called out from the family room.

"Not yet." She peeked into the family room, but his attention was laser-focused on the television. "But dinner's ready. Are you hungry? I can fix you a plate so you can eat now." It would keep her mind off waiting for Will to come through the front door.

"I want to wait until Dad gets home." When Zach turned to face her, he was wearing a scowl. "What's taking him so long?"

Kate tried to make her voice sound casual. Unconcerned. "I don't know. He probably got stuck in traffic, but I'm sure he'll be home soon."

Back in the kitchen, Kate crossed her arms against her chest and stared out the window, her breath fogging the glass. She focused on the street until she was convinced she'd jump out of her skin if she went one more second without seeing Will's car. With a groan, Kate wiped the window with her sleeve and began pacing the kitchen.

As she stared down at the tile, her heart thumped. There had to be a reasonable explanation. But if there was, why hadn't Kate heard from him? Will never had any interest in getting a cell phone, but she was planning to insist after tonight.

Thirty minutes later, there was still no call and no Will. Panic started to descend on Kate like a thick fog, surrounding her and seeping into her pores until she couldn't see past it. Where the *hell* was he? Kate pressed her lips together to keep from screaming and scaring Zach. Her gaze drifted from the clock to the window. Again, and again, until she felt ill.

Kate wrapped her hand around her stomach as tears sprung to her eyes. Swiping at them, she glanced toward the family room. She didn't want Zach to know she was worried.

She parked herself at the front window, her gaze glued to where Will's car would come from. Nothing. Kate's nerves buzzed under her skin.

This didn't make sense. Her gaze drifted upward, and in the glow of the streetlight, she could see the snow was still falling. From where Kate stood, she could see the accumulation on top of the mailbox. It wasn't *that* much. The main roads had to be drivable. Nothing about the weather would warrant Will being this late.

Kate drew in a deep breath and exhaled loudly as frustration surged through her. She had no idea where her husband could be. No clue what was taking him so long. He hadn't called to tell her not to worry. When he finally walked in, she was going to—

"Mom, I'm hungry," Zach yelled.

Kate turned from the window and headed to the family room.

Zach hung over the back of the couch. "Why isn't Daddy home yet?"

"Soon, bud. Let me make you something to eat." A welcome distraction. Kate bustled back into the kitchen, pulled a small plate from the cabinet. "You want carrots and potatoes too, right?" she asked. Without waiting on his response, Kate yanked open the silverware drawer and grabbed a serving spoon.

At the sound of a car, the utensil fell from her hand. It clattered against the counter as Kate spun around and rushed toward the window. She peered down the street, her breath coming quick and shallow. Headlights. Kate's heart thumped wildly. Will would never hear the end of this.

As it neared the house, the car slowed, but it wasn't Will's. A choked whisper. "No. Please, no."

Kate willed the vehicle to keep going. It didn't. When it pulled into their driveway, her throat tightened, Zach's dinner forgotten. She stood hunched over, arms wrapped around her middle. Watching. Waiting. She heard herself whimper.

On top of the white sedan, rotating red and blue lights lit up the night and then went dark. The driver's side door swung open, and a policeman stepped out.

The officer pulled his coat collar up against the back of his neck and headed toward her sidewalk. A heaviness gripped Kate's chest. She heard him on the front porch, stomping his boots, no doubt ridding them of snow. Then his knuckles rapped against her door. Deliberate and urgent.

Fear paralyzed her. She knew he held the answer for why Will wasn't home yet. Kate pressed her trembling hands against her mouth to stifle her scream.

CHAPTER 7

*K*ate pounded on the door to the emergency room. The wind blew the falling snow against her face, and it stung her skin with tiny pinpricks. A security guard turned his head at her insistent knocking.

"Ambulances only." He jabbed the air with his index finger. "You need to go to the other door. Registration."

"My husband was in an accident," Kate said, her voice frantic. "They brought him in by ambulance. The police told me to come to the ER."

The security guard nodded but didn't move from his folding chair. "Okay, but you still need to go through registration. Someone there can let you know what's going on with your husband."

Kate didn't think to say thank you. She spun around and raced off in the direction the security guard had indicated. A quick glance up and the outside lights revealed the snow was falling harder now. She left a trail of frenzied footprints in the snow that had accumulated on the concrete behind her.

She hurtled through the automatic doors, and her gaze swept through the maze of people as she looked for someone who could help her. When she located what appeared to be the registration window, she hurried toward it.

Two people in front of her stood between her and Will. Anxiety always turned Kate's insides into a churning pit, and she wrapped an arm around her stomach to try to keep the nausea at bay. At least she hadn't eaten anything that could come up.

She tapped her foot and scrutinized the woman in front of her with an annoyed scowl. No blood was dripping. No bones protruding through flesh. Kate expelled a loud exasperated sigh. There should be a separate line for people who actually had a dire emergency. She drew in a deep breath. Will was fine, she told herself. He had to be.

After a moment, Kate went around the people in front of her. With an urgent stare, she rapped on the Plexiglas between her and the person checking people in.

The woman glanced up. "I'll be with you in a—"

"My husband was in an accident. He came in by ambulance," Kate cut in, her tone urgent. She had no time for small talk—or waiting.

The woman's face softened. "Okay, hon." She rose slightly up out of her chair and glanced around. Her hand went up into the air as she appeared to communicate non-verbally with a woman standing near the front door.

The woman nodded and hurried over to Kate. "Can I help you?" she asked.

Kate looked her over with dismay. The woman wasn't a nurse. The nametag pinned to her crisply ironed shirt said she was a volunteer.

"I don't know if you can." Kate's tone held little confidence this woman could provide her with the information she needed. "My husband was brought here by ambulance. He was in an accident."

"Your name?"

"Kate Kennedy."

The volunteer consulted her clipboard and then nodded. "Okay, Mrs. Kennedy." She gestured toward a bank of chairs off to the side of the large waiting area. "Why don't you have a seat and let me see what I can find out."

Kate dropped into the chair and swallowed hard, desperate to know Will was okay. As she stared through the Plexiglas, she observed chaos. Nurses ran around. A team of paramedics with someone on a gurney shouted vitals. A woman cried.

Her husband was back there somewhere. As Kate watched the woman sob, her head pounded. Something terrible must have happened to someone she loved. Kate wrapped her hands around her head and stared at the floor. The melting snow dripped from her hair and left wet splotches on the tile.

The volunteer returned a few minutes later. "A nurse will be right out to give you an update."

A nurse. That sounded reassuring. If it was serious, wouldn't it be a doctor that needed to give her an update?

When the nurse approached, Kate got to her feet, her pulse racing. "Is my husband okay?" she asked, worry creating a deep divot between her brows.

The nurse gestured back at the chair Kate had jumped from and took the seat next to her.

"Hi, Mrs. Kennedy. I'm Cathy. What do you know so far about what's happened to your husband?"

Kate held her hands out helplessly and shook her head. "Nothing really. The police—the police came to my house. They only said there'd been an accident and he'd been transported by ambulance to this hospital. They didn't know anything about his condition."

Cathy let out a small breath. "Okay. Then let me tell you what I know since I was part of the team that worked on your husband. It appears your husband pulled over to help a woman with a flat tire and was struck by another car. When he was brought in, he was not awake."

Kate let out a gasp. What did *that* mean?

Cathy placed her hand over Kate's before continuing. "We immediately helped him to breathe and worked to stabilize his vital signs."

Kate's eyes welled up with gratitude, her shoulders relaxing. Will was breathing now. Stable. All this worry had been for nothing.

The nurse patted her hand, almost as if she'd seen the relief in Kate's face and dreaded what she was about to say. "His right leg was broken, but of more immediate concern was a head injury he incurred. We did a CAT scan which did show there had been damage to his brain."

Kate pulled her hand back, and it flew to her mouth. Her eyes grew wide. "Is he—" She couldn't finish the thought, her words muffled and soft behind her hand.

Cathy folded her hands in her lap. "Your husband is in surgery. They took him into the OR to stop the bleeding and try to relieve the pressure the swelling was causing."

"So, they can do that? They can fix it?" Kate had hope again as she pinned her gaze on the nurse. She knew nothing about all this medical talk. Maybe this was more routine than she thought. She prayed that was the case.

"They'll know more once they get in there to see what's going on," Cathy said in a gentle tone. "A CAT scan can only tell us so much." She stood and glanced at her watch. "They should be finishing up within the next hour or so, and then the doctor can speak to you. There's another waiting area for the families of patients in surgery. I'll take you there."

Kate rose from her seat in a daze. Thoughts churned through her head as she stumbled behind Cathy through a maze of hallways. She glanced over her shoulder, wondering if she'd be able to find her way back out. When she went someplace without Will, he always wrote down detailed directions for her. Then he'd laugh when she still managed to get lost.

Kate's throat tightened as they approached the waiting area.

"You can have a seat here." Cathy gestured at an area of chairs. "As soon as there's any news, one of us will be out to share it with you."

Kate's gaze drifted to take in the other families waiting. Solemn faces. A man drinking coffee. An elderly woman engrossed in a paperback. She glanced around for an isolated seat. She wasn't up to small talk.

Sweating now, Kate shrugged her winter coat off onto the chair next to her. She slumped over and stared at the design of the carpet underneath her. It was a dark, busy pattern. Forgiving, she figured, if a heartbroken family spilled a beverage or two in their time of grief.

In time, the adrenaline of waiting wore off, and Kate couldn't sit still anymore. She sat up, rolled her neck in a circle. Her shoulders felt like they were made of stone. She glanced around and spotted a payphone.

Should she call Will's parents? Kate's chest tightened as she imagined what she'd say. They lived in Florida, so if Will's situation was serious, they'd have to fly up. She decided to wait. Until she knew more, she'd leave them in their blissful ignorance that everything was fine with their only son.

Kate stood and made her way to the phone. When her call was finally answered, she wasn't sure she could speak.

"Mom?" The word escaped her lips as a high-pitched squeak.

"Katie? Is that you?"

She swallowed down the lump in her throat. "Yeah, it's me," she said, her voice soft and serious.

"What's wrong?" Her mother's question came abruptly. Somehow, she always knew something was wrong just by the sound of Kate's voice.

"I'm at the hospital."

"The hospital?" She heard her mother shout out for her father. "Steve, come quick. Katie's in the hospital."

LIANE CARMEN

"I'm *at* the hospital, but it's not me, Mom. It's Will. There was an accident. He's in surgery."

"Will's in surgery, Steve," her mother called out.

Her father picked up the second extension. "Katie, it's Dad. What happened? Did he have a car accident in the snow? Were you with him?"

"I wasn't with him." Kate let out a heavy sigh. "Will was on his way home from work. All I know is he pulled over to help someone with a flat tire." A realization hit Kate in the middle of her chest. It was her fault. By asking Will to come home early, she'd put him in the path of the driver who needed assistance.

"I don't understand," her mother said. "So, Will stopped to help—"

"While he was standing on the side of the road, someone hit him. His car wasn't even damaged." The car was fine. Her husband was not. Kate felt in the back pocket of her jeans for the card the policeman had given her. Danny's Towing. Will's Toyota had been towed for safekeeping.

"How badly is he hurt?" her dad asked.

"They're not sure yet," Kate said, her voice breaking. "I should know more when he comes out of surgery. His leg is broken and —" She hesitated, not wanting to say the words out loud. "There's some damage to his brain."

Her mom gasped. "Oh, sweetie."

Kate blinked hard as tears filled her eyes. "They're operating to stop the bleeding and reduce the pressure. I'm waiting for an update."

"Okay, Katie, we're here to help," her father said matter-of-factly. "What do you need? Where's Zach?"

With the arrival of the police, his dinner had been forgotten. "I took him to the Griffins next door. They said they'd keep an eye on him until I got home ..." When exactly *would* she be going home? Kate's stomach twisted with the knowledge she'd be leaving the hospital without

54

Will. Recovering from brain surgery couldn't be a quick or easy process.

"We'll come to the hospital and wait with you," her mom said. "What about Will's parents? Have you called them yet?"

Kate pressed her palm against her forehead. "No. I wanted to wait—I figured I should wait until I know more. If it's serious, I'll have to tell them to book flights."

"What hospital are you at?" her dad asked.

Kate told him, then noticed a doctor scanning the seats in the waiting room before glancing over toward the payphone. "Hey, let me go. I think maybe Will's surgery is finished."

"Mrs. Kennedy?" he asked when she approached him. When she nodded, he extended his hand. "I'm Dr. Miller. I operated on your husband."

Her shoulders tensed. Kate could see something in his eyes. His tone was professional, but his face was serious and tight.

"Is he okay?" She held her breath, waiting for his response.

"Mrs. Kennedy, your husband was brought in with a broken leg and, more concerning, a head injury. A subarachnoid hemorrhage is what it's called. He wasn't awake, and he wasn't breathing on his own. They inserted a tube to help him breathe, but a scan showed bleeding in your husband's brain, which was creating pressure on his skull. There was no time to wait for you to arrive. We needed to operate as soon as possible to stop the bleeding and try to relieve the pressure."

Kate nodded and waited for the doctor to tell her the only part that mattered. Was Will going to be okay?

The doctor rubbed his temple. "While it's a useful tool, A CAT scan can't tell us everything. Specifically, about brain function. When we relieve the pressure, we look to other signs to tell us if there's been damage. When we remove the sedation, we hope to see vitals start to improve."

"And my husband? When will you be able to tell—"

"What we're finding with your husband is that some of his

vitals aren't improving the way we would have hoped. Machines are breathing for him, but his heart rate's low, as is his blood pressure. His pupils are dilated."

Kate raised a clenched-up fist and held it against her lips, her throat thick with panic. "What does that mean?"

"We're not seeing the signs of improvement we would have hoped to see after surgery. They also set his broken leg, and your husband's now in recovery." The doctor placed his hand on her arm. "You can sit with him, but I'm afraid you'll need to be realistic about the prognosis. You should be prepared."

Kate's eyes widened as she searched nearby for something to lean on. "Prepared? My husband's not dead. I mean, he's not dead, right?"

The doctor's face softened. "His body is still alive because the machine is keeping him that way by breathing for him." His voice was matter-of-fact but gentle. "We'll watch him for a bit, but I suspect brain activity has ceased. I'm very sorry, Mrs. Kennedy. Tests will need to be done to confirm it, but it's likely your husband is brain dead."

CHAPTER 8

*W*hen Kate slipped her hand into Will's, it felt warm. His chest rose and fell. She tried to focus on his breathing and ignore the sounds of the machines in the room. The soft brown curls that usually fell against his forehead were gone. White gauze encircled his shaved head, and his eyes had been taped shut. What if he tried to open them?

Aside from several abrasions on his face and a bandage on his left arm, he was still her Will. His face was its usual color.

His chin bore the stubble that was always there by the end of the day. He liked to rub it on her when he kissed her and then laugh as she shrieked about his face feeling like sandpaper. Kate reached out and stroked her finger against it. If she got him back, it would never bother her again. Nothing would.

Will's broken leg had been suspended off the bed, and Kate could imagine Zach wanting to color on the white cast when his daddy came home. Will had to get better. This didn't feel real.

They were supposed to be having a snowball fight or watching Zach break in his new snow tube. There would have been hot chocolate. Kate stifled a sob. Zach was ten years old, and he adored his father. There was no way she could tell her son his daddy wouldn't be coming home. No way.

A nurse was fiddling with some of the machines, making notes onto a chart. "I'm Heather. If there's anything you need to know, just ask me. I'm here until seven tomorrow morning."

"He seems fine," Kate said, mostly for her own benefit. "He looks like he's just sleeping." She glanced up at the nurse. "Is it possible he hasn't come out of the sedation yet?"

"Probably not," she said, her tone gentle as she shook her head. "They used propofol to sedate him for surgery. Once they shut it off, he should have come out of it fairly quickly."

Kate squeezed Will's hand, every fiber of her being willing him to squeeze back. He would show them. The people at this hospital didn't know her husband the way she did. He was a fighter.

"His hand—his hand is warm," she said.

The nurse's voice was soft but sure. "His hand is warm because the machine is breathing for him."

"Oh," Kate said, the word leaving her mouth as a whisper.

"I'll be back in a little bit. Do you need anything before I leave?"

Kate still wanted to believe Will's eyelids would eventually flutter, and those green eyes of his would turn to look at her. Well, now this was a pretty crappy day, he'd say, and she'd smile at him because, yes, it had been a bad day, but it was nothing they couldn't overcome together. They were a team. How many times had they said that to each other?

"His eyes. Can you take off the tape?" Kate asked. "What if he tries to open them and they're taped shut?"

Heather hesitated. "They put that on during surgery to keep his eyes from drying out."

Kate shrugged slightly. "Well, then he doesn't need it now, right?"

Heather made her way to Kate's side. "Keeping his eyes taped shut leaves his eyes moist. He can't—he can't keep them closed on his own. I can take them off for a minute if you want, but it's standard procedure to leave it on—to protect them."

Kate stiffened. "I guess it's okay to leave it for now." When Will woke up, she'd take it off herself if it came to that.

"Do you have anyone that can come be with you?" Heather asked.

"My parents are on their way."

Heather nodded. "Okay, I'm glad to hear that. You need support."

"He's still in there," Kate said, her mouth trembling. "I know he is."

Heather rested her hand on Kate's shoulder. "We're going to keep an eye on him, don't worry. I'll leave you alone with him for a little bit, but I'll be back."

When the door closed behind the nurse, Kate picked up Will's hand and brushed her lips against it. "You need to fight, honey. Fight to come back to Zach and me. We can't live without you. We need you." Her eyes welled up with tears as she heard a soft knock behind her.

The floodgates opened when the door opened and Kate saw her parents.

"It's okay, sweetie. We're here now." Her father squeezed her shoulder.

When Kate stepped back, he used his thumb to wipe the tears from under her eyes. He glanced over at Will, lying motionless in the bed except for the steady rise and fall of his chest.

"What did the doctor say?" he asked.

Kate shook her head. "It's not good, Daddy. They aren't seeing any improvement since the surgery." She could see her pain reflected in her father's face as he listened. "The doctor thinks it's possible—" She choked out the words. "Will might be brain dead."

59

Kate's mother sucked in a sharp breath. "Oh, no, sweetie. Did you call his parents?"

She nodded, her vision blurry with tears. "And his sister. His parents were going to book the next flight and try to get here late tonight. Lisa's driving." Kate hadn't looked out a window in hours, and it was now dark. Will's sister, Lisa, lived in Rhode Island. She'd insisted on getting in the car and driving down by herself, but she was over four hours away. "The weather—"

"It stopped snowing, and it looks like it's going to change over to rain," Kate's dad said. "They should have no problems flying in. The main roads aren't too bad, and I don't think they got any snow north of us. Will's sister should be fine to drive."

Kate felt her chest loosen. Will's family needed to be here with him.

"It doesn't sound like they know anything for sure yet, right?" Kate's mom asked.

Kate wiped her eyes with her fingers. "They're supposed to do testing at some point. That will tell them for certain if there's any brain activity."

"Tonight?" Kate's dad asked.

She shrugged. "I'm not sure."

Kate's mom reached for her arm. "We'll stay with you, don't worry. What about Zach?"

Kate hadn't called the neighbors back, and it was getting late. "Could you go get him from the Griffins? Take him back to the house and maybe make something for him to eat? I was making his dinner when the police came, but I—I just left everything."

"Sweetie, it's almost nine o'clock," her mother said. "I'm sure the Griffins have fed him by now."

"Oh, right." Kate had lost all concept of time. "In that case, maybe you can get him settled and into bed. Can you stay—"

Her mother nodded. "We'll stay with him as long as you need. Your father can drop me off and go back to our house to pack a few things. Don't worry."

"I don't know what to say about school in the morning. If you let Zach stay home—" Kate pressed her lips together as her throat tightened. "Somebody needs to call the school. Will's school. Tell them … tell them …" She let out a heavy sigh. "I don't know what to tell them."

Kate's dad put his arm around her. "I'll take care of it. They'll need to know to arrange a substitute for his class."

Concern crossed her mother's face, and she then glanced at her father. "Steve, you stay with Kate, and I'll take the car to the house."

Kate shook her head. "No. I don't want you driving in the snow, Mom."

Her dad rubbed Kate's arm. "I'll run your mom to the house and drop her off. I can be back in a half-hour or so."

"Okay," Kate said with a slow nod before turning to her mother. "Mom, please don't tell Zach anything yet."

"Oh, honey, I wouldn't."

"Don't give him any false hope either. You know, *Daddy will be home tomorrow.*" Kate's mouth pinched. "Maybe say we're both at the hospital, and you're not sure how things are going."

Her mother's face fell. She fought back tears and nodded. "Okay, if that's what you want."

"It's not what I want at all, but I think it's better." Kate exhaled. "In case something happens, I don't want him to think you lied to him. But you should go. It's getting late for the Griffins, and I'm sure Zach's wondering what's going on."

Kate's dad gave her shoulder a quick squeeze. "I'll be back as soon as I can."

She gave a grateful nod. "Okay, but don't speed. I'm going to sit with him. Hold his hand and pray. I'll be okay."

Kate was then left alone with Will and only the odd sounds of the machines in the room for company. Random beeping. The steady clicking and whooshing of the ventilator, a constant reminder that her husband wasn't breathing on his own.

Kate studied him, laying there completely still. Peaceful. It was almost as if Will had already accepted what she refused to even consider.

CHAPTER 9

*M*uffled voices woke Kate from the dream she'd been having. Disoriented, she opened her eyes and was dragged back into reality. Will's accident. It hadn't been just a nightmare.

She raised her head and grimaced. Then she dug her fingers into the back of her neck and tried to massage away the stiffness. Sleeping with her head laid on the bed beside Will hadn't been the most comfortable position.

Lisa had arrived at almost one in the morning with the news that her parents hadn't been able to get a flight until six a.m. Kate's father had come back, but when Will's sister got there, Kate insisted he go back to her house to get some sleep. He'd left with a promise to return in the morning.

Heather had been in and out all night but confirmed there'd been no change in Will's condition. She suspected the doctor would be running tests in the morning that would tell them more. "More," Kate feared, was code for the nurse's firm belief that Will wouldn't be recovering.

Until the tests, Kate could still try to convince herself there would be a different answer. Without medical proof, she could attempt to ignore the picture the night by his bedside had painted.

"Hey," Lisa said. "Sorry if we woke you, but I'm glad you finally got a little sleep. Heather's shift ended, and she went home. This is Christine."

The nurse in the room nodded as she wrote some numbers on Will's chart. "I'm very sorry about your husband."

Sorry. That didn't sound like today would bring any sort of good news.

"I'm going to get coffee," Lisa said when Christine slipped out of the room. "Want one?"

Kate yawned and rubbed her right eye. "Yeah, definitely. Thanks." She glanced out the window. Dark and dreary. Rain. It seemed fitting. "What time is it?"

"A little after seven. I called the airline to check on my parents' flight. They took off on time, so they should be here in a few hours."

Kate glanced at Will and exhaled a deep breath. "He looks the same."

"The doctor came by to look at his chart, but I didn't want to wake you. There hasn't been any change." Lisa swallowed hard. "He suspects there isn't any brain activity. Will could be brain dead."

"He told me the same thing after the surgery." Kate didn't even try to fight the tears.

"There are tests they need to run on Will this morning to confirm it, but it's not good." Lisa's voice broke, and now she was crying too. "He said—he said we need to be prepared."

Kate shook her head. "How am I supposed to prepare to say goodbye to the love of my life?"

Lisa laid her hand on Kate's shoulder. "I know. This isn't supposed to happen to someone like Will."

Again, Kate struggled with the role she had potentially played. Her request that Will leave early had put him in the wrong place at the wrong time. If she had let him finish grading his papers at school, would this have still happened? Or instead, would Will be grabbing his coffee right now and kissing her goodbye as he headed out the door for work?

Part of her wished her husband wasn't so damn kind-hearted. Of course he stopped to help someone. If the woman had taken better care of her tires, maybe she wouldn't have had a flat on the side of the road. Was the person who hit him not paying attention? Kate couldn't help but be bitter toward the people involved in the set of circumstances that had put Will in this bed. She included herself in that group.

Lisa wiped her eyes. "I'll find coffee. Be right back."

It was going to take much more than caffeine to get through the day. Kate's chest tightened with dread, terrified she'd be going home alone to deliver heartbreaking news to Zach.

She held Will's hand and brought it to her lips. "I hope you can hear me. You need to fight. Zach and I need you."

Ten minutes later, Lisa returned with two large steaming hot cups of coffee. "I didn't know what you took in it, so I grabbed some sugar and creamers."

Kate used the small table in the room to fix her coffee. At the first sip, she cringed. "This is awful. Your brother would have hated it." Will was a coffee connoisseur. She used to laugh at him as he walked through the specialty shop sniffing the beans. He ground them fresh every morning before making a pot for both of them.

Kate stared off as the visual of Will savoring his coffee like a fine glass of wine played in her mind. She let out a long slow breath and ran her hand over her face. Coffee. Such an ordinary thing to think about amidst surreal circumstances.

"Did the doctor say what time?" Kate tried to blink away fresh tears. "For the tests?"

Lisa glanced at the clock over the door. "He said they would wait for my parents to get here."

So, in a few hours, all doubt would be removed. Kate slugged her coffee, hoping it would be able to pass through the tightness in her throat. She glanced at Lisa and dipped her chin slowly. No words were necessary.

After a few moments, Lisa cleared her throat. "A woman I work with—her son was in a car accident." She hesitated. "Her son was brain dead, and they—they donated his organs. I asked Christine about it. You know, if Will …"

Kate stiffened, then drank her coffee to buy her a moment. It was like Will's sister had already given up on him. "What did she say?"

Lisa gave a slight shrug. "I get the feeling it's not her place to bring it up. I guess if it comes to that, there are people from the organ procurement group that handle it. Ask permission. That kind of stuff. But she said organ donation can save up to eight lives. There's even cornea donation, you know, the clear lens over —Anyway, they could help someone see again."

Lisa seemed to be studying Kate for a reaction. "Did Will ever mention anything to you about it? You know, if he would be willing if anything happened to him?"

Annoyed, Kate shrugged. "Not that I remember. But why would it even come up?" Neither she nor Will would have ever thought this was something they'd need to discuss.

Lisa wrapped both hands around her coffee and raised it to her mouth. She peered at Kate over the top of her cup. "How do you feel about it?"

Kate pressed her lips together to keep from screaming. They weren't supposed to be talking about her husband as if he was a used car being sold for parts. "It's hard for me to imagine pieces of him out there and—" Kate sucked in a gulp of air, put her coffee down, and buried her head in her hands.

Lisa moved quickly and put an arm around Kate's shoulders. "I know, but this is *Will* we're talking about. He would have done anything to help anybody. You know that. Maybe it's a way to make something worthwhile come out of this."

Kate winced. How could she wrap her head around the fact that Will's death could in any way be considered worthwhile? "I don't know why we're even talking about this now. We still don't know anything for sure." Her shoulders sagged. "I'm not ready to accept there's no chance—no chance—"

Lisa gripped her tight in an embrace. "I get it. I'm just saying *if* the tests confirm it. I don't think Will would have had a moment's hesitation if he knew he could help others. As his wife, it's legally your decision, but I hope you'll think about what he would have wanted." Her voice was soft but firm. "Burying him with his organs when he could do something good for so many seems wrong. A waste."

Kate knew Lisa was right. She gave a nod but wasn't giving up on a miracle yet. "I'm going to give you a little time alone with your brother. I need to get some air."

The sounds of the machines still echoed in Kate's head as she set out to locate the chapel. She wasn't sure if a prayer for Will said there carried more weight, but she needed somewhere serene and quiet to plead with God.

* * *

After several wrong turns on the way back, Kate found the hallway that led to Will's room. Fear paralyzed her. It was only a matter of time before they'd show up, do the tests. Then it would be official. The doctor would be able to tell her with certainty her husband was dead. Kate's legs threatened to fold under her. She veered toward the wall, her hand reaching out to keep herself upright.

There was a small row of seats next to a few vending machines. Kate stumbled over and sank into a chair. As she slumped over, a weight pushed down on her shoulders. She wasn't ready to say goodbye to Will yet. She bowed her head and tried not to cry.

When a woman passed her, Kate shielded her tear-stained face and puffy eyes from view. She couldn't imagine what she looked like. Melting snow the night before had left her hair unruly. The clothes she'd been wearing since yesterday were wrinkled and slept in. She was in desperate need of a shower.

Snickers bar in hand, the woman walked by again. Just past Kate's chair, she hesitated and then turned. "You look like you could use a shoulder to cry on."

Kate glanced up. Wild brown curls framed a face etched with compassion. A glint of light caught the silver necklace she wore. Two angel wings hung off a chain and glimmered in the hollow of her neck. While Kate would have preferred to be alone, there was something comforting about the woman. She nodded for her to sit.

"I'm Celeste," the woman said as she dropped into the seat beside her.

"I'm Kate."

"It's nice to meet you. I thought—you look like you might be able to use someone to talk to."

"It's my husband." The words broke as they came out of Kate's mouth. "He was in an accident yesterday. And now—now they're planning to do tests today to confirm he's brain dead." Kate had no idea why she was opening up to this stranger, but Celeste was right. She did need someone to talk to. Someone who wasn't related to Will.

The woman sat with her hands in her lap, one loosely holding her candy bar. Her face flooded with sympathy. "Do you think the tests will show he is?"

The realization knocked the wind out of Kate. She drew in a breath and and dipped her head. "He's gone. In my heart, I know that. His body is still here, but he's not in there anymore."

Celeste's eyes were glassy as she placed her hand over Kate's. "I'm so sorry. I lost my husband Ed two years ago. Heart attack."

Kate winced and swiped at her tears. "Oh, I'm sorry."

Celeste gripped Kate's hand. "You won't believe it now, but it does get easier. I'm actually here at the hospital for a grief group I attend. Well, now I help run it." She withdrew her hand from Kate's to glance at her watch. "In fact, they're probably waiting on me to get started."

The woman reached into her purse, pulled out a small piece of paper, and wrote her name and phone number on it. She handed it to Kate. "I'm just a phone call away. Trust me. You're going to need someone who understands. You'll be caught up in the whirlwind for a bit, but when it stops, everyone will go back to their lives. But you? You won't have the life you knew to go back to. It can be rough without support."

Kate folded the paper and shoved it in the pocket of her jeans. Right next to the card for the towing company that had Will's car.

She gave Celeste a grateful nod, but Kate didn't want support. She wanted her husband. "I appreciate it. You're very kind to check on the strange lady crying next to the candy machine."

Celeste offered her a small smile. "You're not so strange." She tilted her head to the side. "Can I give you a hug?"

When Kate nodded, Celeste wrapped her arms around her tightly. "You're stronger than you know." Her words were soft in Kate's ear before she pulled back. "I have to run, but please call me. I mean it. You may want to come to our group when you're ready. Or if you just need a friend, well, that's okay too." With that, Celeste stood and hurried off.

Kate let out a heavy sigh and steeled herself to head back to Will's room. When she got there, her dad was waiting. He wrapped his arms around her, and Kate gave herself permission to break down.

CHAPTER 10

$\mathcal{W}$hen Will's parents arrived two hours later, Kate rose from the uncomfortable chair next to the bed to greet them. She wrapped her arms around Will's mother, Betty, but not before she saw it in her eyes. A mother's worst fears realized.

Kate knew she needed to be strong for them now. They had only now walked into the reality she had been living with since the night before.

With every hour that passed, Kate's heart and brain had fought for control. The understanding was slowly dawning on her that her husband was probably not coming back to her. But her heart? It physically ached to imagine her life without him.

Will's parents moved to his bedside. His mother took his hand, much the way Kate had done for hours, praying she would feel something that would tell her he was still in there.

Displaced, Kate stood awkwardly at the end of Will's bed, her arms hanging slack. Her father moved to her side, and without words, he pulled her close to him.

This new point of view caught Kate off guard. The man lying in the bed was covered in tubes and wires. Connected to machines. It wasn't that he didn't resemble her husband, but as Kate fixed her gaze on him, something was different. Missing. It was like Will had checked out and just left his body behind.

"Have you gotten any updates on his condition?" Will's dad asked.

Kate opened her mouth to speak, but nothing came out. She was grateful when Lisa stepped in.

"There's been no change since last night," she told her parents. "They were hoping when the sedation wore off, Will would wake up, but he hasn't." Lisa pressed her lips together, and her eyes filled with tears. "That's—that's not a good sign."

Will's mother frowned and shook her head, as if she refused to accept what her daughter was telling her. "Your brother looks fine, well, except for the cast and the bandages. Is it possible—"

Lisa didn't let her finish as she rested her hand on Betty's shoulder. "Mom, the doctor said we need to be prepared to say goodbye. Will's not breathing on his own. The machine is doing that for him."

Will's father leaned down and wrapped his arms around his wife as a sob erupted from deep within her throat. "I know, honey," he said, his soothing voice trying to provide comfort.

"The doctor will be in soon," Lisa said, her voice soft. "There are tests they need to do to confirm—to confirm whether he's brain dead. Actually, two doctors need to test him separately. You know, to make sure they both agree." She hesitated. "I asked about organ donation."

Will's mother's head turned swiftly in her daughter's direction, the color drained from her face. "Really?" she asked in an incredulous tone as if she couldn't believe it was something they already needed to consider.

When Lisa nodded, Will's mother bowed her head, her shoulders heaving as she cried. Apparently, she didn't want to think about it either. Her daughter moved to her side and hugged her.

Agony hung thick in the air. They all went silent, the room

devoid of any further conversation. Filling the room instead were the sounds of the machines keeping Will alive punctuated by the whimpers of human pain.

Kate jerked when there was a knock on the door. The doctor who'd performed Will's surgery came in with Christine and a second woman behind him.

"I'm Dr. Miller." He gestured at the woman in the white coat. "This is Alison, a respiratory therapist who'll be assisting me today." She nodded and took her place behind a piece of equipment. "And as you know, Christine is Will's nurse."

Betty shifted in her chair, and Will's father stood behind her. She held up a trembling hand, and he gripped it tight. With Lisa by her side, they presented a united front as they pinned their attention on the doctor.

"I'm so sorry we're meeting under these circumstances," the doctor said. "As you know, Will was brought in yesterday after being struck by a car and suffering a head injury. After a CAT scan, we immediately rushed him into surgery to stop the bleeding and relieve the pressure on his brain. Unfortunately, the scan can't tell us everything we need to know about the totality of his condition."

"But the surgery, you did stop the bleeding, relieve the pressure, right?" Will's father asked.

"Unfortunately, that doesn't always guarantee recovery. After surgery, we look to certain factors to measure improvement." Dr. Miller's gaze drifted around the room at all of them. "Unfortunately, we haven't seen what we needed to see in Will. When we removed the sedation, he should have come out of it and regained consciousness." When he shook his head, compassion crossed his face. "He didn't. We're also not seeing any corneal reflexes."

"So, what does that mean exactly?" Will's father asked.

Even with her father's arm around her, Kate worried her wobbly legs might not hold her up. Twisting the rings on her finger, she stole a quick glance at Christine. The somber expression on the nurse's face told her everything she needed to know. Kate swallowed hard, a sour taste in the back of her throat.

"When we see these kinds of results, we start to consider whether the injury affected more than a CAT scan can tell us," the doctor said. "Specifically, we aren't able to use the results of the scan to determine brain activity before surgery. I'm sorry to say I strongly suspect there's no brain stem function. Whether it had already ceased before the surgery or not, we'll never know."

Betty turned toward Will. She shook her head as her eyes filled with fresh tears.

"There are tests we need to conduct to make a determination of brain death," the doctor said. He made direct eye contact with each person in the room as he spoke. "Essentially, this is death as we know it. An incompatibility for life." His voice was filled with empathy but also matter-of-fact, almost as if he wanted to make sure his words couldn't be misconstrued to leave any room for false hope. "We have Will on a ventilator pushing air into his lungs. The lungs then provide oxygen to his heart which then beats. With brain death, the lungs can no longer function on their own. The brain stem doesn't provide that message to them."

Kate hunched over, her arms crossed against her stomach. She made no attempt to stop the tears as they fell, and several of them landed on the bottom of the bed where Will's feet were covered by a blanket.

Her dad rubbed her back. "I know, sweetie."

Kate wasn't sure she wouldn't have collapsed in a heap on the floor if her father hadn't reached for her arm.

The doctor gripped Will's file in his hand. "I'm going to perform some cursory tests of brain stem reflexes followed by an Apnea test."

"What's that?" Will's mother asked.

The doctor glanced at Christine before continuing. "We'll administer oxygen to Will but then remove him from the ventilator. This allows carbon dioxide levels to increase in his system. This build-up would normally trigger an attempt to breathe, but the lungs won't function without the brain stem telling them to do so. We'll monitor Will's response for eight minutes to see if there's any respiratory response or attempt to breathe on his own."

After explaining more about the test, Dr. Miller scanned the room. "You're all welcome to stay or leave for the tests. It's up to you."

Her father turned to her, and Kate gave a somber nod. They all chose to stay.

A deathly quiet fell over the room as the doctor pressed hard on Will's fingernails and then carefully removed the tape that held his eyelids closed.

Kate caught a glimpse of the green eyes she loved so much, but they weren't the same. The sparkle that was there when he teased her or told her how much he loved her was gone. Instead, they stared out vacantly, as if the life behind them was already gone.

After a nod to Christine, the lights dimmed. Dr. Miller shined a light in each eye and then took a Q-tip and gently touched Will's eyeball with it.

There was no response.

As the lights returned, Kate turned away and wrapped her hands around her head. She stared down at the floor until she finally heard the doctor announce he was getting ready to give Will oxygen. The air in the small room was heavy as preparations were made for the Apnea test. With the doctor and his team on one side of Will's bed and his family on the other, Kate remained near his feet and leaned her hands gently against the railing to hold herself up.

"We're going to turn off the ventilator and proceed with the test now," Dr. Miller said with a nod to Christine and the respiratory therapist. They both appeared to shift to pre-designated positions, their gazes directed at the clock on the wall.

The clock was behind Kate, but she wasn't interested in watching it. She planned to observe Will.

Kate flinched when one of the machines started beeping, but Dr. Miller reached out and pressed a button to quiet it. She could still hear the mechanical sounds of medical equipment but gone was the clicking and whooshing of the ventilator that had been breathing for Will.

All eyes stared upward over her head, but Kate's eyes were anchored on her husband. Even though she couldn't see the clock, she heard the ticking of the second hand in her head. Second by agonizing second, it clicked, counting down the time Will had left to show the doctors he wasn't ready to go.

Dr. Miller and Alison exchanged glances as they watched the monitors. Periodically, the respiratory therapist made notations, jotted down numbers onto a form. Christine's gaze drifted between Will and the clock on the wall.

Kate fixated on Will's chest, her mind playing tricks on her. She clasped her hands together on the railing over his feet. Silently, she spoke to him. Begged him. *Breathe, Will. Fight to come back to us.* For a split second, she remembered his coaching when she gave birth to Zach and didn't think she had anything left to give. *You can do this. Take your time. You have eight minutes.* Or was it only seven now?

The day she'd taken that first pregnancy test flashed through her mind. Three minutes. It had seemed so long as Kate waited for their old kitchen timer to ring. But this wait, the clock ticking on the wall behind her, would never seem long enough. It would determine her whole life. Eight minutes would decide if Will was lost to her forever. *How much time had already passed?*

Kate pleaded silently with him to breathe, all the while holding her own as if maybe she could give her ability to him. *Breathe, Will. Damn it, breathe.*

Her eyes moved to his mouth, his lips dry and chapped. She couldn't help but remember their first kiss. The nervous expression on Will's face as they stood outside her apartment after their first date. His lips on hers, tentative and soft. The slow smile he unleashed when she unlocked the door and dragged him inside. *How much time did he still have?*

Will wasn't moving, his hands by his sides perfectly still. The wedding ring he wore on his finger was a reminder of the scavenger hunt around town he'd planned for Kate's twenty-fourth birthday. He'd sent her on a mad dash to all their favorite places. The last clue had directed her to a gazebo in the park. It was there she'd found Will on bended knee, the ring she now wore on her finger held out in his hand. *I call dibs on you, Katie Matthews. Make me the happiest man in the world. Marry me.*

She brought her hand to her mouth and pressed her lips against her rings. He had made her the happiest woman in the world when he chose her. *How much longer did her husband have?*

When Kate heard the sudden sound of sobbing, a sharp gasp escaped her throat. Will's father was staring at the clock, tears streaming down his face, one arm around his wife and the other around his daughter. They were all crying. *Did that mean Will's time was up?*

Kate's anxious gaze bounced to the medical team. They were professionally and methodically doing their jobs, but their eyes had grown wet, their expressions despondent. Any remnant of hope was ripped from Kate's grasp.

When Dr. Miller gave a curt nod and reconnected the ventilator, Kate wanted to scream at him. *No! Give him more time.* Her gaze flew urgently back to Will. *Quick, before they give up on you. Breathe!*

But there was no more time—nothing else the doctor could do. A heavy silence hung in the air as Alison made a few final notes on whatever form she had that now confirmed Will was gone.

Incompatible with life.

"I'm sorry," Dr. Miller said as Christine pulled the blanket back up over Will's chest.

Kate heard her dad exhale. He turned to her, and she fell into his embrace.

She squeezed her eyes shut. Like a film in fast forward, flashes of her life with Will played out on the inside of her lids. The secluded waterfall they'd found on their honeymoon where Will had insisted no one would see them skinny dipping. The faces on the poor family who proved him wrong. How thrilled he'd been when she surprised him with a trip to Tampa and then handed him Super Bowl tickets to see his beloved Giants play. That mischievous glint in his eyes when he was up to something. He was *always* up to something. Will could make her laugh so hard she thought she'd pee herself.

Kate's stomach clenched as tears fell from her eyes and dampened her father's shirt. It didn't feel like she'd ever laugh again. She took in short, shallow breaths as reality settled over her like an unrelenting darkness. It was over.

Will was never coming home.

"$\mathcal{T}$he service was lovely," Kate's mother said, her hand on her daughter's arm. "All those students. Such a testament to the kind of teacher Will was."

The church had overflowed with so many people, it left many standing in the back. Teachers and students packed into the pews. Teenage girls dressed in their best black dresses choked back tears as they held hands. The football team had come as a group. Some cried openly. The rest looked stunned as if they couldn't fathom how something like this could happen to someone like Will, a man so full of life. Kate didn't understand either.

Will's coaching assistant, Mac, had hugged her tightly after the service. "Will was a great coach. I mean, you know, the whole team respected the hell out of him. What he did for those kids ..." His voice choked with emotion. "The players—they want to put a tribute to Will on their uniform next season."

"He would have liked that," Kate had said, trying to sound appreciative. It was a nice gesture, but his players needed their coach, not some tribute stitched on their jersey.

Mac stood rigid, an awkward silence filling the air. He let out a long heavy sigh. "Damn, Kate, this sucks. I'm so sorry."

She had pressed her lips together. A quick nod before the next person tapped on her shoulder to offer their condolences.

Her friends had all put in appearances. They huddled together looking uncomfortable, their eyes glazed over as if they could lose their husbands by mere association. They obviously wished they could be anywhere but a funeral where they had no idea what to say. It wasn't their fault. Kate didn't know what they could say either.

Even her cousin Melinda, the reason she and Will had even met, couldn't find adequate words. "Oh, Katie," she'd said, her voice choked with emotion. "I'm so sorry," she'd whispered into Kate's ear over and over as she embraced her. When she finally let go, Melinda had shaken her head, tears slipping down her cheeks.

"I wish Adam and I didn't have to run," she'd said next with an apologetic shrug. "The sitter. She can only stay until four."

Kate had murmured all the right things so her cousin wouldn't feel bad. After all, what did it matter? Will was going to be put in the ground whether Melinda was there or not.

As Melinda hurried off to find her husband, Kate heard a female voice behind her.

"Mrs. Kennedy?"

Kate spun around, and her head tipped to the side as she attempted to place the older woman approaching her. Her eyes were rimmed in red, her face blotchy. Was she a teacher at Will's school, perhaps?

"Yes?"

The woman held a pair of black leather gloves, and as she lowered her head and stared at them, she twisted them in her hands. Her shoulders shook as she cried.

Kate reached for her arm, an odd need to comfort this

grieving woman at her husband's funeral. Shouldn't it be the other way around? "I'm sorry, but how did you know Will?"

She brought her gaze back up reluctantly, a pained expression on her face. "Your husband's death. It's all my fault."

Kate flinched, and confusion creased her forehead. "I'm—I'm sorry?"

A shudder went through the woman. She took several breaths while Kate waited, then nodded to indicate she would try to continue. "They said—Triple-A said there was a nail in my tire. I didn't know—they're doing construction by my office. I got a flat driving home, almost lost control, and I pulled onto the shoulder." She bobbed her head insistently. "I would have called Triple-A. My husband got me the membership. You know, in case anything happened." When her eyes met Kate's, it seemed they were searching for something. "But your husband. He pulled right over to help me." The distraught woman shook her head, her chin trembling. "I'm so sorry. It's all my fault."

Kate drew in a deep breath. Nothing would change what happened, and she couldn't let guilt continue to consume this woman. "This isn't your fault. My husband—he was always going to pull over if someone needed help. It's who he was. You didn't do anything to cause this."

The woman hung her head. "But he was on the shoulder because of me. That other car—" Her voice broke. She stared off, almost as if she was reliving the moment in her head. "It just—the driver—the car swerved right into him." The woman pressed her hand to her forehead, the gloves still gripped in her fingers. "I have nightmares about it. That kid needs to pay for what he did."

Kate felt a tap on the shoulder. Her father. "We need to go, sweetie. The car for the cemetery is waiting."

She gave her dad a curt nod and placed a reassuring hand on the woman's arm. "The police—they're looking into what happened, but it's not your fault. I appreciate you coming, but if you'll excuse me…"

With a sense of relief, Kate turned to catch up with her parents. She didn't want to hear any more from this woman. Her chest tightened when she tried to imagine what Will had been thinking as it happened. Was he afraid? Had he known he would never be coming home to them?

The only thing Kate would ever recall about the cemetery was the steel gray sky and biting wind. It cut through the long jacket she wore over her black dress, and her cheeks, exposed to the frigid air, burned in protest.

She'd stared at the casket in disbelief. Beautiful white flowers laid on top were in stark contrast to the way she felt inside. A pit of darkness drowning her. She'd said her final goodbye that morning when she slipped their wedding photo and pictures of Zach inside with him. It didn't seem real.

That person in the coffin was a stranger. He wasn't *her* Will, the always-grinning, playful husband who told her every day how much he loved her. But then where had *that* Will gone? Kate desperately wanted him back, an empty place in her heart where the security of his love for her used to reside.

She'd stood rigid between her parents. At first, she'd stared blindly at the pile of dirt beside the hole that had been dug. The notion that she would leave Will there—bury the man she loved down in the cold ground—was more than her brain could process. So instead, Kate had stared vacantly off into the distance. Pinned her focus on a patch of trees, appropriately devoid of leaves and anything that resembled life. Her ears didn't hear a single word.

Every part of her mentally checked out until her father mercifully squeezed her shoulder. "Time to go back to the house, sweetie."

With a dutiful nod, Kate trudged behind him to the car. She didn't want to ever think about that place again.

* * *

"Do you think there's enough food?" Kate asked her mom as she turned to head toward the kitchen. More people than she had expected had returned to the house after the funeral. At this point, Kate was simply on autopilot. She'd even baked desserts the night before, laid out now on one of the long tables her father had set up.

Her mother reached for her arm. "I'll check on everything in the kitchen. I'm sure it's fine. I can make coffee, too, if you need it."

"That would be great, Mom. Thanks." When this was over, Kate would need something more substantial than coffee. Preferably alcoholic.

Her eyes scanned the room for Zach, but he wasn't anywhere to be seen. The Griffins were there with their two boys, and the three of them had probably fled the somber adult gathering.

The Griffins had taken Zach home for her right after the service. It didn't seem necessary to make Zach go to the cemetery. She hadn't even wanted to be there.

As she tried to locate Zach, she passed Will's mother speaking to an older woman she didn't recognize. "Will's organs saved the lives of five people."

"They told you who got his organs?" Kate heard the older woman ask.

"Not yet. I guess, you know, it could still change—"

"Betty?" Kate cut in as she tapped Will's mother on the shoulder.

At the hospital, the transplant recovery coordinator had offered some vague information about where Will's organs were going right before they wheeled him off. Kate understood it seemed to be giving his family a bit of peace, but she couldn't bear to hear about it anymore. Especially today.

"Have you seen Zach?" Kate asked.

Betty lifted her head, and her gaze drifted around the room. "I saw him before with two other children. I overheard him say something about Legos."

Zach was obsessed with Legos. He and Will had been in the process of building a Lego replica of Giants Stadium. One more thing Zach would no longer have his father to help him with. It was complicated and beyond what Zach could ever finish without Will's help.

As Kate made her way up the stairs, she heard Betty resume her conversation.

"They even used his corneas. They told us—"

Kate's jaw clenched. She'd always liked her in-laws but would be grateful when they returned to Florida. Although Kate had agreed to sign the papers for Will to be an organ donor, dwelling on it wasn't something she planned to do. It hurt too much.

"Hey, buddy." As she thought, Kate spied Zach showing his friends the stadium replica, which sat on the Lego table in his room. "Be careful with that. Maybe—maybe I can help you finish it. Or maybe Grandpa."

"I'm being careful, Mom."

Zach turned back to his friends. "My dad designed this whole thing, and when the stands are finished, we're going to put people in the seats."

Kate couldn't help but notice he was still talking about his father in the present tense.

"Children are resilient," the social worker at the hospital had told her. "He'll accept it in his own time, but he'll also look to you to see how you're handling the loss. Don't be afraid to talk about your husband. Zach needs to feel comfortable talking about his father. He needs reassurance that he's not going to be expected to forget him."

Zach would never forget Will and how much he loved his son. Kate would make sure of it.

"You hungry?" she asked.

Zach shook his head. "No. Grandma made me a sandwich before."

"Okay, I'll be downstairs if you need me." Kate wasn't sure how long her house would be filled with people, but she was ready to be alone. She stood at the top of the stairs, her limbs heavy with exhaustion. As she thumped down the stairs, her father was walking through the front door.

"Hi, Daddy." Kate knew her father could only stand a gathering like this for so long before he'd feel the need to do something useful. In his hands, he carried a small grocery bag and a bouquet of mostly wilted flowers that were well past their prime.

"Did someone send dead flowers?" Kate asked, her tone incredulous. A florist would undoubtedly need to get a call if they had the nerve to send something like that.

"Come with me, sweetie."

Kate followed her dad into the kitchen. He left the flowers and bag on the counter and turned to her.

"I went to the tow yard and got Will's car for you."

"Oh." Kate held onto the table for support as she glanced out the front window. A sea of cars was parked in front of her house.

As if reading her thoughts, her father said, "I parked it down the street, but when everyone leaves, I'll move it into the driveway for you. You'll have to decide if you want to sell it, or maybe keep his instead of yours. Will's is newer, which might be something to consider."

Kate flinched. Drive Will's car? Could she sit in the driver's seat of his car without visualizing him, windows down, belting out *Journey* songs? The smell of his soap would have permeated the driver's seat, a constant reminder filling her senses as she drove. No, it wasn't possible. Kate could never drive Will's car.

Instead of responding, Kate nodded her chin in the direction of the counter. "Where did those come from?"

"The bouquet was on the passenger seat of his car. So was the grocery bag."

That explained the condition of the flowers. Kate stumbled to the counter and peered into the grocery bag. Hot chocolate with marshmallows. Will had stopped as she'd asked to get some for Zach. A small whimper escaped her throat as her legs threatened to collapse under her.

"I know, sweetie." Her dad swept her into his arms. "You're in for a rough ride, but your mom and I are here for you."

Kate wanted to cry but didn't think she had any more tears in her. She pulled back, and her eyes pleaded with him. "Maybe you could start herding people out of here? I just—I need to have this day over with. No more small talk. No more pity. I want to be alone with Zach."

Her dad nodded. "Sure. I can handle that. I'll start winding this down."

True to his word, her father helped clear the house while her mother cleaned up the kitchen and wrapped up all the leftover food. At least Kate wouldn't have to worry about cooking anything for a while. Not that she had any sort of appetite.

When her parents had finally gone home after Will died, Kate had thrown out the pot roast dinner and cake she'd made the night he was hit. Her mother had wrapped it all up for her, but she couldn't bear to look at it, much less eat it. Especially the cake. It had been Will's absolute favorite, and she knew she'd never make it again.

After finally getting Zach to sleep, Kate flicked off the light in the kitchen. Her shoulders drooped, and she rested her palms on the counter to hold herself up. Her lids were heavy, but sleep hadn't come easy in the days since Will died. Sleeping alone in their bed just reminded her why his side was empty.

She drew in a deep breath, then exhaled as she turned the light back on. After running a hand over her face, she bent at the knees and searched the cabinet where they kept the liquor. A bottle of vodka they'd be given over the holidays. Perfect. She set the bottle on the kitchen counter and reached for a small glass.

She poured a healthy shot, slugged it back, and winced as it went down her throat. Another and she felt the heat warm her face.

She'd already gone through the wine they had, the empty bottles placed discretely at the bottom of the trash can before her parents arrived. The night Will died, she'd gone through two bottles of pinot grigio. They'd left her with a throbbing headache as she picked out his casket the following day. She'd blamed it on her grief.

The night after that had been chardonnay. Then last night, she'd finished baking for today's gathering and polished off an entire bottle of red. It had been enough to gift her a few hours of sleep. Sleep was the only respite she could hope for, the only peace she got. If she wasn't awake, she didn't have to feel her insides being ripped out. For a little while, she could forget that Will was never coming back.

Kate had one more shot and then turned off the light. In the darkness, her hands reached for the small glass and the bottle. She took them with her as she headed up the stairs.

* * *

Something was tugging at Kate's arm, but she couldn't move. Her limbs felt weighted down, paralyzed.

The pulling became more urgent until she heard his voice—a plaintive wailing. "Mommy, please wake up. Wake up, Mommy. *Please.*"

Kate tried to open her eyes. They were swollen shut from tears, her lids heavy from far too much vodka. She ran her hand over her face and licked her lips. Her mouth was bone dry. Her bleary eyes took in Will's side of the bed, and once again, she was thrust back into reality. Alcohol only blurred the edges, but right there in the middle was the miserable truth. Her husband was gone.

"Zach?" Kate moaned as she rolled over slowly and turned

toward the sound of the sniffling. Her limbs felt like they were pinned in wet sand.

Panic was etched on her son's face as he perched by her side of the bed. "Mommy! You weren't moving. I was scared you were dead too."

She watched the tears rolling down his face, his breathing ragged as he sucked in huge gulps of air. The heartbreaking sound of her child's panic yanked Kate out of her alcohol-induced grogginess. Of course Zach would now worry about her. He only had one parent left.

She reached for him, her hands rubbing his small shoulders to comfort him.

"Oh, honey. Mommy's fine." Kate heard her voice, the words slurred. She licked her lips and drew in a breath. "I was asleep—I was just sleeping soundly, and I didn't hear you."

A stab of guilt twinged her insides as she saw the vodka bottle on the nightstand, the contents noticeably lower than when she had gone up to bed. That explained the wet sand feeling. Will always said she couldn't handle her liquor.

Zach's blue eyes, rimmed in red from crying, peered up at her. "Can I sleep with you in your bed?"

"Of course you can." Kate let out a soft groan as she lifted him up onto the bed. From there, he crawled over her toward Will's side.

As Kate turned to face her son, his face blotchy and wet, a stark realization hit her. Falling apart was not an option. Zach needed her. What if something had happened to him and she was too drunk to realize it? The fierce love she had for him was more important than anything else she felt, even her own misery.

Zach laid his head on the pillow and snuggled in close to her. "I'm glad you were only sleeping. You don't have to worry about anything. I'll take care of you."

With everything that had happened to her little boy—losing the dad he idolized, sitting through Will's funeral, the houseful of people—Zach was worried about *her*. Kate reached out and ran her fingers through his soft curls. The love she felt for her son overwhelmed her as she brushed the hair away from his face.

Zach's eyes closed as he laid beside her, his fists curled up under his chin.

Kate let out an appreciative sigh as she stared at him. "How did I ever get so lucky to get a little boy like you?"

His voice was soft and sleepy when he responded. "Because I knew you'd need me."

CHAPTER 12

FIVE MONTHS LATER

*K*ate reached for the remote, hit the pause button on the VCR, and tilted her head. Was someone knocking?

Wrapping the blanket around her as if it would somehow provide a shield of safety against danger, she lifted herself from the couch. It had only been five months since Will died, and she wasn't sure she'd ever get used to not having a man in the house for times like this. Crouching down, she made her way to the kitchen and glanced out the front window—no headlights in her driveway. Kate hugged the wall and slipped into the front hall. A shadow was clearly illuminated on the porch through the frosted panes of her front door.

Kate shrank back. Who was on her front porch at this hour? Okay, it wasn't *that* late, but she usually didn't have visitors at eight-thirty at night. Zach had only gone to bed thirty minutes earlier.

Another knock and a voice called out. "Hey, it's me. I see you, so you might as well let me in."

Relief surged through her. Celeste.

It hadn't taken long before Kate realized what she'd said when they met at the hospital was true. Everyone went back to their lives while she had to figure out what hers looked like without Will. She'd saved Celeste's number, tucked it in the bottom of her jewelry box. Just in case.

On an impulse, Kate had dug it out and called her. Two hours later, her doorbell rang. Celeste brought pizza and blew in like a breath of fresh air. Instantly, they became friends as if they had known each other forever. Kate didn't have to pretend to be okay. If she was having a bad day, Celeste understood. She'd been there too.

It was like Kate's other friends didn't know what to say to her. So, they said nothing. Their calls had dwindled down until she barely heard from them. Melinda called her occasionally to check in, but she had three small kids to keep her busy. And a husband. Even though Melinda and Adam didn't make her feel like a third wheel, she was one now without Will.

As Kate pulled open the front door, Celeste rushed in. "It's about time. I was starting to think you were never going to get up to answer the door."

Kate pulled the blanket tight around her body. "What are you doing here? You scared the crap out of me."

Celeste gave Kate a pointed look. "I know what day it is. My neighbor is staying with the kids." She held up a tall brown paper bag that clearly held a bottle. "I brought wine."

Kate was sure it was obvious she'd been crying. There was no fooling Celeste, and yet she tried anyway. "I'm fine. Really. You didn't have to check on me."

Celeste's eyebrows shot up. "Let's just see about that." She scurried down the hallway toward the family room.

"Where are you—hey, come back here," Kate called after her, her socks sliding on the wood floor as she tried to keep up.

Celeste's gaze swept through the room. Crumpled tissues on the coffee table. Stack of videotapes next to the television. Wedding album laying open. The television frozen on an image of Will and Kate standing at the altar.

Celeste put down the wine and turned to face Kate, who offered up a guilty shrug like a little girl caught lying to her parents.

"How did you know?" Kate asked.

Celeste wrapped her in a hug. "Because I did the exact same thing on my wedding anniversary after Ed died. It's normal to be extra sad today, but I didn't want you to have to be alone." She picked the brown bag up from the coffee table and slipped it off the bottle of cabernet. "Want some?"

Kate hesitated, then shook her head. "I would love some, but I have a tendency to go overboard. Like a big old bandage over my feelings." She didn't mention how she'd almost been too drunk to realize Zach needed her and how much it had scared her.

"Sometimes that's okay," Celeste said softly.

Kate pressed her lips together to keep them from quivering. "If I started tonight, I don't think I'd be able to stop. But when I woke up in the morning, I'd be hungover, and Will would still be gone. I'd have to start all over again. I feel like I need to feel the pain to get through it. When I don't *need* it, then I know I'll be okay to have a glass or two without it turning into a bottle or two."

"You know, you can still come to the support group at the hospital. It might help to talk to other women who've been through this. Besides me, I mean."

"I know. Maybe someday." In truth, going back to the hospital where she'd lost Will wasn't something Kate even wanted to think about. "I don't think I'm ready yet."

Celeste nodded. "I get it." She looked down at the bottle she was cradling in the crook of her arm like a football. "So, the wine … am I allowed?"

Kate gave her a small smile. "Of course you are. C'mon, I'll get you a glass. Unless you're planning to drink right from the bottle."

Celeste scrunched up her mouth and tilted her head as if that wasn't such a bad idea.

Kate held out her hand. "Give it to me, and I'll be right back."

When she returned from the kitchen, she had wine for Celeste and a can of Coke for herself. She took a sip and then settled back into her spot on the couch.

Celeste settled in on the other side of her. "So, we're watching your wedding video?" she asked.

Kate nodded and hit play on the remote. Celeste gripped her hand and watched silently alongside her as the ceremony began.

When they got to the part where she and Will left the church, Kate turned to Celeste with a bittersweet smile. "Will wanted to get our vows laminated so we would always remember what we promised that day. But then, of course, after the wedding, he had no idea where he put his. They probably went back to the tuxedo rental place." Kate gave a wistful shrug. "Lost forever, I guess. Or maybe the next groom decided to use them."

"They *were* pretty good."

"His vows were exactly what I would have expected from him." Kate pointed at the screen. "And that's my cousin, Melinda. Will and I met at a Super Bowl party at her house."

As Kate watched her wedding day unfold on the television screen, she couldn't help but think about the anniversaries before Will died. They'd celebrated by sitting right in the same spot watching this video. Sometimes he'd grab her by the hand and dance with her in the middle of the family room as their wedding song played. He'd sing along, mostly out of tune—just like he had done that day—without a care who could hear him.

Now the opening bars of her wedding song prompted tears

instead of the absolute joy she had felt that day. Would that ever change so she could remember the good times without feeling so damn sad? Kate reached for a tissue.

"Your husband—he was the life of the party, wasn't he?" Celeste said finally, after watching Will lead the congo line around the reception hall.

Kate sniffled and blew her nose. "He really was larger than life. People gravitated to him." She rolled her eyes slightly, a small smile taking her by surprise. "I mean, he was a sarcastic little bugger sometimes, but it was all in good fun."

Celeste tipped back her wine glass and took a long swallow. "Well, it's clear how much he loved you."

As the wedding highlights came to an end, Kate mentally steeled herself for the end. She'd watched it so many times and thought nothing about it, but now, she couldn't ignore how naïve they'd both been that day.

As the parking lot of the reception hall faded in, she turned to Celeste. "This is the end of the night, and Will couldn't wait to get me out of there." Kate couldn't help but laugh. "He was ready for the video guy to stop following us around. He said he felt like we had a chaperone all night trying to keep us from sneaking off into a coat closet or something."

The limo was there, ready to take them to the hotel for the night. They only had a few hours before they needed to leave to catch their early morning flight to Jamaica. Kate was still in her wedding gown, the hem dragging against the black asphalt. By that point, she didn't care. The uncomfortable shoes she swore to her mother would be fine for dancing had been slipped off her aching feet and tossed into the back seat. Will had the collar of his shirt unbuttoned and the bow tie in his jacket pocket where it had been since the beginning of the reception. He held a bottle of beer in one hand and Kate's hand gripped firmly in the other.

It had been more than a decade, but she could remember the

moment like it was yesterday. *One final hurrah for the camera guy, and then we can finally be alone.*

Kate's eyes were fixed on the television screen as Will dipped her dramatically with his free hand. He lowered his face to hers and kissed her. Then he locked his eyes on hers and whispered, "Mrs. Kennedy, I can't wait to love you every single day for the rest of your life." His voice had been so low that watching the video, it wasn't clear what he'd said. But Kate knew.

Then she heard her response on the tape. "I can't wait to love you too. Forever."

As Will let her up, he let out a soft growl. He released that slow, sexy smile Kate had come to know meant Will had only one thing on his mind.

He kissed her and then looked directly into the camera. "Mr. and Mrs. Kennedy have to go now. But don't worry, they lived happily ever after."

"Okay, that's the end." Will waved his hands over each other in the air and laughed when his beer spilled onto the pavement. "Fade to black," he told the video guy. "I need to get my perfect bride to the honeymoon."

CHAPTER 13

THREE MONTHS LATER

"This coffee cake is amazing," Celeste said as she sat at Kate's kitchen table on a Saturday morning. "What do you put in here? It's practically melting in my mouth."

"Oh, come on now. I already gave you my cheesecake secret."

"I'm telling you. I treasure our friendship, but your desserts are making me fat."

Kate rolled her eyes. "You are not fat."

"Yeah, okay," Celeste said, popping the button pressing on her stomach. "Tell that to my jeans. They've staged a coup."

Kate glanced out the kitchen window as laughter floated in. Zach was outside on the grass tossing a football to Ben, Celeste's eight-year-old son. Six-year-old daughter Bella shook pretend pom-poms as she cheered them on off to the side. Zach adored both of Celeste's kids, and Kate was grateful they all got along. The kids understood each other because they all shared the pain of no longer having a daddy.

"Hey, you want to take the kids to a movie tonight?" Celeste asked.

Kate hesitated. "Maybe. I'm sure they'd love it, but I'm worried I need to start watching what I spend."

She'd been horrified when the hospital bills started rolling in. The cost for the organ donation had been covered, but the rest was on her. Even after the insurance paid their part, there were still new bills still coming in every day. The ambulance, the hospital stay, the surgery. A small life insurance policy Will had through his job paid out, which helped, but that wouldn't last much longer. Kate's administrative job alone simply didn't pay the bills.

"I may need to find a second job," Kate said with a half-hearted shrug. "Or sell the house. Zach loves his school. I would hate to move and have to put him somewhere where he knows no one. He's had too much change as it is this year."

Not to mention, the idea of selling the house she'd shared with Will seemed so final. Like she'd just accepted what happened and moved on.

Celeste gazed off for a moment, her lips pursed. "You know, I might have something for you."

"Really, what?"

"My friend Liza told me her sister is thinking about starting a catering business. I guess it's something she's always wanted to do, and she finally decided it's now or never. She cooked for Liza's fortieth birthday party. Marcy—that's Liza's sister—is a great cook. The food was delicious, but I heard her tell someone she ordered the cake because desserts weren't her thing. I wonder if there could be something there. Maybe she needs a partner."

"Oh, I don't know. I don't bake well enough for it to be a business," Kate said, her voice filled with skepticism.

Celeste gave her a dismissive wave of her hand. "Of course

you do. You never give yourself enough credit. You make some of the best desserts I've ever tasted."

"You really think so?"

Celeste patted her stomach. "Would you like to ask my jeans?"

Kate laughed. "So, what would I need to do?"

"Let me talk to my friend. See what she thinks." Celeste picked up her coffee cup and took a sip.

Kate's face grew serious as she twisted the rings on her finger. "Can I ask you something?"

"Seriously? You know you can ask me anything."

"When did you stop wearing your wedding ring?"

Celeste let out a breath. "Oh. Right before the first anniversary, I think. People made assumptions. Tell your husband we were here. Ask your husband if he needs the house painted. Stuff like that. I think I finally decided it was time when one of Bella's teachers said we needed to set up a conference. She asked if I needed to check with my husband to see when he'd be free. I hated having to explain it in front of Bella."

"It feels like a betrayal somehow," Kate said, her voice soft. "I still feel married even if Will's not here."

"That's understandable. But some day you may feel ready for a new relationship, and—"

"I don't plan to ever get married again," Kate cut in, shaking her head. "Or even date."

"No?" Celeste asked, surprised. "I'm two years ahead of you. It does take time. You know the invitation stands if you want to come to the support group. It might help."

Kate lifted a shoulder. Talking with other women wouldn't change anything. Will would still be gone. "I've had the love of my life. It wouldn't be fair to make someone else try to compare with that. Will set the bar way too high."

"I understand, but you still have a lot of living left to do," Celeste said. "You might change your mind about wanting to spend it alone. Some day you may decide a little companionship would be nice."

Kate shook her head. "I don't think so. You would get married again?"

Celeste nodded without hesitation. "Yeah, I would. If I found the right person who understood I had a husband I loved. We didn't get divorced. I didn't *choose* to leave him. They'd have to be able to accept that. And the kids, of course."

Kate sighed, then stood. "I'll be right back." She trotted up the stairs to her bedroom.

When she returned, she placed a framed picture on the kitchen table—it was from her honeymoon. She and Will looked tan, content, and gloriously happy.

Celeste glanced at the photo. "I get it, Kate. It's hard to get over them. Trust me, I know."

"Will had this framed for our first anniversary." Kate pointed at the bottom. "Look at the engraving."

Celeste picked it up and read it. "*Like the ocean, we have no beginning and no end.* That's beautiful, but—"

"There is no but," Kate said, her voice firm. "That's how I feel. My relationship with Will won't ever be over, so how can I ever think of being with another man?"

"Don't you think Will would want you to be happy?" Celeste asked. "Even if it meant you were with someone else?"

"I—I don't know." Kate lowered her head. "I've never told anyone this because I was afraid they'd think I was crazy." She brought her gaze up and met Celeste's eyes. "A few weeks after Will died, I had a dream, and it felt like he was back. It was like I had only imagined he died." She shook her head as she remembered it, the memory still crystal clear in her mind. "I'll never forget how real it felt. How happy I was to think the whole thing had just been a horrible nightmare."

Celeste gave her an understanding nod. "I dream about Ed, too, sometimes."

"I've had other dreams about Will, but this one was different. I felt like I could almost reach out and touch him. He was standing at the end of our bed, and he smiled at me." Kate closed her eyes for a moment, and she could almost see him again. The lopsided grin that drew her in like he had a secret only meant for her. The perfect teeth, except for the one tooth on the bottom that was a tiny bit crooked. The crinkles on the outside of his eyes. "It was the way he used to look at me right before he told me how much he loved me."

"I'm sure you needed that," Celeste said, her voice gentle. "It must have—"

"Will told me he was okay. That I didn't need to worry about him. He said he knew I was strong, and I could handle anything life threw at me. And he said—I'll never forget his words—he said, 'Katie girl, you find what makes you happy, and you go do it.'"

Celeste put up her hands. "So, there you have it."

Kate let out a confused moan. "But what if he meant a job or a new career and not remarrying. How am I supposed to know what he meant by that?"

"Maybe it incorporates anything and everything that makes you happy. I do believe Ed watches over the kids and me." Celeste leaned back in her chair. "Some people believe in signs. A cardinal. A butterfly. Me? I find pennies. When I'm worried about something and need some guidance, I find a penny. I believe it's Ed's way of telling me I'm doing the right thing."

Kate shrugged. "Maybe."

The sound of the kids' laughter filtered in through the open window in the kitchen.

"I'll see if they want to go to a movie later." As Kate got up to call out to them, she stopped and turned, her eyes wide. She raised a finger and pointed at the window. "Celeste, look. Slowly."

There was a butterfly on the other side of the screen perched on a bush with vibrant red berries. White dots framed the rich black wings that blended into a beautiful light blue color. He was just sitting there.

Her friend shifted gradually in her seat and smiled. "Gorgeous. Maybe that's the sign you needed."

With that, the butterfly lifted off the bush, its wings fluttering as it drifted away.

"Maybe Will's telling me I can do the catering business. He did always love my baking." Kate pressed her lips together. "But I'm still not sure I'll ever want to be with anyone but Will. I've had my great love, and now it's time to focus on me. Take care of Zach and find a career. One that I love."

"There's nothing wrong with that." Celeste leaned forward and placed her hand on Kate's left hand, covering her rings. "Will's only been gone eight months. You are entitled to wear your wedding ring however long you want to, or for the rest of your life if that's what makes you happy. You don't ever have to be with anyone else if that's your choice. No one can tell you what to do or how to feel. Listen to your heart and go from there."

Kate nodded. There was a massive void in her life without Will, but she had to keep living. She was excited about the idea of getting involved in this new business venture. Wherever Will was, she hoped he was watching over her. She wanted to make him proud.

CHAPTER 14

ONE YEAR LATER

The phone rang as Kate was getting ready to head out the door to drop Zach at school. Maybe it was Marcy. It had been a year since they became partners and opened the catering company. They had a luncheon booked for that afternoon, and Kate had stayed late the night before to finish all the desserts. She'd left a note, but maybe Marcy hadn't seen it yet.

"Hello," she said, stretching the phone cord to grab Zach's lunchbox from the counter.

"Hey, it's Celeste—"

"Oh, hey, I'm heading out the door. Can I call you when I get to work?"

"Sure, but I have a quick question. Did you and Marcy cater a huge wedding in Bedminster last weekend? Some ridiculous mansion?"

"Yeah, why?"

"There's a column about you in the paper. Some food critic loved your stuff."

Kate's forehead wrinkled. "A food critic? Like a reviewer?"

"Critic, reviewer. Whatever you want to call it. Yeah, he said, and I quote, 'I normally don't review wedding fare, but the meal served by MK Catering last weekend was hands down the best I have ever had.' Listen to what he said about your cake. 'The wedding cake practically melted in my mouth and left me contemplating whether I should attempt to claim the pieces of the early goers who unknowingly left before it was served.'"

Kate's mouth went slack, and she leaned against the counter. For a moment, she was speechless.

"Wow."

"Yeah, wow," Celeste said in agreement. "Call me when you get to the office. Maybe Marcy doesn't know about it yet."

"What paper was it—"

"Mom, c'mon." Zach grabbed his lunchbox from her hand and shoved it in the top zippered compartment of his backpack. He threw the strap over his arm and held out a large piece of poster board. "I'm going to be late. I need time to drop my science project off in the gymnasium before school starts."

Kate nodded at him. "Okay, bud." She followed the cord back to the phone on the wall. "Celeste, thanks for the great news. I have to get Zach to school and then head to work. I'll call you back in a little bit."

When she pulled into the back lot thirty minutes later, Marcy's car was already there.

They had renovated a perfect space for the business, the entrance right on a main road, sandwiched between a small art gallery and a stationery store. In the front, they had an office and a small conference table to meet potential clients. The kitchen area was a large open area beyond that. They'd installed commercial ovens, prep counters, and a large walk-in cooler adjacent to the back door.

As Kate walked in from the parking lot, she realized someone must have called Marcy too. Her partner had the newspaper spread out on one of the large counters in the middle of the kitchen.

"Have you seen this?" she called out before Kate had even shut the door behind her.

"Celeste called and told me about it."

Marcy picked up the paper and began reading. "The culinary magic of Marcy Walker and Kate Kennedy held its own in the spectacular sprawling Lindsey Brown mansion in Bedminster, the site of the recent nuptials of the new Mr. and Mrs. Ethan Fitzsimmons. I should have had some insight into the delights awaiting me as I feasted on the passed hors d'oeuvres during the cocktail hour. The balcony's panoramic view was the perfect setting for mini crab cakes, drizzled with a cream sauce that held the perfect hint of cilantro. I would love to know their secret ingredients in the corn croquette recipe." Marcy lifted her gaze from the newspaper, a wide smile on her face. "Blah, blah, blah. I've read this whole thing about ten times, so I won't bore you with all the accolades for the appetizers. Let's just say he loved them all."

"How could he not?" Kate asked, thrilled her partner was getting some well-earned recognition.

"Right?" Marcy's gaze dipped back to the paper, and she continued reading. "Feeding two hundred people is no easy task, but these ladies served a perfectly prepared grilled beef tender-loin, topped with morel mushrooms and a pinot noir demi-glaze. To the side was a rich and decadent black truffle risotto. I challenge you to find a risotto equally as good in any five-star Italian restaurant. The same may be true of the chicken marsala. I wasn't lucky enough to have a chance to sample both meals, but the woman next to me cleaned her plate and couldn't stop raving about it."

"Well, damn. Maybe we should send this guy some of your chicken marsala."

"Here comes your glory," Marcy said, jabbing her finger in the air toward Kate. "The pièce de résistance had to be the three-tiered wedding cake that actually tasted as good as it looked. An absolute fantasy for the tastebuds. The frosting was perfection, just a hint of lemon to complement the tartness of the raspberry filling nestled between layers of rich vanilla cake." She glanced up. "And then he basically said he wanted to steal pieces from the people at his table who left early."

"Yeah, that was the part Celeste read to me on the phone." Kate shook her head in disbelief. "That's pretty much a fairy tale of a write-up. I would think that might drum up some new business for us. Did he include our contact information?"

Marcy's eyes drifted to the bottom of the article. "He included our phone number."

"That was nice of him," Kate said with an appreciative nod. "Pretty impressive he wrote up a catering company at a wedding. I mean, he's a food critic, right? They don't normally do that, do they?"

Marcy shook her head. "I don't think so. He's got a column recommending restaurants for the most part. There's a bit of a bio on him at the top. I guess he used to be a chef. He also owned that pretty restaurant on South Street in Morristown. The one with all the twinkling white lights on the patio."

"I know the one." Every time they passed by it, Kate told Will they needed to check it out. From the outside, it looked like it would be a romantic spot for a birthday or anniversary. They'd run out of time, never making it there before Will died.

Kate leaned down toward the paper. "So, what's this guy's name?"

"It's at the top." Marcy pointed with her finger. "Sam Winston."

"What's the protocol here? Do we call and thank him?" Kate asked as she skimmed the article for herself.

Marcy shrugged as she pulled on an apron. "I don't see why

we couldn't. We probably have to reach out to him through the paper. Do you want to try to see if you can get in touch with him? I've got to get the ricotta tarts in the oven for the luncheon today."

"Sure. I finished the dessert order for that last night before I left. It's all in the walk-in."

With the folded newspaper in hand, Kate headed to their office. She dropped into the seat at the large desk they shared and wrote the number she got from information on a Post-it.

"I'm trying to reach a Sam Winston," she said when a gruff voice answered the phone. "He has a column in your paper."

"Sam? Sure. Hold on, I think he's here today."

There was ringing, then an upbeat male voice answered. "Sam Winston here."

"Um, hi, Sam." Kate tapped her pen against the desk. "My name is Kate Kennedy, and my partner is Marcy Walker. You were nice enough to write a column about our catering company. We wanted to say thank you for your review."

"Well, hello, Kate." The voice on the other end was warm and friendly. "The Fitzsimmons wedding, right? Audrey and Ethan. Wedding food can be … well, not the best. I thought I might go hungry but was pleasantly surprised they found your catering company. I'm sure it was Audrey who found you. Ethan's actually my accountant. Doesn't tend to be too creative."

Kate laughed. She remembered the couple well. "It actually *was* Audrey that did most of the planning. Ethan did show up for the final tasting, but she had already decided on everything she wanted. Pretty much all he did was nod and write the check."

"Yup, that sounds about right. But seriously, everything you served was incredible. I felt obligated to write it up. Felt it was my duty to let future brides know they don't need to serve dried-out rubber chicken at their weddings." He laughed. "You know, in case I happen to get invited."

Kate couldn't help but smile. There was something charming about Sam Winston. "Well, we certainly appreciate it. Although Marcy mostly does all the food. I'm strictly desserts."

"Don't tell her, but the wedding cake might have been my favorite part. Probably the best I've ever had. Is that all you do is weddings?"

"Oh, no." Kate leaned back in her chair. "We do all kinds of events. Corporate meetings, family reunions. You name it. I even sell some of my pies and cakes to restaurants."

"Really?" Sam sounded intrigued. "Do you have a listing of what you offer?"

Kate pulled open a drawer in the desk and reached for the folder that held copies of the menus.

"Sure, do you have a fax number? I can send you the dessert selections. Or I can drop it in the mail for you."

Sam seemed to hesitate for a moment. "Actually, where are you located?"

"We have an office and kitchen space in Madison," Kate said as she pulled out menus for him. "We meet potential clients here and do tastings. Well, in addition to all the cooking and baking, of course."

"Of course," Sam said. "If it's okay with you, maybe I'll stop by and get that list. I'm not far, and I have to head in that direction anyway. If you fax it, some editor will scoop it up off the machine, and it'll be buried under the piles of paper on their desk before lunch. Besides, I need to see where all the magic happens."

Kate laughed as she put the papers for him aside. "Sometimes I wish I had a magic wand I could wave to make five hundred chocolate mousse cups appear. But sure, if you want to come by here, that would be fine. Depending on when you show up, you might not get to meet Marcy. She has to run some food to a luncheon around eleven, but I should be here. Probably until at least three-thirty." She needed to make sure she left in time to make Zach's science fair at school.

After Kate gave him the address and hung up, she reported back to Marcy as she put the last of the tarts into the large commercial oven.

"Well, Sam Winston couldn't have been nicer. When I told him I baked for some of the restaurants around here, he seemed interested. He wants to come by and get the menu of what desserts we offer."

Marcy wiped her hands on her apron. "Well, he did own that restaurant I told you about. Maybe he's bought another place or has some sort of financial interest in one."

Kate tilted her head as she considered it. "Maybe." As she reached for the order form to pitch in, she was surprised to realize she was curious about learning more about the food critic, the man behind the friendly, inviting voice.

Just before eleven, Kate went out back with Marcy to get everything packed in the van they owned.

"You're sure you're okay taking this over by yourself?"

Marcy nodded. "I've got this. Besides, I don't want you to miss the review guy if he stops by. It could lead to some more restaurant business."

No sooner had Kate walked in through the back door and someone was coming in the front entrance. As she made her way toward him, she knew it had to be Sam Winston, who was surprisingly easy on the eyes. She wasn't sure who she'd expected, but it wasn't the person coming toward her—a handsome man who appeared to be in his early forties. Tall and fit, his sandy brown hair was flecked with a tiny dusting of gray at the temples. He was dressed casually in jeans paired with a light blue button-down shirt with the sleeves rolled up.

"Hi, there," the man said. "Sam Winston. Are you Kate?"

Her feet froze as she stared at him. She knew she was looking at him in that inquisitive way that left a deep wrinkle between her eyebrows. Celeste had already warned her that if she didn't stop, one day that crease wouldn't go away.

He winced slightly at her seemed confusion. "Um. Kate said it was okay if I stopped by. I wanted to get a list of the desserts ..."

She shook her head to help her reset their introduction. "Sorry." She extended her hand. "I'm Kate. You just look so familiar. Maybe I saw you at the wedding."

He smiled, and a small dimple appeared in his right cheek. "I was the dashing one in the black tux."

Kate laughed as all the men had been in tuxedos. "Perhaps. Come on in, and I'll show you what we have."

She led him to their office, where she gathered up the papers she'd set aside for him before settling into a chair at the round table. Sam hesitated, then pulled out the chair next to hers and sat down.

He leaned toward her. With his forearms resting on his thighs, he clasped his hands together under his chin, right below the small smile that played on his full lips. "I'm looking forward to this."

Kate swallowed hard at his close proximity and quickly realized Sam Winston was as charming in person as he had been on the phone.

"So, let me show you what we have," she said, spreading out the papers.

As Kate went through the dessert lists, Sam's gaze drifted from the papers on the table to her face. As she spoke, his eyes studied her intently. Eyes she realized were blue—almost a perfect match to the color of his shirt.

"You make all of these yourself?" Sam asked, sounding impressed.

Kate was relieved to slip into business mode. "I do. And if you had a special request, I'm always open to that as well. We also change it out seasonally, so right now, we're offering a caramel apple torte, and around the holidays, we'll have a delicious eggnog cheesecake."

"Eggnog cheesecake? Wow, that sounds good." Sam moistened his lips, and once again, Kate froze. That feeling of déjà vu was back.

Her face grew warm. "I just—I can't shake this feeling we've met before. Do you have kids?" Maybe he was one of the dads from Zach's school.

Sam shook his head and leaned back in his chair. "I wish I did, but it wasn't in the cards for me. I started as a chef and then owned a restaurant in Morristown."

Kate nodded, breathing easier now that he had put some distance between them. "My partner, Marcy, mentioned that. I always admired it from the outside. I'm sorry to say I've never been there. You don't own it anymore?"

Sam pursed his lips and stared off for a moment before answering. "The restaurant business is rough on a marriage. You spend a lot of time there instead of at home. I finally sold the restaurant …" he hesitated for a moment as if choosing his words. "I sold it for a lot of different reasons." He shrugged, and the corners of his mouth lifted slightly. "Turns out it wasn't the restaurant that was causing the rift in my marriage. It was my wife's golf instructor. We got divorced about two years ago."

"Oh, I'm so sorry," Kate said, but inside she had to wonder. What the hell did the golf instructor look like? Sam had admitted to spending a good deal of time away from home, but still.

"Nothing to be sorry about. It was for the best," Sam said with a nod. His words seemed sincere. "A friend of mine offered me the gig at the newspaper at just the right time. I invested the money when I sold into a small group of restaurants, and that's where I thought your stuff would be perfect. They have nothing like what you have on their menus, so I'm thrilled I found you … and your desserts. They're going to love what you have to offer."

"Well, that sounds great."

Kate reached for the menus as Sam leaned forward to grab

them. As their hands brushed against each other, she caught her breath. Her cheeks went hot.

"Um, you can take these." She scooped up the papers and held them out toward him.

Now, Sam was frozen. "What?" he asked, his gaze lingering on her face.

"The menus," Kate said.

Sam glanced down, took them from her, and stood. "Okay, great. Thanks. Let me see what their interest level is, and I'll get back to you. Sound good?"

"Sure." Kate stood as well, her hand reaching out for the edge of the table when she found her legs were a bit shaky.

Sam reached for her hand, but it felt different than when he'd arrived. This time his handshake wasn't quite as firm or businesslike. He slipped his palm into hers, then brought his other hand around until her hand was between both of his. The warmth of his skin on hers left her insides rolling, and as he said goodbye, she was sure her face was flushed.

The gaze he fixed on her was intense. "It was nice to meet you, Kate."

She tried to respond, but nothing came out. She cleared her throat. "Yes, you too, Sam. Thanks for coming by. It's always more personal than sending stuff over a fax machine." Who was she kidding? This man she'd just met had her mind reeling. Not to mention some other body parts that had lied dormant for a long time.

A smile grew on Sam's face, and that endearing dimple was back. "Talk to you again soon, Kate."

He wasn't out the door for more than a few minutes when Marcy came in. "Was that the food critic? The tall, good-looking man in the blue shirt and jeans."

"Uh, yeah," Kate said, still trying to catch her breath from the goodbye with Sam. She stared down at the desk as she tried to busy herself with some papers. If she looked up, it would be written all over her face. She'd felt something for Sam. She hadn't expected it, and it had left her with a pang of guilt.

For the first time since Will died, Kate wondered if it was time to take off her wedding ring.

CHAPTER 15

FIVE YEARS LATER

"I'm starting to regret I didn't wear gloves," Kate said as she and Celeste made their way onto the bleachers. "It's freezing out."

"Well, it is November." Celeste reached into her jacket pocket and pulled out an extra pair of gloves. She handed them to Kate. "Do I know you or what? I'm glad this is the last football game. I hope they win it since it's the championship, but these Friday night games are turning frigid."

Kate shook her head as she settled onto the bleacher, cringing at the cold metal underneath her. "I can't believe Zach's a senior. This is the last high school game he'll ever play in. It went so fast."

"How are the college applications going?"

"They're all in. Now we wait." Kate cringed. "And then I figure out how to pay for it."

"The catering business is still doing well, right?" Celeste asked, tightening her scarf around her neck.

"It's doing great, but have you seen the price of some of these colleges? Zach has his top choices of where he'd like to play football, but he's going to have to wait and see who offers him a scholarship. Otherwise, he'll be at a state school I can afford."

"I'll be right behind you, and I have two to pay for."

"Luckily, he has the grades to get in almost anywhere." Kate waved at another set of parents settling onto the bleachers below them. Their son played on the team as well. "I certainly never had the kind of grades he gets. He must have gotten that from Will."

Just then, Zach's team took the field. Kate saw him squint into the bleachers and then hold up his helmet in her direction before slipping it over his head and fastening the chin strap.

"His dad would have been proud of him," Celeste said.

"If Will was sitting here, he'd take all the credit." Kate lowered her voice to do an imitation of him. "That's my boy. Who do you think taught him how to throw a perfect pass like that?" It was good to talk about Will, but Kate's insides twinged that he wasn't here to see his son play his last high school football game. She was sure Zach felt it too.

Celeste put her arm around Kate and squeezed her. "Well, you may not have taught him to throw a perfect spiral, but you did good too, Mom. It wasn't always an easy road, but you two made it together. Zach's a great kid."

"I wouldn't have made it without you." Kate turned to face her. "I don't know how I got so lucky that you needed a Snickers at precisely the moment I needed you."

Celeste gave an exaggerated wince. "Well, truth be told, my regular vending machine was empty that day."

"Really, you have no idea how much your friendship means to me. Isn't it ironic?"

"What's that?" Celeste asked, rubbing her hands together as she sat hunched over.

"If we both hadn't lost our husbands, we wouldn't even know each other."

Celeste thought about it a moment, then gave a slight shrug.

"Maybe we would have met some other way. You know, like we were destined to be friends one way or another."

"I guess that's possible. But it still wouldn't be the same friendship we have now," Kate said. "For so many years, it's just been the two of us. And the kids, of course." She gave her friend a pointed stare. "You still haven't told me. How was the date with the dentist last weekend?"

"Ah, Bruce. You mean other than the fact that I was worried I had salad in my teeth all night?" Celeste nodded, a smile on her face. "It was nice. Really nice. I haven't been out to dinner with a man in so long, I'd forgotten what it's like. It was refreshing to have a glass of wine and not have to referee arguments for the kids." Celeste tipped her head to the side as if remembering their evening together. "He makes me laugh. At my age, that's important. I was getting ready to give up on ever finding anyone I could enjoy spending time with."

Kate had long since settled into her single life. Her focus had been on getting Zach through school and building up the catering business with Marcy. She didn't like to casually throw around the word success, but her chest puffed with a little bit of pride when she considered how far she'd come. When Will died, she didn't know how she'd survive on her own. But she had, and she was doing well.

Aside from a brief encounter with Sam, the food critic from over five years ago, Kate never considered dating anyone. She'd felt something for Sam, but it was short-lived. After their meeting, he'd given the information about her desserts to the restaurants. They'd been ordering directly from her for years, but Sam had sailed off into the sunset.

Kate had long ago decided it was probably for the best. She'd resolved that she was better off on her own, but Celeste was another story. Her best friend wanted to find another relationship, and she'd dated nothing but duds for the last couple of years.

"So, are you going to see him again?" Kate asked. "Bruce, the dentist, who makes you laugh."

A glimmer in her friend's eyes told her the answer before her words did. "We're going to dinner and a movie on Sunday."

"Look at you." Kate was happy for her friend. "A second date. Could this one be a keeper?"

Instead of responding, Celeste nudged Kate as the game started and the crowd began to cheer.

Zach was virtually flawless, his team scoring two touchdowns in quick succession. As they neared half-time, the other team put seven points on the board.

Kate glanced at the scoreboard as the clock ticked down. "I'm heading down before halftime to get some hot chocolate. Want one?"

Celeste's teeth chattered as she answered. "Y-y-yess."

Kate ducked down until she got to the aisle to try to block as little of the game as she could for the other fans. When she reached the last step at the bottom, she glanced over and let out a groan. A line was already forming at the concession stands. The metal thumped loudly under her feet as Kate rushed across the platform of the bleachers. She hurried down the small set of steps to the ground.

As Kate took her place at the end of the concession line, she turned up the collar of her coat in an attempt to keep the wind out. While she stood there, the whistle sounded to announce the official end of the first half. The fans descended in thundering droves down the metal bleachers.

Kate bounced from one foot to the other to keep warm. Volunteers manned the concessions during the game, but speed wasn't their strong suit. As she glanced behind her at the long line forming, she was grateful she'd thought to come down early. Those unlucky enough to be at the end of the line would never make it back to the stands in time for the kick-off of the second half.

The teenage girl hesitated before placing the two large Styrofoam cups on the table in front of Kate. It was almost as if she hated to give up the warmth they were providing to her red, chapped hands.

"That's four dollars."

Kate gripped Celeste's glove with her teeth to pull it off. She made a mental note to replace them rather than give them back with her teeth prints on the fingers. She fished a five-dollar bill out of her jeans pocket and handed it to the girl.

"Keep the change." It was the least she could do. The poor girl looked frozen.

After wiggling her fingers back into the glove, Kate picked up a cup in each hand and relished the warmth.

"Excuse me," she said as she tried to work her way out of the concession crowd. Kate put her head down and pressed forward, trying to dodge the families and young children who weren't watching where they were walking. As she eventually made her way into a bit of open space, her shoulders relaxed, and she exhaled.

She turned to head toward the section of the bleachers where Celeste waited, then winced when she felt the thud. Now, she was the one who hadn't been paying attention.

"Oh, I'm sorry, I didn't mean—"

"Kate?"

She blinked hard as she stared at the man bundled up in the soft black leather jacket, a knit cap over his head. Finally, she was able to place the face. "Sam?"

"Hey, I thought that was you." He gestured for her to step out of traffic so she wouldn't get swept up and moved along in the stream of people. "You know, my restaurants love your stuff. I stop into them every so often to get my fix, and they always tell me what a hit they are with the customers. I mean, that chocolate brownie cake you make now is incredible. If I'm not careful, I'm going to need some new holes in my belt."

Kate nodded, but unless his coat was hiding something unexpected, he didn't look like he had put on a single pound since she last saw him. His cheeks were red from the cold, and maybe he had a few more laugh lines, but who didn't? It had been more than five years, after all.

Kate shivered. It was cold, but she couldn't deny it was also the effect Sam was having on her. She brought her arms in closer to her body, hoping he wouldn't notice the cups shaking as she held them. Every part of her was trembling.

"Thanks. I'm glad you're all happy with what they've been ordering." She was careful not to let her expression show how disappointed she was that he'd never called her after their initial meeting. At least he had turned over the information, and his restaurants had been great customers.

"So, what are you doing at the game?" Kate recalled he had told her he didn't have kids, and she'd never seen him at a Monarch game before.

Sam pulled his hat slightly down over his ears and shoved his hands deep into the pockets of his coat. "My girlfriend's daughter is a cheerleader for the Knights."

Her stomach twisted. Girlfriend. Well, of course he wouldn't still be single after all this time. Someone passing by jostled her elbow, and she glanced at the hot chocolates in her hands to ensure nothing had spilled. Now, she was grateful for Celeste's gloves that covered her hands and hid whether she was wearing a wedding ring. As far as Sam knew, he had his girlfriend, and she had a husband. Kate wasn't sure why it mattered. It wasn't like it was a competition.

"What about you?" Sam asked.

"My son is the quarterback for Monarch." Kate's chest puffed out, and she spoke with the tone of a proud mother.

Sam lifted his eyebrows. "Wow. He's having quite a game. He's a senior?"

She bobbed her head. "He is."

"Any plans to play in college?"

"He's hoping to. We're still waiting to hear. I'd cross my fingers, but—" she raised the cups in the air.

As fans started to ascend the bleachers, the whistle blew for the start of the second half.

"I guess it's game time," Kate said. "I'd say good luck, but since we're rooting for opposing teams, I'll just say it was nice to run into you instead." It would have been much more enjoyable to run into him had he not mentioned he was there with another woman.

"It was *really* good to see you, Kate," he said, and he sounded sincere. "I've often wondered how you were doing, but you … you look great."

His gaze made her knees threaten to buckle.

Kate groaned silently. Why did he have to look at her that way? It felt like he could see right through the casual façade she tried to put up.

Sam lingered for an awkward moment as if he had something else to say. Then he leaned in close, and Kate caught her breath as a hint of his cologne wafted over her. "Don't tell anyone on my sideline, but good luck with the game." His blue eyes lingered on hers, and as she let herself disappear into them, the noise of the stadium and the fans rushing past her disappeared.

"You better go," Sam said finally, breaking the spell. His eyes drifted to her hand. "I'm sure someone's waiting on that other hot chocolate." He turned, and after he waved goodbye over his shoulder, he took a right and headed off to the other set of bleachers.

Someone's waiting. What did he mean by that?

When Kate handed Celeste her hot chocolate, her friend took it and raised her eyebrows. "So, who was that hottie you were talking to?"

Kate laughed. "You don't miss a thing, do you? Remember that review in the paper several years ago? That was the guy who wrote it."

"I remember how much he loved your wedding cake." Celeste sipped her hot chocolate and stared at Kate. "I have a finely tuned sense of people's body language—some might even call it a superpower." She cocked her head. "From here, it sure looked like that man was interested in much more than just your baking skills."

Kate scrunched up her face. "You're crazy." She settled back down on the bleacher holding her cup carefully so as not to drop it. "Besides, he's here with his girlfriend. Her daughter's a cheer-leader for the Knights."

Celeste shot her friend a dubious stare. "I'm not usually wrong about these things. Are you telling me my Spidey sense is off?"

"This time it is. Sorry, super Spidey." Kate sipped her hot chocolate and turned her attention back to the field. She glanced at the scoreboard. "I can't believe I already missed a field goal."

Kate watched as the other team went three downs and out and then kicked the ball back to Monarch. The wind took the short kick off-kilter to the right. They'd given Zach excellent field position. After three first downs, he had them back in the red zone. Zach threw a slant to a running back, but he was stopped with only a two-yard gain. He tried a different play, but that didn't gain much more than a yard.

"Third and seven," Kate said, stomping her foot against the metal bleacher. "Come on, Zach," she yelled at the top of her lungs. "You got this!"

Zach stepped back to throw, but even Kate could see someone had run the wrong play. He had no one open. After hesitating for a moment, he took off running. Kate held her breath as the defense for the other team hurtled toward him.

She leaped to her feet, willing him to outrun them. Instead, Zach seemed to slow and collapse just short of the goal line. The defense seemed equally surprised, one of the players leaning in for a late hit. Zach's body moved with the force of the impact but then lay crumpled on the field. Kate's cup slipped from her hand, tipping as it hit the bleachers, the chocolate liquid running over the edge.

The referee's whistle shrilly sounded as yellow flags went flying through the air. Kate's heart beat wildly in her chest, She squinted at the field, but she was too far away to see much. Only that Zach wasn't getting up. Coaches and staff from both sidelines raced across the grass toward him.

"Oh my god, I think he's really hurt." She turned swiftly to Celeste, who had risen to her feet beside her. "Why isn't he getting up?" Kate asked, her voice taut.

Celeste shook her head. "I don't know what's going on, but Zach's young. Healthy. He's going to be fine."

Kate whimpered and turned her attention back to the field as a crowd surrounded her son. Now, she couldn't see anything. She yanked at the scarf around her neck. It felt like she was being strangled.

She tried to swallow past the lump in her throat. "What the hell just happened? It looked like he went down before the guy even hit him. I'm scared, Celeste."

Kate's attention was riveted to the field, her hands clutched to her chest while she waited. He'd get up, she told herself. Walk off to the sideline with an arm around the coach's shoulder. The crowd would erupt in applause that their star quarterback was fine.

But as she watched, none of that happened. Instead, a hush of deathly silence hung in the air.

Kate's insides churned. "Please, no. Not you too," she whispered.

CHAPTER 16

The tires on the car screeched as Celeste careened to a stop at the front of the ER. "Go find Zach. I'll park the car and wait for you inside."

Kate nodded and threw open the car door.

As she rushed toward the registration desk, reminders of another cold night she'd been in this hospital raced through her head. That was a memory she'd long ago tried to push from her mind—desperately trying to find Will, praying he was fine. But he wasn't. Nausea hit the pit of her stomach. She was determined she wasn't going to lose Zach too.

A nurse hurried out to get her, and she led Kate to the room where Zach was lying on a bed. Electrodes attached to his chest were connected to a machine, but he was conscious. He gave his mother a feeble smile.

Kate's legs wobbled as her hand covered her mouth. Tears of relief filled her eyes. "Thank god you're okay."

The nurse nodded at the doctor in the room. "This is Mrs. Kennedy, Zach's mom."

"Your son's a lucky kid," the doctor said as she extended her hand. "I'm Dr. Rachbind. To be honest, I'm surprised he's sitting here."

Kate flinched and stole another glance at Zach. He seemed okay. "Why?"

"Sounds like he had a quick intervention on the football field," Dr. Rachbind said. "The fact that the other team's coach was so experienced in CPR may have saved your son's life today. It's what got him to the hospital so we could get his heart back into a normal rhythm."

"His heart?" Kate asked, confused. "I don't understand. I mean, he didn't even get hit that hard—"

"Zach has a couple of broken ribs. Those could be from the hit he sustained, or it's also possible they're from the CPR itself. Done correctly, it can actually be pretty violent." The doctor's gaze drifted to Zach. "But it seems your son actually collapsed *before* the hit."

Kate had thought the same thing when it happened. Was the doctor saying Zach's heart had stopped? Her insides twisted as her gaze settled on the machine the doctor was standing in front of. "What's that doing?"

"This machine is used for an echocardiogram. It uses sound waves to produce images of Zach's heart."

"But he looks fine now," Kate said, frowning. "Is it looking for something specific?"

"It allows us to see his heart beating and how it's pumping blood. I suspect your son has something called IHSS. It stands for idiopathic hypertrophic subaortic stenosis."

Kate's eyes glazed over at the confusing medical term. "Idio, what?" It sounded serious.

"Basically, IHHS is an inherited disease of the heart that causes thickening of the heart muscle and other changes that significantly impair the heart's ability to pump blood."

Kate's eyes widened. "So—so, what does that mean?"

"It means that Zach's extremely fortunate to be alive right

now," the doctor said. "IHHS is pretty rare, but most athletes don't survive when something like this happens. In fact, they don't even know they have it until they collapse." The corners of her mouth lifted. "Usually, I based my opinions solely on medical facts, but your son must have had an angel watching over him today. Maybe the coach who knew to immediately start CPR and not stop until the ambulance got there."

Kate exchanged a look with her son. She knew they both had the same thought—Zach's angel had been his dad.

"IHSS can also be genetic. Do you know if there's a history of heart issues on either side of his family?"

Kate shrugged and then shook her head. "Not that I know of."

"Zach said he didn't have any siblings, but it's a good idea for you to get tested. His father too."

Kate thought briefly about the baby she'd lost. She always did when someone asked how many kids she had. "His father passed away about seven years ago."

It amazed her to realize it had been that long ago. Some days it felt like yesterday, and sometimes she feared she was forgetting what Will's voice sounded like.

"Oh, I'm sorry. Not heart-related, correct?"

Kate shook her head. "No. It was—it was a car accident." She didn't feel the need to go into any additional details.

"I'm sure that was hard for both of you. If there was an autopsy done, the ME would have found evidence if your husband had it as well."

They wouldn't have had his heart for an autopsy, but she didn't tell the doctor that. Kate also hadn't wanted one done. Will had been cut apart enough, and it wasn't like she didn't know how he died.

Kate thought of Will's heart beating in someone else's chest. They had run so many tests before all the surgeons arrived to recover his organs. She reassured herself that they wouldn't have given it to the recipient unless it was perfect.

She opened her mouth to ask Dr. Rachbind but then glanced over at Zach. She'd never told him about his dad being an organ donor. He was so little at the time, and since then, she'd tried not to think about it. Maybe someday she'd tell him. This didn't seem the appropriate time to have that conversation.

When Kate didn't reply, the doctor gave her an intense look that suggested the severity of what she was about to say. "If anyone else has it, they probably don't know, but it could trigger a cardiac event. I'd strongly suggest any living members on either side be tested. Just to be sure."

Kate nodded as she imagined having to call Will's family with this news. "Okay, we will. So, if Zach has this idio—IHSS—is it something that requires surgery?"

"I've asked for a cardio consult," Dr. Rachbind said. "My guess is because of what happened today, they won't let him leave without an internal pacemaker and defibrillator. Just to make sure his heart keeps working the way it should." She took in Kate's wide eyes and offered a reassuring smile. "It's a simple procedure, don't worry."

Kate exhaled and nodded at Zach. "So, he gets the surgery, and he's fine?"

"The cardiologist will be able to give you more specifics. If he follows all the precautionary advice, there's no reason to think he can't live a normal life."

"What about football?" Zach asked, his brows knitted with apprehension. "I'm hoping to play in college."

The doctor pressed her lips together. Her face softened as she shook her head. "I'm sorry, Zach. Any strenuous activity could put you at risk. I think your football playing days, at least competitively, are over."

Zach sucked in air, and Kate reached for his hand. "We'll figure out college even if there's not a scholarship. Don't worry."

"I just always thought—Dad—" Zach's eyes were wet.

"Your dad would be so proud of what you've accomplished. Don't you for one second think any part of this is a failure."

Zach swiped at his tears. "I know he would have loved to see me play college ball. Like all that time he spent with me in the backyard finally paid off." He caught the stare from the doctor. "Don't worry. I get it. It'll just take some getting used to. Football's been a part of my life for so long."

"I'm sure if your dad was around, his priority would be your health." Dr. Rachbind turned to Kate. "When the echo is done, the cardiologist will be in to go through the results with you. I'm sure he'll be able to answer all your questions."

Kate pulled the chair in the room beside Zach's bed. "Well, then I'm not going anywhere."

"I'm surprised how fast you actually made it here," Zach said.

"Oh," Kate said abruptly, her memory jogged. "Celeste dropped me off and went to park the car. She's probably wondering what's happening." She turned to the doctor. "He'll be okay if I go find my friend?"

Dr. Rachbind nodded. "He'll be fine. If you need to take a few minutes, he's in good hands."

"Okay, I'll be right back."

Kate rushed out the door and back to the lobby. Zach's teammates were there in the waiting room, still wearing their uniforms, solemn expressions fixed on their young faces. When they saw her, they nudged each other and stood as a collective group. The coach held up his hand to hold them back.

"How's Zach?" he asked as the spokesperson for the team. He studied Kate's face as if hoping her expression might give him a clue before she spoke.

Kate offered him a tentative smile. "A couple broken ribs, but he's going to be okay." She didn't mention Zach's heart condition, the possible surgery, or that he wouldn't be playing football anymore. That would be his news to tell if and when he felt comfortable sharing.

"Oh, that's such a relief." The coach removed his hat and ran his hand over his face.

"Tell him we won the game for him," one of the players called out. "He's still our MVP."

Kate dipped her chin. "I'll tell him. And I know he'll be happy you won the championship. You all worked so hard to get there." For Zach, it would be a bittersweet ending. "I don't think he'll be allowed any visitors today, and they'll be keeping him at least overnight. You guys should go celebrate the win. He'd want you to do that."

Kate's gaze drifted over the players' heads, and she saw Celeste stand from a seat along the wall. She lifted her hand to acknowledge her. "If you'll excuse me, I need to fill in my friend."

As she wove her way through the waiting room to where Celeste stood, a couple approached her. A slightly balding man was wearing a Knights cap and hooded sweatshirt with their logo embroidered on the front.

"Is your son going to be okay?" he asked, his face scrunched up with earnest concern.

The woman he was with wore a similar expression on her gently lined face as she waited for Kate's response.

"You're the Knights coach?" Kate asked, although it was obvious he was someone from the opposing team.

"I am." He brought his palm to his chest. "I'm Charlie." He used his other hand to gesture to the woman next to him. "This is my wife, Janet. We've been frantic to know your boy was okay ever since the ambulance took him away."

"The doctor told me you were the one that did CPR. I don't know how to thank you." Kate didn't mention the broken ribs. If they happened with the hit or the CPR, it didn't matter. "The doctor said he's going to be fine, but they're running some tests now."

The coach exhaled loudly. "Oh, that's such a relief. My wife's had heart issues, so I always—I always had to be ready. Luckily, I never had to perform it on her, but I always renew my certification. We have three kids ourselves, so when I saw your son go down, my instinct kicked in."

"Well, we're both certainly glad you're so well trained." Kate rested her hand on the woman's arm, and her gaze drifted between the couple. "If not for both of you, I'm not sure he'd be alive. I don't know how I could ever repay you." She leaned in and wrapped her arms around both of them.

"I cherish every minute I get with my wife," the man said in a soft voice. "Do the same with your son, and that will be payment enough for both of us."

CHAPTER 17

3 YEARS LATER

Kate's cell phone rang as she pulled into the parking lot at work. "Hey, buddy. How's school?"

"Things are great," Zach said. "I've been studying like crazy, but it's all good. *Really* good."

"You're coming home at the end of the month for Celeste's wedding, right? I know she'd love to see you. Bella and Ben too."

"I wouldn't miss it." He hesitated. "Do you think she would mind if I brought a guest?"

Kate and Marcy were catering. It was a small wedding, but Zach was like family to Celeste. "I doubt it's an issue, but I'll ask. Who did you have in mind?"

"I, uh, met someone, and we've been spending a ton of time together. She's a junior like me, and we have a class together. Her name is Sarah. I want you to meet her."

"Oh, really?" Kate's voice lifted.

"She's great, Mom. You'll love her."

"If she's the reason you sound so happy, then I'm sure I will. Let me double-check with Celeste, and I'll call you back. Okay?"

Kate smiled as she snapped her flip phone closed and pulled open the back door to the office. Zach had dealt well with having to go to a state school. It was still a great university but much more affordable. Though Zach missed playing football, he'd adapted well and found new interests. Apparently, one of those interests was a girl named Sarah.

"Good morning." Marcy stood at the long kitchen counter, placing miniature quiches on a baking tray.

"I was just talking to Zach. Sounds like he has a new girl-friend." Kate shrugged her bag off onto her counter.

Marcy spun around. "Oh, that's exciting. So, when do you get to meet her?"

"He wants to bring her to Celeste's wedding."

"I'm sure she won't mind." Marcy bit back a smile. "By the way, you had a guest stop by right before you walked in. Said he'd be back in a little bit."

Kate couldn't imagine who'd be looking for her that would have her partner looking so entertained. "Really? Who?"

"The handsome food critic has reappeared." Marcy seemed to study Kate's face looking for a reaction.

Kate didn't give her one, though the mention of Sam made her pulse race. She worked to keep her voice from revealing the flicker of excitement she felt about Sam's reappearance. "Hmm. I wonder what he wants."

A couple of days after the football game, Sam had reached out to make sure her son was okay. Since then, he'd gone radio silent. Three years of not hearing a word from him.

Kate wasn't sure what she'd expected. The fact that he'd checked in on Zach was sweet, but she'd thought maybe—he'd seemed genuinely happy to run into her. He'd admitted he'd wondered how she was, remarked she looked great.

She'd dissected every moment of their brief encounter. Sam

was charming. It was possible he made every woman he met feel like there was a spark between them.

Besides, Sam probably thought she was married, and he'd told her he had a girlfriend. They could even be married by now. Celeste had met Bruce around the same time, and her wedding was right around the corner.

Kate pulled her folder with the week's orders and tried to get organized, but her gaze kept drifting back toward the door.

"You're like a nervous little bunny." Marcy's eyes narrowed. "Is there something going on I don't know about? If so, work on him for another rave review."

Kate snorted and shook her head as if the idea there was something between the two of them was ridiculous. "Of course not. I'm just debating if I want to start rolling dough for this week's pies if he's going to come strolling in the door."

"Oh, the *pies*." Marcy stretched out the last word with a knowing smile. "That makes sense. You wouldn't want to start making pies if Mr. Perfect was going to come strolling through the door."

Mr. Perfect. Kate had never called him that, and she wasn't even sure why Marcy was so convinced something was going on. She'd mentioned running into Sam at the game when it happened and that he'd called to check on Zach. Since then, Kate hadn't brought him up at all. Marcy knew better than anyone that Kate hadn't dated since Will died.

Kate rolled her eyes at her partner and then reached into the shelf below the counter for the large measuring bowls. She bustled around her baking space to make a statement, not only to Marcy but to herself. Obviously, she wasn't waiting for Sam if she was getting everything ready to bake. Kate rooted around in the cabinets for her dry ingredients, then yanked out the over-sized bag of flour, which landed with a thump on her work surface.

Marcy turned slightly at the sound, an amused smile lifting

the corners of her mouth. "Everything okay?"

"Fine. Everything's fine." Kate would never be able to play poker well. She couldn't bluff worth a crap. She threw on her favorite apron. "Need anything from the walk-in?" she asked as she tied the strings around her waist.

When Marcy shook her head, Kate headed to the cooler for butter and eggs. Once inside, she shivered. She wanted to blame it on the cold air, but her body had reacted to the news that Sam would be back.

Arms overflowing with ingredients, Kate leaned her body against the handle to release it, then lifted her foot and kicked the door.

As it flew open, Sam was standing on the other side. Kate's forehead creased at the notion that she might be hallucinating. Maybe her imagination had concocted a visual of Sam because her brain hadn't stopped spinning at the idea of seeing him again.

"Whoa, ninja." Sam raised a hand and stepped out of the way of the heavy metal door.

The hallucination spoke. Clearly, he was real.

The items in Kate's hands wobbled, and Sam reached to catch the large package of butter before it hit the floor.

"Here, let me help you." He grabbed a carton of eggs perched precariously on Kate's arm.

"Oh, I told Sam you were in the walk-in cooler," Marcy called out. Kate was just in time to see her poor attempt to stifle a satisfied smile.

"Thanks." Slightly miffed, Kate shot Marcy a look before unloading the remaining items in her arms onto the counter.

Sam added the butter and eggs he held and then leaned toward her with his forearms resting on the countertop.

Kate gestured at her partner. "So, I see you met Marcy. She's the genius behind all the food here."

Marcy turned with a wave. "That review you wrote about us was much appreciated."

"Your food's incredible. It was well-earned," Sam said before directing his attention back to Kate. "You look busy." He cringed slightly. "I probably should have called first. I have something to talk to you about, but I can come back another time."

Kate was intrigued. When Sam was all bundled up at the football game, she hadn't been able to get a good look at him. Now with him standing right in front of her, she worked to keep her staring subtle. He looked slightly older than when they'd first met, but in a good way. He'd aged well. His hair was thinner on top, a bit more gray. His face was still warm and friendly, the crinkles around his blue eyes slightly more evident.

Although she'd only seen Sam twice over the past eight years, he still seemed as familiar as ever. Like she'd seen him last week and not three years ago at the football game. The effect he had on her was instantaneous, and the only other person who'd ever made her feel this way was Will.

There was no way she was willing to wait until another time to see what Sam wanted.

Kate shrugged. "Well, I suppose I haven't really gotten started yet."

With a side glance toward Marcy, Sam stood awkwardly on the other side of the counter. He lowered his voice. "I was kind of hoping maybe we could grab a cup of coffee."

"Oh." Kate's breath hitched in her throat at the idea that Sam wanted to talk to her alone. She glanced at the ingredients laid out. "Um, okay, I can do that. I just have to put this stuff back."

"I can help you." Sam gathered up the items on the counter and followed her. She pulled the door handle, and he made his way past her into the cooler. "This good?" he asked as he placed everything on the first shelf right inside the door.

Sam couldn't see her expression, but as Kate caught a whiff of his cologne, she realized him being this close to her was good. Very good. She didn't much care where he put the eggs and butter.

"Sure, that works."

As Sam made his way toward the front door to leave, Kate untied her apron. She threw it on the countertop and reached for her purse. "I'll be back in a little bit."

"I'll be here filling quiches," Marcy said louder than necessary. "Lots and lots of little quiches."

Sam held the door for Kate, and they walked out together into the sunny autumn afternoon.

"Your partner, she's not mad you're leaving, is she?" he asked.

Kate shook her head. "No, not at all. That's just Marcy."

They stood for an awkward moment on the sidewalk before Sam gave a slight shrug and stuffed his hands in the pockets of his jeans. "It's beautiful out. Should we walk to the coffee shop?"

She offered a brief nod. "Sure."

They made small talk as they walked, but Kate's heart was skipping in her chest, her focus on not accidentally veering into him. What she really wanted was to reach out, yank his hand from his pocket, and slip her palm into his. Hell, part of her wanted to throw him against the wall in front of the furniture store they passed. Kate was almost forty-seven, and yet Sam made her feel like a giddy teenage girl.

It had been twenty-four years since she'd first met Will and felt this way. But that relationship had been different. So easy. From the moment she met Will, there'd never been a single doubt about how he felt about her. There'd been none of the uncertainty she felt with Sam.

At the coffee shop, Kate found an available table and sat down, stealing a glance at Sam as he placed the order for her latte. Though she tried not to stare when he handed it to her, she couldn't help but notice. He wasn't wearing a wedding band. That didn't necessarily mean the girlfriend wasn't still in the picture, but it didn't seem they'd gotten married. At least not yet.

Kate held her coffee cup up to take a sip and casually laid her left hand flat against the top of the table. Her fingers were bare.

The diamond from her engagement ring now sat in a pendant on the chain that hung around her neck. Her wedding band was tucked inside her jewelry box.

Sam settled into the seat across from her and placed his cup on the table off to the side. He folded his hands in front of him and met her curious gaze.

"So, I have a bit of a business proposition for you."

Kate fought to keep her expression from betraying her disappointment. Any anticipation she'd had sunk to the bottom of her stomach with a resounding thud. This excursion for coffee wasn't any sort of date. It was about business.

Kate attempted to appear casual as she slowly pulled her hand from the table and leaned back in her chair. If Sam noticed or cared, he didn't show it. She took a sip of her latte to buy herself a moment to recover.

She gave a curt nod. "Okay. I'm all ears."

"I ran into a friend of mine from college. He was with his wife eating at one of my restaurants. He works for one of the big publishing houses, and I was telling them about your spectacular desserts." Sam laughed. "His wife had a bite of every single one of them. The manager was ready to kill me over his food costs, but she agreed your desserts were fantastic."

So, Sam was talking about her to other people. Even after all these years. And yet, he didn't seem to have an interest in making any proposition that wasn't business-related. Kate had clearly been kidding herself that he might have felt something more for her.

She furrowed her brow and immediately thought of Celeste's warning about wrinkles as she tried to relax her face. "I'm not sure I understand what that has to do with me."

"Oh, sorry. My friend is in the department that publishes mostly cookbooks." Sam unfolded his hands and reached for his coffee.

"Okay …" Kate waited to see if he'd add more after he sipped from his cup. She still didn't understand what any of this meant for her.

"The publishing company he works for is running a contest—sort of a bake-off. The winner of the whole thing gets a contract for them to publish an entire cookbook of their original recipes." Sam paused while he studied her reaction. "It's a pretty lucrative offer if you win."

Kate's eyes narrowed. "So, what are you saying? You think I should—"

"His wife couldn't stop raving about your creations. He pretty much begged me to get you to enter."

So, this is why Sam had reached out. His *friend's* insistence. Kate rested her arms on the table in front of her and shrugged. "I don't know, Sam. I mean, I know you like my desserts, but compete? I'm sure there are bakers much better than me out there. I'm not—"

"Don't," Sam said, shaking his head. Leaning in across the table, he stared directly into her eyes. When he moistened his lips, Kate held her breath. For a moment, she was convinced Sam was going to kiss her. Her face grew warm, his gaze so intense, she had to fight the urge to look away.

Sam's lips parted, the moment suspended in the air between them. Then he wrapped his hand around her arm. "Don't you dare say you can't win this," he said firmly. "Because I know you can." His eyes were anchored on hers for a moment before he finally released his hold on her. "So, will you enter?"

Kate released a shallow breath and leaned back. To cover the flush she felt on her face, she lifted her cup to her mouth. She needed a minute to regain her composure, her dignity. Silently, she chastised herself for expecting more. Sam's intensity had been about a baking contest. Not her. Well, not about kissing her anyway.

Kate tipped her cup and drank her latte while she regrouped. She considered Sam's request. The catering business was going well, but she could feel Marcy pulling back. It was possible she was growing tired of the long hours, time on her feet cooking, weekends spent working. If Marcy decided she'd had enough, Kate didn't have the cooking skills to fill her shoes.

If she agreed to participate, wouldn't Sam stay involved to see how she did? Attend the bake-off, root for her from the sidelines? It's not like Kate expected to win, but it could be an opportunity to figure out where she stood with him.

Since Will died, Sam was the only man who'd made her feel anything. Kate could swear he felt something too. But time and again, she'd been left to wonder. Was she imagining it? Maybe it *was* all in her head simply because she wanted to believe he shared her feelings. She needed to figure out the truth, once and for all. This was her chance.

Kate rubbed the back of her neck and then slowly drank the rest of her latte. Dragging it out. Leaving Sam to wonder if he'd convinced her.

He didn't take his eyes off her as he waited for her to say something. Kate noticed the throbbing in his right temple, Sam's rapid pulse betraying how badly he wanted her to say she'd enter. She resisted a smile. As her silence hung in the air, she could almost hear the music from *Jeopardy* playing.

Kate already knew what her answer would be, but she enjoyed the apprehension in Sam's eyes as he waited. It only confirmed her belief. His interest in her *was* more than business. For some reason, Sam was fighting the way he really felt, and she was determined to find out why.

Kate pursed her lips and placed her empty cup down on the table. She allowed her gaze to linger on Sam's anxious face. Led him to believe she was still unsure.

Then she drew in a deep breath and gave him what he wanted. What they both wanted.

"Okay, I'll do it."

CHAPTER 18

THREE WEEKS LATER

*K*ate waited on her coffee to brew while she stifled a yawn. The wedding the previous night had been beautiful, but it had been a late night for all of them. Zach and Sarah were both still asleep upstairs. At least Kate assumed they were.

When they'd both arrived together, she'd told Zach he needed to put Sarah's things in the guest room. He hadn't argued. When they all got home from the wedding, the two said goodnight and went to their separate rooms. Whether they'd stayed there or not was anyone's guess. Kate knew they could do anything they wanted when they were at school, but she felt odd giving them the green light in her house. Besides, they'd only known each other a few months.

Still, Zach had been right about Sarah. Kate did love her, and she especially loved how happy she made her son.

Kate pulled her cup from the coffee machine and added a bit of milk. It wasn't the same as the pots of aromatic coffee Will used to make. Just one more case of how her life had divided itself into how it was before Will died and how it was after. Now she had a machine that used pods—coffee for one.

When her cell phone rang, it sounded slightly muffled. Kate's gaze drifted around the kitchen until it settled on the small clutch she'd carried the night before.

"Well, good morning, Mrs. Knecht," she said when she answered. "How does it feel to wake up as a married woman?"

Celeste laughed. "It's not that much different from how I felt when I woke up yesterday." Bruce had already moved into Celeste's place. They'd decided it would be easier on the kids if they didn't have to relocate. "The man even packs for himself."

"A week in sunny Key West. I'm jealous." Kate sipped her coffee. "What time are you leaving for the airport?"

"In about an hour. My parents will keep an eye on the kids, but they know if there's anything they need, they can also call you."

"Of course. Whatever they need." Kate brought her coffee to the kitchen table and sat down.

"You and Marcy did a great job last night. Everyone loved the food, and the wedding cake was incredible. Even better than the one you did for the tasting."

"I'm so glad you liked it. The whole night was magical, and your new husband is absolutely perfect for you." Kate took a long swallow of her coffee.

"He is, isn't he?" There was a pause. "I know you always say you're not interested, but Kate, you deserve to find someone. You deserve to be happy too."

Kate rested her mug on the table and adjusted the phone against her ear. "I am happy."

It wasn't a lie. She'd gotten to a point where she'd accepted the life she had. She loved the catering business, and Zach was doing well. That was enough, wasn't it? Her thoughts drifted to

Sam, but she couldn't say he made her happy. More than anything, he just left her confused.

"You know what I mean," Celeste said. "Trust me, I thought about Ed yesterday and my first wedding. How different I was then. But the truth of the matter is, the woman Ed married isn't the same woman Bruce married, but both those women deserve to be happy." Her voice softened. "I have no doubt if Will were still alive, you'd be happy and evolving together, but he's not. I'm sure he wouldn't want you holding onto a ghost. He'd want you to move on."

Kate was quiet while she considered her friend's words.

"You still there?" Celeste asked when there was no response. "I'm not trying to come down on you. You know that."

Kate realized her best friend had taken her silence for aggravation. "No, I know you're not. I was just thinking about what you said."

Celeste let out a sigh. "I love you, Kate. It took me a long time to find Bruce, but he was worth the wait. I just don't want you to close yourself off to the idea of finding someone. You deserve a wonderful man to love and cherish you too."

Kate sipped her coffee as her gaze drifted out the kitchen window. She wasn't rejecting the idea of finding someone. That person could be Sam. There was no denying Kate felt a spark with him. One second, she'd be convinced he felt it too, but then his interest would slip away like grains of sand through her fingers. Yet, she had hope. Now that she'd said yes to the bake-off, she was determined to find out how he really felt. Maybe it would lead somewhere.

She didn't say any of this to Celeste. If her friend knew she was interested in someone and believed there might be something there, she'd probe continually. At this point, Kate simply had nothing to report.

"I'll think about it, I promise," she said instead. "For now, you two go off and have a wonderful time, and don't worry about a thing. I know it's only going to be a week, but I'll miss you. Do you realize we've never gone a whole week without seeing each other since that first night you came over toting a pizza?"

"Hmm. I never thought about that, but you're right. Don't worry, I'll be back in a week, tan and relaxed. But you're still my best friend, and there's not a thing—or a husband—that's going to change that."

Kate smiled even though she knew things would have to be different. Bruce was a great guy, but he'd undoubtedly want time with his wife. Married couples needed to spend time together. Once again, Kate would be the third wheel, and while she knew Celeste would want to include her, that wasn't always going to be fair to Bruce.

"You'll always be my best friend too. Go have fun. Do lots of honeymoon … stuff." Kate laughed. "Not that I'd remember anymore what that is. I'll see you in a week."

Kate downed the rest of her lukewarm coffee and then made herself a second cup. When it was finished, she dropped back into the kitchen chair and shuffled through the papers for the bake-off. Celeste had been so busy preparing for the wedding, Kate hadn't even told her about it yet. Part of her knew it was because Sam was part of the story.

The week before, he'd dropped by unexpectedly with the entry forms and thrown Kate's emotions into a tailspin. Did he always have to look so good? She'd raced out of the house that morning in a panic. No makeup, her long blond hair wound in a bun on top of her head. After making cupcakes all day, she'd been covered in a layer of flour when he walked in.

Sam had stifled a smile as he made a motion with his finger across his cheek. "Is that …?"

"What? Do I have something on my face?" Kate swiped where he was indicating, her fingers coming away with frosting on them. With a shrug, she licked her finger. "Godiva fudge frosting."

Remembering what he said next made her dizzy even now.

He leaned into her, so close she could feel his breath on her neck. "It would be rude to lick it off your face, right?"

If that wasn't flirting, she didn't know what was. But then, just as quickly, the moment evaporated. With Marcy nearby observing every nuance of their encounter, Kate wiped her face with a dish towel before retrieving one of the freshly frosted cupcakes for him.

"It's my lucky day," he said as he took it from her, his lips curving into a seductive smile that left her insides in a puddle on the floor.

Then he handed her the pile of papers he held in his other hand. "Here are the entry forms for the bake-off. The deadline is November 15th, so make sure you get them turned in before then." His eyes scanned the countertop where she was working. "Do you have a pen?"

When she handed him one, Sam dug into his jeans pocket, pulled out a grocery receipt, and wrote his number on the back. "If you have any problems filling out the forms, give me a call."

Talk to you soon, Kate. That was what he said before he peeled back the paper from his cupcake and took a large bite.

He used his tongue to lick the frosting from his lips, and Kate had to keep a moan from escaping her own. A dab of chocolate remained on the tip of his nose. She laughed, rubbing her finger against her own nose much the way he had when she had frosting on her cheek. Sam swiped at it.

"This cupcake is ridiculously good." He gave her a knowing nod and smacked his lips together. "You're going to win this whole thing, Kate. Mark my words." And with that, Sam had strolled out, leaving Kate staring longingly after him.

That was three weeks ago, and not a word from him since. Kate picked up the receipt with his number on it. She flipped it over. Sam was a man who bought bananas, tomatoes, two-percent milk, and bulbs of garlic. The last item made her smile.

Peanut butter cups. She, too, was guilty of the impulse buy at the register.

Kate agonized over his phone number. *If you have any problems filling out the forms, give me a call.* That was what he'd said. It hadn't sounded like an invitation to call about anything else.

If she asked Celeste, she knew her friend would say she was being silly. *Of course you should call him. Why would he have given you his number if he didn't want you to use it?* Kate wasn't comfortable putting herself out there. Except for Will. Even then, he'd made the first move. She had just willingly followed.

Marcy had grilled her mercilessly after Sam left. "C'mon," she said, pleading like a high school girl needing good gossip. "Tell me what's going on. I saw the way you two were looking at each other, and damn, that man's good looking."

Kate wasn't sure how Marcy would feel about the bake-off competition and hadn't planned to mention it yet. If she didn't get chosen as a finalist, it wouldn't even matter. But then Sam came in, waving the entry forms and expressing a desire to lick frosting off her face. Kate had no idea how she'd held herself together.

After Sam left, she relented. She told Marcy about the bake-off, mostly so she'd stop sniffing around thinking there was more. In a way, Kate felt vindicated. If Marcy thought there was something between them, maybe it wasn't just her imagination. Not that it meant anything. The only thing that had come out of Sam's supposed interest was the bake-off and his belief that Kate's Godiva frosted cupcake was her greatest attribute.

To her surprise, Marcy had been supportive of her entering the contest. "If you do well, it will only reflect well on the catering business."

"I have no idea how long it will take them to go through all the entries to pick the finalists. If I make it in—not that I will— it's six weeks of competition, and they're being held on Saturdays in New York City." Kate had no idea how she could handle that since most of the significant events they catered took place on weekends. "That's going to be rough."

"As long as you get the orders done, we can manage. This is why we hired staff, remember?" Sam seemed to have been forgotten as Marcy patted her on the arm. "It's about time the rest of the world knew the kind of talent you have."

To enter the competition, Kate had to submit an original recipe to the selection committee, which would then be scored on a variety of factors. She thought it odd that the committee, not the bakers entering, would be making the recipes to narrow the field to only twelve contestants.

From there, the bake-off competition would pit the final twelve against each other in the six weekly baking competitions. Their creations would be scored. The two with the lowest score would be eliminated each week until it was narrowed down to the final two, who would compete for the publishing contract.

Sam had been right. If she won, it could mean a significant amount of money. Kate also couldn't deny the prestige of having her name on a cookbook of her own recipes would be incredible validation for her. While she'd started with Marcy as a way to make more money, she still didn't think of herself as a professional baker. If she won, that would change.

Deep down, Kate knew she'd be lucky to even make it to the bake-off. The competition was open to anyone, professional or amateur. She'd be up against some serious heavy-hitters. Who was she to think she could compete, much less win?

Footsteps sounded on the steps as Zach came down, followed by Sarah.

"Good morning, you two. I'm surprised you're up. There's a big selection of coffee pods if you want to make some."

"I got this," Zach said, gesturing for Sarah to take a seat at the table.

Kate stifled a smile when Sarah slipped into the chair sporting a gray Dallas Cowboys hoodie. Zach had found himself a fellow football fan, but she wondered how they handled their teams' rivalry.

"So, do you two have plans today?" Kate asked when Zach handed Sarah a mug and slid into the seat next to her.

"I want to show Sarah around a little bit," Zach said as he poured milk into his coffee and stirred it. "Then I think we're going to meet some of my friends at the sports bar to watch football. Giants play at one."

Zach was wearing one of Will's old sweatshirts, and sometimes he reminded Kate so much of his father she had to catch her breath.

"And you're bringing the Cowboys fan?" Kate smiled so Sarah would know she was teasing.

"I know, right? But she insists on tagging along." Zach leaned over and kissed his girlfriend. "It's okay. Cowboys fans need love too."

Zach had inherited so much from his father. She recalled the way Will had teased her, but it was always with so much love. Sarah offered Zach a tolerant smile, much the way Kate had always taken Will in stride.

"So, how in the world did a Jersey girl become a Dallas fan?" Kate asked as she sipped her coffee and tried to ignore it was barely warm anymore. Zach had mentioned Sarah's family lived in South Jersey about ninety minutes from them.

"I haven't always lived in New Jersey, Mrs. Kennedy," Sarah said. "I actually grew up in Frisco, Texas. Well, for a while anyway."

"Oh, I didn't know that. And please, call me Kate."

Sarah smiled as she wrapped her hands around her coffee mug. "Okay … Kate. We left Texas when I was in fourth grade. We'd moved there for my dad's job, but—" She shrugged. "We had no relatives there. My mom's two sisters live near Princeton, and my dad's family is mostly in Pennsylvania, right near Philly. One day, my parents sat my sister and me down and said we were moving back. They decided they needed to be near family."

"I can understand that," Kate said with a nod.

She thought wistfully of Will's family. His sister, Lisa, and her husband had two kids in Rhode Island, including a seven-year-old son she'd named after her brother. The kids were busy with karate and gymnastics, and Kate and Zach hadn't seen them in years.

Kate had tried to insist they all come for Christmas during Zach's senior year. With the news that his heart condition could be genetic, they all needed to sit down and have a conversation. Still, the best Will's family could manage was a short lunch with her and Zach. They'd agreed to get tested and said they had to be on their way. Kate sometimes wondered if it was painful for them to see Zach, who looked and acted so much like his father.

Aside from cards at the holidays, they had drifted away. Kate was disappointed for Zach's sake. He'd already lost his dad. Then a set of grandparents and an aunt, uncle, and cousins had disappeared too.

"So, your sister? Is she older or younger?" Kate asked.

"She's two years older than me," Sarah said as she sipped her coffee. "She graduated last year and got a teaching job. Sixth grade."

Kate tipped her head to the side. "Interesting. Zach's dad was a teacher. Eleventh grade English."

"I know. He told me." Sarah reached out and squeezed Zach's hand.

"Do either of your parents teach?"

Sarah shook her head. "Oh, no. I have no idea where my sister got the idea. My dad's an engineer. My mom went back to school after we moved and became a nurse. I'm actually a business major with a focus on marketing."

"Seems like a similar path to you, Zach." He wanted to be

involved with sports, even if he couldn't play. He was pursuing a degree in Sports Management with a marketing minor.

"We met in our advertising class."

"That's great," Kate said. "You must be able to study together."

The two exchanged a glance that said they might have started as study partners, but that wasn't where they'd left it.

Kate sipped her coffee and let it go. It was still hard to think of her little boy in a serious relationship. He'd had several girl-friends in high school, even a couple in college, but he'd been casual about them. Sarah seemed different.

"What's this?" Zach picked up the papers about the bake-off.

Kate shrugged as if it wasn't important. "Oh, it's a baking competition. The prize is a publishing contract for a cookbook."

Zach's eyes widened. "Wow, that would be awesome for you, Mom."

Sarah glanced over his shoulder at the contest papers. "Zach told me you made the wedding cake last night. It was delicious."

"Thanks. I'm glad you enjoyed it. I'm still considering whether I want to enter or not." That wasn't entirely true. Kate had promised Sam she would, but part of her still wanted to save face if she didn't get picked as a finalist.

Zach frowned. "Why wouldn't you?"

Kate lifted a shoulder. "I don't know. There's going to be some pretty stiff competition."

"So? I'm sure none of them can hold a candle to your stuff."

A surge of pride came over her. She had raised a great kid.

Zach turned to Sarah. "My mom's an incredible woman. When my dad died, she didn't know how we would make it, but she wanted something and went after it. She was always baking—pies, cakes, cookies, these incredible molten chocolate cherry cupcakes. Those were my absolute favorite. I'd come home from school, and they'd still be warm. You'd cut into them, and the insides would ooze out. Melted chocolate, tart cherries." He rolled his eyes toward the ceiling and moaned. "She drizzles this stuff on top— she won't tell anyone what's in it, but it's like heaven."

Zach turned to Kate and clasped his hands together in front of him. "Mom, you have to make those while Sarah's here. Please. She hasn't really lived until she's had one of those."

Kate leaned back in her chair and downed the rest of her coffee before giving him a consenting nod. "Sure. It's been a while since I've made anything in my own kitchen. It's not the same without my taste tester around."

"You're the best." He leaned in over the table and whispered loudly behind a cupped hand. "Thanks for helping me win over the pretty lady." He used his chin to point in Sarah's direction.

Sarah giggled. "I'm sure they're delicious, but you've already won me over."

"Aw, babe." Zach leaned over and kissed her.

Kate stifled a smile and studied them. Was her son in love?

"The cupcake will just seal the deal," he said. "Just wait. I promise you've never had anything like it. My mom makes some pretty amazing stuff, but these are my absolute favorite."

"Really?" Kate asked, surprised.

Zach gave her an enthusiastic nod. "Oh, yeah. Those cupcakes are the bomb."

Kate rubbed her chin thoughtfully. "The bomb, huh?"

And that was when she knew exactly which recipe she would use to enter the bake-off.

CHAPTER 19

FIVE MONTHS LATER

*a*s Celeste held out a twenty-dollar bill for the toll collector, the horns of impatient drivers and the smell of exhaust fumes wafted through the open window. She collected her change and rolled the window back up.

"That's enough of that."

Kate looked out into the sea of cars. They were all exiting the long row of toll booths and trying to work their way into two narrow lanes that headed into the tunnel. It seemed to be a bit of a free-for-all.

"I appreciate you driving into the city. I'm already so nervous about today."

Kate glanced at her watch. They'd made good time—only about forty-five minutes and they were heading through the tunnel which would put them in mid-town.

"Traffic's not bad. I guess it's good they've got this scheduled for a Saturday afternoon."

"Some of this may even be matinee traffic," Celeste said,

glancing in her rearview mirror. "You have the address where we need to go, right?"

Kate read her what was on the paper she'd been sent, and Celeste made a left as they exited the tunnel. She made her way down Twelfth Avenue before aggressively working her way through the sea of cars and yellow cabs to put herself in the right-hand lane.

"Just trying to avoid the theater district," she said as she made the turn on Fifty-Eighth Street. "We can take this down to Seventh Avenue and then over to Fifty-Seventh. I'm sure there's got to be parking somewhere near the test kitchens."

Kate nodded, but her insides were swirling in nervous anticipation. When she got the call she'd been picked as a finalist, she was shocked. Four months had passed since she entered. She'd started to wonder if the whole thing was a scam.

The notification had come from an outside company managing the contest. Then, two days later, a packet arrived. Inside were all the details and logistics for the competition, but still not a peep from Sam. Not a word since the day he'd dropped off the entry forms.

His lack of communication had left Kate with conflicting emotions. She was thrilled she'd been chosen, but Sam was the only reason she'd even entered. It was supposed to be a way to spend time with him.

She pressed her lips together as she remembered waiting one day, then two, then a week before finally accepting the hard truth. Sam wasn't going to call, not even to congratulate her.

At least she no longer needed to figure out where she stood with him. She stood nowhere. Shaking her head, Kate tried to clear the disappointment from her mind. She needed to be focused today. Trying to figure out Sam's obvious lack of interest was the last thing she needed.

Celeste pulled the car into a driveway for a parking garage. "This is as close as we're going to get." She reached for the claim ticket the parking attendant handed her and tucked it into the side of her purse. "Don't let me lose this, and between the two of us, we need to pay attention so we can find our way back to the garage."

Kate cringed. "You know about my sense of direction. If you're depending on me, we might need to walk back to New Jersey."

"Okay, okay." Celeste rolled her eyes as they exited the garage. She glanced at the sign on the corner to get her bearings, then began walking in the other direction. "So, what did you decide to make today?"

"I hate that bread is the first category that will determine if I move on," Kate said with a slight scowl. "It's not really my specialty, but I decided to make the pull-apart bread with brie and cranberry."

Kate had been testing recipes all week, and Celeste had sat in her kitchen night after night—a willing test subject for most of them.

Celeste moaned. "Oh, I loved that one. Good choice."

As they strolled toward their destination, Kate's nerves escaped in a loud exhale. "I hope the judges think so." When she'd received the paperwork, it had said there would be five to-be-determined judges, and she would find out who they were when she arrived for round one. "I'm not sure if it would have helped to know the judges ahead of time or if it would have made me more nervous. I guess it doesn't matter. I mean, I probably won't even make it past this first week."

Celeste came to a dead stop in the middle of the sidewalk and turned to Kate. As aggravated pedestrians expressed their displeasure, she rolled her eyes and waved her hand for them to go around.

Kate glanced around, confused. "What are you—"

Celeste gripped Kate by the shoulders. "Listen, you need to believe in yourself. You're an amazing baker, and these judges will know talent when they see it." She tilted her head. "Or I guess I should say *taste* it. I won't stand for any of this 'I don't stand a chance' nonsense. You hear me?"

Kate nodded like an obedient child. "I hear you. But could we keep moving?" She aimed her chin in the direction they needed to go. "Before we cause a riot here on the sidewalk by disrupting the flow of traffic."

Celeste huffed but resumed walking. "Like I care? They'll survive and get where they're going just fine, but you—you needed the pep talk."

"Maybe, but it probably could have waited—" Kate glanced down at the paper in her hand and then looked up at the numbers on the building they were standing in front of. "This is it." She let out a deep breath and pulled open the heavy glass door. "Here goes—" Kate noted the stern look Celeste was shooting at her and changed the way she was going to end her declaration. "—everything. Here goes everything."

Celeste gave an approving nod. "Positive thinking. I like it."

As they approached the security desk to check-in, Kate spun around to face Celeste and jabbed her finger in the air to help make her point—to her friend and to herself. "Not only do I plan to bake like a rock star today, but I'm taking home the big prize at the end. I'm not settling for anything less."

Celeste clutched her hands to her chest. "I'm like a proud mother getting ready to watch my baby bird fly. And I don't have a single doubt you'll be the last one standing."

After signing in, the guard handed them guest badges. "Good luck today. You need to go to the tenth floor."

The elevator doors opened, and they stepped out into a posh reception area, but no one was behind the desk to greet them. Behind the glass office doors, Kate could see empty offices and cubicles.

Before she could lower herself into one of the plush chairs, a casually dressed girl in her early twenties was on the other side of the glass. She pushed open the door and held a clipboard in her hand.

"Hi, I'm Max Preston's assistant, Abby. I'm here to take you back to the test kitchens. You are?"

Kate stepped forward and extended her hand. "Kate Kennedy."

Abby noted something on her clipboard and nodded. "I need to see some form of identification. It should have mentioned that on the paperwork you were sent."

"Oh, right. It did." Apparently, they didn't want anyone stepping into Kate's slot to bake in her place. She reached into her purse and pulled her driver's license from her wallet.

Abby glanced at the license and then up at Kate before handing it back to her. "Great. Follow me."

Kate noticed Abby was wearing some sort of headset. As she stood with her back holding open the door so they could enter, she pushed the mic closer to her mouth. "I'm bringing Kate Kennedy back."

Kate's stomach was swirling with excitement as they followed her down a long hallway. She glanced back and forth between both walls trying to take in the framed images that lined the walls. There were cookbook cover images, authors with awards, well-known chefs, and photos of every kind of mouth-watering food imaginable. Kate's eyes grew wide. She nudged Celeste and aimed her chin at the picture of Sarah Jessica Parker standing beside an incredible wedding cake, a man in an apron beaming by her side.

Abby glanced back to make sure they were still behind her and noticed Kate's gaze aimed at the photo. "That was her wedding day. Can you believe she wore a black dress? I guess she wanted it to be a surprise and didn't want the guests coming to know it was actually going to be her wedding. But hey, it worked. One of those great celebrity couples who are still together."

Abby stopped and pulled open the door to an enormous

warehouse space. Kate could see the gleam of stainless steel, white counters, and several other finalists already in their designated kitchens. Her pulse ramped up. The bake-off was starting to feel real.

"Here we are," Abby said. "I'll take you in and show you your kitchen set-up for today."

As Kate and Celeste followed her, Abby stopped suddenly and spun around. "I want to introduce you to my boss, Max Preston. He heads up the cookbook division of Diamond Publishing. This contest was his idea." She gestured at a man who was in the midst of a conversation with several other people.

Kate nodded while they stood awkwardly off to the side to wait. Finally, Abby tapped his arm gently. She leaned in and whispered something to him. He turned, a broad grin on his face. He stepped out of the small circle of people he was in and headed toward her.

"Kate Kennedy," he said, extending his hand. "I'm Max Preston. I've heard some wonderful things about you."

She smiled as she shook his hand. "You're too kind."

"Well, you certainly have a fan in Sam. I know I have him to thank that you even entered." Max stepped backward and tapped someone in the small huddle on the shoulder.

When the man turned around, Kate's stomach dropped.

CHAPTER 20

"Kate." Her name slipped from Sam's lips with the breath he expelled.

As he moved toward her, his full lips lifted into a smile, his intense gaze anchored on her as if she were the only person in the room. He searched her eyes for a moment before pulling her into an embrace.

His touch made every nerve she had tingle, and Kate hated how weak she was. Everything in her body's reaction betrayed how disappointed she'd felt that he hadn't called for months, hadn't even congratulated her for making the finals. She'd been more than disappointed. She'd been angry at herself for letting him be her ulterior motive for entering in the first place when he didn't seem to care.

Kate let her eyes close. As she breathed in Sam's familiar scent, her anger evaporated. His arms were wrapped tight around her, his body against hers. Her heart skipped inside her chest, a dead giveaway of what being this close to him did to her.

Sam finally released her and stepped back. He reached for her hands and held them, his eyes never leaving hers.

"Congratulations, Kate. I knew you'd make it."

She stood there trembling, intensely aware of his warm hands clutching hers.

"Thank you," Kate managed to eke out with a feeble nod. She desperately needed to regain her composure. With a hard swallow, she pulled her hands from his to turn and gesture behind her. "This is my best friend, Celeste."

He reached out to shake her hand. "Hi, Celeste, I'm Sam."

"Sam. Good to meet you."

There was no misinterpreting the look Celeste shot her next. *Aha! I was right that night of the football game. My superpower remains intact.*

Max cleared his throat. "So, Kate, Abby will get you set up in your kitchen, and maybe you and Sam—maybe you can finish catching up when it's over?"

Max's assistant gestured for Kate to follow her.

Celeste hurried along as well, a quick glance over her shoulder as if she was worried someone might try to stop her. "Am I allowed to go with her?"

Abby nodded. "Sure. Until the actual competition starts. Then you'll have to leave and stay in the area designated for spectators." She pointed off to a roped-off section that had rows of seats set up.

Celeste grabbed Kate's hand as soon as they were alone. She smiled as she glanced around to see if anyone was watching them. Then she clenched her teeth as if she was worried someone might read lips. "Okay, that's the hot man from the football game. You'd better start talking."

Kate offered her an innocent shrug. "There's nothing to tell."

Celeste kept the smile pasted on her face, and for that, Kate was grateful. She would be mortified if Sam knew they were talking about him.

Her friend squeezed her hand hard, and Kate winced in protest. "Ow."

"I call bullshit. I didn't get a hug like that, and you two practically spontaneously combusted right in front of everyone." Celeste narrowed her eyes at Kate. "You had me doubting myself, but it seems my superpower is working just fine. Better than fine if you ask me."

Kate rolled her eyes, but Celeste shook her head and let out an incredulous chuckle.

"Don't even try it. I have eyes, you know."

Kate wrenched her hand free from her friend's grip. "I'm telling you the truth. Sam was the one who told me to enter the bake-off because Max is a friend of his from college. But that's it. Nothing's happened."

"Yet." The word was crisp on Celeste's tongue. "I'm going to need every single detail on the ride home."

Kate hesitated before finally relenting with a nod. It would be good to have someone help interpret Sam's mixed messages. "Okay, deal, but I hope you're not expecting much, or you're going to be disappointed."

Kate opened the small refrigerator in her kitchen. "Now, let me make sure I have everything I need for my bread recipe. It's going to be hard enough to concentrate with, you know, the hottie sitting out there watching." She wagged her finger at Celeste. "And don't you sit next to Sam and say a word. I mean it."

Celeste threw her hands up. "Okay, I promise, but can I make sure no one else tries to flirt with him?" She lifted her eyebrows and grinned. "A man that handsome should not be left unattended."

"Yes. That you can do." Kate glanced at her watch. "Now go. We start in twenty minutes. I need to get organized, not to mention figure out how in the world I'm going to be able to focus on making bread."

"Okay, okay, I'm going."

When Celeste turned to leave, Kate grabbed her arm. "Don't forget your promise," she said, her voice a stern warning.

"Oh, I won't. But later, you're spilling it all."

Then, with a knowing smile, Celeste meandered out of Kate's kitchen.

* * *

"I knew that one judge loved your bread by the way he licked his lips after he tasted it," Celeste said as they climbed into the car to head home.

Kate was exhausted but exhilarated she'd made it to the next round. "I thought so too. Did you see the face of the pastry chef after she tasted that first guy's Irish soda bread?"

"Oh, I know." Celeste fastened her seatbelt. "For a second there, I thought she was actually going to spit it out. Did you see how fast she reached for her water glass?"

The whole day had been an eye-opening experience for Kate. There was a panel of only four judges, not five, as the paperwork had stated. Two were from highly regarded New York City restaurants. One was a baker at one of the oldest bakeries in the city, and the fourth had her own cable show, *All Things Sweet*.

Kate had watched as they scored each person's entry on taste, overall appearance, and creativity. They hadn't been pushovers, and they provided critical feedback to each contestant as well as positive comments.

Kate's bread had placed third. She now understood the importance of creating a visual experience for the reviewers. The woman with the best score had plated her praline-topped apple bread with a spray of paper-thin apple slices. It was so beautiful it looked like art.

Celeste pulled out of the garage and headed toward the tunnel to take them back to New Jersey. Not a word so far about Sam. Not that Kate was naïve enough to think the conversation she'd promised to have wasn't coming.

While concentrating on making her bread, Kate had deliberately kept her eyes from straying to the spectators. It was easier on her nerves. Only after the judges announced the final scores had she glanced out into the crowd, smiling as Celeste stood and cheered for her.

Once Kate knew she was moving on, she was already looking ahead to the following week. Another chance to prove herself. It felt great to win, but all night she'd imagined Sam being part of the celebration. Maybe a congratulatory kiss. As she searched the crowd for him, she realized she'd set her hopes too high. He had already left.

"So, let's go back. How long has this non-thing with Sam been going on?" Celeste asked. "You know, where you pine for each other, and you never mention a word of it to your best friend?" She shot Kate an aggravated look. "I can't believe you kept this from me. All along, I've wanted you to find someone, and he's been out there for *years*."

After a deep sigh, Kate told Celeste how they'd met at the office after his review and how he'd let the restaurants make contact with her instead of following up himself. She'd seen him at the football game, as Celeste already knew, but Sam mentioned he was there with a girlfriend. Maybe he still had one.

Then she told Celeste how he'd come by her office to take her out for coffee, but only to pitch the bake-off. She mentioned he'd also dropped off the entry forms to her but left out the suggestive comment he made about the chocolate frosting on her face.

"I haven't heard from him since that day," Kate said, her face tight. "He never even called to congratulate me."

She didn't tell Celeste she had Sam's phone number because she would never have used it to tell him she was chosen as a finalist. If Sam wanted to know if she'd been selected, all he had to do was ask Max. The ball had been in Sam's court. He simply had no interest in playing.

"And then he showed up today, which you witnessed first-hand." Kate shrugged. "I've always felt there was something between us. There were times I was positive he felt the same, the

way he'd look at me …" her voice drifted off. "If he was interested, he never made any effort to pursue it. Maybe there's
someone else. I think it's probably time for me to give up and
accept all we might be is friends." She thought about him leaving
before the judges even announced the scores. "If we're even
that."

Celeste had listened quietly, nodding every so often.

Finally, she glanced over, and Kate shrugged. "That's it. I told
you not to expect too much."

"So, I did sit next to Sam during the competition." Celeste's
hand went up before Kate could chastise her. "I only promised I
wouldn't say anything about you to him, and I didn't."

Kate let out a breath. She was relieved Sam had left for something better and not because Celeste said something that scared
him off. Maybe he had a date. "Well, I appreciate that."

"I didn't have to say anything about you." Celeste glanced over
at Kate and smiled mysteriously. "He did all the talking."

"Really?" Kate's voice lifted. "What did he say?"

"He told me he had no doubt you'd get picked as a finalist.
Apparently, Max asked him to be a judge and wouldn't tell him
anything as they went through the entries. Max kept pushing him
to be the fifth judge, but Sam was so sure you'd be in the final
twelve. He said there was no way he could be unbiased toward
you, so he finally convinced Max he couldn't do it. Just last night.
He didn't know you'd made it until you showed up today."

Kate let out her breath. So, that was why he hadn't called to
congratulate her.

"And then—" Celeste turned her head to make sure Kate was
paying attention. She grinned like someone about to impart a
huge secret. "Then I heard his friend Max say to him, 'Well, now I
understand *completely* why you couldn't be a judge.'"

Kate's eyes grew wide. "What do you think he meant by that?"

Celeste rolled her eyes. "C'mon. That hug he gave you? The
way he looked at you as if you two were the only people there? It

practically screamed of his inability to be unbiased toward you—or anything you might bake."

Kate frowned. "But he didn't even stay to hear the judges' scores."

"Oh, that. Right. I haven't even gotten to that part yet."

Kate stared at her friend expectedly. "What part? Did he say something before he left?"

Celeste lifted a shoulder. "He got a call, some sort of emergency with his mom." She glanced over briefly at Kate. "He had to go, but he told me to tell you to call him and let him know how it went." She pressed her lips together before turning her attention back to the road. "He said you have his number, which I found interesting. Very interesting, indeed."

"Well, he gave it to me in case I had any questions about filling out the entry forms. Not to call him for a date. He could still have a girlfriend, for all I know. Think about how stupid I would have felt."

Celeste shook her head. "Oh, there's no girlfriend."

"How do you know?"

"I mentioned I had recently gotten married and how happy I was."

Kate let out an exasperated breath. "Really, Celeste, that wasn't a little obvious?"

Her friend scowled as she pretended to be offended. "Hey, he asked."

"Maybe he was actually interested in *you*."

Celeste glanced over and rolled her eyes. "Stop being ridiculous. Sam told me he thought my rings were beautiful, and I mentioned I was a newlywed. He told me he was divorced and that he used to be a professional chef. Said he still loves to cook, but sometimes it wasn't worth the effort to always cook for one. For *one*, Kate. That doesn't sound to me like there's anyone else in the picture."

"Wow. He told you a lot." Sam had also told Kate his wife had been cheating on him with the golf instructor. He seemed to be a person who didn't mind sharing.

"That was all he told me," Celeste said. "And that was pretty much the only time he wasn't gushing about you."

Kate let out a sigh. "A lot of good it does me."

Celeste's eyes drifted off the road for a quick moment while she gave Kate an encouraging nod.

"Hang in there. I'm not sure why, but I don't think Sam realizes yet how in love with you he really is. When he figures it out, it's going to hit that man like a ton of bricks."

CHAPTER 21

SIX WEEKS LATER

"I'm proud of you, Mom. I knew you'd make it to the final two."

"Oh, you did, did you?" Kate said, studying her son. "I wish I'd been as confident. It's been a nerve-racking five weeks. Every week I thought, well, crap, this could be it for me."

As soon as the words were out, she wanted to snatch them back. She could picture Celeste's frown if she heard Kate talking like that. Especially heading into the last week.

Zach pulled open the refrigerator and stared inside. "Did you decide what you're going to make yet? The coconut cake you made was good."

She'd been testing recipes all week. Zach had been her willing taster for most of them.

"Really, the coconut one?" she asked. "But still, *good's* not going to win. I need great. Phenomenal. Spectacular. What about the mocha one with the fondant icing?"

Zach scrunched up his face. "The one that tasted sort of like tiramisu?"

She shrugged slightly. "Yeah, I guess it did. No good?"

"It was beautiful, but ... eh. Not a fan of that stuff on the outside."

"That's the fondant," Kate said with a small smile.

"Not my thing, I guess," Zach said. He pulled out a soda, popped the top, and took a sip. "Celeste still can't take you Saturday?"

Kate shook her head as she leaned against the counter. "No, it's Bruce's parents' fiftieth-anniversary party. She'd never make it back in time."

"I asked around to see if anyone could cover my shift. No luck."

"Don't worry about it. You don't need to be rocking the boat at the restaurant anyway, especially since they decided to let you become a bartender." Zach had only been home a few weeks from college and had been lucky to find a job where he was making good money. "I'll figure something out."

Zach glanced at the clock. "Oh, hey, I have to go." He raised his eyebrows. "If you try anything else out tonight, leave it for me, and I'll be happy to sample it when I get home."

Kate nodded, then plopped down into a seat at the kitchen table. "You got it. I have to decide by tomorrow so I can send in the list of ingredients. I need to choose something pretty quick here. It's just—" She pursed her lips. "Nothing's thrilled me yet."

"You'll figure out something amazing." He gave her a wave, and she heard the front door slam behind him.

Kate planted her elbows on the table and rubbed her face with both hands. What *was* she going to make for the final round? The clock was ticking. When her cell phone rang on the counter, she let out a deep sigh as she stood to answer it.

"Hey, it's Sam, and it's Wednesday." His voice sounded more upbeat than she felt. "This is it. Got your final recipe ready?"

"I wish I did." Kate pulled open the refrigerator door and grabbed a bottle of water. "I'm stuck. Really stuck." Her eyes drifted to the window—crystal blue sky and sunshine. With the phone to her ear, she strolled through the family room and pulled open the sliding door to head outside.

"You have to get the ingredients to Abby by noon tomorrow."

"I know, I know," Kate said, lowering herself into a lawn chair. "No pressure or anything, Sam."

After he'd left early the first week of the competition, Celeste had relayed Sam's request for Kate to call him. With a solemn vow to make her friend pay dearly if she was lying, Kate had dug up the receipt with his number on it.

They spoke for an hour, the conversation light and easy. Comfortable, even. It had ended with no plans for anything else. Saturday at the next round, there he was again. This time Sam had stayed long enough to hear she'd be moving on before he disappeared.

The following Wednesday, her cell phone had rung. "So, whatcha making this week?" he'd asked casually, like him calling her was an everyday occurrence.

And so it had gone, week after week. Seeing him in person was frustrating, but on the phone, Kate could distance herself. He was a different Sam when they spoke. Friendly. Supportive. Not that he wasn't that way at the bake-off rounds, but that Sam came with a smoldering gaze that made her want to pull him into her kitchen and have her way with him.

How she got a lick of baking done, she wasn't sure. It wasn't only the oven warming her station. Kate could feel the heat of Sam's stare as he fixed it on her while she baked.

At least she had Celeste in the spectator section, parked right next to him, her Spidey senses on high alert. Looking for anything. A clue. A slip of the tongue. There hadn't been much. Her best friend was still firmly convinced Sam was harboring a deep-seated love for Kate. A love that, for some reason, he seemed to have no interest in pursuing. Celeste was just as confused as Kate.

At this point, Kate had to wonder if all she and Sam might ever be is friends. Her heart didn't want to accept it. If she was being completely honest with herself, a few other body parts firmly rejected the notion as well. She just wasn't sure she had another choice.

"Do you have any ideas?" Sam asked. "Maybe I can help you narrow it down."

"I was talking about it with Zach too," she said. "He's been a good sport this week, trying everything I put in front of him."

"So, was there something he was crazy about?"

"Nothing that's coming through as the clear winner. He liked this coconut cake I made, said it was *good*. But you know as well as I do, good's not going to beat Bryce." She twisted the cap off her water bottle and took a long swig. "I wish I knew what he was going to make."

"He's a slimy guy, always looks like he's up to something," Sam said. "There's no way you're going to let him take this from you. Who cares what he's working on? It won't be as good as whatever you choose."

"Which is what?" Kate let out a moan. "Why is this so hard? The other weeks were so much easier."

There was a moment of silence on the line.

"Maybe because this is the end," Sam said finally. "There's a lot on the line."

Kate ran her hand through her hair. "I know. And I'm starting to realize something important."

"Oh, yeah, what's that?" Sam asked in a soft voice.

Kate wondered if he thought she was prepared to say something about the two of them, but that wasn't what was on her mind. Not in that instant anyway. With Sam safely on the other end of a phone line, she could think clearly about the competition.

"I want to win this, Sam. I mean, *really* want to win. The first week, even the second, I felt like I was just lucky to be there."

"It had nothing to do with luck," Sam said, and by his tone, she could picture the scowl on his face. "You deserve to be there. You deserve to *win*."

Kate pressed her lips together. "I think that's why I want it so much. From the start of the bake-off, I felt like—" Her shoulders rose. "I don't know, like I snuck in somehow."

"You mean like I had something to do with you being a finalist?" Sam sounded offended. "I swear, I didn't—"

"No, that isn't what I meant," Kate said insistently. "More like, somehow I got selected, but eventually it would come to light that I'm not as good as they thought I was."

"That's crazy. Obviously, it hasn't happened so far. You had the top score for the last two weeks. That means the judges all agree. You're good, Kate."

"I guess if I win, then I'll have to believe it, right?"

Sam let out an amused chuckle. "Well, when you win, I plan to be right there to tell you I told you so."

Kate's gaze drifted out over the backyard as she let her mind wander. When this was over, she was hoping Sam would tell her a lot more than that. Would he continue to call her? There'd be no reason.

She tipped her head back and let out an audible sigh. Let Sam assume her distress was about the contest. Now it was actually about them. As much as she was starting to enjoy this Sam—this *friend* Sam that seemed to have emerged—in her heart, she knew. This wouldn't be enough for her.

Sam moved into fix-it mode. "Okay, start from the drawing board. Would any of the desserts on your catering menu work?"

Kate squeezed the water bottle in her hand as she thought

about it. "Not really. I mean, they all *taste* good, but they're designed to be quick to make. You know, I bake a bunch at a time. There's not the wow factor of that one-of-a-kind dessert I'm sure the judges will be looking for."

"You're probably right," Sam said. "What about … Go back into your past. Maybe when you first started baking. Anything you used to make that you haven't made in a long time? You know, something you were experimenting with and sort of forgot about?"

Kate went quiet, her mind a million miles away. She'd already considered the obvious choice, but just as quickly, she'd dismissed the idea. She wasn't sure she could make it again. She had sworn she would *never* make it again.

"You got something?" he asked after a few moments of silence.

Kate chugged some water, the sun warming her and the conversation leaving her throat dry. "There is a cake I haven't made in a long time," she said, hesitation in her voice.

"Okay, that sounds promising."

Kate's face grew tight, and she shook her head, even though she knew Sam couldn't see her. "I don't—it's not the right choice. I'll come up with something before tomorrow. I work well under pressure." She didn't, but she needed time to sort this out in her head. "I'm going to go through the binders where I keep all my ideas. There's probably something in there I've forgotten."

"Okay. If you need to talk anything through, call me later," Sam said. "If not, I'll see you Saturday. You can win this, Kate. Go find something amazing."

She hung up, leaned her head back, and closed her eyes. As the sun washed over her, Kate tried to convince herself. It really was the best dessert she made. It had been a long time, but the recipe was ingrained in her memory. She could make it visually stunning to look at, and she knew the taste could help her win. She drew in a deep breath, released it. Could she handle it emotionally? Would it throw her off, the origin too much of a distraction for something with stakes this high?

She opened her eyes. There was only one person she could ask.

CHAPTER 22

"*J* can't believe after all this, I have to miss the final round." Celeste took the coffee Kate handed her and slid into a kitchen chair. "Do Bruce's parents really have to have their anniversary party *tonight*?"

"You mean on their *actual anniversary*?" Kate asked. "It's okay. Listen, I appreciate Bruce sharing you with me all the other weekends."

"Did you decide if you're going to drive in?"

Kate shook her head. "I'm not comfortable with it. Will always drove when we went into the city. You know, to see a show or the tree at Christmas. I'll be nervous enough."

"What about Marcy or Zach? Can't one of them take you?"

"Marcy has a bar mitzvah we're catering. Zach has to work. He tried, but he couldn't get out of his shift tonight."

"Do you want me to ask Bruce if …"

"No. Absolutely not."

Celeste gave her a hesitant look. "Why don't you ask Sam to take you? I'm sure he'll be there anyway."

Kate leaned back in her chair, her hands wrapped around a coffee mug. "I thought about it. Really, I did." She stared off for a moment. "Talking on the phone with him is one thing. Spending an hour in the car with him is another." She shook her head firmly. "I can't. I'd be a hot and bothered mess by the time I got there."

"I get it, I guess. So, how *are* you planning to get there?" Celeste asked.

"There's a park and ride lot on the other side of the tunnel in North Bergen. I can catch the bus there, and it will drop me at Port Authority. I'll just grab a taxi from there."

Celeste bit back a smile. "Grab a taxi? Do you even know how to hail a cab?"

Kate put her arm up in the air. "Taxi," she said in a loud voice. She rolled her eyes at her friend. "I've seen Will do it. I think I can handle it."

"You know, it's not that far from Port Authority. You could walk," Celeste said, shrugging.

Kate shot her a look. "Can you imagine? With my sense of direction, I'd end up in Brooklyn."

Her friend burst out laughing. "So, you're planning to swim?"

"Whatever," Kate said with a huff. "Don't worry, I'll figure out how to get a cab."

"I'm sure you will. You should hail it going uptown, which should be easy from Eighth Avenue." Celeste sipped her coffee. "I still feel bad bailing on you for the last week."

"Don't feel bad. It meant a lot to me that you were there through all of this."

"And miss the Kate and Sam weekly Saturday saga? Are you kidding?" Celeste held her coffee cup up in Kate's direction. "And my best friend kicking ass and taking names. That's been fun too."

"I still can't believe I'm one of the final two."

"You deserve it. And c'mon, Bryce? You can beat him with one hand tied behind your back. Did you decide what you're going to make? I mean, you've already done cookies, pies, cakes, and what was the second week?"

"Breakfast baked goods."

"Oh, right. Those maple bacon muffins you made were crazy good." Celeste's gaze drifted around the kitchen. "I would kill for one of those right now. I'm not kidding. You could sell those. Not to mention those chocolate-dipped cannoli cookies last week. That was the highest score you've had. Bryce's score wasn't even close."

Kate's lips curled up in a satisfied smile. "It wasn't, was it? I wish I had someone else to compete with for the final two. He's so smug. I wonder what he's planning to make."

Celeste waved her hand dismissively. "I wouldn't even worry about him. Did you save something good for this last round? You can make anything you want, right?"

Kate released a puff of air. "I've been baking all week. Trying out every great idea I had." She chuckled. "Poor Zach was overloaded being my taste tester."

"So, what did you finally decide?" Celeste asked. "Was there one Zach liked best?"

"There was nothing that jumped out as the obvious choice for either of us. But I had an idea." Kate pursed her lips. "When Will and I first married, I was goofing around in the kitchen one Sunday afternoon, and I concocted this cake. I perfected it over time, and it was Will's favorite. A dark chocolate cake covered in this rich chocolate glaze I made with red wine."

Celeste tilted her head, and her face lit up. "Oh, I like anything that involves wine."

Kate rolled her eyes. "I know you do." Her face grew serious. "The last time I made it was the night Will died."

Celeste's face fell, and she reached for her friend's hand. "Oh, Kate."

"I swore I'd never make it again. I never put it on the catering menu. Never offered it up for anyone. It was kind of sacred, like some sort of exclusive tribute to Will."

"And that's what you're thinking of making?" Celeste cringed. "Are you sure you're up to using *that* recipe for this?"

Kate set her mug on the table and leaned in, her arms folded in front of her. "The other day, I was talking to Sam. I was sitting outside in the backyard, and we were talking about what I should make."

"You told Sam about Will's cake?"

Kate shook her head. "Not exactly. But I mentioned I was considering something I hadn't made in a long time."

"And what did he say?"

"It wasn't anything Sam said that convinced me."

"Okay …" Celeste looked at Kate expectantly.

"All this worrying I've done about whether I could handle making it again got me thinking. Will would have supported anything I did. He would have been there, right in the front row, cheering me on. But I also realized something important. If Will hadn't died, I wouldn't have had the nerve to reach out to Marcy. I'd have never quit my dead-end admin job and started catering with her. I certainly wouldn't have thought I could enter, much less win, a contest like this. And if I win, there's going to be a cookbook with my name on it. My recipes. It's something I wouldn't have dreamed could come true for me."

"Don't shortchange yourself," Celeste said. "There's still a chance you would have found this path even if Will were alive. I'm not sure you give yourself enough credit."

"I appreciate that." Kate then shook her head. "But I don't think so. I was happy with my life the way it was." She hesitated, her gaze drifting off. "At least I thought I was. I was Will's wife. Zach's mother. It never occurred to me to follow my passion and do something just for me."

"So, is that what convinced you to make the cake for the last round?" Celeste asked.

"Not really. After I hung up with Sam, I was sitting outside enjoying the sunshine. I still wasn't sold on the idea. I couldn't decide if it was right to make Will's cake—you know, with Sam there." Kate shrugged. "It felt, I don't know … wrong. The whole thing had me so confused. Not that anything is happening with Sam. Sadly, I think we've moved directly into the friend zone."

Celeste shook her head. "I don't think that's what's happening, but let's come back to that. Tell me what helped you decide."

Kate knew Celeste would understand why what happened felt so profound. Why it convinced her Will's cake wasn't off the table.

"I was sitting out there, not knowing what I should do." Kate lifted her hands up in a helpless gesture. "So, I decided to ask Will." She let out a laugh. "If anyone saw me, they would have thought I was completely nuts talking to myself, but I didn't care."

"What did you say?"

Kate gave a slight shrug. "I said, 'Tell me what to do. Do I make your cake? Is it bad karma since Sam got me into the contest?' I wanted to know if Will was okay with everything that was happening for me. What if something did happen someday with Sam? Was it okay with him? I wanted—I needed some sort of sign."

Celeste nodded in understanding. "I told you I find pennies when I need an answer from Ed. I believe they can hear us. So, did you feel like you got an answer?"

A smile tugged at Kate's lips as she gave a slow nod. "I felt something—just the tiniest little vibration on my hand. When I looked down, this beautiful butterfly was sitting there, flapping its wings ever so slowly. Celeste, I swear it was looking right at me."

Celeste threw her hand in the air. "There's your sign."

"There's more." Kate moved her fingers to her face. "As it flew away, I felt something on my cheek. Tiny flutters. Like butterfly wings gently flitting against my face."

Celeste's eyes narrowed. "But the butterfly flew—"

"Away. Yeah … he did. I think the butterfly was sent to get my attention but the flutters on my cheek? That was Will. That was him letting me know he's still watching over me, and he's okay with where I'm at. He's proud of me."

"And what about Sam?"

Kate was quiet for a moment. "Will would want me to be happy," she said with a confident nod. "I don't think he'd want me to be alone. I wouldn't want that for him if I had been the one to die first."

"Of course you wouldn't."

"In all the years since I lost Will, Sam's the only one who ever made me consider being with someone else. I'm just not sure he's on board in that way."

Celeste groaned. "I disagree, although I admit I understand why you'd be confused. I don't get it either. His whole face lights up when he sees you, and trust me, I'm the one who sits next to him week after week. He talks about you non-stop. But when it comes time to put his money where his mouth is, Sam slinks off like some sort of clueless schoolboy. It's like he can't handle being close to you, or he's holding back—" Celeste shrugged. "It's like he's waiting for something, but I have no idea what."

Kate let out a wistful sigh. "He's been supportive through every round of the contest, but it hasn't gone anywhere. He always leaves right after they announce the scores. It's the oddest thing. I see him on bake-off day, and then he calls during the week to find out what I'm making. Usually Wednesday, since I have to turn in the ingredients I need to Abby on Thursday. It's sort of becoming our routine, but that's as far as Sam seems to want to take it."

"Well, he'll have to break routine soon if he wants to stay in touch," Celeste said matter-of-factly. "This is it. If he doesn't come up with a new plan, he won't know where you are every Saturday, and he'll have no reason to call."

The same thought had occurred to Kate. "That's what I was thinking. And if he doesn't, then I guess it's not meant to be."

Kate couldn't admit that if Sam drifted away when the contest was over, she'd be crushed. If that happened, she needed to walk away from him. No looking back. Despite how Sam made her feel during their phone calls, her heart couldn't take it anymore. She didn't want Sam as her friend. She needed more.

Celeste rubbed her chin while she stared at Kate. Her friend was studying her, no doubt trying to figure out if this could be it for Kate and Sam. Celeste would be disappointed too. She'd been so convinced they'd figure it out, but so far, she'd been wrong. Her Spidey senses might not be all she thought they were. At least as far as Sam was concerned.

"So, you turned in the ingredients for Will's cake?" Celeste asked. "You decided to make it?"

"Sort of. I sent the list of ingredients for the original cake to Abby on Thursday, but then I decided—" Kate bit back a nervous smile. "I decided I'm different now than when I first made it. I want to make it as much for *me* as for Will. So, last night I decided to give it an update."

Celeste winced. "At the last minute?"

Kate scrunched up her face, her shoulders lifting. "What can I say? I had some ideas to make it even better."

Celeste cocked her head. "Do tell."

Kate leaned in across the table. "I added a crust of chocolate cookie crumbs at the bottom, and now it has a chocolate cheese-cake layer nestled into a layer of the chocolate cake. I added a thin layer of soaked raspberries on top, and then I topped it with a second layer of cake on top of that."

Celeste smacked her lips. "I'm in overload. You didn't get rid of the glaze, did you?"

"No, but that's why I need the cake layer around the cheesecake. The glaze is key." Kate's eyes lit up. "But last night, I tried something different. Instead of red wine, I used Chambord."

Celeste let out a long moan. "That sounds incredible. Wait, is that what you soaked the fresh raspberries in?"

Kate nodded. "Just a little. Also, I decided last night that I need to hit the presentation out of the park. I'm using edible gold leaf sprinkled across the top. I'll pipe whipped cream rosettes around the bottom with fresh raspberry centers."

"That sounds beautiful. But changing it at the last minute?" Celeste cringed. "But wait, didn't you already send Abby the ingredients you needed?"

"I did." Kate stood and strode to the counter, where she picked up the cooler bag she'd set next to the Chambord bottle. "That's why I'm packing a bag to take the additional stuff with me."

Celeste gave an approving nod. "Look at you. You've got my mouth practically watering. Please tell me you'll make this at home sometime so I can taste it."

"Funny you should ask. I invited you for coffee because I wanted you to try it." Kate lifted the cover off her cake plate to reveal the test cake she'd made the night before. She'd taken it out of the refrigerator before Celeste got there so it would come to room temperature. "As long as you don't mind cake for breakfast."

Celeste's hand flew to her mouth as Kate set it in front of her. "It's stunning, and c'mon, have you ever known me to turn down cake? Who cares what time it is? If it tastes as good as it looks, you're a shoo-in today."

Kate pulled a fork and her cake knife from the silverware drawer and then grabbed a small plate from the cupboard. She set them on the table.

Celeste was studying the swirled pattern of the gold sprinkles. "Is it my imagination, or is this a—"

Kate nodded with a slight smile. "It is. Do you think anyone else will notice?"

Celeste scrutinized it for a moment, then shook her head. "I don't think so. It looks like a design, not a letter."

"I just wanted something to pay a little homage to Will."

"I think it's perfect." Celeste picked up the fork. "Now, let me at it."

Kate cut a generous slice, then carefully slid it out onto the plate. The crumbs on the bottom, the layers, the glaze. Perfection.

Kate held her breath as Celeste lifted a fork full of cake to her mouth. Her eyes closed. She seemed to be savoring the flavors in her mouth before she finally swallowed.

"Well?" Kate asked finally, the anticipation killing her.

Celeste blew out a puff of air. "That was quite possibly the most amazing bite of anything I've ever had. Sorry, but that was even better than the wedding cake you made for me." She gave Kate a solemn nod. "I'm so proud of you. If you don't win this whole thing, those judges are out of their minds."

CHAPTER 23

*K*ate clutched her purse and cooler bag as she sat on the rattling bus, which seemed to hit one pothole harder than the one before it. The air conditioning on board was minimal at best, but at least the humidity hadn't yet kicked into high gear. Still, perspiration beaded on Kate's forehead as she sat wedged in beside the man sprawled out next to her.

At least this wouldn't be a long ride. As the driver glided them into the bus lane, they started to pick up speed. Before Kate knew it, they had left the long line of cars behind and were flying through the tunnel.

As she stepped off the bus at the terminal, Kate glanced around, determined not to look like a lost tourist. All she needed was to get robbed. She put her purse around her neck and laid the strap across the front of her body like she'd seen other women do while walking in the city.

She gripped the handle of her cooler bag and let out a nervous sigh. Finally, she spotted a sign that directed her to the street level.

Once outside, the city was awash in movement and noise.

Cars and taxis impatiently tried to make their way through traffic, buses whooshed by, there was a steady hum of voices as crowds of people walked along the sidewalk. Kate imagined even the rumble of the subway underneath her was coming up through the grates.

Her eyes drifted down the street, looking for the best place to hail a cab. Kate shielded her eyes with her hand as she peered into the sunlight at the street sign and remembered what Celeste had told her. She was on Eighth Avenue, and it went uptown. Perfect.

Kate lifted her hand into the air like Will had always done, but there wasn't a cab in sight. Finally, just as panic set in, a taxi pulled to the curb a bit further up from where she stood. She let out a sigh of relief.

Kate rushed toward the yellow cab, but someone else got there first. A woman who looked to be in her late twenties was gripping the handle of what appeared to be a violin case as she opened the back door of the taxi. Kate's taxi.

Kate's face fell. "Oh."

As the woman was about to step into the cab, she stopped short at the sight of Kate's distress.

"Hey, you okay?"

"Um, sure. I just thought—I never come into the city by myself, so I wasn't sure—"

The woman's face softened. "Where are you going?"

Kate handed her the piece of paper that had the address on it.

The girl nodded. "Okay, so this looks like you need to go to Fifty-Seventh between Broadway and Seventh. I'm heading to Lincoln Center, so we can take Eighth Avenue, and you're pretty much on my way. Hop in. We can share a ride."

Kate hesitated for only a moment. The woman's face was kind, and her instincts told her it would be fine. Besides, she'd be happy to have someone help her make sure she got to the right place. She already knew she would never mention this to Celeste.

She could hear her now. *You what? You got in a cab with a complete stranger?*

Kate silenced the voice in her head. She slid into the back with the kind stranger, her violin case on the seat between them. She was a woman carrying a musical instrument. What could happen?

"Thank you so much for letting me ride with you," Kate said as she settled in.

"Two stops, please," the woman told the cab driver. "Fifty-Seventh and Eighth and then up to Lincoln Center. Sixty-Second and Amsterdam is fine. If you could take Eighth to the circle and then head west on Sixtieth, that would be great."

As the cab driver set the meter and pulled off into traffic, the tension slid off Kate's shoulders. "Wow. You really know your way around. My name is Kate."

"I'm Luisa. I was coming in from my parent's house. I live here, but I don't have a car, so I usually take the bus back in."

"I've been coming in for the last five weeks, but I have a friend who usually drives me." Kate missed the security of having Celeste with her. "This is the first time I've ever taken the bus in by myself."

"You were doing fine," Luisa said to reassure her. "You were just hailing a little too far south, but it's no big deal. We're going the same way. So, what brings you to the city?"

The smell of exhaust fumes wafted through the open windows. The lemon air freshener the driver had hanging from the rear view mirror wasn't putting a dent in the smell that permeated the back seat.

Apparently, there was no air conditioning and no real hope of a breeze with the stop-and-go traffic. Kate's clothes were starting to stick to her. She shrugged her cooler bag off her shoulder and lifted the strap to her purse so she could shake the front of her shirt in an attempt to cool off. It didn't do much.

Luisa cringed and lowered her voice as she leaned toward

Kate. "I'm never lucky enough to get a cab with AC. I think there's like two of them in the whole city."

Kate smiled appreciatively, grateful that her travel companion didn't blame the offending smell on her. "I'm actually here for a baking competition."

Luisa's eyes grew wide. "Baking? Wow, that's interesting. I can't bake—or cook for that matter."

"Well, I can't play the violin, so I guess we're even."

As Luisa laughed, Kate continued, her nerves propelling the conversation. "This is the final week. It started six weeks ago with twelve of us, and only two of us are left now. Me and a young guy who doesn't look old enough to know how to bake. Bryce." Kate said his name like a teenage girl might mention a boy she didn't care for. "But I guess the judges like him because his stuff is—" Kate held up her hands, her mouth open but frozen as she searched for the right word. "Edgy. I guess that's what it is. I'm more traditional, I suppose."

"Wow, that's exciting to make it to the last round," Luisa said. "What do you get if you win?"

"It's sponsored by a publishing company. The person who wins gets a publishing contract for a cookbook of their recipes."

"That would be awesome, huh?"

"It would be incredible validation for me." Kate was surprised at how comfortable she felt talking to Luisa. "And you? I know you play the violin, but where do you do that?"

"I play in the Philharmonic. We have a matinee today at two o'clock."

"Wow, I'm impressed. My husband loved classical music. In the summer, he used to sit out back under the stars with a glass of wine and his Mozart CD playing in the background. Have you played for a long time?"

"My parents started me when I was young. I took a bit of a break but then ended up going to Julliard."

"So, you must—"

"First stop," the driver announced.

"Oh, okay." Kate glanced out the window and frowned. Nothing looked familiar. The parking garage Celeste usually parked in must have been in the other direction.

Luisa seemed to sense her confusion. "You want to make the right here on Fifty-Seventh." She pointed out Kate's side window. "Walk down until you cross Broadway, but stay on Fifty-Seventh. Your address is about halfway up before you get to Seventh Avenue. It should be on the right-hand side, so you might want to cross over to the other side of the street here or at Broadway." Luisa smiled. "I wouldn't recommend crossing in the middle of the street. I doubt they'd get you for jaywalking, but the taxi drivers around here drive like maniacs."

Their driver shot Luisa a look in his rearview mirror.

Luisa met his eyes. "Not you, of course. But you know some of them do drive a little nutty."

The taxi driver nodded slightly but said nothing.

Kate was too busy trying to remember everything Luisa told her to smile at their exchange. "Thank you so much, Luisa." She caught sight of the meter as the red numbers clicked to increase the amount of the fare. "Oh." Kate's face grew warm. She'd been ready to leave without paying for her share of the ride. "Let me give you some money."

Luisa dismissed her offer with a flick of her wrist. "Don't worry about it. Just go bake yourself crazy today. Go kick that young kid's butt. That *Bryce*." She used the same tone Kate had used to say his name.

Kate laughed. "I'm going to try. Thank you again." She opened the cab door and slid out, her thoughts already focused on where she needed to go. She turned back before slamming the door. "Have a great concert. It was nice to meet you."

Kate merged herself into the foot traffic on the sidewalk and headed in the direction Luisa had sent her. She had plenty of time to walk slowly and calmly, but she couldn't. She practically ran. Once she found the building and was inside, then she could relax.

She followed Fifty-Seventh Street across Broadway, and it slowly started to look familiar. When Kate saw the gold numbers on the building, she exhaled in relief and pulled the handle for the heavy glass door. She'd made it.

"Well, hello, Miss Kate." The security guard offered a friendly smile that showed off the slight gap between his two front teeth. "No Miss Celeste today?"

Kate shook her head. "Nope. She had to hang with her husband. It's just me today." She gave the guard a nervous smile. "This is the last week. I'm going to miss seeing you every Saturday."

"I'm going to miss having your pretty face brighten up my weekend. Good luck today." He pulled a card off the desk he stood behind and held it out for her. "Here you go."

"Thanks, George." Kate grabbed her building credential and gave him a wave as she headed to the elevator. They had become old friends over the last six weeks.

As the elevator deposited Kate on the tenth floor, the tension slipped from her shoulders. Nothing had gone wrong, and she was on time. Celeste would be proud.

Before she could even take a seat in the reception area, Abby was out to get her.

"Kate's here. I'm bringing her back now," she said into her headset. "This is it. The final two. Nervous?" Abby asked as she pulled open the door to the offices.

"Uh, yeah," Kate said with a chuckle. She could pretend she was calm and collected, but she wasn't sure anyone would believe her. As she followed Abby down the long hallway, she stared at the pictures that had left her so impressed that first week. Maybe someday soon her cookbook would be up there too.

Kate's gaze drifted around the warehouse space as they entered, but there was no sign of Sam. He'd said he was coming, so maybe she'd just gotten there before him. Still, Kate's stomach twinged at the idea that he might not show up. If that happened, she'd never be able to concentrate on making her cake.

Abby gestured for Kate to follow her toward her assigned kitchen for the day. "All your ingredients are either on the counter or in the refrigerator," she called out over her shoulder as they walked. "I don't think you had anything for the freezer." She stopped when they got to a kitchen setup that was marked with Kate's name. "Here you go. Take a few minutes to make sure everything you asked for is here. You have a little time to relax before we get started."

Kate glanced over at the station next to hers. Bryce was already there, busying himself and pretending not to notice she'd arrived.

She noted the bottle of cabernet on her counter and held it up as if studying the label. Just to mess with Bryce. She hoped his brain was spinning as he tried to figure out what she was making that included wine. It was even funnier because she didn't even need it anymore. Kate bit back a smile. Her cake would be even better with the Chambord.

She reached for the strap of the cooler bag, but as her hand patted her bare shoulder, her eyes went wide. Panic set in as her mind reeled. Where had she—

Kate's eyes brimmed with tears, the realization of what she'd done slamming into her. It felt like she'd been punched in the stomach, the wind knocked out of her until she couldn't breathe. She bowed her head and berated herself for being so careless.

She'd left her bag in the cab.

CHAPTER 24

*K*ate struggled to gather her thoughts as she dropped her elbows on the counter and wrapped her hands around her head.

Bryce seemed to take pleasure in her obvious distress. "Everything okay, Kate?" he called out with a smirk on his face.

Kate set her jaw. The worst part about not winning would be losing to Bryce. She wasn't about to give him an ounce of satisfaction. "Everything's perfect."

She opened her refrigerator and hid behind the door as her mind searched for a way to fix what she'd done. It was useless. There was no way she'd be able to find the cab she'd been in. Kate didn't even have the receipt that might give her the taxi number or the driver. Luisa would have that.

She'd come so far, made it all the way to the final round. Now it had come down to this. Her eyes welled up again. How could she have been so—

"Kate?"

She flinched at the sound of his voice. Reluctantly, she backed up and closed the refrigerator. She turned to face him.

"Hey." Sam's face softened when he saw how glum she looked.

He entered her station and placed his hand on her shoulder. "I just got here. What's wrong?"

Kate threw a glance over at Bryce's station and gave her head a quick shake.

Sam lowered his voice. "Sorry. Don't let your nerves get the best of you. You're going to do great today."

Kate moved closer to him. "It's not that. Well, it is, but it isn't."

Sam gave her a puzzled stare. "I don't—"

"I don't have everything I need to make my recipe for today." Kate hung her head. "I messed up."

Sam looked confused. "What do you mean? You got Abby the list of ingredients you needed Thursday, right? Did she not deliver everything you asked for?"

"She did, but—" Kate was sure she looked like a little girl caught doing something sneaky. "I altered the recipe. Last night. I needed some new ingredients, but I brought them with me—in a cooler bag. I had to take a cab here from the bus terminal and—" She pressed her lips together and avoided his stare. "I left the bag in the taxi."

"Wait, the *bus* terminal?" Sam's gaze flew abruptly to the spectator section. "Where's Celeste?"

"She couldn't come today. Her husband's parents are having an anniversary party."

Sam's expression turned incredulous, a deep divot between his brows. "So, you took the *bus* in? You could have ridden in with me. Why in the world didn't you call me?" His tone clearly indicated he thought calling him would have been the obvious choice. So obvious he was utterly astonished it hadn't occurred to her.

Kate shrugged helplessly. It wasn't like she could tell Sam the truth. That the idea of sitting next to him in the car, being so close but not able to grab his hand or lean over and kiss him, was more than she could have handled today. That even now, the only thing she wanted was for him to wrap her up in his arms. That she'd feel better if he told her it would all work out because no matter what happened, they had each other. She couldn't admit any of that. Kate suddenly realized that her need to hide how she really felt about Sam may have cost her the win anyway.

Sam was studying her, still searching for an explanation as to why she hadn't called him. When it became clear Kate wouldn't offer one, he shifted instead into an attempt to fix the situation.

"Okay, let's think about this. You have all the ingredients for the original recipe, right? Is there a reason you don't want to make that?"

"I can. It's just …" Kate's confidence had been lost with her cooler bag. "It had evolved into something similar but—but so much better." She'd let herself down, and Kate knew disappointment was written all over her face.

Sam held her gaze, then twisted his wrist to glance down at his watch. "Okay, is there time to run out and get what you need? I can run to the store. We still have about twenty-five minutes until it starts."

Kate threw a glance at Bryce, who was far too interested in what was happening in her kitchen. She moved to offer him a view of her back instead of their conversation. This was bad enough without his gloating.

"You'd need a grocery store and a liquor store," she said. "I went to the farmer's market at the crack of dawn to get the fresh raspberries. I'm sure D'Agostinos won't have any nearly as good."

Sam placed his hands on Kate's shoulders and looked her in the eye. "I'll taste every one of them until I find the ones that taste like they were picked this morning." He glanced around and yanked open a small drawer under the counter. He pulled out a small pad and a pen. "Make me a list, and I'll go get what you need as fast as I can."

Kate let out a defeated whimper as she reached for his arm. "Sam, I appreciate it. Really, I do, but you won't make it back in time." Once the competition started, no one was allowed anywhere near her station. "I'll go back to my original recipe and hope for the best." It had been good enough on Thursday when she turned it in. She'd make it work. There was no other choice.

Sam's chest deflated with resignation as his eyes searched hers. He placed his hand on the side of her face. Soft and gentle, his thumb caressed her cheek. "Okay, but Kate, I just want—"

The sound of her name echoed throughout the warehouse—Abby's voice calling out to her. Kate pretended not to hear it. She needed to know what Sam had been about to say.

"What were you saying?" she asked.

But Sam's hand had fallen away, his attention diverted to the entrance. Kate didn't care what Abby wanted. Sam had been about to tell her something that seemed important, and she desperately wanted to know what it was.

And then her name was repeated louder. Abby sounded irritated, as if she knew Kate was choosing to ignore her.

With an aggravated sigh, Kate whipped her head toward the voice calling her. She then brought her hand to her mouth, let out a sob, and raced out of her station.

Sam followed as Kate rushed through the warehouse to where Abby stood. Luisa was standing beside her. One hand gripped her violin case, and the other held Kate's cooler bag.

"I can't believe this." Kate shook her head in disbelief.

Luisa held out her bag. "I remembered the address, and luckily, I realized you forgot this before the cab driver got too far. It looked important, so I told him we had to go back."

Gratefully, Kate took the bag from Luisa's hand and turned toward Sam. He grabbed it so she could wrap both arms around the girl who had gone out of her way to help a stranger. "You don't know how much I appreciate this." Kate pulled back, and concern slid across her face. "Don't you have a matinee to get to? You're going to be late."

Luisa nodded with a half-shrug. "Probably." Her gaze drifted to Sam as if she was wondering who the handsome man was to

Kate. "Hey, if I'm late, the other violins will cover for me. Things happen, right?"

Kate worried the show would start with one lone empty chair in the violin section and hoped there wouldn't be any repercussions. "Well, I'm going to come to see you play one of these days, and be prepared because I'm going to bring you the biggest basket of baked goods you've ever seen." Kate leaned in. "And when I win this whole thing, thanks to you, there's an autographed cookbook with your name on it."

"It's a deal." Luisa's eyes scanned the warehouse and all the kitchen stations. "This is a pretty sweet setup here." She brought her gaze back to Kate and lowered her voice. "The guy with the nosy look on his face. Is that him? *Bryce?*"

Kate followed Luisa's gaze and bit her cheek to keep from laughing. "Yeah, that's him."

"He's all bugged out right now wondering what's going on over here." Luisa gave Kate a confident nod. "You got this. Go bake circles around him."

As Abby walked Luisa out, Kate reached for the cooler bag in Sam's hand. She wrapped her arms around it, tucked it tight against her chest, and headed back to her station. Sam walked beside her, wearing a thoughtful expression as if he was trying to put the pieces together.

"We shared a cab," Kate said, trying to explain as she unpacked the contents of the bag onto the counter. "She plays violin for the Philharmonic, and this will probably make her late for the matinee."

"You found an angel on the streets of Manhattan." Sam rubbed his chin as he leaned against the counter next to her. "That *has* to be a sign of good luck."

Maybe it *was* a sign. Was there a chance Will had sent Luisa? She'd never know. Kate's gaze drifted over Sam's head, where she caught Bryce's narrowed eyes staring back at her.

Sam turned his head to see what had caught her attention. As

Bryce jerked his gaze away, the corners of Sam's mouth lifted. "You're making the competition nervous."

"Good." Kate allowed herself a satisfied smile. "When you first came to me with the idea of entering, I thought you were crazy. I didn't think I'd ever be selected as a finalist, much less one of the final two. But now—now I *want* to win. When I look at where I started to where I am right now, I'm so damn proud of myself." Her voice cracked slightly. "But *winning* this would mean everything to me."

Sam reached for her arm and turned her to face him. "It doesn't matter what that final score says, Kate. You're still a winner."

Strength surged through her. Kate still wanted to be with Sam, but if he didn't feel the same, she'd be okay. She'd made it to the final round. Sure, that was a big deal, but if she won the whole thing? That was when Kate would know she'd really succeeded.

As Abby called for the contestants to get ready to begin, Sam leaned in and hugged her. Not a distracting embrace that made her heart thump in her chest but a hug that told her, if nothing else, he cared about her.

"Good luck."

As Kate watched Sam walk off to sit with the other spectators, she knew. She *could* win this. When she did, life would take her where she was meant to go. Kate would just have to wait to see if that journey included Sam.

* * *

Hours later, Kate rubbed the back of her neck, digging in with her fingertips to try to break up the knots. So far, everything had gone perfectly. She'd already advised the judges her glaze would need time to fully set before she'd be ready. They had agreed.

Dinner was being brought in for her and Bryce since they weren't allowed to leave their stations.

Kate allowed her gaze to drift to the spectators for the first time that afternoon and caught Sam staring. He gave her a supportive smile, and she dipped her head to let him know so far, everything had gone according to plan.

Kate had no interest in peeking into Bryce's station. Whatever he made didn't even matter anymore. This was hers to win.

"Hey," Abby said, handing her a bag. "The salad you ordered for dinner."

Kate dragged a stool to her counter, and as she collapsed down on the seat, she glanced back at the spectator section. It was empty. Kate turned her body to give Bryce a view of her back, pulled out her salad, and stared at it. Her shoulders sagged. The adrenaline of the last few hours had abated, and Kate's limbs were sore and heavy.

She was too tired to eat. It had been a long day to get to this point. Up early to go to the farmer's market and then the breakfast visit with Celeste. The bus trip and then the taxi ride. Losing her cooler bag. The sheer exhilaration at seeing Luisa standing there. Hours of baking and assembling her cake so it was perfect. By the time they announced the winner, Kate wasn't sure she'd still be standing.

She glanced at her watch. Celeste would already be at the anniversary party with Bruce, wondering, no doubt, about the results. Kate was disappointed her friend wasn't there. If Sam pulled a disappearing act, Kate would pat herself on the back for a job well done. She'd given it her all.

Finally, Abby approached her station. Her gaze settled on Kate's uneaten salad, and then she announced they were getting ready to start up again.

"You each have thirty minutes to finish up. The judges will be by each of your stations to score the appearance of your dessert overall. When they're finished with both of you, the timer will reset. You'll then have twenty minutes to plate your dessert for each of the four judges."

Kate nodded as she stood. With a quick glance at Bryce, she reached with her hands high in the air to stretch out the aching muscles in her shoulders and back. This was it.

Now that the glaze had set, it was time to pipe the whipped cream rosettes with raspberries and apply the edible gold. Like a nervous athlete, Kate drew in a deep breath and shook out her arms. The gold sprinkles had to be precisely the way she pictured them. She needed a steady hand.

Tuning out everything around her, Kate visualized the final product in her mind and got started. When she was finished, she stepped back to admire her work. She couldn't help the smile that slipped across her face.

It was perfect.

When the judges came by to score her, Kate bit her lip, her heart skipping wildly in her chest. Her cake looked breathtaking. Although the judges tried to keep their faces neutral, Kate could tell they were impressed. If it tasted as good as it looked, she had no doubt she could win this.

When the timer reset, Kate started carefully slicing and plating. She only had twenty minutes.

The raspberry puree was already made. She scraped some in a bowl and added the sugar and heavy cream before beating it into peaks. It was as she'd envisioned—her whipped cream the palest shade of lavender. Kate piped it onto the smear of raspberry puree she'd added to each judge's plate and added several fresh raspberries on top. She added another small peak on top and sprinkled that with a dusting of gold sprinkles.

When she was finished with all four plates, she gave an affirmative nod. Abby appeared and placed them all carefully on a large tray to take them to the scoring table.

Kate's shallow breathing quickened. She clasped her hands

together and rested them against her face while she watched and waited.

The judges started with Bryce. The remainder of his cake was on display, six thin layers in progressively darker shades of orange. His plated slices did look light and refreshing—perfect for a summer dessert. The cake frosting on the outside started in pale orange at the bottom. It then intensified in color as it went up the sides toward the top. An interesting technique.

Bryce had frosted the top of the cake with oversized white flowers, which Kate had to begrudgingly admit looked gorgeous. His piping technique was flawless. They were supposed to be orange blossoms, maybe, and in the middle of each was an orange candy. An odd choice. They resembled the sugared jelly slices most people were familiar with but never really ate.

Dead silence filled the room as the judges held up their plates and studied Bryce's plating from every angle. He had paired his slices with a sprig of fresh flowers that must have been fragrant. One of the judges leaned down to sniff hers.

Next to the flowers, there appeared to be a puff of white spun sugar, almost like cotton candy, with several orange candies nestled inside. The judge with the cable show picked one up and took a tentative nibble. Immediately, her face scrunched up.

Kate would have loved to have seen Bryce's expression, but instead, she shot Sam a look. He winked, and Kate bit the inside of her cheek to keep from smiling.

After putting the plates back down, each judge took time to scribble notes on their white cards. Unlike the first five rounds, the two finalists wouldn't hear any feedback until they announced the scores and the winner.

The judges then tasted Bryce's cake, putting their forks down to fill out their small white cards. They would have made great poker players. Kate had no idea what they thought.

Then they were on to Kate's entry. She held her breath but knew there was nothing she could do now to change a thing. Her pulse raced, and she scrutinized their expressions while each sampled her cake. Had she imagined the food reviewer with the cable show let out a moan of contentment? Kate observed the bakery judge, who seemed to contemplate a second bite before laying down his fork and picking up his card to enter his comments.

Kate's heart was jackhammering in her chest by the time they turned their cards over to Abby. With a reassuring smile at the contestants, she handed them off to Max.

He took his place in front of the judges' table and turned to glance behind him. "I want to thank our judges for their time and dedication to tasting all our entries and providing their expert feedback." He spun around to face the kitchens. "To our two final contestants, I want to thank you both for the efforts and creativity you have shown throughout the competition. The recipes you've created and made for us here over the last six weeks have been not only innovative but delicious."

He then gestured to the spectator section. "After a long day, we're going to give you all a change of scenery while we tally the scores. We're going to move everyone into the room across the hall where we'll award the trophies."

Kate reached up and released the hair clip that had kept her long hair pinned up so it didn't fall in her cake batter. She washed her hands one last time in the small sink, then pulled off her apron. After she followed the crowd across the hall, she searched for Sam.

He spotted her first and held up his hand to get her attention and gesture her over.

"Long day, huh?"

Kate sank down into the seat next to him and exhaled loudly. "Whatever happens now, I'm just glad it's almost over."

Sam leaned close to her and lowered his voice. "From where I was sitting, you looked like the clear winner. Those judges loved your cake, and it looked spectacular."

Kate hoped Sam was right.

On the table in the front of the room sat the two trophies. The smaller was a black diamond-shaped trophy resting on a silver base. The larger had five small diamond-shaped crystal towers in front of a tall crystal prism in the back. Kate knew which one she wanted to walk out with when this was over.

Abby stood in the front of the room and called out, "If everyone can please find a seat, we're going to get started."

After the side conversations settled and everyone was seated, Max addressed the group. He gripped the stack of cards in his hand before turning them up to face him. "First, I'm going to read the comments from the judges for each of our finalists. Then we'll move on to the final scores, starting with our second-place winner. We'll start with the judge's comments for Bryce Robert's orange creamsicle cake."

Kate nudged Sam. "So, that's what that was. Feels like something you'd make for a kid's birthday party. And did you see the judge's face when she tried that candy? What even *was* that?"

"Whatever it was, she definitely didn't like it. And was that *cotton candy* on the side?" Sam whispered behind a cupped hand as he leaned toward her.

Kate shrugged, but a small smile tugged at her lips. She wasn't even listening to the judges' comments anymore. Sam's hand now rested on her leg as they waited for her results. It was impossible to focus.

"Ready?" Sam said as he gave her thigh a squeeze. "You're next."

Max's gaze drifted to Kate. "Now on to Kate Kennedy's chocolate cake with a dark chocolate Chambord glaze." He looked down at the first card in his hand. "The judges' comments on her cake's appearance overall. *So stunning I almost hated to see her cut it up. I say almost because I couldn't wait for my piece.*" There was a titter from the audience.

After that, Kate only heard snippets as her heart pounded in her ears. *"Breathtaking ... a work of art ... absolutely gorgeous."*

"Kate," Sam whispered in her ear. "I told you they loved it."

She couldn't breathe as Max went on with one accolade after another. *"... melted in my mouth ... an explosion of favors ... meant to go together."* Her insides were swirling with emotion. Satisfaction, joy, accomplishment. No matter the final scores, Kate had never been prouder of anything she'd done in her entire life.

Sam's arm was pressed against hers, and she let out a slow breath as it hit her. She wanted him in her life, but she didn't *need* him. It had taken this contest for her to see her own worth. To taste success.

If Sam faded away again, she'd miss him, but now she was certain. Kate only wanted to be with Sam if he felt as strongly about her as she felt about him. No more wondering, no more doubt. She deserved nothing less.

"Here we go," he said to her as Max picked up the second-place trophy.

"In second place with a total of forty-nine points ..." Max's gaze drifted between the two contestants before finally settling on her competition. "Congratulations to Bryce Roberts."

As Bryce stepped forward to accept his trophy, Kate could see the disappointment etched on his face. The smug look had disappeared. She almost felt sorry for him, but he had plenty of years in front of him to perfect his craft and win other awards.

"Yeah, thanks," he said as he accepted his award. After a handshake from Max, Bryce averted his eyes as he walked by Kate and headed back to his seat.

Max then picked up the first-place crystal trophy from the table. "And now, our first-place winner with a total of fifty-eight out of sixty points." His gaze found her in the audience, and he grinned. "Kate Kennedy."

Even though she'd known her name would be announced, emotions surged inside her as she rose from her seat and stepped forward.

"Congratulations, Kate," Max said, handing the trophy to her.

It was heavier than she expected.

Bryce hadn't said anything when he got his trophy, but Kate didn't care. She was going to celebrate this moment, an acceptance speech springing to her lips. "Thank you so much, Max, and to Diamond Publishing for sponsoring this contest." She nodded at the front row. "And to all the judges as well, for their time and all the great feedback they've given."

Kate studied her award silently as she held it in her hands. More than ten years ago, she'd been widowed, wondering how she could make it on her own. Not only had she survived, but she'd also found her passion—first, the catering company, and now this. Soon, she'd be a cookbook author. As Kate stood there holding her trophy, it suddenly became clear. Everything she'd gone through had led her to this moment. She was exactly where she was meant to be.

Kate brought her gaze back up to the crowd. "I feel incredibly honored to have been able to experience the last six weeks. Winning today feels like a dream. There was a time I'd never have imagined this would be possible for me." She dipped her head thoughtfully. "Even though we can't always see the reasons, sometimes life unfolds exactly the way it's meant to. And for that, I'm grateful."

Kate hoisted her trophy up in the air. A smile tugged at her lips as the overhead lights caught the prisms of crystal and sent rainbows of light dancing across the room.

Her insides were bursting with pride. If it hadn't been for Sam convincing her to enter, she would have never known how incredible this accomplishment would make her feel. This moment belonged to both of them.

Kate's gaze shifted in anticipation to him. But instead of the happiness she expected to find in Sam's demeanor, his body was rigid, his expression blank. He simply stared at her, his eyes unblinking, his mouth slightly agape. Kate reeled back as the smile slipped from her face. After all his support, Sam seemed stunned she'd actually won.

Kate blinked hard as she worked to regain her composure. Sam's reaction stung, but she wasn't going to let anyone steal this moment from her. Not even him.

"We'll be in touch with your contract," Max said as he shook Kate's hand and offered congratulations. "The editors will reach out to you to start working on the recipes and content for your cookbook. But that cake you made today? I think that has to be your cover photo. It was stunning."

Kate nodded and forced a smile to her lips. "I'd be okay with that."

As Max and Abby walked away, Kate's eyes fell back on Sam's seat. Empty. Could he really have left without saying a word to her? Not even congratulations?

In disbelief, she scanned all the other seats and let her gaze drift out into the hallway, but he wasn't anywhere. Her eyes welled up in disappointment, mostly with herself. She'd let herself be fooled once again. Damn him anyway.

Kate pressed her lips together to keep from crying. She needed to escape as soon as possible before someone pinned her down with small talk she couldn't handle right then.

Dread hit the pit of her stomach at the thought of having to find her way back to the bus terminal, toting her trophy no less. Maybe she could ask Abby to help her get a cab. As Kate's gaze bounced around the room searching for Max's assistant, she felt a tap on her shoulder.

When she wheeled around, her stomach lurched. It was Sam. Kate froze, the intensity of his gaze stealing her breath. His blue eyes drew her in and held her until she got lost in them, everything around her disappearing into a blurry haze.

He took the trophy gently from her hand and carefully set it back on the table. With his eyes locked on hers, he reached for her and pulled her in close to him. A gasp escaped Kate's lips as he pressed himself against her, his heart thumping against her body as he held her in his arms.

Sam's breathing was quick and shallow. His eyes lingered on her face, almost as if he was seeing her for the first time.

"Kate," he whispered.

The tender way he said her name made her breath catch in her throat. Kate swallowed hard, her need for him to say more etched on her face.

Sam's lips parted slightly, his eyes searching hers as if they needed her consent to continue. Without breaking his gaze, she gave him a subtle nod.

The corners of Sam's mouth lifted ever so slightly. He gripped her tighter, his fingertips pressed into her back. Their hearts thumped rapidly in concert until she couldn't tell which was his and which was hers.

Sam tipped his head slowly toward hers, and the words she had longed for, the admission she'd needed, tumbled out. "I'm in love with you, Kate." He lifted his shoulder in a sheepish shrug. Then he gave her a hesitant smile, almost as if he was unsure how she'd react to his unexpected declaration. "I'm so in love with you. I don't know why—"

"Sam—"

"Shhh." He put his finger to Kate's lips. "What you said up there. Things unfold the way they're meant to." His gaze was as intense as his words. "*We're* meant to happen. You and me."

When Kate nodded in agreement, the corners of Sam's mouth slowly lifted until the smile he wore reached his eyes. He leaned forward, cradled her face in his hands, and brought his lips to hers. A tentative kiss. Kate's body tingled with anticipation. The kiss, soft and gentle at first, grew more passionate as if releasing the longing built up between them. Kate shuddered when Sam ran his fingers through her hair.

Finally, she was precisely where she'd wanted to be for so long, but she couldn't continue. Kate pulled back, reaching for

Sam's hands. She pulled them from around her neck and held them in front of her.

"Sam …" Her breathing was as heavy as his. "There's still a lot of people in this room."

Sam glanced around as if he'd forgotten where they were. "How about I grab your trophy, and we get out of here?" he asked with a seductive smile. "Somewhere where it's just the two of us." His eyes caressed her, and every part of her body ached for him.

"That sounds like a perfect plan," Kate said with a nod as Sam tucked her trophy into the crook of his arm. "And Sam …"

He glanced down at her, and his tender gaze tugged at her heart. "Yeah?"

Kate reached for Sam's hand and slipped her palm inside his. It felt as wonderful as she had always imagined. "I'm in love with you too."

CHAPTER 25

"*H*ey, you still at work?" Kate asked when Zach answered his cell phone.

"Yeah, it's busy," he said. "I should make good money. We're on a wait, so there are lots of people at the bar."

"Okay, I won't keep you, but I didn't want you to worry." Kate perched on the edge of the bed as she slipped off her shoes. Her eyes strayed to Sam, who reclined beside her. "I'm going to stay in the city tonight. You know, it's getting late, and my car is at the park and ride."

Kate heard someone call out for a beer.

"I'm sorry again I couldn't take you. So, tell me quick, how'd it go?"

She couldn't help but grin. "I won, Zach."

"Oh, Mom, that's amazing. Not that I had any doubt you would." Kate heard glasses clinking in the background. "I had a piece of that cake in the fridge. If that was the test run for today, I'm not surprised the other guy didn't stand a chance."

"I almost didn't make the one you had, but that's a story for tomorrow when I get home. I should be back—" Kate looked to Sam for confirmation as he crawled on the bed toward her.

Late, he mouthed. *Very late*. He wrapped an arm around her, planting gentle kisses on her neck that tickled. Kate stifled a giggle.

"You okay, Mom?" Zach asked.

She tried to wave Sam off so she could concentrate on her call, but he ignored her. "Yeah, I'm fine. I'll see you … tomorrow."

"Okay, sounds good. I gotta go. Oh, one more thing, when you get home, I have a favor to ask."

Kate shut her eyes as Sam's lips probed and explored.

"Mmm, hmm. Whatever you need, sweetie. I'll see you tomorrow."

After she tossed her cellphone aside, Sam's lips hungrily found hers. He parted her lips with his tongue, and when Kate finally came up for air, she let out a contented sigh. She had wanted this for so long.

"You know, I didn't exactly plan on staying over tonight," she said. "I don't have a single thing with me."

Sam held up his index finger and picked up the phone in the room. "Hi, yes. Apparently, I forgot our toiletry bag. Could you send up two toothbrushes and toothpaste?" A short pause. "Okay, thank you. Oh, if no one answers, you can leave them outside the door." He threw a glance at Kate and lifted his eyebrows. "Oh, and a bottle of champagne with two glasses. We're celebrating tonight." His face scrunched up into a frustrated scowl. "Okay, that's fine, but could you ask them to rush it. Thanks."

"What was with the face?" she asked.

"I have to sign for the champagne, which means I need to get the door which means …"

Kate didn't find out what Sam was going to say as he laid his body over hers. She let her fingers wander into the hair at the nape of his neck. His lips brushed her cheek and then her face. Slowly. Tantalizing. Until finally, his lips found hers again, and she shivered. It had been so long since she'd felt a man's mouth on hers.

Every sense she had was heightened as he brought his hands up to cup her face. Her eyes closed as his tongue flitted against hers. She could feel his heart thumping against her chest, and hers had quickened as well. Above the sound of his breathing, heavy and urgent, came the rap of knuckles on their door.

Sam let out a frustrated groan but kissed her on the lips before scooting off the bed. "Don't move."

As if she would.

As she tried to catch her breath, she watched him open the door a crack. Sam signed the receipt in the leather folio handed to him, and then the door opened slightly wider.

"I got it from here," he said to the person in the hall. "Thanks."

Sam turned with the tray that contained the bucket of ice with the champagne bottle and two flutes. The toothbrushes and toothpaste were laid on a white linen napkin. After setting the tray on the dresser, he grabbed the bucket and glasses and placed them on the nightstand.

He twisted the cork on the bottle of champagne, and Kate jumped when it popped louder than expected.

His expression turned lustful as he poured them each a glass. "Oh, the things we need to celebrate tonight."

He handed a flute to her and held his up.

"First of all, I have something that has to be said before anything else. I can't believe I didn't say this right after you won." Sam grinned at her. "But to be fair, I *was* slightly distracted by the whole I'm madly in love with you thing." He tapped her glass with his. "But you did win tonight, so I promised to say I told you so."

When Kate rolled her eyes and began to sip her champagne, Sam put his hand out. "There's more." He raised his glass back up in the air. "To your well-earned success, a best-selling cookbook, and our future which starts tonight." His eyes danced playfully. "As soon as possible would be preferred. We could have driven to my house, but your car is at the park and ride lot, and well, quite simply, I didn't think I could stand to wait one more minute."

She held up her glass and clinked it against his. Kate was too old to deny she didn't want him just as much. Besides, if she was being honest with herself, she had wanted it from the first moment she'd laid eyes on him. She was more than ready.

Kate took a sip of her champagne and gave him a coy smile. "A toothbrush is great, but I don't even have a change of clothes. I've been baking all day in these." She thought of the ride in the cab and wondered if the smell had clung to her skin.

Sam leaned over, and when he kissed her, she could taste the champagne on his lips. "There's nothing wrong with chocolate and raspberries."

He took the flute from Kate's hand and returned it to the nightstand next to his.

The corners of his mouth lifted mischievously. "It's not like I packed a bag either, but I'm not worried about it."

Sam sat up slightly and reached over his shoulder to the middle of his back. His hand grabbed his T-shirt, which he then pulled over his head. Dramatically, he tossed his shirt to the floor and crawled back over to where she lay on the bed.

"I don't think you have to worry either." He moved over her and straddled her body between his knees.

She marveled at how perfect he looked, her hands desperate to feel the warmth of his skin under her fingers. "No?" she asked with feigned innocence.

His head went back and forth slowly as his eyebrows lifted ever so slightly. "Nope."

He leaned over and kissed her lips as his fingers deftly undid the bottom button of her sleeveless shirt. "This okay?"

Kate couldn't speak. Instead, she murmured her consent as she pressed the back of her head deeper into the pillow.

With a glance down between each gentle kiss, Sam unfastened one button after another until he reached the top. When he used his hands to push aside her shirt, her shallow breathing quickened at the feel of his warm fingers against her bare skin.

Sam reached for his champagne glass on the nightstand. Tipping the glass ever so slightly, he dribbled a small amount on her stomach. Then, with his eyes anchored on hers, he lowered himself to run his tongue slowly over the liquid. "We are celebrating, right?"

He downed the rest of his glass and brought his lips, wet with champagne, back up to kiss her neck. Then he pulled back, his eyes locked on hers. "Do you know how long I've wanted this?" His mouth drifted down toward hers until he was tantalizing her with a soft, gentle whisper of a kiss. He let his lips brush ever so lightly against hers before he pulled them away. Again and again, he teased her until she thought she might come out of her skin.

Finally, Sam slipped her shirt off one arm and then moved to the other, raining lingering kisses along each shoulder. The feel of his soft, warm lips on her skin made her quiver with pent-up anticipation. Every time Sam stopped, for even a second, every part of her body tensed as she willed him to continue.

After tossing her shirt aside, Sam trailed his lips down her neck toward the edge of her bra. When he slid his tongue slowly under the black lace and then inside, she arched her back and couldn't suppress the soft moan that escaped her lips.

Sam's eyes bore into hers while he slid both hands under her back. With one motion, he released the clasp. Leaning over her, he took one of the straps between his teeth. He tugged it down her shoulder, past her elbow, and then slid it over her wrist. He kept his gaze anchored on her face before he moved to her other shoulder to do the same. Sam's lips turned up in a satisfied smile as he used one hand to toss the black lace bra off the bed to the floor.

"See why you don't need to worry?" Sam asked with a slight shake of his head. "It's not like you're not going to need a single stitch of clothing for what I have planned for tonight. I mean, if that's okay with you ..."

Kate couldn't speak but managed a nod. As his soft hands roamed her body, she sucked in a deep breath. With her arms wrapped around him, her fingers trailed down his back. She closed her eyes and stopped thinking about anything other than the way his touch made her feel.

Sam was right. She didn't need to worry about anything anymore.

CHAPTER 26

*K*ate laid in Sam's arms as his fingers slowly drifted across her shoulder. "This has been the most incredible day of my life."

"The day was incredible?" Sam leaned his head closer to hers. "Or the night?"

Kate leaned over him to glance at the alarm clock before settling back into the crook of his arm. They hadn't slept yet, and sunrise was only a few hours away.

"I guess technically, it's tomorrow now, but you know what I mean. Winning the bake-off was like a dream come true." Kate shifted so she could look up at Sam. "You were a different kind of dream. To get both in the same day seems surreal."

He rubbed her shoulder. "When I saw you with that trophy, it was like my eyes were opened. I kept thinking, what am I doing? The contest was over, and I couldn't let you walk away. It made me realize I needed to tell you how I felt, and if you didn't feel the same—"

Kate sat straight up to face him. "Didn't feel the same?"

"I didn't know. I felt like I was putting it all on the line and taking the risk of being rejected."

Her head jerked back. "How could you say that? From the first time I met you, I knew there was something between us." Kate wagged a finger in the air at him. "I know you felt it too."

"I did." Sam offered a slight shrug. "But I didn't think there was anything I could do about it."

Kate frowned, studying him to see if he was serious. "That's crazy."

Sam nodded at the bucket with the chilled champagne. "I might need another glass."

Kate slid over toward the nightstand and refilled his glass. As Sam propped himself up against the headboard, she handed him the flute.

Sam tipped it back and took a long swallow.

Kate wrapped herself up in the bedsheet and sat facing him on the bed, her arms around her knees. If Sam had an explanation for why they had played this cat and mouse game for so long, she wanted to hear every word of it.

Sam drew in a long breath, then released it slowly. "When I wrote the review and then came to see you, I thought you were married. I had no reason to think otherwise. But after I left, I couldn't stop thinking about you." He took another sip from his glass before continuing. "But you know—I told you. My wife cheated on me when we were married. I would *never* do that to anyone else's marriage." He gave his head a slight shake. "I had to step back. That was why I had the restaurant managers all call you directly."

Kate realized with a twinge of guilt Sam's explanation made sense. "It bothered me that I didn't hear from you again. I thought maybe you didn't feel what I felt." She dipped her head. "But I get it. Why wouldn't you think I was married?" Kate thought back to the conversation she'd had with Celeste about when it would be appropriate to take off her wedding band. "I did wear my rings for a long time. It was hard—I had a hard time letting go, but finally, I accepted it was time. I had taken them off by the time I saw you at the football game, but—"

"But I had a girlfriend," Sam cut in. "I still didn't know—I didn't know your situation. I had no idea anything had changed. You were wearing gloves. You had *two* hot chocolates," he said pointedly.

"One was for Celeste."

Sam rolled his eyes. "Well, *now* I know that." He paused for a moment. "That girlfriend and I actually broke up that weekend. The day after the football game."

Kate tilted her head. "Really?"

"Yeah. I knew I was never getting married again unless I found the perfect person. She wasn't it. It wasn't fair to keep seeing her. And seeing you at the game—well, that stirred up all the feelings I had for you. It confirmed she and I weren't meant to be together."

"Hmm." Kate studied his face, but his expression confirmed his sincerity.

"About a week after that, I was at the Fitzsimmons' house for dinner, and I mentioned running into you at the game. Audrey knew I had written the review after their wedding. Even that the restaurants were serving your desserts. When I brought you up, she got this serious look on her face and said something about it being so sad that your husband had passed away. I was shocked. I thought it had happened recently, but Audrey said no, it had happened way before the wedding." He pressed his lips together. "That caught me by surprise."

Kate nodded slowly, imagining how shocked Sam must have been. "I can understand that. Marcy and I had been working together for over a year by the time we catered her wedding."

Sam went quiet, his gaze drifting down to his hands as if he was deep in thought. When Kate gently nudged him, he lifted his eyes to meet hers. "Audrey told me you'd mentioned to her—" His mouth pulled tight. "She said you were adamant you were never going to get married again or want to be with anyone else. You said your husband had been the love of your life and—"

"And what?" Kate searched her memory, trying to remember what she'd said.

Sam held her gaze for a moment, then looked away.

Kate grabbed his arm. "Sam, I didn't—"

"Audrey said you told her your husband had been the love of your life, and no one else would ever be able to compare."

Sam shifted uncomfortably against the pillow as if reminding Kate what she'd said might cause her to change her mind about him. Or maybe it hurt for Sam to acknowledge his belief that he could never compete with Will for her heart.

Kate moved closer to him and placed her hands on the sides of his face. "I do remember saying that. It was the day she came to taste wedding cakes, and at the time, I believed it. When Will died, I didn't think anyone could ever make me feel the way he did. And then I met you." Kate held Sam's gaze, her eyes begging him to believe her. "And you looked at me in this way that ..."

"That what?"

Kate took in a deep breath and wondered if she could make him understand. "The way you looked at me made me feel like you could—you could see into my *soul*. I'm not sure I can explain it. You felt ..." She stared off as she tried to figure out how to put it into words. "Being with you reminded me of the way you feel when you've been away on a trip. You walk into your house, and you think, oh, it feels so good to be home. That was how you felt. Like I was right where I belonged when I was with you." Kate groaned. "But at the same time, my insides quivered every time I saw you like I was a smitten teenager."

Sam gave her a crooked smile. "A teenager, huh?"

Of course that was what he would take from what she'd said. "You know what I mean."

"I do. I felt like a teenager too. One with raging hormones that went off the charts every time I saw you." Sam grabbed her play-fully and nuzzled his face into her neck.

Kate pulled back and swatted him lightly on the arm. "That day we went for coffee, I thought—I wondered if maybe it was something more. Which was crazy. I hadn't seen you in three years, but that day—" She covered her face with her hand.

Sam pried each finger gently away. "What about that day?"

Kate's face grew warm. "I can't believe I'm admitting this to you now. That day in the coffee shop, you leaned over the table. You put your hand ... on my arm. I thought—I thought you were going to kiss me."

"You have no idea how much I wanted to," Sam said. "I told you about the bake-off because it was the right thing to do. You absolutely should have been competing in it. But at the same time, I was sure I was going to get *crushed*. Spending time with you. Rooting for you to win. I thought it would *kill* me to know you'd never want anything more."

Kate moaned. "But I did."

Sam threw his hands up. "I didn't know. You never said anything. I was worried about doing anything that might make you uncomfortable."

Kate huffed. "Oh, really? What about the frosting on my face? What the hell was *that* about?"

"Okay, but it's not like that was *my* fault," Sam said, attempting to plead his innocence. "How was I supposed to restrain myself? You looked so beautifully disheveled, covered in flour with this—this swath of chocolate across your face." Sam gave her a wicked grin. "Trust me. Licking that off your face wasn't all I had planned for you that day." He offered a shrug as he attempted to appear serious. "But I put it out there. You were the one that didn't accept my offer. We could have ended up in this position much sooner, you know."

Kate smacked him gently with a pillow. "Do you remember

Marcy? Standing right there?" Her face turned serious. "And then you disappeared after that day for months."

Sam's face fell as he ran a hand through his hair. "I know. I'm sorry. Trust me, I thought about you all the time. I knew you had my number, but when you never called—I figured Audrey was probably right."

Kate let out a grunt and threw her head back against the pillow. "Do you know how many times I looked at that stupid receipt with your number on it?"

"So, why didn't you call?"

Kate answered with a sigh. "I guess I was afraid. I was sure I wanted more than you did. And then when we finally start talking about the bake-off—"

"I felt myself falling more and more in love with you," Sam said. "Our conversations—"

Kate let out an exasperated groan. "I thought we were moving into the friend zone. All we did was talk on the phone."

"That was because I didn't trust myself to be alone with you." Sam raised a hand in the air. "On the phone, it was safe. When we would talk, it felt so—so comfortable. I think I'd decided that if all I could have was your friendship, I would try to accept that."

"I had decided the same thing, I think. I knew I couldn't be alone with you either." Kate chuckled. "Why do you think I took the bus instead of asking you for a ride?"

Sam raised his eyebrows and shot her a roguish grin. "I'm not sure you would have even made it to the bake-off. I might have whisked you off to this hotel instead."

"You wouldn't have done that."

"Oh, but I would have wanted to." Sam grabbed her and pulled her to him.

Kate kissed him and released a contented sigh as she curled up next to him. "I won twice today. The bake-off and you. I've wanted you for so long, but I think—"

Sam squeezed her shoulder. "You think what?"

212

"I think it was better we waited until the contest was over. I had things to prove to myself. When Will first died—" Kate paused. "Being here with you like this, it feels wrong to talk about Will. Does it bother you? You can be honest."

Sam seemed to consider it for a moment, then shook his head. "It actually doesn't. Your life with him made you who you are today. Someone that I love."

"I think it's the opposite," Kate said matter-of-factly.

Sam frowned. "You think that I *don't* love you?"

"No, silly."

Sam studied her through narrowed eyes. "Then what do you mean, the opposite?"

"Will and I were happy—absolutely—and I loved him. Honestly, our life seemed perfect." Kate observed Sam's expression as she explained. He didn't flinch. "But it was his *death*, I think, that made me who I am today. If Will were alive, I would still be baking in my kitchen and spending my days working in a crappy office. I would have been Will's wife and Zach's mother. Not Kate, the woman who goes out and finds her own success."

She waited to see if Sam would say anything, but he simply watched her and listened. "Don't get me wrong. I would have been happy with the life I had. But only because I wouldn't have known how fulfilled I could be doing something I felt passionate about. Something that was only for me." Kate paused, worried it sounded like her husband didn't support her. "It's not that Will would have ever stopped me from doing anything I wanted to do. It's more that I don't think it would have ever occurred to *me* that trying something new was an option."

"I think I understand."

Kate sat up. "When Will died, I didn't know if I could afford to keep the house, pay the bills. It was Celeste that encouraged me to call Marcy, who was in a similar position to me. Cooking was her passion, but she never thought it would be possible to open a catering company. I'm not sure what flipped the switch for her, but she finally decided she wasn't getting any younger. She wanted to follow her dream."

"I didn't know that. I like Celeste. I think she knew before either one of us that this was going to happen."

Kate smiled as she remembered that cold night at the football game. "She absolutely did. She swears she has a superpower."

Sam's forehead creased. "A superpower? What kind of superpower?"

"I'll let her fill you in after I tell her the good news." Kate winced. "She's going to *kill* me for hanging her out to dry about the results of the contest, and just so you know, I *may* have to kiss and tell. She is my best friend, after all."

Sam's dimple made an appearance as he grinned. "If you must. Make sure you build me up properly when you tell her."

Kate tilted her head up and kissed him and his male ego. "Trust me, I don't need to build you up. Or tonight. We had, what, nine years of foreplay?"

Sam laughed. "There were times it felt like even more, but you can tell Celeste whatever you want. I like that she's been such a good friend to you."

"That's another thing she and I always talk about. Do you know how we met?"

Sam seemed to consider it, then shook his head. "No, she never told me. In all those times we sat and watched you bake, she let me do most of the talking."

Kate gave his arm a reassuring pat. "That's all part of her undercover spy strategy."

Sam looked confused but then shrugged as if accepting Celeste was part of the package. "This is going to be some chat. I can feel it."

"Celeste and I met at the hospital," Kate said. "I was crying in a chair by the vending machine. She got a candy bar, and as she was walking away, something made her turn around. She had lost her husband too."

"She told me she just got married again. A dentist, right?"

"Yeah, Bruce, and he's perfect for her. But her first husband died about two years before Will. A heart attack. When Celeste and I met, she was leading a grief group for women who'd lost their husbands. Right there at the hospital. And there I am bawling because my husband was dying."

"Sounds like you two were meant to meet."

Kate nodded, happy that Sam understood. "I think so. Celeste says if it hadn't happened at the hospital, it would have been somewhere else. Like one way or another, we were destined to be friends."

"Like the way we were destined to find each other?" Sam leaned down and kissed the top of her head.

"Maybe," Kate said softly.

It wasn't like she'd wanted Will to die. But he had. Kate had been left to struggle and grow as she found her way in a life without him. She'd found success, but she'd also put herself on a path toward finding another chance at love. A path that led to Sam.

"It's crazy how things unfold," she said. "I meant it when I said that today. If Will hadn't died, I still say I might not have met Celeste. She wouldn't have told me about Marcy's catering business. You wouldn't have written that review—"

"If only we'd figured it out sooner," Sam said, a wistful expression on his face. "I guess the universe was conspiring against us for a while."

Kate shook her head and nuzzled in close to him. "I think it all happened exactly the way it was supposed to and at the right time." She ran her hand across his chest. "Although, I might not have agreed with that before when my insides were aching for you."

"Aching?" Sam pulled back and grinned, like a schoolboy with a crush who's found out the little girl on the playground likes him too.

LIANE CARMEN

Kate rolled her eyes. "Yes, *aching*. But like I said, I think it was important for me to feel like I had accomplished something before I became defined as another relationship."

"And how *are* you defining us?" Sam gave her a pointed stare.

Kate hesitated while she considered her response. "You're the second chance at love I never knew I wanted. But right now, being here with you, I realize exactly how much I needed you."

"So, have you changed your mind about never wanting to get married again?"

Kate bounced that ball right back. "Have *you* met the perfect person that makes you want to get married again?"

Sam kissed her as his way of answering her question. "I have."

Kate gazed into his blue eyes. "Me too."

She couldn't help but smile. Just wait until Celeste heard about this.

CHAPTER 27

*H*er best friend stormed in like a hurricane, huffing and puffing. "Why couldn't you tell me what happened on the phone? Did you win? I left you about ten voice-mails last night because I just couldn't fathom *why* you wouldn't be answering your phone."

Celeste stood just inside Kate's front door, her hands on her hips. "So, there I am at the party making small talk with the senior citizens and waiting for you to call with the results. But nope, I hear nothing. Then, I'm thinking, well, crap, you had to find your way back to that dark, deserted park and ride lot, which made me worry." Celeste's index finger jabbed at the air in front of Kate's face. "And then I thought, maybe you got off your 'oh, no, I can't be alone in a car with Sam' soapbox and accepted a ride home with him."

Kate stifled a smile as her friend did her best imitation of her.

Celeste then tapped her index finger against her lip. "But then this morning, when you said I *had* to come over, I thought, well, *maybe* it's because I need to take you back to the parking lot to go *get* your car." Celeste threw up her hands. "Except when I get here, your car's already in the driveway." She took in a deep breath and crossed her arms over her chest. The pointed stare she gave Kate meant she needed to start explaining.

Sam had taken Kate to get her car when they left the hotel. He'd wanted her to come to his house, but Kate had insisted she needed to go home. She needed to prepare for the outrage that would be Celeste. Kate had no doubts she'd be forgiven. After all, she had news to share. Monumental news.

Once Kate spilled the previous night's details, she hoped her friend had advice about what to tell Zach. Kate worried her new relationship could come as a shock. She hadn't been with another man since Will and had no idea how her son would take it.

"Okay, calm down," Kate said, trying not to laugh at her friend's dramatic entrance. "I'm sorry I worried you. I'll make you a cup of coffee and tell you everything."

Celeste followed Kate into the kitchen.

"What is *that*?" She marched over to the trophy sitting on the counter. "First Place?" She spun around. "You won! I knew you would." Celeste threw her arms around Kate and squeezed her tight. But when she pulled back, her lips were pursed. "I still don't understand why you couldn't have told me last night or on the phone this morning. What's up with that?"

Kate popped a pod into the coffee maker and set a cup for Celeste underneath. "I did win, which was pretty amazing. You should have seen Bryce's face when he realized he only got second place."

"Oh, I can't believe I missed it. What did the boy wonder make?" Celeste slipped into a chair at the table.

Kate told her about Bryce's creamsicle cake and weird candy as she set sugar and creamer on the table.

Celeste frowned. "That's like something you make for a kid's birthday party."

"That was exactly what I said." Kate handed Celeste her coffee.

"So, what was the final score?" she asked, adding a hefty pour of vanilla creamer to her cup.

Kate couldn't help but grin as she slid into a chair across from her friend. "Fifty-eight to forty-nine."

"Nice. Take that, Bryce." Celeste sipped her coffee. "I knew the judges would love that cake." She glanced in the direction of the refrigerator. "Speaking of which, got any left?"

"Probably. I know Zach had a piece, but I wasn't home last—" Kate froze mid-sentence, but it wasn't quite in time.

Celeste cocked her head, narrowed her eyes, and pointed her finger at Kate. "You weren't home last night? That means you ... *slept out.*" Her eyes grew wide with excitement. "This is big. Were you with Sam?"

Kate's cheeks warmed. She hadn't gossiped about a man in years. Decades actually. "Well, technically, I didn't get much sleep." Kate let the implication sink in, enjoying how Celeste's attention was now laser-focused. "But yes, I *was* with Sam."

Celeste let out a squeal. "The hell with the winning trophy." She placed her elbows on the table and clasped her hands together in front of her. "Tell me everything. And no skipping the good parts."

Embarrassed, Kate shrugged, but Celeste wasn't having any of that.

"Oh, no, you don't. I've been invested in the Kate and Sam saga for far too long for you to hold back now."

"Well, okay, if you *insist*," Kate said, leaning in.

She relayed how Max had announced her as the winner, but when she'd looked for Sam, his seat was empty.

"So, you thought he left again?" Celeste asked, nodding. "You must have been *pissed*. You were pissed, right?"

Kate shrugged. She'd been more hurt than angry. "I was ... slightly disappointed."

Celeste rolled her eyes and took a sip of her coffee. "Right," she said with a dismissive shake of her head as if she didn't buy it.

"Okay, so you were pissed because you thought Sam left." She rolled her hand in the air. "Continue."

Kate rested her arms on the table. "As I was looking around the room trying to figure out if he left, I felt a tap on my shoulder."

"It was Sam?" Celeste asked before smacking her hand against her forehead. "Duh, why am I even asking? Of course it was Sam."

Kate shot Celeste a look that said her interrupting was only slowing down the story. "Are you going to let me tell you what happened or what?"

Celeste drew her fingers across her mouth. "Zipped shut. I won't say a word until you're done. Go on."

Kate let out a breath. "Okay, so when I turned around, Sam was standing there with this look on his face." She planted her elbow on the table and set her chin in her palm. "I'm not even sure I can explain it, but then he …" Kate knew she probably had a dreamy look on her face, but she couldn't help it. "He took the trophy from my hand and put it on the table. Then he grabbed me and pulled me into him."

Eyes wide, Celeste pressed her lips together hard, her expression saying what she couldn't. Kate tried not to smile. She knew her friend had to be *dying* to say something.

"And then Sam looked deep into my eyes, and he said …" Kate paused dramatically and let her gaze drift off, knowing full well the torture she was inflicting.

Celeste didn't say a word. Instead, she expelled a loud, drawn-out groan through her pinched lips and pounded the heel of her hand against the table.

Kate couldn't help her laugh but quickly composed herself to continue. "As he held me, there in the room where they awarded the trophies, he looked deep into my eyes. Then he whispered to me, 'I'm in love with you, Kate.'"

Celeste crossed her hands over her chest. She let out a loud moan but then caught herself. She held up her hand in apology and ran her finger across her lips again.

"Then he kissed me, soft and sweet." Kate shivered, remembering the moment. "And then it got intense. I mean, he was *really* kissing me, until finally, I had to stop him." She wrapped her hands around her head as she admitted the truth. "I got embarrassed."

Celeste frowned, her annoyance loud and clear. Kate knew what she would have said if she'd been allowed to speak. *Who the hell cares who's watching?*

Kate gave a helpless shrug. "I mean, really, we were in a room full of people making out like teenagers at a high school dance. There were people in that room I'll be working with for the cookbook, and who knows who else. It's not like I *wanted* him to stop, but it didn't seem … appropriate."

Celeste brought her fist to her mouth and then rolled her eyes to let Kate know where she stood on her need to be appropriate.

Kate shook her head as she dismissed her friend's approval of their very public display of affection.

"So, then Sam said, 'let's go someplace where the two of us can be alone.' The next thing I knew, we were checking into the Marriott." Kate tried to fight a smile, but there was no way she could. "We never even made it out of the city. And yes, we had *quite* the night."

Celeste nodded repeatedly and pointed at her mouth. Eyes wide, she shot Kate an urgent stare.

Kate answered her with a nod of her own. "Yes, you can speak. I'm finished."

Celeste slammed both hands down on the table. "I told you I had a superpower!"

Kate laughed. "Okay, you were right. Although Sam and I did a lot of talking—"

"Talking? Are you kidding me?" Celeste scowled in disappointment. "Must you ruin it for me?"

"Okay, we did a lot of talking *after*."

"After *what?*" Celeste raised her eyebrows, her face lighting up. "Say it."

Kate shook her head and covered her face with her hands.

Celeste reached across the table and pulled her hands away. "Oh, no, you don't. Say it."

Kate scrunched up her face, her cheeks burning. "After the mind-numbing sex that made my toes curl." With her admission out in the open, Kate leaned back in her chair, her eyes wide. "I know it's been a *long* time, but wow. It was even better than I imagined." She grinned. "And trust me, I've spent a good amount of time imagining it."

Celeste stood with a satisfied smile. "Okay, that'll do for now." She made her way to the refrigerator. "This requires a piece of the winning cake."

Kate watched as Celeste pulled it out of the refrigerator and cut herself a slice.

"You should let it come up to room temperature."

Celeste gave her a defiant stare as she dug her fork in. "Desperate times. I need this right now." She took a bite, exhaled loudly, then dipped her head. "Okay, I'm better. Please continue."

"Well, after the mind-numbing you-know-what, we did talk about why we never got together. First, Sam thought I was married. You know, me wearing my rings. Then the football game. I had gloves on, so he had no reason to think I wasn't still married. And then Audrey—"

Celeste glanced up from her cake, confused. "Who's Audrey?"

"Fitzsimmons. Marcy and I catered her wedding—the one that prompted Sam to write the review. Her husband is Sam's accountant. Anyway, Sam was at their house for dinner. Audrey happened to mention in passing that Will had died. Which, of course, Sam thought had just happened because he thought I was married when we met. But Audrey said no, it happened long before her wedding. And then she told Sam …" Kate let out a slow breath. "Audrey told Sam I said I would never get married again because no one could ever compare to Will."

Celeste's fork paused in mid-air. "Why would she tell him that?"

Kate shrugged, but she knew the guilty expression on her face told the story.

"You said that?" Celeste asked, her face screwed up in disbelief. "To Audrey Fitzsimmons, the wife of Sam's accountant?"

Kate held up her hands in a helpless gesture. "At the time, I thought it was true. I mean, I hadn't even met Sam yet."

Celeste cringed and took another bite of her cake. "So, how did he take that news when he heard it?"

Kate's expression turned somber. "She had Sam thoroughly convinced I wouldn't ever be interested. In him or anyone. All the phone calls about my recipes and what I was going to make every week? He was trying to accept that all we'd ever be is friends. But then, at the awards, he said a light went off in his head. He said he knew he had to try. He was convinced he'd make this huge declaration, and I would turn him down."

Celeste licked the glaze from the back of her fork before giving her head a shake. "Your new man—not very good at reading signals, is he?"

Kate couldn't argue with that. "I think it all happened the way it was meant to, even the timing. We're together now, and that's what matters." She couldn't help but smile. "I just want to keep saying it. *We're together now.* I get this wonderful second chance at love. I understand now what you said about Bruce. Being with Sam doesn't change the way I felt about Will. It doesn't change a thing about what Will and I had together."

"Of course not. And don't you dare feel guilty."

Kate tilted her head as she considered it. Did she feel guilty, like she was in some way betraying Will? It took her a moment, but finally, she shook her head, surprised at the realization. "I don't. I loved Will, but Sam's not competing with what Will and I had. We'll have our own relationship, completely separate."

"Good. I'm so happy for you. So, where do you go from here?"

"That's why I wanted to talk to you. What do I tell Zach?"

"What do you mean, what do you tell Zach? You tell him the truth. Well, you know, the PG version of it."

"How did Bella and Ben take it when you told them about Bruce?"

"It took them a bit to warm up to the idea, but Kate, we don't have little kids anymore. Ben's going to college next year, and Bella's only two years behind that. Zach's *twenty-one*. He has a serious girlfriend." Celeste pushed her empty cake plate to the side and leaned in. "We've done our time. For a good part of their childhood, we raised them alone. I mean, I'm grateful we had each other to lean on, but ultimately, we had to figure it all out ourselves. We sacrificed, and we knew it was all on us to turn decent human beings out into the world. And you've done that."

Kate nodded in agreement as she listened to her friend. "Zach *is* a great kid."

"He is. You did an amazing job, but he's *not* a kid anymore. Your job is done. Now it's your time. You deserve to be happy, Kate, and you don't need to feel bad that you don't want to go to bed alone anymore. You've earned that right." Celeste's tone was firm. "Don't you think Zach would want you to be happy? And Sam makes you happy."

Kate nodded thoughtfully. "He really does. You know, when I first met Will, our attraction was instant. I knew we would end up together. It was all so easy. I never had one single doubt about us." She let out a puff of air. "Sam, on the other hand, well, that wasn't so easy. Obviously. It took a long time for us to figure it out, but last night when we were together, I was as sure about Sam as I had been about Will." She grinned. "And he was worth the wait. Oh, was he worth the wait."

Celeste laughed. "Look at you, feeling all sorts of frisky now.

Don't worry, Zach will understand." She cringed. "Maybe don't mention the moms gone wild thing." She picked up her empty plate and coffee mug and stood. "Where is he, by the way?" she asked, opening the dishwasher.

"I'm not sure," Kate said. "His car wasn't here when I got home. Maybe they called him in for a lunch shift."

"How's he liking the summer job at Attilio's?"

"He's started to bartend there. Makes great money, especially on the weekends."

Celeste leaned against the kitchen counter. "What about Sarah?"

"Still hot and heavy. Zach had a couple of days off this week, and he drove down to see her. I like Sarah. I wouldn't mind if they eventually ended up getting married."

Celeste's eyebrows rose. "Wow. Talking about your baby getting married. Maybe you can have a double wedding."

"Well, maybe not a *double* wedding, but Sam and I *did* talk about it."

"Oh, *really*? So—"

The front door opened and then slammed shut. Celeste shot Kate a look.

"Hey, Mom. Hey, Celeste," Zach said, walking into the kitchen and heading for the refrigerator. He pulled out ingredients to make a sandwich and then carried it all to the counter. He was unloading his arms when he noticed her award.

"Hey, is this your trophy?" He picked it up with one hand and flinched. "It's heavy." His eyes drifted down to the engraving. "First place. Way to go, Mom."

"Thanks, sweetie."

"So, when does the cookbook come out?" he asked.

"I guess we'll start working on it soon. They have to send over contracts and stuff."

Celeste watched as Zach made himself a sandwich and then

cleared her throat. "All right, I have to go. Kate, give me a call later. Bye, Zach."

He waved over his shoulder. "See ya."

Kate waited until Zach had his lunch ready. "Hey, sit and eat. I want to talk to you about something important."

He set his plate and water on the table, then slid into the chair across from her. "I have something for you too."

CHAPTER 28

"*Y*ou go first," Kate said just as Zach took an enormous bite out of his sandwich.

He chewed for a moment before finally swallowing. "Sorry, I'm starving."

Kate glanced at the clock. "Were you at work? It's early to be home from a lunch shift."

"Nope, the mall. Sarah's birthday is next week."

For a minute, Kate wondered if he was planning to propose or do something crazy. She hoped he wasn't planning to ask for her engagement ring. Her hand drifted to the necklace she now wore around her neck.

"Did you find something nice?" she asked.

"She wanted one of those iPod Nanos. It's small, so she can use it while she works out."

Kate exhaled. She wondered if she needed to prepare Zach that she no longer had her engagement ring. For if and when the time came.

"I'm working the dinner shift tonight. Which is actually what I wanted to talk to you about."

Now Kate had no idea what Zach could want. "Okay …" she said, confused.

He dropped his sandwich to the plate, then took a long swallow from his bottle of water. "So, you know I've been bartending these last few weeks."

"Yeah."

"Well, this guy comes in a few times a week. Always eats dinner at the bar, but he never has anything to drink. He told me he works the night shift at the supermarket down the street. I guess he stocks shelves."

"That's a rough schedule. He's your age? Maybe he's not old enough to drink yet."

Zach shook his head. "No, he's older. I'd say maybe he's in his thirties."

"Is he married?"

Zach shrugged. "If he is, he never talks about his wife."

She still wasn't sure where Zach was going with this. "So, you feel sorry for him? Because he seems lonely? Is that it?"

"Sort of, I guess. He's a decent guy. Always makes sure he leaves on time, so he's not late for work. I thought maybe …"

"Maybe what?" Kate asked.

Zach picked up his sandwich. "Maybe you and Marcy could think about giving him a job. A second job, I guess. You're always hiring servers for the events you cater, and I know he could use the money." He took a bite and looked expectantly at his mother.

"Oh, is that it?" Kate relaxed her shoulders. "Sure, tell him to come by the office and fill out an application with your name as his referral. I'll let Marcy know to keep an eye out for him too."

"Thanks, Mom. I appreciate it." Zach opened his mouth as if he had something else to say but then closed it.

"Is there more?"

"Mmm …." He pursed his lips and picked up the other half of his sandwich. "Nope, you go."

Kate's pulse quickened. "Okay. So, the bake-off. I actually entered on the advice of a food critic."

"The guy who wrote the review when you and Marcy first started?"

Kate was surprised Zach remembered. "Right. The same guy. He found out about the contest and thought I could win."

"You did win, so that was pretty smart of him," Zach said as he ate.

Kate's lips lifted into a small smile. "I guess it was. Anyway, we've kept in touch over the years. In the past month or so, we've been talking every week about the contest. What I should make the following week. You know, that kind of stuff."

"He obviously gave you good advice. Does he get anything if you win?" Zach asked.

"As far as the publishing contract? No, but—" Kate sighed. "It's been a long time since your dad died. I still miss him terribly, but there comes a time—" She waited for him to look up, and she caught his eye. "I'm ready to move on. It's time."

Zach's mouth was open, about to take a bite of his sandwich. Instead, he dropped it to his plate. "So, what are you saying?" he asked, confused. "This guy, the food critic—"

"His name is Sam."

Zach's eyes narrowed. "Are you dating this Sam?"

"It's more than that. I'm—I'm in love with him."

Zach lifted his hand in the air, a frown on his face. "Wait, what? You don't even know this guy."

"But I do," Kate said, her tone insistent. "We actually met nine years ago."

"But you haven't been *dating* him all that time."

"No, I haven't," she acknowledged. "But I've known—I've known for a while there were feelings there. We both did. Now that the contest is over—"

Zach pursed his lips. "Is that who you were with last night? When you called me."

Kate hesitated and then nodded, remembering what Celeste said. She had earned the right to be happy. "We decided to celebrate." She hoped Zach wouldn't ask for more details than that.

Her son gave her a hard stare, his mouth pinched tight. "Are you sure this guy's not trying to ride your coattails now that you're going to have this cookbook coming out and who knows what else?"

Kate flinched as his words landed heavily on her. She hadn't thought he would take this direction for their conversation.

Zach's shoulders sagged. "I'm sorry, that's not cool. I'm not suggesting this guy wouldn't want to be with you without having an ulterior motive because, of course, he would." He ran his hand over his face and sighed. "I just feel like you worked hard. You *earned* your success. I want to make sure this guy's intentions are in the right place."

"You don't have to worry." Kate met Zach's probing gaze, her voice firm. "No one could be more supportive of any success I have than Sam. When you meet him, you'll realize he's a decent man." Her voice was soft. "And Zach, Sam loves me too."

Zach let out a breath and leaned back in his chair. "It's hard to think of you with someone that's not Dad."

"I know."

"But I realize it's been a long time," he said thoughtfully.

"More than ten years."

"He makes you happy? This Sam?"

Kate nodded. "He does. You know, your father—when we fell in love, I knew right away I wanted to spend my life with him."

"That's how I feel about Sarah," Zach said, his face serious.

Kate flinched at his admission but recovered quickly. "I thought—I thought your dad and I would have a long, happy life together. I remember one night—you were a toddler—we'd gotten you to bed, and we were sitting in front of the television. We were both utterly exhausted from chasing you around all day. We were having a glass of wine and trying to stay awake so we could spend a little time together—just the two of us. And I remember saying to your dad, 'This won't be forever. Zach will get older. Things will get easier.'" Kate laughed. "Do you remember that stain that was on the old family room couch?"

"The pink one?"

"Well, it started out red, but that's the one," Kate said. "That stain was from that night. We were sitting there on the couch when the show we were watching ended. Your dad was quiet, so I asked him if he was ready to go to bed, but he didn't answer me. When I looked over, he was already sound asleep. Still had the wine glass in his hand, but unfortunately, it was upside down pointing at the couch." She shook her head and smiled. "Wine everywhere. Red wine, of course."

"Wasn't he snoring?" Zach asked. "That should have been a dead giveaway."

Kate shrugged. "Maybe I was sleeping too. I don't know. I guess the point of my story is that your dad and I—all of us—we didn't get enough time together. He should have been here to watch your football games, to see you graduate high school, even to meet Sarah. We should have dropped you off at college together and then come home to enjoy our empty nest. We should be sitting in the backyard on a nice night, holding hands, celebrating the place we've gotten to in our lives."

"I know, Mom. It wasn't fair."

"It wasn't fair to either one of us. But it's the hand we were dealt. And you know what, we not only survived, we triumphed."

Zach pressed his lips together. "I know you gave up a lot for me."

Kate shook her head. "I didn't give up anything for you. While you were growing up, everything I had was *for* you." She leaned in toward him. "You were my heart. I would have done *anything* for you. But now—"

"Now you want something for you," Zach cut in. "Or *someone*, I guess I should say."

"Not someone. *Sam.* I'm not trying to replace your dad. I couldn't if I tried. What Sam and I have is different—not worse or better—just different. And it should be that way. Sam's his own person. He doesn't deserve to live in Dad's shadow."

"Do you think he and Dad would have gotten along?" Zach asked.

Kate thought about it and then nodded. "I do."

"He'd better treat you right, or I'm going to have to kick his butt."

Kate laughed at the idea of Zach defending her honor against Sam. "I'll let him know."

"I'm sorry for giving you a rough time. I don't want you to be alone. I'm only home for another month or so, and next year things are about to really change." He looked Kate straight in the eye. "For both of us."

"In what way?" she asked, tilting her head as she stared at him. Zach still had one more year of college. She'd always expected he'd come home to live after graduation while he searched for a job.

"Well, that's the other thing I wanted to talk to you about."

Kate now realized Zach had led with the guy who needed a job to lull her into a false sense of security. Her intuition had been correct— he *was* considering proposing to Sarah. They were both still so young. If she did nothing else, she needed to get them to agree to wait until after they'd graduated and found decent jobs.

"Are you and Sarah—are you thinking about asking her to marry you?"

"There is that," Zach said, a nervous smile playing on his lips.

Just as she'd feared. "Oh, Zach, What's the rush? You're both young. You still need to graduate college."

"I know, but we'll figure it out," Zach said, trying to reassure her. "Remember how you knew Dad was the one? I *know* Sarah's the one for me."

Kate had known he'd use that comparison because she wouldn't be able to argue. "Right, I understand feeling like that. But Sarah's not going anywhere. If you two want to be together, a couple of years won't make a difference. You'll just be better equipped—"

"I want us to be married before the baby comes," Zach said, blurting out the news he'd been holding back.

Kate's mouth went slack and her stomach lurched. "What?" she asked, choking out the word.

"You're going to be a grandmother, Mom. Sarah's pregnant."

CHAPTER 29

"I'm so happy for you." Marcy glanced up from the counter where she'd been chopping vegetables. "Winning the bake-off, getting your own cookbook. That has to bode well for the catering business."

"I think so too." Kate had taken off the day before, and Celeste had driven her into the city to meet with Max. "I know I've needed time off, but I'm back. I appreciate you pitching in so much."

"Did they tell you how the cookbook is going to work?"

Kate leaned on the other side of the counter. "I met with my publishing team yesterday. They gave me the contract, and I sent it to a lawyer to look at. Not that I have any doubts it's on the up and up, but you can't be too careful. I think once everything is signed, they'll want to set up another meeting to put together a game plan." She winced slightly. Here she had said she was back, and the cookbook could already be interfering with her regular work. "I'll do my best to take as little time as possible away from the business, don't worry."

"We'll figure it out. This is a great opportunity for you." Marcy resumed chopping. "Oh, by the way, a friend of Zach's

234

came in and filled out an application yesterday. He doesn't have much experience serving. Or doing much of anything."

"He's been having dinner a few days a week at the restaurant where Zach works. He works the night shift at the supermarket, but he's looking for a second job. Maybe we can give him a chance, see how he works out?"

"Your call," Marcy said with a nod. "I'm fine if that's what you want to do." She used her knife to gesture toward the office. "His application is on the desk."

Kate's cell phone rang, and when she answered, it was Sam. Her lips lifted into a sappy smile at the sound of his voice. "Hey, you."

She turned and walked toward the office and out of earshot of Marcy. Kate hadn't mentioned anything yet about their new status.

"So, I was thinking ..."

"About how much you miss me?" Kate asked. It had been a few days since they'd spent the night together, and she couldn't wait to see him again. A weight had been lifted off her by telling Zach, and she felt relieved he'd finally given her his blessing.

"I wish I could be even a little cool about it," Sam said. "But, damn, I can't stop thinking about you."

"I can't stop thinking about you either." Kate started to laugh. "Oh, geez. The two of us. We sound like a bunch of love-struck high school kids."

"There's nothing wrong with that. Come over after work tonight, and I'll make you dinner."

"You're going to cook for me?" Kate asked, her eyes downcast as she absent-mindedly ran her foot back and forth on the floor.

"I was a professional chef, you know. Owned my own restaurant."

"Oh, *right*," Kate said, her voice lifting as she teased him. "I believe you mentioned that when we first met. Although, if I remember correctly, I had a hard time concentrating that day."

"It's supposed to be beautiful tonight. I'll set the table outside on the porch overlooking the lake. Very romantic. What do you say?"

Kate didn't know Sam lived on a lake. She realized with a start she had no idea *where* he lived.

"How am I completely head over heels in love with you, and I don't even know where you live?" she asked incredulously.

"Well, come over tonight, and you won't be able to say that anymore. Not the head over heels in love part. That part I plan to fully use to my advantage later."

Kate could picture the gleam in Sam's eye that went with his seductive proclamation. She couldn't fight the smile tugging at her lips. "Oh, really? Is that so?"

"You better believe it. Are you complaining?"

"Absolutely not." Kate's insides were already tingling with anticipation. "In fact, it might be all I think about all day, which won't be good because I have a full day ahead. Making your restaurant orders, as a matter of fact."

"Oh. Maybe you'll make an extra one of those brownie cakes. I'll make dinner. You bring dessert." He paused. "Oh, and bring the cake too."

Kate giggled, despite herself. "Don't you worry. I've got you covered."

"I can't wait to see you," Sam said, a boyish excitement in his voice. "Six?"

"Six sounds perfect. I'll see you then." Kate was about to hang up when she realized she still didn't have his address. "Hey, wait, I really *don't* know where I'm going."

After pulling a piece of paper from the printer next to their desk, Kate jotted down his address and directions. She folded it up and tucked it in the back pocket of her jeans.

Marcy stared at her quizzically when she went back to the kitchen to get her day started. "Okay, who's got you grinning like that? That's an I-have-a-new-man smile or—"

Kate lifted her apron off the hook. "I guess it is *sort of* a new man. But not really. I guess it's been a long time coming, but Sam and I—"

"Mr. Perfect—the food critic?" Marcy asked, her eyes wide.

"None other. And I have to say, he *is* pretty perfect." Kate pulled her apron over her head and tied it around her waist.

"Oh, Kate, good for you." Marcy gave her a hug and stepped back. "All that 'I'm never dating again' stuff. It's about time."

Kate didn't bother to mention Audrey Fitzsimmons' role in it taking so long or that it had been Sam who had to come to his senses. "He invited me over for dinner tonight." She raised her eyebrows. "And he's cooking."

"Oh, I'm really happy for you. The last time Sam was here, it was pretty clear you were both working to keep your feelings under wrap." Her face turned serious. "Life's too short. I'm glad you both finally realized it."

"Me too," Kate said as she reached up into the cabinet and started pulling out ingredients. "I guess I need to get to work if I want to make it to my romantic dinner on time."

* * *

By the end of the day, Kate had filled all her orders, an extra cake slipped to the side to take to Sam's. She balled up her apron and tossed it in the laundry basket she'd bring home at the end of the week.

"I'll be in early tomorrow." Kate reached for her purse.

Marcy gave a knowing smile. "Maybe not if tonight goes well."

"I don't think I have the luxury of missing another day or being late. I need to get started on the stuff for that big conference luncheon Thursday. Was there anything scheduled for tomorrow that I need to work on? I got most of the restaurant orders done today."

"I don't remember. Check the book."

Kate made her way to the desk they shared in the office. She shrugged off her purse and rooted around for the scheduling book. When she located it, she flipped it open to the following day.

"I put a note in here to also get started on the cupcake order for the two baby showers this weekend," Kate called out. "I'll make those Thursday and then wait until Friday to frost them. I can also deliver them if I need to. Unless you've got any of the delivery drivers working."

Marcy appeared and leaned against the doorframe of the office. "I've got to send them with the stuff for the Ellender wedding, but maybe they can take your orders on the way."

Kate had just closed the book when she noticed the completed application. "Is this the one for Zach's friend? The one sitting on top of the folder?"

Marcy nodded. "Yeah, Martin something."

Kate's pulse quickened when she picked it up and saw his full name. She desperately wanted to believe it was only an unfortunate coincidence, but it wasn't a common name. As she skimmed it, everything fit. Except for one fact he'd conveniently omitted.

Kate stood, her hand shaking as she held his application. "What did this guy look like?"

"I don't know," Marcy said. "Brown hair buzzed short, brown eyes, I think. Clean cut. Very polite. Why?"

"Was he short, tall, average height?" Kate's voice was taut.

"Oh, he *was* pretty tall. Maybe six-two. And he had something tattooed on the inside of his wrist, but I couldn't see what it was." Marcy frowned. "Is everything okay?"

The tattoo didn't sound familiar, but Kate had never seen him up close. From a distance, the height certainly seemed possible. Kate's legs wobbled, and she reached out for the edge of the desk to steady herself.

Marcy rushed over and grabbed her other arm. "Hey, you

look like you're about to pass out. We don't have to hire this guy if you have a problem with him. Tell Zach it was me that said no. I mean, it's not like the guy had any experience. He'll understand." Marcy searched Kate's face, no doubt looking to see if her solution solved whatever was bothering her partner so much.

There was nothing Marcy could say that would make the heavy feeling in Kate's chest subside. How had Martin connected with Zach of all people?

Kate sank into the chair, tossing the application on the desk like it had burned her fingers. "I know why he doesn't have much on his résumé."

Marcy gave her a quizzical stare. "Why's that?"

Kate planted her elbows on the desk and held her head in her hands. She stared down at the paper, and she knew with every fiber of her being. It was him.

Her breath hitched in her throat as she turned to answer Marcy's question. "Because I'm pretty sure he's been in jail."

Marcy knelt down in front of Kate and gripped the arms of the chair she was sitting in. "In jail? For what? Kate, who is this guy?"

Kate reached for her stomach, anxiety twisting it tight. How was it fair he'd collided with her world again? She'd finally let herself move on, be happy. And now this?

He had the unbelievable *gall* to befriend her son, to come to her workplace and ask for a job. She'd worked so hard to forget he existed, hoping she'd never have to hear his name again.

Kate met Marcy's eyes, filled with concern. She swallowed hard and said, "Martin Kentala is the guy who killed Will."

CHAPTER 30

*K*ate went home for a quick shower, but Zach wasn't there. She had no idea what to tell him about his new friend. She and Marcy certainly wouldn't be hiring him.

For the entire day, Kate had basked in the anticipation of being with Sam tonight. But now, her brain was spinning, her insides in a tangled knot.

As she slid into the driver's seat, Kate glanced at the directions he'd given her. It would take almost thirty minutes to get to his house. She pulled out of the driveway and called Celeste.

"I need to talk to you." Her voice trembled.

"Kate? You don't sound okay. You need me to come over?"

"I'm actually on my way to Sam's. He's making me dinner."

"Is that what this is about?" Celeste said, her tone dismissive. "You're nervous about a romantic dinner for two. I'm sure—"

"Celeste," Kate cut in, her voice sharp. "This isn't *about* the dinner with Sam."

"Oh. So, what is it about?"

"Remember the guy Zach asked me to hire? Well, he came in yesterday to fill out an application. When I saw it today—his name—" Kate's throat grew tight. "I'm almost positive it's the guy who killed Will."

Kate heard Celeste suck in air. "But you're not positive?"

Kate slammed her brakes and came to a stop at a red light.

"I guess not, but the age fits. He didn't list any work experience for the past ten years. And his name—Martin Kentala. That's a pretty unique name." Everything in Kate's gut told her this was the same guy.

"Okay, but do you even know if he's out of prison?" Celeste asked in a calm voice as if she was trying to keep Kate the same way. "How long was his sentence?"

Kate jumped when the car behind her sounded their horn, then hit the gas. "Twelve years, I think. But he could have gotten out early." She moved over a lane so the impatient driver could go around her.

"Did you sign up to be notified when he was released?"

Kate brought her hand to her forehead and tried to remember. "I don't think so. But it never occurred to me Zach would want to be friends with him, or he'd come knocking on my door for a job." She slammed the brakes and pounded her fist on the steering wheel. "Shit, I missed my turn." She leaned forward and squinted through the windshield to see where she could turn around.

"Go concentrate on driving. Let me see what I can find out, and I'll call you back."

When Kate finally pulled into Sam's driveway, she wiped the tears from her face. She'd considered canceling. Her state of mind wasn't conducive for a romantic night, but Sam would have started dinner. Kate wasn't hungry. Her stomach was a mess, and she couldn't imagine the night going the way they'd planned.

Sam was waiting at the door to greet her as she walked up the sidewalk. A slow smile took over his face, and he swept her up in his arms. Kate breathed in his scent, now familiar and comforting. She tried not to cry.

"I couldn't wait to see you," he murmured into her ear before bringing his lips to hers. He pulled back and reached for the cake in her hand. "Here, let me—" His face fell when he saw she was on the verge of tears. "Hey, what's wrong? Come on in." He grabbed her hand and led her into the house.

Kate followed him down a hallway and into a large, bright kitchen. Whatever he was cooking smelled heavenly.

Sam set the cake on the kitchen table, then turned to Kate, his eyes filled with concern. "Too much too soon? Am I overwhelming you?"

Kate shook her head. "No, no. It's not you." She reached for him and let her head fall against his chest, grateful she hadn't canceled. She needed him.

Sam held her close and stroked her hair. "Something you want to talk about? I'm here for all of it, Kate. The good and the bad. We—"

He was interrupted by the ringing of Kate's cell phone. Her purse was still hanging over her arm, and she pulled back and reached inside. It was Celeste.

She put up her index finger. "I'm sorry. I just need a minute."

"Take as long as you need." Sam strode off to give her space and stir whatever smelled so good on the stove.

Kate slipped into a chair at the kitchen table and answered her phone. "Hey."

"Okay, so Bruce helped me find the information, but I think you're right. It looks like he got out about four months ago."

Kate slowly nodded, but the heaviness in her throat wouldn't let her speak. She planted her elbow on the table and let her head fall into her hand.

"You still there?" Celeste asked.

Kate swallowed hard and cleared her throat. "Yeah, sorry. I just got to Sam's. Thanks for finding that out for me."

"Kate?"

She let out a slow breath. "Yeah?"

"He took Will from you. Don't let him take Sam too." Celeste's voice was soft but firm. "Forget about Martin Kentala. He's in the past. You can tell Zach the truth and let that be the end of it."

"Uh-huh." Easier said than done.

"I'm serious. Go enjoy your night with Sam, and I'll call you tomorrow."

After disconnecting the call, Kate remained at the table. Her fingers folded and refolded the corner of a placemat as she thought about what Celeste had said. Martin was out of jail. He'd served his time and was moving on with his life. How he'd managed to cross paths with Zach, Kate had no idea, but it didn't matter. She'd tell Zach who he was, and that would be it.

As Kate sat there, her insides still burning, she knew she had to find a way to let go of the anger. Martin Kentala only had the power to ruin her night if she let him. Celeste was right. Kate had waited so long to be with Sam. She couldn't waste one more minute of her time on Martin. He didn't deserve it.

She came up behind Sam at the stove, hugged him, and rested her cheek on his back.

"Whatever you're making smells amazing."

"Your call—everything okay?" he asked without turning.

"Yup." Kate nuzzled into him. "I'm with you now, so it's better than okay."

Sam spun around and searched her face. He leaned forward and kissed her. "Okay, but I meant what I said." He gave her a crooked smile. "I'm not just here for the hot sex. I'm here for anything and everything you need me for." He winked. "But especially the sex."

Kate swatted at him playfully. "I'm starving. When does the chef think dinner will be ready?"

"Impatient, I see." Sam glanced up at the clock. "Ten minutes, I think." He hooked his arm through hers. "Let me show you to your table."

He pushed open a set of French doors that led to a small deck with an incredible view of the lake.

Kate let out a gasp. "Oh, Sam, it's beautiful."

He'd set the table with a white tablecloth and linen napkins. A vase filled with freshly-picked flowers was surrounded by candles that flickered inside hurricane glasses. A balmy breeze blew her hair gently away from her face, and the sun, just dipping down over the water, washed the sky with shades of orange and purple. It was all wonderfully peaceful, the air filled with the sound of the gentle lapping of the lake below her. Sam pulled out a chair and gestured for her to sit.

"I promised you a romantic dinner, and you should know, I'm an overachiever." He reached for a bottle of wine and poured a healthy amount into her glass. He leaned in over her shoulder, moved her long hair to the side, and placed a soft kiss on her neck. "Relax. I'll be back to serve dinner in a few."

The angst of Martin's release from jail began to ebb away. As she sipped her wine and stared out at the water, the tension in Kate's body lessened and she started to relax.

"Too many people only look at their food and don't enjoy it in every way possible," Sam said when he reappeared, holding two plates high in the air. "Close your eyes."

Kate did as she was told. She heard the sound of a plate being placed down in front of her, the whoosh of her cloth napkin as it was snapped open. The smell of dinner wafted toward her, and her stomach grumbled. Her appetite had returned.

"Keep your eyes closed," Sam said. "It will heighten your other senses. What do you smell?"

Kate inhaled and thought carefully. "Fish. Garlic. Maybe onion? Peppers—green peppers … no red peppers. A hint of lemon. There's another smell that's familiar, but I can't place it."

"Anything else?" Sam asked.

"There's sort of a nutty smell. Like rice, maybe?"

She heard the faint scraping of a utensil against her plate.

"Open your mouth," Sam said as he whispered into her ear.

Kate couldn't help but smirk. "You're going to feed me?" She felt his fingers on her lips.

"Shhh. Behave." Sam was attempting to sound stern, but his tone made her release a nervous giggle instead. "Hey, c'mon, stay with me." Kate could picture his scrunched-up face as he chastised her. "And keep your eyes closed. No peeking." She felt the metal tines gently tap her lips. "Now, open up."

"Okay, okay." Kate opened her mouth and then closed it around the forkful of food. She let out an appreciative moan as the flavors exploded in her mouth. "Oh, wow. This is delicious."

"So, what do you taste now?"

She considered it for a moment. "Fish, but one that's delicate and not overpowering. Maybe grouper?" Kate moved the food around in her mouth while she figured out the flavors. "Definitely peppers. Green *and* sweet red peppers, I think. Oh, olives. That was what I couldn't figure out before. A somewhat … salty olive. Lots of garlic. Just the right amount of onions. Maybe shallots. And there's a spice I can't put my finger on. Maybe that's the slight taste of lemon I detect." She swallowed. "Did I pass?"

Kate's eyes were still shut, but then she felt his lips against hers. Soft. Gentle. Barely a whisper of a kiss. Sam was right. With her eyes closed, every sensation she had was heightened. A longing built inside her—a need for more. Blindly, she reached up until she felt Sam's face. She pulled him closer.

Finally, he left one last lingering kiss on her lips and pulled back. "I want you to eat while it's hot."

Kate let out a deep sigh as she came back to reality. "Ah, is that sea bass?" she asked, glancing down at her plate.

"Correct. You did pretty well. The spice was coriander, and the olives are Kalamata olives which *are* a little salty. It did have a squeeze of lemon too. You were also right about the rice, but I didn't give you any of that in the forkful you got." Sam placed his napkin in his lap. "You're allowed to eat on your own now."

Kate picked up her fork. "It looks—and smells and tastes—amazing. I'm impressed with the chef."

Sam topped off Kate's glass and poured himself some wine. "When I first became a food critic, that was one of the exercises I always tried to do. Not just see what someone had prepared but let all my senses enjoy it. Because does it matter how good something *looks* if it doesn't taste good?"

Kate had never thought of that way. "You're right. I guess it doesn't."

While they ate, the conversation flowed. Like their phone calls, except Sam was sitting across from her. Even better, now Kate knew he was hers. He was easy to talk to, and he didn't push for her to tell him what had been bothering her when she arrived.

When they finished eating, Sam brought the dishes back into the kitchen and returned with two small slices of her cake. "Dessert number one."

He set the plates on the table with a mischievous grin that told her everything she needed to know about what he had planned after the cake.

He took a bite, held her gaze, and licked his lips. "Just as good as I remember."

Was he talking about the dessert or thinking about their night in the city?

When Kate was finished and laid down her fork, Sam reached for her hand. "You know, it's your first time here, and I never did give you a proper tour."

Kate offered a coy smile. "That's true, you didn't."

Sam led her back through the kitchen and into a tastefully decorated family room where a large stone fireplace filled one of the walls. He gestured to the floor in front of it. "When it gets cold, we're going to spend a lot of time right here."

"Horizontal?" she asked, a suggestive smile on her lips.

Sam shook his head, pretending to scowl. "Oh, you naughty

girl." Before Kate could respond, he clapped his hands. "Come on now, let's keep the tour moving."

He popped open the doors to a spare bedroom, a small bathroom, even a hallway linen closet. He waved his hand over them with the flourish of a game show host presenting prize options.

"This is all very nice, Sam." Kate tipped her head to the side. "But there's still one room you haven't shown me yet."

He wagged his index finger in the air at her. "You're quite astute. We are nearing the end of our tour, and it's quite possible I may have saved the best room for last."

Sam pushed open the double doors to the master bedroom. White candles flickered throughout the dark room, bathing everything in a warm, serene glow. Kate's eyes scanned the room to see rose petals had been scattered over the top of the king-size bed. Sam leaned in and pressed a button on the CD player that sat on the dresser. Soft music played.

She reached for his hands. "You weren't kidding about being an overachiever."

Sam's expression turned serious. "You deserve this and so much more. I want to give you everything."

A slow smile grew on Kate's face. She moved to the bed and then pulled Sam down with her.

"The candles and the rose petals and the music—all very nice."

She locked eyes with Sam, pulled his shirt over his head, and tossed it to the side. She let out a contented moan as she ran her hands up his back.

"But I have *everything* I need right here. I love you, Sam."

At that moment, Kate didn't need him to respond. The look he gave her right before his lips found hers told her everything she needed to know.

* * *

As she laid with her head on Sam's chest, Kate could hear the steady thumping of his heart against her ear. She didn't want to keep anything from him.

"Knowing I was going to see you tonight wrapped my whole day in this happy glow." Kate sat up and rested her hand on the side of his face. "What happened before didn't have anything to do with you. Or with us."

Sam nodded ever so slightly and anchored his attention on her, waiting quietly to see if she'd continue.

Kate leaned back on her elbow. "I told you I spoke to Zach, and he understands it's time for me to move on. I think we're in a good place about you and me, but he asked for a favor."

Sam got an apprehensive look on his face.

Kate worked to set his mind at ease. "Nothing to do with us, at least not the way you think. When he brought it up, it didn't seem like a big deal. He met someone at the restaurant where he works, a customer, who was looking for some work."

"He wanted you to give this person a job?"

Kate nodded. "Exactly. Which, like I said, didn't seem like a problem. We're always looking for servers, drivers, set-up people. This guy, he came in Monday to fill out an application. I was out, and he gave it to Marcy."

Sam sat up and leaned his back against the headboard. "Okay."

Kate sat up as well, hugging a pillow to her chest. She crossed her legs underneath her and faced him.

"I was getting ready to leave tonight to come here, and I happened to see it. The application." Kate sucked in a deep breath. "I recognized the guy's name."

Sam's eyes narrowed. "Who is he?"

"I'm pretty sure it's the man who killed Will."

A loud puff of air escaped Sam's lips. "No wonder you were so upset." His forehead wrinkled. "I thought Audrey said it was a car accident."

Kate related how Will had pulled over to help the woman

with the flat tire and how he'd been hit while he was on the shoulder. "It was snowing. I asked him to come home early, but Will was the kind of person who always pulled over if someone needed help."

"He sounds like a good man, but were the roads bad because of the weather? It wasn't like this guy *tried* to hit Will, right?"

Kate shook her head. "No, but—I'm not saying it was *intentional*, but he'd been drinking all afternoon with his friends, smoking pot. He was stoned. His blood alcohol was twice the legal limit. Sam, he wasn't even old enough to drink."

Sam winced. "How old was he?"

"Twenty. After Will died, they charged him with vehicular homicide."

"They convicted him?"

Kate shook her head. "He pled guilty. I was so relieved there wasn't a trial. I only went to one of his court dates. I slipped in, sat in the back." She lifted a shoulder in a shrug. "I had to see what he looked like. I had this image of a monster in my mind, but when I saw him, I was shocked. He was just a scrawny, scared-looking *kid*."

"So, how long did he get?"

"Twelve years, but it appears he got out a couple of years early. That was the call I got from Celeste. She looked him up online and was able to find out he was released a few months ago."

Sam lifted the pillow from her lap and pulled her close to him.

"I need to let it go, let him go," Kate said, shaking her head. "I almost let him ruin our night. I can't give him that much power over me."

"How much do you actually know about this guy?"

Kate's brow furrowed as she gazed up at him. "What do you mean?"

"Well, you said he was twenty." Sam's voice was soft. "That's younger than Zach is right now."

"Right …"

"I guess what I'm getting at—he was pretty young. Yes, he made a stupid mistake, and it cost you your husband and Zach, his father." Sam hesitated. "But Kate, he pled guilty. He accepted responsibility and served his time. What, ten years? If Zach likes this guy, maybe he got his act together while he was in prison."

Kate frowned. "So, what are you saying?"

"You said it yourself. He was a scared kid. Maybe if you consider that, it might make it easier to release it and let yourself move on. I know it was a huge life-altering mistake, but—"

"But what?" Kate cut in, her tone betraying her growing aggravation. Martin Kentala had made a *fatal* mistake.

Sam flinched, his lips pressed together tightly.

"I'm sorry," she said quickly, reaching for his arm. "I want to let this go. I really do. I want your opinion."

Sam studied her for a moment as if he was unsure he wanted to continue. "Kate, we were both young and stupid once," he said finally. "We didn't end up killing anyone, but maybe we were just lucky. I mean, hasn't Zach ever done something that made you wonder what the hell he was thinking?"

Kate considered what Sam was trying to say. Putting it all in the perspective of her own son did make her look at it differently.

Kate wasn't sure she could admit it to Sam yet, but he was right. Zach was a good kid, but he'd made errors in judgment. It hadn't cost someone their life, but he had done something stupid and life-altering.

He and Sarah hadn't known each other very long, and they weren't even out of college. Soon enough, there'd be parents. They'd have a newborn who'd need the constant attention of two people who had no idea how hard it was going to be.

This baby they were having was going to change all their lives.

CHAPTER 31

*K*ate had been trying to find the right moment to tell Zach about Martin, but the two of them had been like ships passing in the night. He'd left to visit Sarah on his days off. She'd been spending much of her free time at Sam's.

"You having dinner with Sam again?" Zach asked, pulling open the refrigerator door. He was dressed for work and hadn't brought up Martin. He hadn't even inquired about whether he'd filled out an application.

"Not tonight. Celeste's on her way over."

Zach was still staring inside the refrigerator, but Kate knew he wouldn't find much.

"I guess I'll head into work early and get something to eat before my shift starts," he said, grabbing a bottle of water.

"Sorry, I haven't done much grocery shopping this week. Can you bring me a bottle of water too, and sit down? There's something I need to talk to you about."

Zach stole a glance at the kitchen clock before slipping into the chair across from her. He slid one of the bottles toward her. "Okay, but if I want time to eat, I need to leave soon."

Kate didn't want to unload this on Zach before work, but he

needed to know in case he saw Martin. She wanted it over. Once Zach told Martin he knew who he was, they could close this chapter. They could all move on.

Kate fiddled nervously with the bottle before twisting the top off. She took a long sip. She had vowed that Zach would never forget his father. Though they often talked about Will, it was mostly memories or funny stories. They almost never talked about *that time*—when their lives were upended after Will left for work and never came home.

Dread pushed down on her. Kate drew in a deep breath, exhaling louder than she intended. "When your dad died, you were so young. There were things I didn't tell you then. As time went on, well, there didn't seem to be a good reason to dredge it all up."

Zach's face grew tight as if he hadn't expected the topic to be his dad's death. He averted his eyes, twisted the top off his water bottle, and took a long swig.

When he was little, Zach had once told her he didn't like to think about when his dad died because it made him so sad. Kate had respected that. She'd always kept the topic of Will light and happy. But now, she had no choice. There were things Zach needed to know.

Kate shifted in her seat. "The way your dad died—"

"A car accident," Zach cut in, his voice matter-of-fact.

"Well, yes … and no."

Zach narrowed his eyes. "What does that mean?"

"It was snowing the day it happened. I had taken the day off." Kate shrugged. "It wasn't even related to the weather, but when it started to come down, I called your dad at work." Her throat went dry, and she took a sip of water. "I wanted him to come home. The snow was getting worse, and I didn't like him driving in it. I never did. Maybe, somehow I knew …"

"Did he leave to come home?"

"He said he was in the middle of grading papers, but—" Kate

bit her bottom lip and then nodded. "He agreed to leave. Said he'd finish them at home."

Kate rubbed the side of her head and let out a heavy sigh. "Part of me thought that maybe—maybe if I hadn't called him, hadn't put him on the road at that exact time …" She couldn't say the words out loud. It had always weighed on her that if she had just let Will leave when he was ready, maybe he'd still be here.

Zach reached for her hand. "You couldn't have known what would happen, Mom."

"I know, but those are the kinds of things you think about. You beat yourself up, even though you know you can't change anything." Kate's throat tightened. Her feelings of guilt, ones she had managed to push deep down over the years, were making it hard to continue.

Zach shook his head. "It wasn't anything you did. You couldn't have changed the weather."

Kate stared down at the table as she tried to regain her composure. After several deep breaths, she brought her gaze back to Zach. "On the way home, your dad stopped at the store." A small smile tugged at her lips. "I wanted him to pick up hot chocolate. We were hoping the snow would stick so we could have a snowball fight—the three of us."

Zach let out a laugh. "Oh, I remember one of those battles. He creamed us."

Kate nodded. "Your father was the champ of snowball fights, for sure." She was grateful for the moment of levity, but she knew she needed to press forward or she'd never get this out. "Anyway, he was on his way home from the store, and he saw a woman pull over with a flat tire. He stopped to help her."

Kate wrapped her hands around her water bottle to give herself something to hold onto. "He got the spare out of her trunk. He was walking back around the car, and—and a car swerved toward the shoulder." Kate flinched. "The car hit him," she said in a soft voice.

Zach stared blankly at her. He seemed to be trying to make sense of what she was telling him, trying to reconcile this new information with what he thought had happened all these years. "So, Dad wasn't even driving when it happened?"

Kate shook her head. "No."

"So, the car that hit him, that was who killed him?"

"Essentially, yes, but not right away." Kate knew she had to tell Zach everything now that she'd started. "They rushed your dad to the hospital. He had a broken leg and a head injury. They set his leg, and they operated to stop the bleeding in his head and relieve the pressure. I prayed, I hoped that he would be okay, that he would come back to us. But, after the surgery …" Kate fought back the tears as those days in the hospital played in her memory like it was yesterday. "Dad didn't wake up. He was brain dead."

Zach sat with his head in his hands. He stared down at the kitchen table as he appeared to be trying to digest the information he'd been given. Finally, he lifted his eyes to meet hers. "So, what does that mean? He was in a coma?"

"No. It means there wasn't any brain activity," Kate said in a gentle voice. "Dad's body was being kept alive by a ventilator, but without it, he wasn't able to breathe on his own."

"So, you made the decision to pull him off? Pull the plug?" Zach stared at her, his eyes narrowed into accusatory slits.

Kate leaned forward in her chair and her voice escalated. "It's not like you're thinking. Zach, he wasn't ever coming back. Essentially, he was *already* dead. His condition was incompatible with life. Those were the words the doctor used when he told us —" She caught her breath. "The machine was breathing for him, but your dad, the father you knew and loved, he was *already* gone."

Zach let out a puff of air and leaned back in his chair. His eyes brimmed with tears.

"Your grandparents and your Aunt Lisa—knowing the kind of man your father was—" Kate drew in a deep breath. "Because your father had been on the ventilator, his organs were still viable. They thought—I agreed—your father would want to help others. We made the decision to donate his organs."

Zach stared at her, a contemplative expression on his face. "So, Dad helped other people?"

"Yes."

"And what about the guy who hit him?" Zach's jaw was clenched. "What happened to him?"

Kate's heart raced. "He was a young kid. Younger than you, actually."

"How much younger?"

"He was twenty."

"So, it was because of the snow," he said. "He was a fairly inexperienced driver, and his car slid onto the shoulder because of the bad weather." Zach seemed to be explaining it to himself out loud. "Is that right?"

Kate hesitated and then took a sip of water before responding. "Maybe."

Zach's brow creased. He leaned in toward her, his arms folded on the table. "What does that mean, *maybe*?"

"The snow may have been a factor, but he'd also been drinking and smoking pot. His blood alcohol was twice the legal limit."

Zach flinched as if Kate's words had punched him in the gut. "What happened to him? Did he go to jail?"

Kate nodded. "He did. He pled guilty."

"Good. I hope he *rots* there."

"I felt the same way," Kate said. "Trust me, I did, but Sam made me see things differently."

Zach scowled and let out a snort. "Sam? What does he have to do with this?"

"The other day, when I went to his house for dinner, I was upset, and we talked about it."

Zach squinted at her. "It came up out of nowhere? After all

this time, you were upset about the guy who killed Dad? While you were with Sam?"

"It wasn't out of nowhere." Kate rested her head in her hands. "It appears he got out of prison a few months ago. I found out right before I went to Sam's."

Zach went silent for a moment. "How do you know he's out? Do you know where he is now?"

Kate met his eyes. "His name is Martin Kentala. He was in prison for ten years, but he got out four months ago. The information is online."

Zach cocked his head. "Why does that name—"

Kate's heart thumped wildly in her chest, perspiration beading on her forehead. "The guy who comes into your restaurant. You sent him to fill out an application for me to give him a job." She leaned over the table and reached for Zach's hand. "That's the man who hit Dad."

Her son's face tightened, and he yanked his hand away. "So, Dad's in the ground, and he's out walking free? Eating dinner at my bar? Having me *wait* on him?" His face screwed up in a look of disgust.

"I doubt he made the connection," Kate said. "I hardly think he would have come to my place of business to ask for a job if he did." She tried to reason with Zach the way Sam had done with her. "He served his time, Zach. I was as upset as you are when I found out, believe me. I was angry, *so angry*, but I realized he was just a kid when it happened. Sometimes when you're young, you make errors in judgment. You've never driven when maybe you shouldn't? Not at college?"

Zach wore a deep, ugly scowl, his eyes dark as he shook his head. "I'm not that stupid."

The look on his face scared Kate. "It's not only drinking and driving," she said, desperate for something to help him relate and understand. "I mean, you and Sarah are going to have a baby. You don't know each other that well and Zach, you have a genetic heart disease. A baby should be something you planned for. Tested Sarah first to find out if she carries the gene."

She saw a flicker in Zach's face that suggested he hadn't even considered that yet.

"I feel bad enough you got it from my side, but your father's side, they didn't have it. You had a fifty-fifty chance of getting it. If Sarah carries the gene, your baby will be *guaranteed* to have it."

Zach shook his head firmly. "I love Sarah, and she loves me. We'll work through whatever happens together. She knows I have a heart issue, and she can get tested. We'll test the baby, and if we have to, we'll watch over him or her. So maybe they won't be able to play sports. It won't be the end of the world. *My* world didn't end, remember? Neither did yours," he said pointedly. "But being young and having a baby, even one that wasn't planned— we didn't *kill* anyone, Mom. It's not even *close* to the same thing."

"I know it's not the same." Her eyes pleaded with Zach to understand. "I'm just saying Martin was young. He made a mistake. Yes, what happened was awful, but I went to court. I saw him. He was a twenty-year-old kid who looked petrified, but he took responsibility. He served his time, and he's out now. You liked him, so maybe he pulled himself together while he was in prison."

Kate released a long breath. "I realized the other night that holding on to this hurts *us*. We need to let go. Martin's trying to move on with this life, and we need to do the same. I'm not saying I'm going to hire him, but—"

"*Hire* him?" Zach asked, his tone incredulous.

"Of *course* I'm not going to give him a job. When you see him, just tell him—"

"When I see him?" He slammed his fist against the table.

Kate reeled back in her chair. For a moment, she wondered if maybe she shouldn't have told Zach about Martin. But Will was his father. He had a right to know.

Zach's jaw was set tight, his hands now clenched into fists on the table. "When I see Martin, getting a job will be the last thing he'll need to worry about." Darkness crossed his face, his eyes squeezed into tiny slits.

As Kate stared at him, the hairs on the back of her neck stood up. She had never seen her good-natured son this angry about anything in his entire life.

"When I see him, I'm going to *kill* him," Zach said, almost matter-of-factly. "*Then* we can move on with our lives."

Kate's mouth dropped open, and before she could close it, he had grabbed his keys off the kitchen counter and was racing out the door.

CHAPTER 32

*C*eleste was pulling into the driveway as Kate came flying out the door trying to catch Zach.

She was too late.

Kate yanked open the passenger door of her friend's car. She dropped into the seat and reached for her seatbelt. "We need to go to Zach's restaurant. I'll explain on the way."

To Celeste's credit, she didn't say a word. Just nodded, put the car in reverse, and headed to Attilio's. She waited patiently for Kate to catch her breath and tell her what the emergency was about.

She'd been as horrified as Kate had been at Zach's reaction.

As they sat in the restaurant's parking lot, Celeste shifted in the driver's seat to turn toward her. "So, is there a plan?"

Kate stared out the windshield and nibbled on her thumbnail. "I didn't think it all through. I just ... went. Well, I had you go."

The idea of Zach being violent had rattled her. She'd tried to convince herself it was merely a knee-jerk reaction. The shock of finding out information Kate should have told him a long time ago. Zach was blindsided—finding out his father hadn't died exactly the way he'd always thought. Learning Will had been brain dead and an organ donor. Discovering he'd actually *liked* the man responsible for taking the father he idolized from him. He'd chatted with him, pocketed his tips, tried to help him get a job. All those years Zach didn't have Will—holidays, birthdays, football games. The blame for that overwhelming loss fell squarely on Martin's shoulders.

Kate couldn't argue her son had more than enough reason to be angry. But his threat had taken it too far.

"Should we warn someone?" Celeste asked eventually. "Maybe you should go in and try to talk to Zach. See if he's cooled off."

"The thing is, I'm not sure I blame him for being upset." The disappointment pushing down on Kate's shoulders belonged to her. "I should have told him—"

"He was only a little boy when Will died." Celeste reached for Kate's hand. "It's understandable you wanted to protect him."

Zach had seemed so small and fragile back then. Or had it been Kate who was fragile? Everything that happened to Will had seemed far too adult for a child to absorb, to understand. *He died in a car accident.* It hadn't been the entire story, but it had been enough at the time. It explained why his beloved father didn't come home, why Will now had to watch over him from heaven.

And then, as the years went on, Kate wanted to preserve the happy memories for Zach. Revisiting the horrible details, facts he never once asked about, hadn't seemed necessary. Knowing how much his father had loved him—that was what Kate had decided was most important.

Over the years, Kate had offered to take Zach to the cemetery to visit his dad's grave. Father's Day. Even Will's birthday. He always declined, so she finally stopped asking. Kate never went herself. She couldn't accept the idea that Will was there, in a box in the ground. It messed with her hope that he was somewhere else watching over her and Zach.

Kate hadn't been to Will's grave since that cold, dreary day he was buried. Not even to see his headstone. His family had etched the date he was pronounced by the doctor as the day he died. Kate always wondered if it should have been the day of the accident.

She wasn't sure Zach even had an inkling of when Will died. He never asked. It wasn't an anniversary Kate ever acknowledged to him. When it rolled around every year, she couldn't fight the sick feeling that sat in her stomach until those two days were over. Why would she want to inflict that on Zach too? Kate always thought it better for him to be blissfully ignorant. The thirteenth of January, the day of Will's accident—just another day on the calendar. She'd tried to spare him. But had she made decisions for him that weren't hers to make?

"Kate," Celeste said gently after her prolonged silence.

"Just thinking," she said before meeting Celeste's eyes. "I tried to protect Zach when he was younger, but he's not a little boy anymore. I would never have lied to him if he asked, but he never seemed like he really wanted to talk about it."

"It's understandable. Why dig it all up? And if this Martin guy had never shown up, it wouldn't even be—"

Kate sat up straight, her attention riveted on the lone figure walking through the parking lot. The man was tall and thin, and unlike the families and couples that had trickled past them, he seemed to be by himself.

"I think that's him."

Celeste pointed her finger at the door. "Go."

"Excuse me," Kate called out as she hurried after him. "Martin?"

The man spun around, his hands still stuck in the front pockets of his jeans.

He glanced around the lot, confused. "You calling me?"

She was right. It was him.

"I was," Kate said with a nod. "Could I talk to you?"

Martin's lips were pressed together, his face tight. "What about?"

"My son Zach is a bartender here."

Martin's eyes narrowed at the mention of Zach's name.

She held her flattened palm to her chest. "My name is Kate. My husband was Will. Will Kennedy."

The air deflated from Martin's chest as he put the pieces together. He looked around apprehensively as if he was in trouble, then a pained expression crossed his face. "I'm sorry. You know, about your husband."

"I just want to talk. Really. I think it might be important for all of us."

Celeste pulled up beside them and rolled down her window. "You don't need me for this, Kate. Call me when you're done, and I'll come back to get you."

Kate held up a finger and turned back to Martin. "So, can we talk?"

When he slowly nodded, she turned back to Celeste. "Okay, I'll call you in a bit."

She and Martin shuffled silently side by side toward the restaurant.

Once inside, Kate spoke to the hostess. "I'm Zach Kennedy's mom. Would you happen to have an out-of-the-way booth I could use? Not for dinner, so I don't need anyone to wait on us. We just—just need a quiet place to talk. We won't take up a table for very long."

After the young girl showed them to a booth in an empty area of the dining room, Kate asked if she could send the manager over.

Kate stood to speak with him in a low voice. "I'm Zach's mom. We have a bit of a family emergency. Is it possible someone could cover for him for about ten to fifteen minutes so he could sit with us?"

She could tell from the manager's bewildered expression that her request was unusual.

"Please," she said. "It's important."

The look on her face must have convinced him. "Okay, but I can't spare him for more than fifteen minutes. I'll get him."

"One more thing," Kate added before he hurried off. "Can you not tell him it's his mom? Just tell him there's someone here that needs to talk to him."

The manager shot her a look, but several minutes later, Zach appeared.

"Mom, what are you doing here? You really don't have to—" His eyes drifted to the other side of the booth, his rage from earlier returning instantly. "What the hell are you doing with *him*?"

"Zach, sit. I think we all need to talk." Kate slid over in the booth and glanced up, her eyes pleading with him. This was as much for them as it was for Martin.

Her son stood frozen, his eyes skewering the man who had taken his father from him.

"Please, Zach," Kate said. "For me."

He hesitated, then let out an aggravated sigh and begrudgingly slipped in beside her. He glared at Martin, his face turning red.

"What the hell, dude?" he asked, his voice loud and angry. "Coming in here all the time—"

Kate reached for his arm. "Zach. Keep your voice down."

He shook his head. "No, Mom, this guy thinks—"

"I'm sorry, man," Martin blurted out. "I didn't know who you were. If I knew, trust me, no way I would've stepped foot in here." He let out a long hiss of air. "Definitely wouldn't have told you my life story—"

Zach huffed. "Right, your life story. Everything except the most important fact. That you just got out of jail—"

"You think I just bring that up?" Martin asked, a scowl on his face. "People know I've been in prison—they keep their eyes on me like they don't know *what* I might do." He shook his head. "I came here, ate dinner at the bar because you—you treated me like I wasn't some piece of shit loser. I mean, you even offered to hook me up with a job."

"I liked you," Zach said, his voice stretched taut with bitterness. "I wanted to help you."

Martin fixed his gaze down at the table. "Nobody, I mean *nobody*, has ever offered to help me." He glanced up, then rolled his eyes. "And me, I was such an idiot. Thought maybe somebody's gonna give me a break for once." He gestured at Kate. "I run off to apply for a job with you." He pursed his lips, screwed his eyes shut. When he opened them and found Kate's gaze anchored on him, he glanced away. "You must have thought it was a bad joke."

Kate couldn't even put in words for him how she had felt that day. "When I saw the application, your name—I was just—"

"I didn't mean for that to happen. I always wanted to say sorry, but—" Martin shrugged. "Words don't mean nothin'. My mom used to tell my stepdad that. I figured I had to *show* you I was sorry. Plead guilty. Do the time."

"So, you pled guilty to apologize? To us?" Kate asked in a soft voice.

"I *was* guilty. Plus, I figured there was probably kids who didn't have a dad anymore. Because of me." His glance flickered to Zach. "And yours seemed like a good one, the way he was helping that lady." Martin's mouth pulled tight, and he looked away. "I never had one. Mine took off, couldn't even wait till I was born. My mom, she tried to keep shit together, but—" Martin shook his head, a frown on his face. "Crappy apartments. Loser guys coming and going."

In an instant, Kate was propelled back to when Will died. Trying to manage her grief with drinking. If she hadn't caught herself, been so worried about Zach, could she have slid down a slippery slope? Taken Zach down with her? Without that turning point, she wasn't naïve enough to believe their lives couldn't have had a different outcome.

"It isn't easy to be a single mom. Trust me." Kate shot a quick glance in her son's direction.

There was a glimmer of compassion in Zach's eyes. Maybe he realized his life could be very different if Kate hadn't been strong enough to make a decent life for the two of them.

Martin bobbed his head. "I know she tried. Married my stepdad like he was the answer." He huffed loudly. "Man, was she wrong about him. They fought. I mean, *all* the time. Scumbag loved his booze way more than my mom. It was *bad*." Martin shrugged, tried to appear indifferent. "She'd throw him out on his ass, but he'd be back. Shit would start all over again."

He rubbed the side of his face, then let out a heavy sigh. "When I got to high school, I had to get the hell out of there whenever I could. You know, try to escape. I hung with a bad crowd, a bunch of older kids. No idea how I pulled off graduating, but you know, it wasn't like there was money for college."

Martin's gaze drifted as a small smile played on his lips. "I got a job fixin' cars. I was actually good at it." He gave a one-shoulder shrug. "Maybe I could've turned it around."

"So, what happened?" Zach asked pointedly.

"I was tryin' to save some cash to get my own place. Came home one day, my shit's on the front lawn. Locks got changed. Stepdad said I had to get out."

Kate reeled back slightly in her seat. "What about your mother? She let him do that?"

Martin leaned his head back and rested it against the booth. "If she crossed him, stuck up for me ... no way would I let her take the fall for me, but I didn't have no place to go. A bunch of guys I partied with let me crash."

Martin's leg bounced under the table, and Kate could feel the vibration as the table shook.

"That night, we were sittin' around, you know, doin' what we did. I was the only one who had a real job, but too many nights of partying—" He pressed his lips together. "Got myself fired." He crossed his arms in front of him on the table and then leaned in toward Kate and Zach. "I wasn't plannin' to drive anywhere, I *swear*."

"So, why did you then?" Zach's tone was sharp, accusatory.

Martin drew in a breath, then expelled it slowly as if buying himself time. "My mom—she called me that day. Said my stepdad found a number in her purse. A guy's number. It was for me, somebody she knew wanted to hire a mechanic. But my stepdad —he freaked. Called her a whore. Started yelling how no wife of his was gonna cheat on *him* with another guy. He threatened to kill her. My mom locked herself in the bedroom, and she was cryin', begging me to help her."

"I should never have got in the car," Martin said, a look of regret on his face. "Should have just called the cops, but c'mon, they don't take that shit seriously. It wasn't snowin' that hard, and I wasn't too far away, so I was gonna drive to her house. I was on the way there, and my mom called again. I could hear shit in the background. That bastard was tryin' to break down the bedroom door."

Martin closed his eyes for a moment, and when he opened them, they were wet with tears. "My mom was *screaming*—all freaked out. *Marty, what do I do if he gets in?* I told her, hang on, I'm almost there."

He slumped over. "Then, I heard it go off. The gun." Martin flinched in his seat and squeezed his eyes shut as if remembering that moment. "So fu—so damn loud. I can't say what happened right then, but all I kept thinkin' was *that asshole finally killed her, and I didn't do nothin' to stop him.* I pounded the steering wheel, started bawling like a little girl. My eyes got all blurry. My car must've drifted, and then—" Martin stopped abruptly, his gaze landing squarely on Zach. "Your dad," he said, his voice a whisper. "He was *right there.*"

Martin held his head in his hands. "I won't ever forget it. Don't *deserve* to forget it." He bowed his head as if he couldn't bear to meet their eyes. "You know the rest."

"What happened to your mom?" Kate asked.

"When the cops showed up, I told 'em what happened. They sent someone to check it out. My stepdad beat her up pretty bad but fired the gun to scare her. They got her to the hospital, told her to file a restraining order against him." He paused. "When I told my mom I was gonna plead guilty, she freaked out. Said she'd have nobody to protect her." Martin pursed his lips. "Not that I'd done a great job."

"But the restraining order? That would have helped, no?" Kate asked.

Martin snorted and shook his head. "Wouldn't have been worth the paper it got printed on. She needed to get away from him. Far away. Before my sentence started, I made my mom move to Florida to go live with her sister. She's still there. Now that I'm out, I'm tryin' to save enough cash to go see her." He held Zach's gaze. "That's why I was lookin' for a second job. It ain't easy findin' someone to take a chance on you when you got a record."

"Did you ever regret pleading guilty?" Kate asked. "There were … extenuating circumstances. You might not have gotten prison time." She wondered how she would have felt about that. But knowing the story now, understanding Martin's life, she felt sorry for him.

Zach was staring at Martin thoughtfully, waiting on his answer.

Martin's shoulders rose and fell with his deep sigh. "I was scared out of my mind to go to prison, but more scared not to. I had to take responsibility for what I did. It *was* my fault. I never should have been driving. I couldn't let myself forget what happened—so when I got out, I could be a better person. I even got a tattoo while I was locked up." He flipped his arm over and laid it on the table to show them.

WK. Never forget.

Zach expelled a deep breath. "I noticed you had that but had no idea—"

"I see it every day, so it can remind me I need to be different now," Martin said. "Doesn't change what I did, but I gotta make something of myself. For your dad."

Kate thought of Will's football team and the tribute they included on their uniforms. Martin wanted to change his entire life in Will's honor.

She rested her hand on Zach's arm. "I think that would have meant something to your father."

"Zach, I swear I didn't know who you were," Martin said. "I just thought you were a nice kid, easy to talk to. If I'd known who you were, I would've run."

"I was furious when I found out who you were." Zach shot a sheepish look at Kate. "I hate when my mom is right, but sitting here tonight, hearing what actually happened that night made a big difference."

Relief loosened Kate's shoulders. Zach's anger toward Martin would have only been destructive for him. And while she didn't want to believe he would have made good on his threat, all that hate inside wasn't good for anyone.

"I didn't deserve the time to talk with you, to try to explain, but I'm grateful for you giving me a chance." Martin shifted in his seat as if what he wanted to say next would be uncomfortable. "Do you think—could you both ever be able to forgive me?"

"It's hard to walk around with all this bitterness inside," Kate said. "Knowing what happened that day, from your side—it really helped me." She turned to Zach. "What about you—"

"I'm sorry to interrupt," the restaurant manager said as he

stuck his head around the corner. "I need Zach back behind the bar. We're getting busy."

With a curt nod, Zach slid out of the booth and glanced at Martin. "You coming to have dinner?"

"Only if it's okay with you."

Zach dipped his head. "It's okay with me."

Apparently, that was how her son planned to convey his ability to forgive Martin.

"What about you, Mom?" he asked. "Hungry?"

Kate shook her head. "I told Celeste I'd call her when we were done. I'll leave you both to it."

Zach leaned down and hugged her. "Thanks, Mom," he whispered before turning and heading back to the bar, leaving her and Martin alone in the booth.

"When Will first died, I was so angry at you," Kate said. "Why had you been so stupid to drive that night? So selfish? When you went to jail, I thought that would be it. I figured I'd never have to think about you again. But then, when I saw your name—the application, I realized that anger was still there, eating me up." She looked Martin straight in the eye. "I'm not angry anymore. You took responsibility and served your time. Your sentence is over. It's time for you to let yourself be truly free."

Martin shook his head. "I don't wanna be free from knowin' what I did."

"My husband was a great man, an understanding man," Kate said. "He taught eleventh grade English and coached football. He wouldn't want this for you. Just like he always supported his students and his players, he'd want you to move on so you could go out there and make something of yourself."

"That's the plan I got."

"What about your mom? How's she doing?"

"She's okay. She won't come back here, but you know, if I didn't go to prison, she might never have gotten away from my stepdad." Martin ran his hand across his face. "Might not even be alive. I thought about that when I was locked up."

"I'll bet she wants to see you." Kate gave him a small smile. "When you get a few days off from your other job, I'll buy you a plane ticket to go see her."

Martin's eyes went wide, then he shook his head. "No way. I can't accept that."

"I'm a mother too. I'm sure she's had her moments of feeling guilty. Of wondering if she hadn't called you that day, maybe you wouldn't have spent all those years in jail."

"Oh, I know she felt like that," he said. "She used to call me and cry that it was her fault."

Just like Kate had wondered about the part she'd played that fateful day. She reached into her purse for a pen and wrote her phone number on a napkin. "I'm serious about that plane ticket. Call me when you're ready."

"Why you being so nice to me? You should hate me."

"There's something about seeing you tonight that helped me understand. I know you didn't *mean* to hit my husband," Kate said, and she knew she meant it. "We all got hurt that night, but like you said, it got your mother away from your stepfather. It gave you the time and purpose you needed to straighten out." She pressed her lips together thoughtfully and held Martin's gaze. "We can live in the past knowing we can't change it, or we can look to the future and make the most of what we have in front of us."

Appreciation flickered across Martin's face. Kate thought about Sam and how he'd helped her see the situation more clearly. He'd convinced her to be open to releasing the anger she felt, and she'd been able to help Zach forgive. They'd all been set free that night.

For so long, Kate hadn't thought she wanted or needed another shot at love. Sam had made her realize she deserved it. It didn't have to change the way she'd felt about Will, but she'd given herself permission to love Sam too. He was what was in front of her. He was her future.

She and Martin slid from the booth, and as they stood there, she gave him a nod that confirmed she had forgiven him.

"I believe we all deserve second chances," Kate said, giving him a small smile. Then, she reached up and gave him a hug.

CHAPTER 33

TWO YEARS LATER

$\mathcal{A}$s Kate's gaze traveled around the room, it seemed surreal. All of it. The entire night was about her success.

She felt Sam's hand on her back as he came around and kissed her cheek. "Hi, beautiful. Max and team did an incredible job here tonight."

She nodded in agreement. "It's magical."

Her cookbook was being released, and the publisher was throwing a launch party. A swanky New York City loft transformed. Table after table of her recipes, presented within showcases of tulle and crystals. A sugar-spun fairytale. Invitees had begun to roam the room indulging in samples.

"I saw your parents," Sam said with a glance toward the table where Max's staff was checking people in against the final guest list. "They just got here."

"Oh, good. I'm glad they decided to get the car service to bring them in. Celeste just called too. She and Bruce should be here any minute, and the kids are driving themselves in. They're bringing the baby."

"Oh, good, I can't wait to see her." Sam gestured toward Max's assistant, making her way through the room, straightening tablecloths and directing the staff. "Abby confirmed that basket you wanted is in the back. The cookbook you autographed is in there too. It's all packaged up beautifully."

"Perfect. I can't wait to deliver it to Luisa tomorrow in person." She and Sam were spending the night in the city after the party and had tickets to the symphony the next day. Without Luisa bringing back her lost bag the day of the bake-off finale, there might not have been a cookbook.

"If that basket is what they sent out to some of the big guests that couldn't attend tonight, they'll be impressed." Sam leaned down and kissed her again. "As they should be. I'm so proud of you."

Kate felt a tug on her arm and turned. Marcy.

"Congratulations." She gave Kate a hug. "You look wonderful. Being a famous cookbook author agrees with you."

She and Marcy had decided a year and a half ago to close down the catering company. Between the cookbook preparation and helping Zach and Sarah, Kate had been running like crazy. Marcy had been ready to move on and give herself a well-earned break. "I proved what I had to prove to myself," she'd said. "I'm ready to go enjoy life."

"I'm not sure I'm famous, but I'm glad you made it." Kate gestured at the room. "Can you believe this?"

"You know I wouldn't have missed this," Marcy said, her gaze drifting around the space. "This place is gorgeous." She glanced down, and her eyes went wide. "And speaking of gorgeous, let me see that rock."

Kate obliged and daintily held out her left hand.

Marcy leaned down and ogled the engagement ring she now wore. "Sam, good job. This is absolutely stunning."

He gave Kate an appraising glance. "How could she wear anything less?"

Kate's parents joined the circle, greeting Sam and leaning forward to kiss her cheek. They already knew about the engagement. Sam had been old-fashioned and asked for their blessing before proposing. "What would you have done if they said no?" she'd asked when he told her. But they hadn't. Her parents were thrilled she'd found Sam. They thought he was wonderful.

"Congratulations, sweetie," her father said. "You probably thought this day would never get here, huh?"

"The last two years have been interesting, that's for sure," Kate said with a slight wince. "But I've enjoyed it."

"Enjoyed what?" Celeste nudged her way in while Bruce raised his hand, greeting the group.

As the crowd around Kate grew, her father placed his hand on her arm. "Your mother and I are going to mingle and check out this beautiful room." He smiled and patted his stomach. "Maybe indulge in a few samples. We'll be back."

Kate turned her attention to Celeste. "Isn't this crazy?"

"Crazy delicious. Goodies everywhere I look." She leaned into Kate and lowered her voice. "I'm kind of glad I brought the big purse."

Kate shook her head and laughed. "You know you can have whatever you want."

Celeste gave a slight shrug, her lips tugging upward at the corners. "It's a little game I play with myself. I convince myself there are only calories if I eat properly from a tiny little plate."

Kate hugged her. "I'm so glad you're here."

"You know I wouldn't have missed your coming-out party for anything. You deserve every minute of this success."

"Your baby bird's flying now, huh?" A satisfied smile slipped across Kate's face.

"You know it." Celeste leaned into her. "I never had any doubt you would," she said in a soft voice. Her gaze then drifted to Sam, who watched the ladies, no doubt wondering what they were talking about. "Aw, your poor fiancé feels left out. You want a hug too, Sammy?"

He laughed and put his arms out. "You know I do." He nodded at Bruce as Celeste leaned in to embrace him. "It's not like we didn't know they were a package deal, right?"

Celeste and Bruce were frequent visitors to the house on the lake. Sam cooked, and the four of them often spent weekends laughing and enjoying each other's company.

Sam had always accepted Kate's friendship with Celeste. He even acknowledged her supposed superpower that had predicted how he felt about Kate before he'd accepted it for himself.

"Everything looks so pretty," Celeste said, her gaze bouncing around to all the tasting stations. "Is Zach here yet with Sarah? They're bringing Jill, right?"

Kate nodded. "They are. Since everyone's here tonight, I told them they should bring her rather than try to find a babysitter or have to take her all the way down to Sarah's parents."

"Oh, I can't wait to see her." Marcy's face brightened. "I haven't seen her in months. She must be getting so big."

"She's walking all over the place." Sam threw an exaggerated wink in Kate's direction. "I'm pretty sure she said my name the other day."

"No way," Kate said. "Not until she says Grandma."

"That's so *complicated*. Sam is so easy to say. It would only make sense she'd say that first."

Kate rolled her eyes. Jill said simple words, so it wasn't out of the question she might have said his name, but Kate would never give Sam the satisfaction of acknowledging it.

"Are they getting ready to move into their new place?" Marcy asked. "I can't imagine how much you're going to miss them."

Kate glanced up at Sam. He'd been wonderfully supportive when she offered to let Zach and Sarah move in with her. Even though it had pushed back their wedding plans, he understood how strongly she felt about helping them while they finished school and found jobs. Kate hadn't regretted a single moment of her decision, but it was time for them to be on their own. It was time for her and Sam to move forward.

Celeste gave Kate a reassuring pat on the arm. "I'm not sure Grandma's going to make it when they go."

"I might not. I think I'm going to be traumatized not seeing Jill every day." Kate winced and then laughed. "Zach, too, of course. But I understand Sarah wants to be closer to her parents and her sister."

Kate had been relieved to find her new daughter-in-law's family warm and easy to get along with. Her parents, Jim and Melanie, were a perfect fit for her and Sam. The two families had meshed wonderfully together, even traveling together to Barbados for the intimate destination wedding.

"I'm sure her parents are looking forward to them being a little closer," Celeste said.

When both families sat down to talk about the pregnancy, Jim and Melanie had been as apprehensive as Kate. The kids were determined to make it work, so collectively, the parents had all agreed to help. Now that Jill was here, none of them could imagine life without her.

"They really are," Kate said. "I know it's been hard for Sarah's family having them all live with me. They make the drive often, but this will make it easier for them. At least once I move to Sam's, they'll only be twenty minutes away. And even though the baby will be in daycare while they're working, I'm sure Zach and Sarah are going to need some time to themselves. Melanie and I may have to duke it out for babysitting time. We'll have to babyproof Sam's house, but he can't wait." She squeezed Sam's hand. "Right, honey?"

"Only if I can teach her to say Sam before she says Grandma."

"Well, maybe she'll call you *Grandpa* instead," Kate said, giving him a playful poke.

"But, how could she? I'm not old enough—"

She narrowed her eyes. "Easy there …"

"There's no way you look old enough to be a grandmother, and you know it." Sam leaned over and kissed her.

"Oh, I don't care," Kate said, waving her hand dismissively. "I'm so proud of them. They both finished school, got good jobs. Now, they get to prove they can do it all on their own." Kate had been relieved Sarah and Jill had both tested negative for the genetic heart condition Zach had. That would certainly make it easier for all of them.

"You were a godsend letting them live with you while they finished school," Marcy said. "What about the house? You list it yet?"

Kate's gaze drifted toward the entrance to see if Zach and his family had arrived. "Not yet, but I'm sure—"

Max Preston had caught Kate's eye. He gestured her over.

Kate nodded at the group. "Won't you excuse me a moment?"

"Here she is, our wonderful bake-off winner and now cookbook author." Max leaned in and gave her a congratulatory hug.

"Everything about tonight has been wonderful. After so much time, to see my recipes in print is quite the rush."

"Your cookbook has been well received already. I have someone who wants to meet you." Max gestured at the man standing next to him. "Peter Symington, this is Kate Kennedy."

Peter was a well-dressed older man. His hair, mostly white, matched his eyebrows, and the smile on his well-worn face was warm and contagious as he greeted her.

"You're not the Peter Symington of Symington Baked Goods, are you?" Kate asked.

He dipped his head and extended his hand. "The one and only."

"Thank you so much for taking the time to come tonight," Kate said as she shook his hand. "I'm honored."

"It's very nice to meet you, but don't be so modest," Peter said, wagging his finger in the air at her. "Max was nice enough to send me an advance copy of your cookbook, and I was very impressed."

"Well, thank you. That means a lot to me. It's been a labor of love compiling all the recipes, testing them, taking the photos." Kate's gaze drifted to Max. "Deciding which ones to save for the *next* cookbook."

"Is that what you're hoping for, Kate?" Peter asked. "A whole line of cookbooks?"

"Well, I wouldn't *hate* it."

Peter rubbed his chin thoughtfully. "I was impressed with the creativity of your recipes, and I have something I want to discuss with you. A business proposition."

Kate couldn't help but smile. The last time she'd heard those words, Sam had been telling her about the bake-off. She remembered vividly the disappointment she'd felt when those exact words came from him. Now, hearing them come from someone with Peter Symington's reputation, Kate was intrigued.

"As you might know, Symington Baked Goods started out as a family business," Peter said. "We evolved fairly quickly, which was wonderful, but like many companies, we had to turn to mass production to be able to make a proper go of it. Now that we have so many successful years behind us, we want to go back to our roots a bit."

"That's wonderful you now have the means to do that. What would it entail?" Kate asked.

"We've been exploring adding a new line of premium cookies," Peter said. "They would come at a higher price to the consumer, but these cookies would feel more like something that came from your mom's oven."

Kate raised her eyebrows and grinned. "I love that idea."

Peter exchanged a knowing glance with Max. "That's good to hear. We're looking to create something new and different. Not the chocolate chip cookies that everyone's mom makes, but something unique and special—you know, those cookies you can't find anywhere else. Ones with the wow factor. We made some of the recipes from your book, just to test them out." He bobbed his head, and his white eyebrows shot up. "Kate, my staff gobbled them up. They insisted I come to see you tonight."

Kate felt her cheeks go warm. "Wow. I'm so flattered you all enjoyed them."

"That we did." Peter rubbed his hands together. "So, I mentioned a business proposition. I'm aware Diamond Publishing owns the rights to your cookbook, and I know that's the content as well. But when you mentioned *future* cookbooks … Kate, I was hoping maybe I could put Symington Baked Goods in line for some of your as-yet-unpublished cookie recipes."

Kate's mouth fell open, and she shuffled back a step. "Oh." For a moment, she was too surprised to say anything. When the shock subsided, her pulse quickened as she considered the potential. "Well, I suppose I do have a fair number of recipes that didn't make the cut this time. And I was experimenting the other day with some new ones." Her gaze bounced to Max. "My win in the bake-off was a contract for one cookbook, but I'm not sure …"

Max patted Kate's arm. "I think what Peter has in mind is a bit more than just a few recipes."

Kate's brow furrowed, and she shifted her attention back to Peter.

He met her curious stare with a whisk of a smile. "We're looking for someone who'll be not only the creator of the recipes but also the face of the brand."

Kate's eyes narrowed as she struggled to understand. "I'm sorry I don't—"

"Kate's Cookies," Peter said, waving his arms in the air in a dramatic flourish. "Don't you just love the sound of that? We want you to come on board to lead up the new division. *You* would be the Kate in Kate's Cookies."

She swayed on her feet, dazed as his words settled over her.

She blinked hard and laid her palm against her chest. "Oh, wow. That's—I don't know what to say."

Kate tried to be subtle, staring off as if she was digesting the information. She caught Sam's eye as he stood with Celeste and Bruce. He dipped his head to acknowledge her telepathic message had been received and made his way in her direction.

"Oh, honey, this is Peter Symington of Symington's Baked Goods," Kate said, trying to sound casual as if she hadn't just summoned him. "Peter, this is my fiancé, Sam."

Peter shook his hand and then gestured at Kate. "So, as I was telling your lovely fiancée, we want her to consider coming on board as the face and creator of our new premium cookie line. Kate's Cookies."

Sam's eyes widened slightly, and Kate knew he was probably as shocked as she was. "Wow, that's wonderful. I guess you've made the rounds trying the samples of her recipes here tonight."

"I actually tried some of them before the party," Peter said. "And she knocked my socks off. Isn't that right, sweetheart?" An older woman had sidled up beside Peter. "Kate, Sam, this is my wife, Liz. She's been making the rounds trying everything tonight. She's a huge fan."

"A *huge* fan." Liz turned to Peter, her eyebrows lifting inquisitively. "Have you asked her yet?"

"I have." Peter gave Kate a knowing smile. "I do believe she might be considering it."

"Oh, Kate, I hope so," Liz said, her voice lifting. "Maybe you could set up some time next week to get together with Pete and hammer out the details."

Kate tensed up and shifted her gaze to Max, her brows knitted slightly. She was uncertain what the protocol was here, but he was the one who'd introduced her to Peter.

"This is all up to you," Max said, giving her an approving nod. "But it's a great thing from my point-of-view. It will only drive demand for your cookbook. And I'm certain you have other recipes aside from cookies." He gave her a wink. "In case we want to do another cookbook of say, cakes and pies only ..."

Kate's shoulders relaxed, and she laughed as she turned back to Peter. "Well, okay, then. Next week would be perfect."

Peter pulled out a business card and handed it to her. "Call my secretary to schedule something when you're available. I'll let her know to expect your call."

As she took Peter's card, Kate noticed Zach coming toward her pushing the stroller. She raised her hand and gave a wave. "My son and daughter-in-law are here with my granddaughter."

"*You* have a granddaughter," Liz said, eyes wide. "I can't believe it."

Kate beamed. "She's the light of my world."

"Hey, Mom," Zach said as they edged closer. "Sorry, we're late. It took a while to get out the door with all the baby stuff, and then naturally, there was traffic trying to get through the tunnel."

Kate made introductions. Then she leaned down, unbuckled her granddaughter from the stroller, and swooped her up into her arms. "This pretty girl is Jill."

As she held her, Kate stared in awe into her innocent blue eyes and smiled. She'd loved every minute of having them all live with her, but there was something extraordinary about the bond she shared with Jill. It went beyond being her grandmother. They had a connection she could never quite put into words.

Kate's gaze drifted around the room. Everyone she truly cared about was there to celebrate her success. Wistfully, she realized that no matter how much time passed or how in love she was with Sam, it always felt odd that she couldn't share any of it with Will.

What would he think if he could look down and see how they had all changed? Did he know Zach now had a wife and daughter? She bowed her head against the baby's soft brown curls that looked so much like Zach's when he was little. Kate hoped wherever Will was, he could see Jill. He would have loved being a grandfather, lapped up every sweet minute with her.

On this night especially, Kate wanted to know if Will was proud of the woman she'd become since he died. Her mind drifted to Peter's offer. *Kate's Cookies.* Will would have thought that was incredible. Her heart needed to believe he was watching and celebrating right along with her. She craved confirmation he was there, still part of her life somehow.

Kate's eyes welled up, and she closed them for a moment. Then, remembering the flutter on her cheek years ago, she silently asked Will to send her some sort of sign.

When she opened her eyes, she blinked away her tears. Kate shifted Jill in her arms so the little girl faced out and could observe the room.

"Oh, she is just the most precious thing," Liz said, leaning in toward her. "Hello, sweet girl."

Jill's wide blue eyes watched her with curiosity and then fixed on the pendant Liz wore on a short chain around her neck. Fascinated by the vibrant colors, her chubby little hand reached for it.

"Oh, be careful," Sarah said, a warning in her voice. "Jill *loves* necklaces." She winced. "Loves to grab them and break them mostly."

"Oh, that's okay," Liz said with a smile. "I'm used to it. I have three grandchildren of my own. Do you like it?" she asked Jill, whose eyes remained hypnotized by the necklace. "It's pretty, right? It's a *butterfly*. Can you say butterfly?"

"Buh fwy," Jill parroted back.

Sarah's mouth dropped open, and the group cheered in surprise. When Jill saw everyone's reaction, she clapped her hands, absolute glee lighting up her small face.

"She's never said anything like that." Sarah shook her head in disbelief.

Kate wasn't quite as surprised as Jill's mother. Her gaze drifted toward the ceiling, and she bobbed her head, a grateful smile playing on her lips. Will hadn't missed her celebration, after all. He was still there, still part of all of their lives.

Happiness swelled inside her that Will knew all about the beautiful girl she held in her arms. Maybe Jill knew about him too. After all, she'd helped him send his sign.

CHAPTER 34

SIX MONTHS LATER

*Z*ach wiped the dust from his nose with the back of his hand. "I think this is the last of my stuff I want to take," he said, setting the large cardboard box on the coffee table. "I separated the rest into two piles. Trash and donate."

Kate was sitting on the floor, clearing out the cabinets in the wall unit. She stood and groaned. Getting up wasn't as easy as it used to be.

She reached into the box, a wistful expression on her face. "Your first football. I remember when your dad got this for you. You going to let Jill play with it?"

"Yeah, I feel like I'm kind of passing it down." Zach glanced around at the half-empty room. "It's so weird to see the house like this."

Kate had sold some of the furniture already and taken all the pictures off the walls. Sam was on his way over to help her pack up her clothes. Their wedding was in three weeks.

Her gaze drifted around the room as she nodded. "I know. It's hard to think someone else will be living here soon. So many memories." Kate reached into the box and pulled out a large manilla envelope. "What's this?"

"I was going to ask you," Zach said. "It's from Grandma and Grandpa, but it was on the top shelf of my closet, stuck in the back. It's addressed to you, but it doesn't look like it was ever opened."

"It's from my parents?" Kate asked, confused.

"No. Dad's parents."

"Oh." She hadn't heard from Will's parents in years. "I'm not sure what it could be. Go ahead and open it if you want."

Zach slid his finger under the sealed back flap and removed a folder.

Kate gestured at the note stuck to the front of it. "What's the Post-it say?"

Zach read from the yellow square, "*We weren't sure if you would ever want these, but just in case, we wanted you to have them.*"

"Hmm. What's inside?" she asked, settling onto the couch.

Zach moved his box to the floor, then sat on the coffee table in front of her. He opened the folder in his lap, a confused frown on his face as he shuffled through the contents. "It seems like it's a bunch of letters."

"Letters? From whom?"

Zach picked up the first piece of paper and laid the folder with the rest of the contents on the table beside him.

He began to read. "*I've wondered for many months what I could possibly say that would convey my gratitude for the selfless donation you and your family made. It was never far from my mind that your loved one had to die—*" Zach abruptly brought his gaze up to Kate. "Are these—you said Dad was an organ donor. Is this from someone who got one of his organs?"

Kate's stomach twinged as she considered the possibility. "Maybe. When everything happened, your dad's family was very much in favor of donating his organs. It was—" She bowed her head, remembering. "It was hard for me to imagine parts of him would still be out there. Somewhere else. I signed the papers because I knew it was something your dad would have agreed to, but I—" She gave her son an apologetic shrug. "To be honest, I never wanted to think about it again."

Zach studied her, a curious expression on his face. "Really? I think it's a great thing to be able to help someone like that. Now I kind of wonder who these people were. Are you okay if I finish reading?"

Kate steeled herself but then realized enough time had passed to soften the pain. This was about Zach's dad. If he wanted to know, she could handle it.

"Sure," she said with a quick nod. "Go ahead."

Zach found the place where he'd left off. *"It was never far from my mind that your loved one had to die for me to have the life I have today. I will always be eternally grateful as I'm sure in your darkest hour, organ donation was not an easy decision."*

Zach glanced up at Kate and offered a small smile of acknowledgment before continuing. *"I was diagnosed with poly-cystic kidney disease, which caused my kidneys to develop cysts that fill with fluid. I tried to manage it for many years, but eventually, they began to fail. For over three years, I needed dialysis three times a week to do the work my kidneys should have done. I needed it to live but strapped to a machine for hours at a time—it wasn't really living. I was on the transplant waiting list for almost two years before I finally got the call."*

Kate winced. "Oh, wow. That sounds terrible."

Zach nodded in agreement. *"After my transplant, I finally felt free. My passion had always been cooking. I had always wanted to make it my career."* He laughed, shot Kate a look. "This person sounds like you a little."

She smiled. "Yeah, that's kind of funny."

"My health and dialysis had always limited what I thought I could do. With my new kidney, I decided to pursue my passion. I opened up

—" Zach suddenly stopped reading, his brows knitted together as he skimmed silently.

"Opened up what?" Kate leaned forward on the couch. "Finish reading it."

Zach rubbed his hand against his chin as he continued. *"I opened up a catering company. I always tried to manage my disease by eating healthy and wasn't much of a baker. So, I got a partner who handles the desserts, and we're making a go of it. None of this would have been possible without the gift of life you so graciously offered."*

"Really?" Kate asked, a deep divot between her brows. "Must be a crazy coincidence. It can't possibly be—" She reached for the letter. "Is it signed?"

When Zach handed it to her, Kate's eyes skipped to the bottom. The signature had been crossed out with a black marker. "I guess the organ procurement group took out any identifying information." Her head was spinning. "Is it possible? I mean, do you think …"

Zach held out his hands and shrugged. "I don't know what to think. Marcy never said anything about being on dialysis before she opened the business?"

Kate rubbed her temples as she tried to remember. "I don't think so, but you know she can be pretty private. There *were* a few times I saw her taking some pills. Back when we first started." She gazed off as she tried to recall what Marcy had told her when she asked about it. "She mentioned something about being sick and finally feeling better. She said she took the pills because she wanted to stay that way." Kate held the letter up to the lamp next to her, trying to read the signature.

"Can you make it out?" Zach asked.

Kate frowned and shook her head. "It *has* to be Marcy, don't you think? I mean, it would be a crazy coincidence if your dad gave her a kidney and then she gave me a job." Kate nodded her chin toward the folder. "Read the next one."

Zach put Marcy's letter off to the side and reached for the one on top. He let out a deep breath and began reading. *"I will forever be grateful to you and your family for your decision to allow your loved one to be an organ donor. I am married with three children and was in end-stage heart failure. What most people don't realize about needing a heart transplant is that you don't make it to the top of the list until you're so sick you could die. My family watched me suffer, and it was agony for them."*

Kate scrunched up her face as she listened. She couldn't imagine which was worse—what she had gone through with Will or watching someone dying slowly over time, waiting for the one thing that could save them.

Zach continued, *"My husband was petrified I would die in his arms or when he wasn't with me. It's an awful feeling for a man to feel so helpless. He coaches high school football and was scared to death to leave me alone. He wanted to quit, but I wouldn't let him."*

Kate tipped her head to the side, her eyes narrowed. "Read that again."

"He wanted to quit, but I wouldn't let him."

She shook her head. "No, before that."

"He coaches high school football."

Kate pursed her lips and closed her eyes. "His name was Charlie."

"Whose name was Charlie?"

"Shh. I'm trying to remember his wife's name."

"Mom, who are you talking about?" Zach asked, sounding exasperated.

Kate put up her finger. "Hang on one second." She took herself back to the hospital—to the night of Zach's last football game. She could hear the coach's voice when he came up to her in the waiting room. *My name is Charlie. This is my wife, Janet.*

"Janet was the wife of the Knights coach. The one who did CPR on you when you collapsed on the field. He said they had three kids, and he told me that night his wife had heart issues too. That was why he was trained in CPR—he said he'd never had to use it on her. He told me to cherish my time with you, the way he did with his wife."

"I'm sure it can't be the same person."

"It sure sounds like it could be. If I remember correctly, I overheard the transplant coordinator saying the heart was staying local." Kate leaned forward and put her hand on Zach's knee. "Remember at the hospital—the doctor said you had an angel looking out for you?"

"I immediately thought of Dad." Zach's voice was soft.

"Me too, and I think maybe we were right." Kate's theory made her lips lift in a smile. "Dad saved Charlie's wife, and Charlie saved you." She nodded at the letters. "What else you got?"

Zach rooted through the file. "Hey, wait, what's this?" He pulled out correspondence that appeared to be typed on professional letterhead. "This looks like it was sent to Grandma and Grandpa in May of 1998."

"Okay, so a few months after Dad died. What does it say?"

"It's some information from the organ procurement people about where Dad's organs went."

Kate sat up straight. "Really?"

"Don't get too excited," Zach said, holding up his hand. "There's not much. *We gratefully acknowledge your selfless donation. Your loved one's organs saved the lives of five people.*"

"They told us at the hospital it looked like it would be five people. But they said it could change. Things happen at the last minute. That kind of thing."

"It gives some basic information about the recipients." Zach lifted his eyebrows and gave her a sly smile. "Let's just see what it says about the person who got Dad's kidneys."

Kate held her breath even though she already knew in her gut what it would say.

"Okay, one kidney and the pancreas went to a forty-year-old

man in Connecticut. The other kidney went to a *New Jersey woman*." Kyle glanced up with a smile. "How old is Marcy?"

"She's four years older than me. So, in January of 1998, she would have been …" Kate scrunched up her face as she did the math and factored in Marcy's birthday. "Forty-two."

Zach grinned. "Ding, ding, ding. We have a winner."

"I *knew* it."

"It looks like the liver went to a woman in New York, the heart to a New Jersey woman, and both lungs to a man in Pennsylvania. Oh, and both corneas went to a man in New Jersey."

"See." Kate jabbed the air with her index finger. "A New Jersey woman got your dad's heart. How old was she?"

Zach glanced down at the paper. "Forty-eight."

"So, that would have made her about fifty-five at the time of your football game. Sounds about right for the coach's wife." Kate eyed the folder, a small smile on her lips. She was now sure her theory was correct. "Read the rest."

"Okay." Zach let out a deep breath and reached for another letter. "*I was always in shape, so when I started having shortness of breath, I was surprised. I was only forty-three years old. A chest X-ray showed I had lung disease, something called pulmonary fibrosis, which damages and scars your lungs. Eventually, it felt like trying to breathe with someone's hand over my mouth and nose. There's no cure aside from a lung transplant, but I really had a hard time with that. I couldn't root for someone else to die. It didn't feel right.*

When my doctor told me I needed to get my affairs in order because I wouldn't live without a new set of lungs, I agreed to be put on the transplant list. I had a wife and two little girls, and I was worried I could die. I moved—" Zach's mouth went slack. He shot a look at Kate that said she wasn't going to believe what she was about to hear. "*I moved my whole family from Texas to New Jersey so my wife would have her parents to help her with the kids if I didn't make it.*"

Kate gave Zach a dubious stare. "I know it *sounds* like Sarah's family, but you said the lungs went to someone in Pennsylvania. What else does it say?"

He held up his hand. *"We got a call two months later that there was a set of lungs from a donor in Pennsylvania, which is where we were staying with my brother while we waited for our new house to be ready."* Zach glanced up. "Aha. So, they *were* in Pennsylvania at first."

"Right," Kate acknowledged but then frowned. "But the letter says the lungs were *coming* from Pennsylvania."

Zach scowled. "Well, that doesn't make sense." He continued reading. *"When we got to the hospital, we learned something had been wrong with them. The transplant was canceled. I went home to die, but a few days later, we got another call. This time the transplant happened. I can breathe again. I may not live forever, but I'll be blessed enough to see my two girls grow up."* Zach's eyes glistened, and he choked up. *"Maybe even live long enough to get grandkids someday if I'm lucky. This is because of your family and your selfless donation. I can never thank you enough. After everything we went through, my wife is even going back to school to be a nurse. We've decided to stay near both our families to enjoy every moment we get with them."*

Zach glanced up and exhaled. "Sarah mentioned once her dad had health issues when they lived in Texas, but she never told me what they were. Jim's got Dad's lungs. I can't believe this."

"Do you realize if they hadn't moved here from Texas and you had gotten one of those football scholarships, you and Sarah might never have met?" Kate frowned. "There would be no Jill."

Zach slumped over, held his head in his hands. "I would like to think we would have met anyway, but my mind's officially blown. Wait till I tell her." His eyebrows lifted. "There are a few more."

Kate threw up her hands. "Well, don't stop now. This is incredible."

Zach reached for the next letter. *"I was only nineteen when I* discovered I was in acute liver failure. I had been playing the violin since I was a little girl—"

Kate leaned forward. "I'm sorry. Did you say the *violin?*"

"Yeah, why?"

She let out a puff of air and gave Zach a head bob. "Keep reading."

"*I had gotten an audition with Julliard, which was my dream. I practiced obsessively. I didn't eat. I didn't sleep. Playing the violin puts an enormous amount of stress on your hands, neck, shoulders. Pretty soon, everything hurt. Instead of slowing down and allowing my body to rest, I tried to manage the pain I had with excessive amounts of Tylenol. I started to feel absolutely terrible, but there was no way I could stop until the audition was over. When I was finished, I collapsed. I went from my audition directly to the hospital, where the doctor told me I could actually die. All that acetaminophen had damaged my liver.*"

Zach glanced up. "Do you know who this is?"

"I think so. Keep reading."

"*They immediately put me on the transplant list. I've never prayed as much as I did that night. The next day they told me that miraculously there was a liver for me. If you had not agreed to organ donation, I'm not sure I'd be alive today. I don't think there's a way to truly express how grateful I am.*

"*After all that, I did get accepted to Julliard. I tell my story to my fellow classmates, so no one has to go through what I went through. It's my dream to play for the Philharmonic. If that ever happens, it will be because your loved one made it possible.*"

Zach rested the letter on the table. "So, you know this girl?"

"It's a long story, but I'm pretty sure I do. She lives in New York City. The final week of the bake-off—remember I had to take the bus in? She and I shared a taxi from Port Authority. I left something in the cab. Something important. She found it after I got out and brought it to me. I always thought she played a part in me winning that day." What was it Sam had said that day about finding an angel on the streets of Manhattan? A smile tugged at Kate's lips. "And she does play for the Philharmonic, which I guess is thanks to Dad. Sam and I actually went to see her play."

"Well, that's pretty cool." Zach shuffled the remaining letters. "Two more. You read them."

"Okay." Kate reached for the first one. *"I was diagnosed with type one diabetes at age sixteen. I managed to get by for many years with daily insulin injections. Later in life, I transitioned to an insulin pump and a glucose monitor. I kept to a strict healthy diet and managed to keep my diabetes under control. But by the time I was in my late thirties, it all started to go downhill fast.*

They put me on the transplant list for both a kidney and pancreas. After nine months on the list, I got the call. Because you decided to donate these organs, I am now healthy and free of the symptoms of diabetes. It has been so long since I could eat whatever I want that it is still hard for me to accept some days. I work for a company that—" Kate groaned under her breath.

Zach gave her a hard stare. "I'm assuming this one is someone you know too?"

"Oh, yeah, I do." Kate picked up where she left off. *"I work for a company that publishes cookbooks, and I'm so used to letting my wife be my taste-tester. Someday I'll accept that I can have a piece of cake or a cookie without worrying about my blood sugar. It's a hard habit to break.*

"You think it's your publisher, Max?"

Kate rolled her eyes. "Who else would it be, right? He does live in Connecticut, and you said the recipient was what, forty when the transplant happened? Max and Sam went to college together and are about the same age, so that fits. Now that I think about it, I never saw Max try much of what we tested for the cookbook. Even before the contest, Sam said it was Max's wife who tried everything and raved about my desserts."

"This is insane." Zach rubbed the side of his head. "All these letters have been sitting in this folder, in my closet. For years. All these people, and we never knew." He then said what she'd been thinking. "It's like Dad somehow sent these people to us."

Kate nodded slowly. "I don't know what else to say. Imagine that. Your father has rendered me speechless, and he's not even here. But it's impossible to think this was all just a coincidence."

"Read the last letter."

Kate picked it up. *"When the doctors told me I could lose my sight, I had pretty much accepted it. It had been deteriorating for some time and had gotten to the point where nothing helped. I changed my life to accommodate the news, but then my eye doctor told me there was a possibility of getting a cornea transplant. I always thought—"*

"Hey, you two." Sam leaned against the doorframe and glanced first at the papers scattered on the coffee table and then at Kate. "What are you doing?"

"Oh, hey, honey, you're here. Zach and I are just—"

"What I mean is …" Sam's narrow gaze was fixed on the paper in Kate's hand, his forehead creased in confusion. "How do you have my letter?"

CHAPTER 35

*K*ate's eyes dropped back down to the letter. Sure enough, looking at it again, she recognized his handwriting. Sam too? Dazed, she stood and staggered toward him.

"I don't—I can't explain any of this."

"Come here." Sam took the paper from Kate's hand and held her up as his gaze drifted to Zach. "Where did you both get this?"

Zach gestured toward the folder on the table. "You'd better sit down with her. I wouldn't have believed any of this if I hadn't seen the proof with my own eyes. None of it makes any sense."

"Okay," Sam said, his voice wary as he led Kate back to the couch. She sank back down into the cushions while Sam settled next to her. He rested his hand on her leg, an expectant gaze on Zach. "So, go ahead. Explain."

"I was cleaning out my old room." Zach leaned toward Sam, his forearms on his thighs. "Packing up stuff that I wanted to take and sorting the rest. I found a large envelope on the top shelf of my closet. Tucked against the wall. It was from my grandparents —my dad's parents. It was addressed to my mom, but it had never been opened."

"I don't remember putting it there," Kate said, her shoulders rising. "I don't even remember getting it in the mail. The first year after Will died—" She shook her head as she took in the bewildered expression on Sam's face. "It was a blur."

She tucked her leg under her and turned to reach for Sam's hand. "The accident. Will had a head injury. They operated, but —" Kate swallowed hard, her throat bone dry. "He was brain dead, Sam. They wanted to know if I would be willing to donate his organs." Her mouth pulled tight, her admission on her lips. "I didn't want to. Selfish, I know, but I just—I couldn't deal with it. His parents, his sister, they convinced me it's what Will would have wanted." Kate laid a palm on Sam's cheek. "They were right. I knew that. I signed the papers, but I listed Will's parents when the organ donation network asked for contact information. I wanted to forget it had ever happened."

Sam slumped over, his head bowed down as he stared at the floor. "So ... the cornea donation?" he asked, bringing his gaze up to search her face. "They came from Will?"

Kate dipped her head slowly.

Sam sat back and ran his hand through his hair. "Wow, okay. This is a lot to take in."

Zach stood and reached for his box. "I'm going to leave you two to talk. Mom, I'll call you tomorrow. I won't say anything to Sarah yet."

Kate met her son's eyes with a nod. "Okay, sweetie. Give Jill a kiss from me."

"I will."

When she heard the front door shut behind him, Kate leaned her head against Sam's shoulder. "I'm sorry you had to find out like this. Obviously, I had no idea."

Sam put his hand under her chin, tilting her head up. His eyes probed hers. "How do *you* feel about it? Does it change the way you feel—the way you feel about me?"

Kate shook her head firmly. "No, of course not. I *love* you. This doesn't change that. I just never knew—never thought—"

Sam rested his hand on his forehead. "I wasn't keeping anything a secret from you, I swear. I didn't tell you about the surgery because, honestly, it was so long ago, I don't think about it much. I check in with my eye doctor once a year, and that's about the extent of it."

Kate's winced slightly. "So, were you ... blind?"

"I had something called Keratoconus. It affects the shape of your corneas, and over the years, I had glasses, contacts, hard lenses. Finally, nothing worked anymore. My vision was blurry. I was seeing double. At the time, I owned the restaurant. I was still cooking and—" Sam let out a heavy sigh. "I started to become a danger in the kitchen. So, when I was offered the gig at the newspaper—"

"The food review column."

He nodded. "Right. I took it. I figured even if I couldn't see—"

"You could smell, and you could taste," Kate said, finishing his thought for him, the corners of her mouth lifting. It all made sense now. "That was why, that night at dinner—"

"I'd made my mind up that I would find another career that would still be centered around food," Sam said. "I sold the restaurant and bought into the other group of restaurants as an investor." He let out a puff of air. "Oh, and I set my wife free because whether I could see or not, there was nothing about that relationship worth keeping."

"So, the surgery ..."

"I had pretty much accepted my fate when my eye doctor told me a cornea transplant would help. In fact, the first time he mentioned it, I said no." Sam shrugged. "But then he brought it up again, and something, I don't even know what—I changed my mind and said okay." Sam held Kate's gaze. "I know you said it was hard for you, but it was a selfless thing you did. I'm sure Will helped other people too."

"You have no idea, Sam. This whole story is even more astonishing than the fact that you have Will's corneas."

He pulled back to look at her. "What do you mean?"

Kate gathered all the letters into a pile. She then moved to sit on the coffee table across from Sam, exactly where Zach had been sitting when they read them.

"So, one of Will's kidneys went to a woman who opened a catering business," she said, her eyebrows lifting. "A woman who took on a partner to make all the desserts."

Sam pursed his lips. "Okay, I see where you're going with this. Did Marcy ever say she even had a transplant?"

"Not exactly." Kate handed the letter to him. "But she said something that makes me think it's definitely possible. The age, her location. It all fits. I'm pretty sure Marcy has one of Will's kidneys."

"C'mon, even if she did have a new kidney, what are the chances she would have gotten Will's?"

Kate shot him a look. "You mean, the way *you* have his corneas? Hang on tight. There's more." She pulled the second letter. "When Zach collapsed on the field during the football game, the Knights coach ran out and did CPR. He pretty much saved Zach's life."

Sam's eyes narrowed. "Don't tell me he had an organ transplant too."

"He didn't, but I'm pretty sure the letter is from his wife. At the hospital, the coach told me he was so well-trained in CPR because his wife had heart issues."

"Okay, now you're stretching. That could be anyone—"

"It could be," Kate agreed with a nod. "But did I forget to mention the woman wrote that her husband was a *high school football coach*?" She handed Sam the next letter so he could read it for himself. "Go ahead. Read this one."

Kate stayed silent while he scanned the page.

"Luisa?" Sam met Kate's eyes, a baffled expression on his face.

"What are the odds you would have met the person with Will's liver in a taxi in New York City?"

"What are the odds of any of these?" Kate asked, throwing up her hands. "Much less *all* of them?"

"There's more?"

"It appears Zach's father-in-law has Will's lungs."

"Jim too?"

Kate nodded. "Yup. And had they not moved the family here, maybe Zach and Sarah wouldn't have met. Who knows, maybe there was even a reason why the first transplant didn't work out for Jim. Can you imagine if the two of them hadn't gotten together, if we didn't have Jill in our lives?"

Sam sucked in a deep breath, then exhaled. "But it's not like Will could have played any part in—"

"He was still on the ventilator when they made these decisions," Kate said. "The organ transplant network, that is. At that point, we weren't even positive where any of his organs were going."

"So, is that all of them?" Sam asked hesitantly. "Any other surprises?"

Kate handed him the last letter with a lift of her shoulders. "Did you know Max had type one diabetes?"

Sam shook his head as he skimmed the letter. "No. I didn't know him that well in college. He was actually my roommate's buddy. I do remember that night at the restaurant—I was trying to get him to try your desserts. His wife mentioned something about him finally being able to have a taste without worrying. I didn't know what she meant." He huffed. "My head didn't exactly go to organ transplant. I thought maybe he'd been trying to lose weight." Sam crossed his arms against his chest and continued to shake his head. "I just don't understand how any of this could be possible."

"It's not logical," Kate said, her face serious. "That doesn't mean it all didn't happen. It's like Will was—somehow watching over everything."

Sam stood and paced as if that might help him figure it out. Kate knew he was looking for an explanation he could wrap his arms around, but he wouldn't find what his brain needed. There was only one possibility. Will.

"But how could he have planned all this?" Sam raised a hand in her direction. "I mean, you meeting me? How could Will have known that would even happen?"

"I don't have the answer, but think about it," Kate said, standing as well. "Despite what Celeste thinks, the only reason I met her was because I was at the hospital when Will died. If it wasn't for her, I would never have known about the job with Marcy."

Sam rubbed his chin thoughtfully. "Well, if it wasn't for Will's kidney, it sounds like there wouldn't have been a catering company."

"You're right." Kate reached for his arm. "And it's because of the catering company that I met you."

Sam tipped his head, studying her thoughtfully. "So, you honestly think Will *planned* for us to meet?"

Kate lifted a shoulder. "Maybe. Indirectly, Celeste led me to you. But think about it, Sam. Without you, I wouldn't have entered the bake-off. I wouldn't have the cookbook or the deal with Symington."

Sam went quiet as he considered it. "So, you're saying you think somehow Will had a hand in all of it?" He slid open the door to the backyard. "I need some fresh air."

"I know it's hard to believe, but what other explanation could there be?" Kate asked, following him. "The odds of all of this, knowing everyone who got his organs, you getting his corneas— that's way too big of a coincidence."

"Maybe it was some sort of divine intervention?" Sam gestured for Kate to sit in one of the patio chairs. He took the other chair and pulled it so he could sit across from her. "Let me ask you something," he said, leaning forward. "Do you think somehow Will knew he was going to die?"

Kate pinched her lips together with her fingers as she thought about it. "The day it happened? I don't think so. But—"

"But what?"

"When Will and I got married—" Kate squirmed in her seat. "I don't know, Sam. It doesn't feel right to talk about some of this with you."

He rolled his eyes. "Would you stop? Every time I look at you, it's through your husband's corneas. I think we're way past feeling uncomfortable talking about your marriage to Will. I owe him a debt of gratitude I could never repay, and nothing will ever change the way I feel about you."

Kate swallowed hard and met his eyes. "Okay. When you and I first met, there was something about the way you looked at me." She held his gaze. "I felt drawn to you. Every time I saw you, it was the same."

"You think—you think I was looking at you the way Will did?" Sam hesitated, then glanced away. His shoulders sagged. "Do you think maybe you were really falling in love with him again and not me?"

Kate slid forward in her seat and grabbed his hands. "No. Don't think that. Maybe that was what caught my attention. Made me realize you were someone I needed to know more about. Trust me, I love *you*, Sam. Every single thing about you. Even Will's corneas are part of you now."

There was no need to bring up the vows Will had made on their wedding day. At the time, Kate hadn't thought too deeply about what he'd said. But now? She could still hear his words. *For the rest of your life, I intend to take care of you and show you just how much I love you.* Not his life. *Her* life. Had Will somehow managed to keep that vow?

301

And then, with a start, Kate recalled what else he'd said. *Even death won't stop me from loving you.*

She gazed off thoughtfully and then dipped her head in a grateful nod. Will's organs had gone to people who'd played important roles in her life. Zach's life too. In her heart, she knew. Will had kept his promise to love her, to always take care of her. Even death hadn't stopped him.

Kate moved to Sam's lap, her eyes locked on his as he wrapped his arms around her. As he held her tight, a sense of peace swelled inside her. She now had no doubt. Will had loved her enough to send her Sam.

CHAPTER 36

TEN YEARS LATER

"*I* think that might be my new favorite restaurant." Kate was pleasantly full, a content smile tugging at her lips.

"Really? Mine too." Sam inserted his key into the lock. "We'll have to go back with Celeste and Bruce."

He pushed open the front door, and as they stepped inside, the house was cloaked in darkness.

In an instant, Kate heard the familiar clicking of nails racing toward them. A large head butted up against her thigh. "We're home, Tuck." Kate reached down to pet him.

The dog's tail wagged furiously, whipping first her legs and then Sam's. His brown eyes gazed up expectantly, then he turned and sprinted down the hallway toward the kitchen.

"What's with him?" Kate asked as they followed him.

Sam shrugged while fighting a smile. "You wanted a puppy. What do you expect?"

"He's not really a puppy anymore—" Kate's foot landed

squarely on Tucker's squeaky toy. Stumbling, she reached for Sam's arm. "We probably should have flicked on the lights."

In front of her, the kitchen was pitch black. The blinds to the deck were closed. There wasn't even a hint of moonlight to illuminate her path.

"I mean, seriously, I can't see a thing," Kate said, her steps cautious. "Hon, hit the switch, would you?"

When the room lit up, a chorus of voices exploded. "Surprise!"

Kate stuttered backward, her mouth slack. Her birthday wasn't even until the following weekend. Shaking her head, she now realized she'd been deliberately led astray by her husband and best friend. Hushed conversations conveniently overheard. They'd left Kate convinced they were in cahoots to throw a party the following weekend at Celeste's house.

This explained Tucker's exuberant behavior. A houseful of people who might drop food.

"Happy birthday, honey." Sam placed a kiss on her cheek. "So, how does it feel?"

"Well, I'm not *quite* there yet, but age is just a number." Kate's lips lifted in a playful smile. "You should know. You hit sixty before me."

They'd been married for almost ten years, their relationship loving and uncomplicated.

"Happy birthday, Grandma." Jill threw her arms around Kate's waist.

Sam gave his wife's shoulder a squeeze and then made his way toward the French doors that led to the deck. Soon, Kate heard music playing. She could now see the moon reflecting off the lake and their backyard lit up. The chatter of voices outside mingled with Sam's playlist.

"Were you surprised?" Jill asked, the little girl's eyes lighting up.

Kate nodded at her. "I was. You all got me good."

"Hey, Mom, happy birthday." Zach came up behind his daughter, leaned in, and gave Kate a hug.

"Thanks, sweetie. Where's Sarah?"

"She's putting Aidan to bed," Jill answered for her dad. She thrived on being the big sister.

"Yeah, the little guy was nodding off. We tried to keep him up for you, but he wasn't going to make it. Hope it's okay they're in your room."

"Of course." Kate scowled. "I'm disappointed he's asleep already."

"I'll check on them, but I doubt he's still awake." Zach laughed. "It wouldn't surprise me if Sarah's in there sleeping next to him. We forgot how hard a baby could be, probably because we had you to help with Jill."

Tucker swept by them just then, absolute glee in his eyes.

"How 'bout you bring the dog outside for me?" Kate asked Jill as she reached for his collar.

The little girl nodded and took control. "Let's go, boy. *Outside*," she said, her voice commanding and authoritative.

Kate had to laugh. Jill was growing up to have way more confidence than she'd had as a child.

"How is it the birthday girl doesn't have anything to drink?" Celeste sidled up next to her and handed her a glass of wine.

"You deliberately tricked me—you and Sam. I was firmly convinced the surprise was happening next weekend at your house."

Celeste lifted her shoulders as a satisfied smile slipped across her face. "You still underestimate me after all these years."

Kate sipped her wine. "Is Bruce here?"

"We're all here," Celeste said with a nod. "Ben's here with Mia. Wait until you see how much she's popped. Two more months, and you won't be the only grandmother in town."

"It's about time. What about Bella?"

"She's out back with you know who." Celeste was not a fan of her daughter's boyfriend. So much so that she barely ever said his name. "I'm surprised he wanted to come, to be honest. You might want to hide the good silverware."

"Celeste." Kate admonished her friend with an eye roll.

She shrugged. "I'm just sayin'."

"You should give him a chance. It might make all the difference." Kate couldn't help but think of Martin and how far he'd come. "You know Martin's wife is expecting a baby too."

"Another one?"

"Yup, although Jen said this is it. I guess it's rough being pregnant with the humidity down there. She's dying."

Martin had moved to Florida to be near his mom, and shortly after, he'd met Jen. She knew about his past and had expressed her gratitude to Kate and Zach.

"It's because of both of you that I have the husband I have," she'd admitted after their wedding. Martin had invited them, which was touching, and Kate and Zach had made a weekend of it. It had been February, cold and dreary when they flew out of New Jersey and headed to eighty degrees.

Jen kept in touch regularly. Martin had a hard time singing his own praise, but she wanted Kate and Zach to know his promise to make something of his life had not been forgotten.

"What about the business?" Celeste asked. "Is it open yet?"

Martin had found a partner and was opening a car repair shop. "I think they're putting the final touches on it now." Kate's gaze drifted as Sam came toward them.

"Hey, Sammy. Am I hogging the birthday girl?" Celeste asked.

"Nope, you're good. Just need to get some stuff out of the garage refrigerator."

"Too bad he took you to dinner first." Celeste gestured toward the backyard. "You should see the spread he and Marcy put together."

Kate glanced around. "Where *is* Marcy?"

"Outside in the back." Sam pulled open the door to the garage and lifted his eyebrows. "And yes, the spread is quite spectacular."

As she and Celeste went out the French doors and down the stairs to the yard, Kate took in the decorations and small candlelit tables set up on the grass. "Is all this your doing?"

"Maybe." Her best friend smiled. "Not quite as elaborate as the wedding setup you had, but not a bad effort if I do say so myself."

"It's beautiful." Kate's gaze drifted to Jill standing near the water's edge with Marcy's granddaughter, Ava. Tucker was fixated on whatever she had in her hand. "Jill, sweetie, keep an eye on Ava. And whatever you do, don't let Tucker go swimming."

"We're being careful," Jill called back. "Grandpa gave us some bread to feed the ducks. And I told Tucker if he goes in the lake, he's in *big* trouble."

"Don't worry. I've had my eye on them." Marcy leaned in and gave Kate a hug. "Happy birthday."

"Well, thank you. Is the rest of the family here?"

Marcy spun around and pursed her lips. "They're here somewhere." Her gaze settled, and she pointed. "Over there with Bruce and Zach. I saw Sarah's family. Is she here with the baby?"

"They're in my bedroom. Sounds like Aiden nodded off. Maybe Sarah too." Kate laughed.

"I'm sure it's not easy with the baby, but at least Jill's old enough to help." Marcy raised her eyebrows. "Seems like she might even be running the whole show."

"No kidding." The awe Kate felt when Jill was an infant had never lessened. Her eyes drifted to the tables set with food. "I heard there was quite the spread out here."

"Where'd you hear that?" Sam came up behind her, balancing a large tray on his palm.

"A handsome birdy told me."

When Kate looked at Sam, she still saw the man who'd walked into her office all those years ago. The one who made her cheeks flush and her heart race. Though he now wore glasses, Sam still had that way of looking at her that made a room disappear. It had nothing to do with Will's corneas. What Kate felt for Sam had a life all its own.

"He's got all your new cookies out," Marcy said with a nod. "Kate, they're amazing."

Celeste spun around to look and then scowled. "You've been holding out on me?"

Kate held up her hand. "The samples *just* came in yesterday, *and* I got the proof for the new cookbook. Desserts in the Insta-pot."

"Amazing." Marcy shook her head. "I don't know where you find the time. Is that your fifth or sixth one?"

"The seventh, if you can believe it. Even Max is surprised how well they're selling. He said he can't retire until I stop putting out new ones."

Kate felt a tap on her shoulder. When she spun around, a sleepy Sarah stood there with a wide-awake Aiden. "He insisted on staying up to say happy birthday to you, Grandma."

Kate reached for him. "Hey, Aiden. You giving your mommy a hard time?"

Sarah stretched her arms above her head and let out a yawn. "How old was Jill when she started sleeping through the night?"

Kate shrugged. "Who remembers? Go ahead and get something to eat. I've got him." She scanned the backyard. "Your parents are over by the big tree eating with your sister and her husband."

As Sarah staggered off, she bumped into one of the lit tiki torches. Kate gasped, but Zach had raced over to steady both his wife and the flame heading for the grass. He held up his hand in Kate's direction. "Don't worry. I've got her."

Kate let out a deep breath and squeezed Aiden. "Your poor Mommy's exhausted." She watched as Zach guided his wife into a chair beside her father.

Kate couldn't help but smile when she saw Jim, knowing that a little bit of Will came with him. When he died, the idea of him being an organ donor had been hard to accept, but now the bigger picture was right in front of her. It wasn't only Jim he'd helped. It was also his family and Sarah's sister's family. It was Zach and his kids. It was because of Will that Marcy's family had their wife, mother, grandmother.

She thought back to what Lisa had said at the hospital. *Burying him with his organs when he could do something good for so many seems wrong. A waste.*

Kate had pondered it obsessively over the years. She'd been tempted to say no when Will died, but would fate have allowed that? Her entire life had unfolded in the glorious way it had because she'd said *yes*. Had she not listened to Will's family, not known in her gut it was what her husband would have wanted, a completely different life might have been waiting in the wings for her.

It wasn't something Kate wanted to imagine—different people surrounding her, not having the career she loved. No Sam by her side. It hadn't always been easy, but as Kate soaked in her friends and family, contentment settled over her. She wouldn't have chosen a different life for herself. The one that had found her was perfect.

GOING HOME

*K*ate felt a force push her upward. A whoosh of release, and she was freed from her physical body. Slightly disoriented, she looked back and stared at the frail frame lying on the bed. It looked old and tired and … empty. She now felt weightless, the heaviness gone.

She reached out to touch Zach's shoulder, but he didn't turn to acknowledge her. Something was wrong.

He was holding her hand, talking to her. "It's okay, Mom. I know you were ready." His voice was low, his shoulders sagging. "I'll see you again when it's my time. Tell Dad I said thank you." He choked back a sob. "I love you."

Now Kate understood. Zach's words meant she was dead, but it made no sense. She felt incredible, more alive than she had in years.

She held her palm against Zach's cheek. He flinched, then closed his eyes. His hand reached up, his fingers rubbing his face in a gentle circular motion. He'd felt her.

As he nodded, a small smile tugged at his lips. "I know this isn't goodbye," he said in a whisper, his words soft but sure.

Kate was relieved. Sarah and the kids would help Zach

through this, but he knew she would watch over them all. Much like they both believed Will had done.

They'd never told anyone what they'd found in that folder. Not that they worried others would think them crazy, though there was a bit of that. They'd feared relationships might change if the recipients knew, placed a burden of guilt they didn't want anyone to feel. So instead, they'd tucked their insight away, something special they shared. Sam knew, of course, but she'd never even told Celeste.

There was no other explanation for what had happened with Will's organs. Kate believed, without a doubt, he'd played a part in taking care of her and Zach even after he was gone. It had brought them both to the same comforting conclusion—death wasn't the end.

After Sam passed away, Kate was ready. Even though she loved her son and his family dearly, she'd lived her life. It was time, and every hope Kate had was pinned on being reunited with the people who'd been so important in her life.

She and Zach had often joked about Will and Sam being up there together or wherever they might be. Were they friends? Celeste was there too. She was sure her best friend was getting a kick out of seeing Kate's two husbands together, probably laying bets on who Kate would be with once she died.

Kate had a feeling she wouldn't have to choose.

She'd been blessed to have been loved by two incredible men. Despite how devastated she'd felt when she lost Will, it hadn't broken her. She'd survived. It had taken time for her and Sam to get together, but it had been worth the wait. What they'd shared for almost twenty-five years fulfilled Kate in a way she wouldn't have thought possible.

Will had married young, naïve Kate. She'd deeply loved him, but when she challenged herself later, she couldn't admit she'd loved *herself* as much as she should have. His death had forced her to figure out exactly what she wanted from life. She had gone forth and conquered.

By the time she married Sam, Kate had blossomed into the woman she was meant to be.

She remembered what Celeste had said when she married Bruce. *The woman Ed married isn't the same woman Bruce married, but both those women deserve to be happy.* It was true, and both Kates *had* been happy. An abundance of love, a son she adored, grandchildren who filled her heart with joy, and the kind of career most people only dream about.

Her success would be her legacy. Zach now worked for Symington's and would ensure the household name that *Kate's Cookies* had become would continue without her.

As Kate prepared to leave the life she knew behind, she felt only overwhelming gratitude. She had no regrets.

Soon, surrounded by a humming and buzzing sensation, Kate felt herself being gently pulled away. There was no fear, only curiosity. As she moved away from her physical body, a sense of freedom enveloped her. Off in the distance, she saw a brilliant whiteness. It beckoned to her.

She was pulled, more deliberately now, through a tunnel, almost as if she were being summoned. Euphoria overwhelmed her. The beautiful light—it was waiting for *her*. A foggy mist led into stillness, and then the light expanded out in front of her. With it, the humming now became more musical. A beautiful sound, unlike any Kate remembered.

Thoughts and memories swirled around her, a kaleidoscope of the life she'd just lived. There was an overwhelming sense of self and harmony. Now Kate knew. She'd taken this warm, comforting journey many times before. She was going home.

Anticipation swept through her as she approached the gateway to the spirit world. Lights—orbs of energy—drifted toward her. As they came closer, they sent her images and thoughts. The shapes changed into people. They assumed their human appearance so Kate would recognize them without fear or apprehension.

Those in the back were hazy as one soul moved to the front. It was Will! The many lives they'd spent together tumbled over each other. These other existences had been lost to her when she incarnated. In this realm, they came rushing back. Vivid memories of each lifetime were imprinted on her soul.

Will had been her husband many times before, but Kate could now see clearly how one life had played an important role in his purpose for this one. When she'd met with her soul circle to plan this lifetime, he'd shared his desire for karmic payback. Despite his plan to depart early, Kate had chosen to marry him because of lessons she still needed to learn to help her soul evolve.

Kate could now recall the life they'd shared when an accident in the snow had paralyzed Will. She'd been left to take care of him, the farm, and their animals. She had no idea how they'd survive, no memory she'd agreed to play a part in the lesson her husband needed to learn in that life.

He'd been unable to run their farm, and Will's domineering personality in that life had struggled. Friends and family stepped in to help, but he needed to learn to relinquish control and welcome their assistance. Ultimately, his disability led him to feel gratitude instead of bitterness. The experience had helped his soul evolve.

Kate now saw the rest of them as they stood beside Will. There was Max Preston, who'd been Will's uncle in that lifetime. His appearance shifted, and she nodded in recognition when she saw him in the faded brown hat he always wore to plow their field.

Sarah's father, Jim, was there as well. He took on his appearance from that life to show himself as the neighbor who'd owned the plot of land beside theirs. Jim smiled at her and reached up to wipe his brow. His other arm cradled a basket of corn he had helped pick from their farm.

The others from that difficult lifetime huddled behind them. When they changed form, Kate recognized Janet and her husband, Charlie. They'd been friends who planted their crops. Marcy and Luisa were church members who'd helped take care of their horses.

As that lifetime replayed in front of her, Kate's soul felt overwhelming appreciation. The emotion was even stronger after the roles they'd all played in her most recent life.

She could now understand the reason behind Will's accident and resulting brain death. Those who had helped them in that previous lifetime on the farm were to be repaid in this one. Will's soul had played a part in guiding Kate to consent to the organ donation. Now it made sense. His organs were meant to give the recipients additional time and perspective. In turn, they'd agreed to help the family Will left behind. They had all played a part in laying the foundation for Kate's future.

Sam's orb moved to the front, and Kate felt uneasy as his appearance shifted. He now was Kate's husband in the lifetime where Scarlet Fever had cost him his sight. He'd refused to let Kate help him as he became surly and resentful. She'd held fast to her wedding vows, refusing to leave him, but his misery made him incapable of reciprocating. She could still remember the disappointment and frustration she'd felt as his wife. He hadn't honored his soul contract to learn from his disability. He'd let her down.

She could now recall planning her most recent life and Sam's desire for another chance. His soul needed to make amends, to show her the love he'd denied her then.

Sam had promised he wouldn't repeat his past mistakes. He'd committed to meet the challenge of blindness this time and move past it, and Will's soul had agreed to help him if he succeeded. By shifting careers when he thought he would lose his sight, Sam had set the wheels in motion for a future with Kate. He'd been gifted Will's corneas, and his new job as a food critic was what had placed him in her path.

Now, it was also clear why Sam had continually slipped away. As frustrated as Kate had been at the time, that had been her soul's doing. With her own lessons to learn around overcoming loss, achieving independence, and establishing her sense of self-worth, she'd set conditions around giving Sam another chance. Laid out rules. She needed to attain her own measure of success first.

Sam had agreed to hold back, to suppress his true feelings. He'd promised to wait for Kate's sign she was ready, that she'd achieved her goal. When she won the bake-off, her crystal trophy had sent rainbows of light not only across the room but also deep into Sam's subconscious. He'd known she was ready to give him his second chance.

Now Sam's appearance changed again, and he was the husband she'd had in the life they'd just shared. Love swept over Kate. He'd made good on his promises, and their time together had left her with nothing but happy memories.

Oh, it's so good to see you again, she told him.

I've been watching over you and the family, waiting for you to return. I'm glad it didn't take very long.

It was hard for me without you. Kate didn't still feel the emotions she'd felt on Earth but did have the memory of how much she had missed him when he died.

You were ready to come home.

She agreed. *I was, except it was difficult to leave Zach and the grandchildren. Jill is going to law school.*

When Sam smiled, it was just as she remembered. *I know. Will and I both saw her receive the acceptance letter—a full scholarship. Zach was dancing in their kitchen.*

No fair, Kate teased. From this side, her two husbands had both been able to see a moment she'd missed while in her human form on Earth.

Zach knows you'll watch over him and the family. You'll still have part of them all in this world.

Souls were not all or nothing, forced to make a choice to be on one side or the other. When they departed for a new life, they always left a piece behind in the spirit world.

Until it was Zach's soul's time to return home, Kate would have the energy he'd left on this side. The same was true for the others still living on Earth. While their human counterparts mourned her death, they'd all sent their soul energy to welcome her back.

Zach and Martin now made appearances as that energy allowed them to show themselves. Again, Kate was taken back to their soul circle planning prior to this life. She could now recall Martin's soul's decision to play a part in causing Will's death. He'd agreed to take responsibility, and Zach's lesson in this lifetime had been to find forgiveness.

Kate also knew why it had been necessary, the slate of a previous life that still needed to be wiped clean.

Zach had been her son, and Sarah had been Martin's daughter. The two had been married in that life as well, but their time together had been short-lived.

Scenes from that life played out, and Kate could see the moment Zach inadvertently tipped over a kerosene lamp while pitching hay in their barn. She observed the fire as it spread quickly and saw Zach manage to escape. But what Kate could now see was something Zach had been unaware of as he watched the structure burn. His wife had come to the barn looking for him and was trapped inside. She'd been pregnant with their first child, and both she and the baby had died.

Their souls had dissected the actions Zach took next when he returned. It was then that Kate learned he'd feared retribution from Martin over the death of his daughter and unborn grandchild. That was why Zach had abandoned his home and family and disappeared. The fire had been an accident, but Zach's self-imposed guilt at not saving his family punished him more than Martin ever could.

The actions he'd chosen had taken a toll on Kate in that lifetime as well. Word had gotten back to her that her only son had been alone when he died of influenza.

Losing her child had destroyed Kate in a way she hadn't been able to overcome. She'd used alcohol to ease her pain but could never drink enough to fill the emptiness she felt inside. Eventually, her husband in that life left her. Kate had defined herself as a mother and a wife, but when she was neither, she felt she had no purpose. Her self-worth in that life became non-existent.

She had drifted aimlessly until she finally drank herself to death. Her soul had then returned to the other side early, and while Kate wasn't met with judgment, she was regretful of her decision to give up. Her soul had much to take from the experience, but in reality, she hadn't escaped anything. The lesson still needed to be learned. She just had to start over again with a new body in a new existence.

Kate had chosen to confront loss again in this recent life, and Will's purpose had provided her the opportunity. She knew now they'd gone through the miscarriage first, so Will could be there to support her. To help prepare her. But his death had been Kate's real challenge. She needed to endure it to learn to make better choices and find her own purpose.

Will's departure could have easily sent her spiraling down the same path as her previous life. She could have chosen to succumb to her misery just as she had done before. And she almost had. Kate could now recall viewing that possibility on one of the screens in the selection room. Her life and her son's had looked very different.

Zach smiled at her now, and she realized there was a reason he'd chosen Kate to be his mother. She recalled the night he'd woken her up as he cried by the side of her bed. He'd been put in her life to help her realize giving up wasn't an option. It was because of him that Kate had found the strength to push forward.

Jill's energy then appeared and gripped one of Zach's hands. In her, Kate now recognized the soul of the baby she'd miscarried. Jill's soul conveyed to her that she'd agreed to return during Kate's lifetime, specifically to be born to her young, unprepared parents. Kate had been guided to let Zach and Sarah move in with her. It was her opportunity to briefly play a parental role to the soul she'd lost before birth.

Zach's other hand gripped Aiden's energy—Jill's brother had the soul of the child Sarah lost in the fire. They'd been given another chance to be his parents, and Kate had the opportunity to finally be his grandmother.

She would miss these beautiful children but was grateful for her time with them on Earth. A wondrous lifetime had unfolded for her. For Zach too. Will's death put them both on the paths they were always meant to take.

That included meeting Celeste, and Kate recalled their souls planning their time together. She'd been shown the necklace Celeste would be wearing when they met—silver angel wings hanging in the hollow of her neck. They were to let Kate's subconscious know she was meant to play an important role in her journey. Celeste had chosen a similar lesson for this lifetime so she could support Kate. Her friend had been her rock, the lens through which Kate saw herself.

Celeste's soul moved forward, and the energy flowed between them. Oh, to be back wholly with this beautiful essence! As part of the same soul circle, they'd been together many times. Siblings, mother and daughter, best friends.

Kate knew it was almost time to move on now. She'd return to her soul cluster and see her parents and the others. Then it would be time to analyze the life she'd lived, the decisions she'd made, and what she'd learned.

As the group in front of her faded to the background, Will's soul came forward. He'd been patient. The others had gotten their chance to greet her, but it was time he had a moment all his own.

Their souls had no need for familiar appearances. As two masses of brightness, they whirled around, then enveloped each other in a brilliant white light. It was an embrace of a spiritual essence, unlike any she'd ever encounter in her human form.

Though their time in this past life had been cut short, Will had played an essential role in helping Kate's soul learn and evolve. She was filled with an overwhelming sense of peace and love as he shared his message with her.

Welcome home. I've missed you

FROM THE AUTHOR

Thank you for reading *When Wings Flutter*. If you've enjoyed this book, a rating or review would be much appreciated. Reviews and referrals help other readers find my novels and allow me to keep writing them.

If you enjoy mystery and/or suspense, please also consider checking out the *Investigation Duo* series:

Where the Truth Hides – Book 1
The Dark Inheritance – Book 2
Memory Hunter – Book 3
For Just a Minute – Book 4 (coming in 2022)

About *When Wings Flutter*

I don't always tell the back story of how my books came to be. Mostly because if my readers knew what rattled around in my head, it might scare them!

I've always been fascinated with life after death, reincarnation, and things that can't easily be explained. I believe it started with a term paper on life after death for my eleventh-grade English class. My initial research was written on index cards, and the hefty stack wrapped in a thick rubber band came back from my teacher with one word: "voluminous." At the time, I had to look up what that meant, but the real explanation for my extensive research was obvious. I was obsessed with what I found.

If you've read my Investigation Duo series, you may know I'm intrigued with what DNA testing can uncover. Several years ago, I had a reading with a medium, and I spoke to her about an adoptee I'd been helping. This woman had always wanted to know more about her birth parents but died before she got those answers.

"Does she get to know who her birth parents are now that she's passed away?" I asked the medium. I'll never forget her response. "Oh, she knows who they are. They're in the same soul circle and have been in many lifetimes together. In this life, they just chose a different type of relationship because of the lessons they each needed to learn."

Yup. Now you're starting to see the whispers of inspiration for *When Wings Flutter*.

But there's more to this story, and it arrived with one of those proud mother moments. My teenage son had gone to get his driver's license. Standing there in the DMV, the woman asked if he was willing to be listed as an organ donor.

That boy of mine didn't hesitate for a second. "Of course," he responded as if she'd asked a silly question. "Why wouldn't I? It's not like I'll need them if I die." Indeed.

Organ donation can be a touchy subject. Though some situations offer the possibility of using a living donor, most of those desperate for a chance to survive need someone else's loved one to pass away.

I had already finished writing this book when I discovered the obsession that is Tik Tok. It was there that I stumbled across a sweet, smiling face talking about her need for not one organ but five! **Sarah Granados**/@SavingSarah is one of the toughest and most inspirational warriors I have ever come across. I'm sure many of her followers feel the same, but I felt an immediate connection to her. (And this was before I even knew she was a fellow kitten foster mom!)

I'm not sure I'll ever forget the tearful video she posted. She was offered organs and couldn't make it from her home to the Miami transplant team in time. I immediately invited her to move into my home in South Florida! She gets her nutrition through a central line, and I don't cook much. I figured we would be a perfect match.

Alas, we were not destined to be roommates. She's now looking to the midwest for her miracle, but she's more than aware her chance to live comes at a cost to her angel donor's loved ones. But as my teenage son so eloquently stated, no one needs their organs once they leave this existence. But others here desperately do.

I hope that in telling this story, I've enlightened people to the plight of those like Sarah. If you're not already, I hope you'll sign up to be an organ donor (www.registerme.org) and share that choice with your family. Those that can selflessly think of others while enduring their worst moments are true heroes.

If this book piqued your interest, I strongly suggest you read *Journey of Souls* by Brian Newton, PhD. It was there that I began my research for this novel, although it wasn't where it ended. I read everything on the topic I could get my hands on and found myself fascinated with the similarity in people's stories.

There were days I felt this book wrote itself, and I sat mesmerized as it unfolded on my computer screen. I have a regular group of beta readers who always read the early drafts of my books. It's their feedback that helps polish my manuscript into the final version.

One of my first readers is always my brother. I remember sending him this manuscript and warning him it was very different than my other books. "It's more of a romance," I told him. "I'm not sure you'll like it."

But, when he was done, his impression was vastly different. He loved it. "I wish you wouldn't bill this only as a romance," he said. "It's really a story for anyone who's lost someone they love."

And once we hit a certain age, who doesn't have someone they wish was still here? If we believe an emotion as powerful as love can't die, that those we've lost are still part of our lives, the ache of missing them might be a little less painful. It gives us hope that when it's our turn, they'll be waiting on that other plane of existence to welcome us back.

And who knows? After we celebrate our joyous reunion and take a brief interlude to reflect, maybe, just maybe, we get to make a plan to share yet another lifetime of lessons with the people we love.

ACKNOWLEDGMENTS

To **Mark Summers**, you had the patience of a saint when I became all-consumed with telling this story. For that, I am truly grateful.

To my editor, **Jonas Saul**, who continues to amaze and motivate me. I'll never forget that Sunday morning when I got your notes on this novel. I always thought this story was special, but you helped me realize I wasn't the only one who thought so. The feedback you gave me will be a high bar to hurdle for future novels.

Thank you, **Sarah Granados**, for helping me put a human face on the plight of needing and waiting for an organ transplant. You have educated your many followers on what it means to have unwavering faith, hope, and love. You handle your journey with a strength that seems unfathomable most days, and I know I'm not alone in praying you find your miracle.

In my life, I've been fortunate to never be thrust into a medical emergency. **Cathy Mutascio** was kind enough to take me into the world of a trauma nurse so I could tell Will's story. She answered my questions patiently and helped me realize it isn't only the families that feel the pain when a patient loses their battle.

I'm grateful for the work **Mara Barlow** and the Sharing Network of New Jersey do for organ donor families and recipients. I'm so grateful she agreed to share her knowledge to ensure my portrayal was accurate.

One organ donor can save eight lives and enhance the lives of up to 75 with the donation of corneas and tissue. Unfortunately, there is a drastic shortage of organ donors in this country, and the demand far exceeds the supply. Over 100,000 men, women, and children await life-saving organ transplants, and 17 people die each day while waiting. You have the power to help change that by registering today as an organ and tissue donor at www.registerme.org.

Sometimes it feels like there are no coincidences. Finding fellow author, **Cindy Nolte,** and learning she's a past life regression hypnotist proved that. She generously offered to help me go back, and I'm not sure I was *that* surprised to see a familiar face. Turns out, that unexplainable connection to someone in my life had a reason after all.

Most of the desserts in this book are derived from my imagination or inspired by recipes found online. The idea for Kate's winning dessert in the bake-off (before she made changes, that is) was loosely based on a recipe by **Dorothy Reinhold**. You can find it at shockinglydelicious.com.

Thank you, **Peyton Regalado, Woody Kamena, Brenda Staton, Stacey Halpin, Stacy Ostrau, Donna Stubock, Brittany Schroeder, Melanie Bollinger, Lacey Stephens, Linda Martin, Claire Cone, Sharon Savoy,** and everyone who agreed to read this book ahead of the curve to provide feedback. I'm so appreciative.

To **Rebecca Pena, Elisa Toucet, Minerba Calero,** and **Faith Rayne-Brennan**, it's because of all of you that I believe in things I can't see with my own eyes.

ABOUT THE AUTHOR

Liane Carmen is the author of *When Wings Flutter* and the Investigation Duo Series. She regularly suffers from insomnia as book ideas rattle around her head until she gives in and starts writing. At this point, she might not sleep again for the next decade.

Her goal is always to deliver that unexpected twist in her books. She enjoys writing stories that revolve around strong women and the relationships that drive their lives. Sometimes, there's also a murder or two.

She's an avid reader, true crime enthusiast, and genealogy buff who's been known to lose large blocks of time researching her family tree. She fosters tiny kittens and attempts to convince them Tucker, her golden retriever, is not actually their new mommy. Unfortunately for him, it doesn't always work.

For more information and to subscribe to her newsletter, visit her website at www.lianecarmen.com.

Made in the USA
Columbia, SC
29 October 2021